INTO A DREAM . . .

Paulina knew only that she was warm and comfortable and that she felt secure. Her sleep instantly thrust her into a wonderful world of dreams and happy memories, and the fog swirling about her pulled her along on a journey that would not be soon forgotten.

Into a netherworld she was destined to travel . . . into a world of excitement, with the man who lie at her side . . . the man whose musky manliness and nearness was all she wanted.

DISCOVER DEANA JAMES!

CAPTIVE ANGEL   (2524, $4.50/$5.50)
Abandoned, penniless, and suddenly responsible for the biggest
tobacco plantation in Colleton County, distraught Caroline Gil-
lard had no time to dissolve into tears. By day the willowy red-
head labored to exhaustion beside her slaves . . . but each night
left her restless with longing for her wayward husband. She'd
make the sea captain regret his betrayal until he begged her to
take him back!

MASQUE OF SAPPHIRE   (2885, $4.50/$5.50)
Judith Talbot-Harrow left England with a heavy heart. She was
going to America to join a father she despised and a sister she
distrusted. She was certainly in no mood to put up with the insulting actions of the arrogant Yankee privateer who boarded her
ship, ransacked her things, then "apologized" with an indecent,
brazen kiss! She vowed that someday he'd pay dearly for the lib-
erties he had taken and the desires he had awakened.

SPEAK ONLY LOVE   (3439, $4.95/$5.95)
Long ago, the shock of her mother's death had robbed Vivian
Marleigh of the power of speech. Now she was being forced to
marry a bitter man with brandy on his breath. But she could not
say what was in her heart. It was up to the viscount to spark the
fires that would melt her icy reserve.

WILD TEXAS HEART   (3205, $4.95/$5.95)
Fan Breckenridge was terrified when the stranger found her near-
naked and shivering beneath the Texas stars. Unable to remember
who she was or what had happened, all she had in the world was
the deed to a patch of land that might yield oil . . . and the fierce
loving of this wildcatter who called himself Irons.

*Available wherever paperbacks are sold, or order direct from the
Publisher. Send cover price plus 50¢ per copy for mailing and
handling to Zebra Books, Dept. 4394, 475 Park Avenue South,
New York, N.Y. 10016. Residents of New York and Tennessee
must include sales tax. DO NOT SEND CASH. For a free Zebra/
Pinnacle catalog please write to the above address.*

CAROLINE BOURNE

EMERALD DREAMS

ZEBRA BOOKS
KENSINGTON PUBLISHING CORP.

ZEBRA BOOKS are published by

Kensington Publishing Corp.
475 Park Avenue South
New York, NY 10016

First Printing: December, 1993

Printed in the United States of America

Part One

What dreams await me when day is done
In the magical realms of the "Midnight Sun"

One

Brett McCallum folded back the lapels of his jacket and narrowed his blue eyes to take a long look at the village of Skagway. Though he had a bit of a nefarious background himself, he hated what he saw before him. In its first year of existence in the Alaskan frontier, the settlement was a nightmare of lawlessness. Since Captain Billy Moore had staked out a squatter's claim to one hundred sixty waterfront acres, saloons and tent establishments catering to debauchery and decadence had popped up along a boardwalk suspended above the muddy Alaskan earth. Captain Billy, gambling on a big gold strike on the upper Yukon, envisioned that Skagway would be the best place for overland shortcuts into the interior. Land values would go up, and he would be rich.

He hadn't, however, counted on the small armies of unsavory characters who did their prospecting in the pokes of honest, hardworking gold miners. Those were the men Brett McCallum, in his risky line of work, had to watch out for.

Traveling the past six weeks from the interior, and having paid little attention to his personal needs, Brett now made his way to a tent advertising baths, shaves, and haircuts for twenty-five cents apiece. When he emerged an hour later, his bronze skin had lost a layer of grime and his chestnut-colored hair, swept neatly back from his forehead, glistened. His fingers rose to caress the sharp line of his clean-shaven jaw, feeling the loss of the coarse bristles that had hidden—he chuckled to himself, remembering the words of a woman he had met—his rich good looks.

Lazily stretching to his full height of six feet two inches, Brett McCallum flicked his wide-brimmed hat back from his forehead. He prided himself on being self-reliant and individualistic to a fault. He cared not a whit what anyone thought of him and took humble pride in his ability to meet the challenges of Alaska's wilderness. He had been born at the base of Denali, and he had no doubts that there he would die one day. He sought the civilized world only to break the monotony of life in the tundra and to fulfill a promise to Gruff, his friend and partner. The only thing resembling a doctor within a hundred-mile radius of Nuklukayet had broken the news to Gruff that he was dying. A cancer was growing inside his head and he'd be dead within a year. Brett and Gruff had been partners for seven years, and Brett wanted the last year of his life to be his best.

To finance his return to the tundra, Brett would pick up an easy fare guiding some half-frozen greenhorns along the gold-rush trails toward the Yukon. He preferred Alaska, hardships and all, to any other place on earth.

As he stood upon the boardwalk, his thumbs tucked casually into the waist of his trousers, his gaze swept over the motley makings of the town, settling momentarily on Clancy's Saloon across the mucky street. He'd spied only one female since entering the settlement, and she'd had

10

three sniveling boys dragging at her skirts and another child on the way. He'd heard of a ramshackle dance hall at the south end of town and, gaining his footing upon the shaky boardwalk, ambled lazily in that direction. He had to see a pretty female face before he withered and died from the lack of it. And maybe there he would find the means to fulfill his promise to Gruff.

He had scarcely moved a hundred yards before a shadow emerged from a tent behind his back. Preparing to remove one of his pearl-handled Colts in defense against the attack he expected, Brett was immediately seized upon the shoulder by a grizzled old prospector he knew only by the name of Obadiah.

"What the hell, you old bear." Brett half chuckled the greeting. "I could have blown a hole in you an army could have marched through."

"But ya din't, eh, Cap'n? The old man's grin betrayed black spikes that might once have been teeth. "What ye'll be doin' in Skagway?"

"Spotting some sourdoughs," Brett replied, referring to the outsiders—anyone not from Alaska—who flooded the interior looking for gold. He wished the old man wouldn't refer to him as Captain, the only reminder he'd had in many months that he'd spent four long years away from his beloved Alaska, serving a hitch in the American cavalry. That was an adventure he never wanted to repeat.

Again Obadiah grinned, his gnarled hand landing harder upon the taller man's shoulder. "How 'bout a whiskey, eh, Cap'n?"

"My coin or yours, old-timer?" Brett asked, knowing full well the man never had a penny to his name. "Come on . . . I'll buy you one."

As Brett was maneuvered along the boardwalk to a tent saloon, Obadiah filled him in on the happenings

11

since Billy Moore had laid out the plans for Skagway. By the time they sat down in two rough-hewn chairs and felt canvas scraping against the backs of their heads, Brett had learned the names of every murder victim who had made a less than gallant exit from Skagway. With the third whiskey beneath his malodorous buckskins, Obadiah began to quiet.

"Say you're lookin' fer sourdoughs, eh, Cap'n?" he asked, stirring Brett from a quiet moment.

"That's what I said," Brett replied absently, overlooking the glass before him to take a drag of whiskey straight from the bottle.

Obadiah leaned across the table, one eye widening while the other narrowed. "I overheerd a thin scrap of a lad askin' about a guide yest'idy, promising to pay twice the normal rate."

Brett's eyes widened in amusement and surprise. "And you didn't jump on the lad for such a fee, old-timer?"

"Me . . . hell, Cap'n. I'm a-waitin' for that load o' dancin' ladies Cap'n Billy's been a-promisin'. Them down at the south end's sows 'n' drags with thighs wider'n a well-fed Lapp . . . swindle a man out of his longjohns and narry bat a blackened eye fer it."

Brett had heard that Obadiah's eyesight had been failing the past couple of years. Rumors were that he could scarcely find an outhouse without unnecessary detours, let alone lead sourdoughs into the interior. "You still down on the Laplanders, eh, old-timer?" he replied after a moment, steering the conversation away from Obadiah's poor eyesight. "The Eskimos would be running the Siberian reindeer into gorges if the Lapps hadn't come here to teach them to herd. Now . . . tell me more about this lad . . . American? Or did you say?"

"Few words he spoke sounded fair American to

12

me . . . real quiet that one. Din't say one word more 'n necessary. Seen him late last night takin' sup alone at Big Pat's place down by the wharf. Prob'ly has a room there . . . Pat's got a soft spot fer the weaklin's. Say, you take him on, Cap'n, how about payin' me a paltry fee fer the lead?"

Brett McCallum's grin betrayed the scar in his right cheek where he'd been struck by the powerful paw of a grizzly some years back. The other scars were somewhere beyond the line of his thick, dark hair. "You know what river the boy'll be wantin' to prospect on?"

Obadiah released a hearty laugh. "Ain't no gold that boy'll be wantin'. He'll be wantin' his pa. Got a map on him that shows where the fella's a-prospectin'. He just wants to join his pa . . . git him to go home to Utah. I 'spect that boy's in a heap o' trouble back yonder south o' the border . . . real 'spicious like . . . keeps his hand on a sidearm strapped to hips that look sorta girllike, if'n you ask me, Cap'n."

"I'll look up the lad."

"Better be careful, Cap'n. Ol' Soapy Smith done got his eye on that one. Thinkin' maybe he'll make a good thief."

Brett stayed in the interior ten months of every year, but Smith's reputation had reached him nevertheless. He had ambled into the new town with five small-time hoodlums, a trip financed by the proceeds of cons he'd operated since leaving Colorado. He'd come by his nickname through soap scams, wrapping money within the wrappers of bars of soap, then putting his shills up to buying the marked bars and flaunting the money, which had prompted suckers to spend their cash for nothing but soap. He hadn't been satisfied with the small-time swindles and so had cut a swath to Skagway, where he'd promptly rescued a man from the lynch mob and set himself up with the townsfolk as a man of high principles. It hadn't mattered that the fellow had been guilty of two murders; Soapy had simply raised fifteen hundred dollars to console the unfortunate widows. Thereafter, Jefferson Randolph Smith—that kindhearted, upstanding gentleman—had been given leave to run the town.

"What yer thinkin', Cap'n?"

Stirred from his reminiscences, Brett allowed the front legs of his chair to hit the packed dirt. "I'm thinking, Obadiah, that I need to locate the boy before someone else does. I'd rather take one boy—or a woman for that matter, God forbid—into the interior to find his pa than a hundred greedy sourdoughs looking for gold."

"Easier to handle, eh, Cap'n?"

"I'd say that one strap of a lad would be a lot easier to handle than red-eyed devils."

At the moment the strap of a lad was proving to be a handful for Soapy Smith, whose large hands held fast to flailing arms. A small, booted foot landed full upon Soapy's shin and, with a surprised yelp, his hands jerked from his prey to cover the throbbing wound.

"Ya blasted little whelp!" the big, surly, full-bearded man, hopping like a banty rooster, yelled at the lad. "I'll hog-tie and whip you for that!"

"You won't be catching me!" the breathless warning came out, along with a menacing pistol that wavered before the good citizen of Skagway. "You touch me again and I'll put a hole in you."

Soapy Smith had prided himself on having full control in Skagway. Why, then, was he having such a time with a slim, effeminate young fellow as green as springtime clover? "I was just goin' to offer you a job, boy.

Needn't get so riled." Calmly, Soapy brushed at the sleeves of his brown corduroy coat, his narrowed gaze daring the few men in the saloon at Big Pat's to continue their gloating laughter.

"You should'na picked on the boy," Big Pat pointed out from behind the bar. "A simple 'Do you need a job?' might have been enough."

Not many men spoke up to Soapy Smith. Most men, even the bastard now rubbing a wounded shin, would have admired the courage it took to speak up. But not Soapy. He decided in that split second that Big Pat would soon join the casualties of Skagway's growing crime rate, along with that blasted boy whose tattered clothing was several sizes too large.

The quiet exchange of venomous glances between the two men gave the "lad" a moment to rush from the saloon. A moment later, the cot in the back room of Big Pat's place cushioned a slim, sobbing body.

Paulina Winthrop wasn't sure why she was crying. She'd encountered nastier men than Soapy Smith since she'd left Turkey Gulch and crept aboard the riverboat *Sadie Mae* bound for Seattle. Two long months of stowing away had frazzled her nerves. She wanted to wear a dress again, she wanted to curl her hair, wear a little lip color . . . she wanted to look like a lady again. With an angry "Pouf! Men! I've no need of them!" Paulina pushed herself into a seated position, which gave her a direct and very distorted view of herself in a small, cracked mirror perched atop a rickety dresser.

How awful she looked! If there was a lady beneath that smut and grime and the drab, baggy clothes a sympathetic young boat hand aboard the *Sadie Mae* had given her, she couldn't see her. She'd dragged her wheat-colored tresses upward, securing them with pins beneath the floppy hat she wore, and she'd bound her

15

breasts beneath several yards of polished cotton she'd purchased from a merchant aboard the steamboat during one of her bold excursions on deck. She had successfully managed to transform herself into a boy as far as observers were concerned . . . but mentally, the lady within her was crying for release.

With shivering revulsion she recalled the day, two months earlier when she faced the old monsters of the Turkey Gulch, Utah, town council. They thought they'd gotten the best of her, that their patronizing taunts and challenges had run her out of town, but . . . blast it all! She'd be back! She would show them . . . and she would have the last laugh!

For the first time that morning, Paulina allowed herself the indulgence of a smile. She missed Uncle Will and her sister, Lillian, who was holding down the fort in Turkey Gulch, and dear, dear young Matt! How she missed the boy who was like a brother to her. He had wanted so badly to travel north with her.

Thinking of their last moments together made her feel warm and snug inside—Uncle Will and Lillian expressing their shared concerns, and Matt, hoping to the last that she might change her mind about traveling alone. When she gave him a hug, he had smiled broadly, informing her in a deep, resonant voice that surely must have pained him, "You need a man to take care of you, Miss Paulie. A man just like me!"

Rising, tousling Matt's dark hair, she had replied, "If I did, you rascal, it would be you. No, Uncle Will and Lillian need you here. I promise, Matt, when I return to Turkey Gulch, no one . . . especially those old poots and those horrid Bartletts, will be laughing at me . . . at us. You just wait and see."

Only a glimmer of disappointment had darkened his eyes as he'd chuckled. "That'll sure be a sight, Miss

Paulie, you standin' before the town council with ol' Millburn's ear pinched twixt your fingers. Heck, Miss Paulie, ol' Millburn prob'ly take you cros't his knee and bare your bottom!"

"Don't be disrespectful." Paulina had tried not to smile, but that had been an impossible chore. Her memories of the boy's loving features were a beacon in the fiercest of storms, keeping her from crashing upon the rocks. "Now, you three," she had said in departing, choking back the lump in her throat as she'd hugged Matt, Lillian, and her uncle for the last time, "when you again see me . . . well—" She shrugged then, unable to speak without emotion.

Thus, finding herself the butt of the city council's joke, and with a few dollars collected from among the sympathetic residents of Turkey Gulch, she had set out on her trek northward, donning men's clothing and praying to the almighty that she could reach the Yukon without her true gender being detected. She thought she had weathered the hardest leg of her journey along the western coast; now, as she trembled in the decadence of Alaska's newest settlement, she had no doubts that the journey into the interior would prove a challenge, one she *might* survive, with great difficulty.

Oh, but she mustn't think glum thoughts. She had come this far and was still alive. . . . Except for the amiable Big Pat, the only person in whom she had confided her true identity—and her gender—she had gone undetected for two long months. Most men had looked at her, peering bashfully from beneath the rim of an oversize hat, as nothing more than a prepubescent boy taking on a mighty big challenge. She had to find a man—a man blind enough not to recognize her gender, a man her gut feeling would compel her to trust—who would lead her to Millburn Hanks. She would feel safe with an older man, perhaps one of Uncle Will's age, who could move quickly enough to cover the distance without dallying, but a man she could easily outdistance if the need arose. There had to be such a man among the various and sundry rogues who inhabited the village of Skagway. Big Pat had promised to keep a lookout for a dependable guide, and she trusted him to do just that.

"Big Pat." The words left her lips in a weary sigh and she responded only with a small jerk when gunfire erupted from the muddy street. "Please . . . please, find that special person before I go absolutely mad."

An irate Brett McCallum jabbed his finger through the bullet hole in his hat. Groaning his displeasure at the assault, he dragged the gun-wielding drunkard up from his slumped position and held him tight by the lapels. "Do you see what you did to my hat?" Brett half hissed the words. "It's chilly enough without a whistle-way through my scalp. What're you going to do about it, man?"

The fellow being held up by the strength of Brett's left hand alone scarcely managed to crack his bloodshot eyes. His breath reeked of cheap gin. "Weren't aimin' fer ya, Mister. Aimin' "—his attempt to raise his hand resulted in the loss of his handgun, which Brett kicked aside with his boot—"fer that orn'ry mule yonder what done kicked me in the backside."

"You missed him by a mile, fella, and I wouldn't suggest you try again. Another man might have returned fire." Brett knew the fellow hadn't meant him any harm, but on the other hand, accidents had laid a good many men in the ground. He wasn't ready to be a casualty. Smoothing down the lapels of the man's shirt in a move to regain his own lost composure, Brett suggested, "You'd better find a place to sleep it off."

"Sure, Mister." The drunkard's hand moved to tip his hat, but met only an empty space above his unkempt hair. The hat was in the muddy roadway, along with his sidearm, being trampled by a slow-moving wagon. "Blast . . ." Swaying when he turned, the man slurred, "That'uz the bes-durn-hat-I-ever-wore," then hopped unsteadily into the knee-deep slush to retrieve his possessions.

Brett's ample mouth twisted into a smile. Smoothing back his thick chestnut locks, he turned to resume his walk to Big Pat's Saloon. Momentarily, he entered what appeared to be the most solid of the buildings on Skagway's Broadway Street and flipped his hat back from his forehead. His eyes narrowed as they swept the large room, as much to assess the layout as to ward off the thick smoke of tobacco billowing from curled, sneering mouths. Then he spied the big man behind the bar, his balding pate and handlebar mustache every bit as comical as he'd expected from Obadiah's description. Tucking his thumbs into his waistline, away from his pair of sidearms, Brett ambled between the chairs and tables and soon dropped to a barstool.

"What'll be yer pleasure, Mister?" Big Pat inquired, absently cleaning out the inside of a beer glass with a cloth.

"Whiskey," Brett replied, tossing a coin upon the bar.

Big Pat eyed the gold piece. "That'll buy you the best bottle in the house, and a little more."

"I'll take that bottle . . . and the 'little more' I'll take by way of information."

Eyeing him suspiciously, Big Pat brought out a bottle of whiskey and set it, along with a shot glass, on the bar

19

in front of Brett. "What kind of information will a fellow like you be wantin' in Skagway?"

Pouring his first glass, Brett replied, "I hear there's a greenhorn boy here and about looking for a guide into the interior."

Silence. Big Pat's eyes narrowed as he studied the angular lines of Brett's face. This was not exactly the kind of man he had been looking for to take the disguised and very nervous young woman into the interior in search of her father. When Brett's eyes lifted to his own, Big Pat said, "There might be. Tell me, fella, what business are you in?"

"Like a lot of others here and abouts—leading the greenhorns and sourdoughs into the gold pastures of the Yukon." Brett gulped his drink and poured another. "You going to tell me if the lad's still around? Or you going to wait for credentials?"

"Anybody here and about know you, Mister?"

Brett's clean-shaven features settled into a half-grin. "I heard you took a fatherly interest in the lad. If you want to check me out, ask old Obadiah. He'll vouch for me."

"You know Obadiah?"

"Bartend! A whiskey over here!"

Taking a bottle of watered-down liquor from beneath the bar, Big Pat moved to his left to fill the bellowing customer's glass. When he returned to Brett, he repeated the question, "You know Obadiah?"

"We've crossed paths off and on for the past four years." With an amused grin, Brett continued. "You want me to get Obadiah over here to vouch for me before you'll give me word on the boy?"

Big Pat's burly forearms landed full upon the bar, one hand closing over the other. His eyes were mere inches from Brett's. "I know Obadiah. I don't know you, Mister. You tell me your name and I'll ask Obadiah about you when he comes in again. If he ain't got nothin' good to say about you, then I ain't got nothing to say to you . . . period. Now, you be drinkin' up and let me get on about my business."

Paulina was not sure exactly what had compelled her to eavesdrop on Big Pat's conversation with the customer. Perhaps the rich, resonant voice had sparked her curiosity. Perhaps the fact that she was the "lad" looking for a guide had justified the small vice she would not normally have engaged in. She knew only that she had to see the face of the man who was interested in forming a temporary business alliance with her.

She had been insane to advertise her ability to pay twice the given rate for a guide. This was a wild land and these were wild men. She had just over one hundred and eighteen dollars in her pocket, and at least half that would be required by the man she hired to buy necessary supplies for the trip. What would she say if he requested payment of his fee before they reached Millburn Hanks? "Sorry, Mister, but I have only a few dollars left." She knew that was a chance she had to take . . . a chance that her guide would not abandon her the hundred or so miles into the interior when she explained that she had no money to pay the fee.

Now she peered like a timid child into the angular features of a man who might be in his early thirties, though it was hard to tell. He could be younger, or older, depending on how kindly the Alaskan outdoors had treated him. The gentle lines at the corners of his eyes indicated maturity, but the set of his features, faintly smiling and mischievous, would almost put his years at scarcely beyond her own. His hair, wavy and unruly, was the color of the rich dark chocolates they sold in their mercantile, and his eyes were so piercingly blue, she was sure they could see into the darkness of the small ante-room where she stood, spying upon him. She saw strength and honesty in his square jawline and strong chin, and gentleness in the lazy way he sat at the bar, refusing to react, as most men would, to Big Pat's sarcastic, accusing tone. He appeared to be a man who would be outraged that she would lie to him about having adequate funds to pay him, but one who would not physically vent his frustrations upon her or abandon her to the timber wolves.

At Big Pat's rather rude dismissal, Brett McCallum climbed to his feet, betraying his impressive stature to the disguised young woman standing in the shadows. His hips were narrow, his black trousers hugging his muscular thighs, the strength of his sinewy chest straining against the fabric of his black shirt. When Paulina gasped, so surprised was she at finding no fault in his appearance, those piercing blue eyes turned in her direction. She jerked to the security of the wall, sure that he had not seen her. A moment passed before she ventured another look and caught sight across the crowded room of his tall frame emerging into the afternoon sunlight.

At that moment, with a strange warmth rushing though her slender frame, she decided that Brett McCallum was the man she could trust to be her guide. It did not occur to her that such a man might easily recognize her tethered femininity beneath the men's baggy clothes.

But she had to take the chance. Most of the men she had met in Skagway were hairy and grizzled, reeking of gin and filth, and wiping tobacco juice from lecherously grinning mouths. But the man who had introduced himself to Big Pat as Brett McCallum had been clean-shaven and remarkably handsome, and though he had worn two Colts at his hips, he had not appeared to be a man who would use them with reckless abandon.

Before emerging from the shadows, Paulina searched the room for the presence of Soapy Smith. When she did not see him, she crept up behind Big Pat and tapped him on the shoulder.

"What you doin', Pauli—"

"Careful, Big Pat." Paulina favored him with a warning smile when he almost spoke her true name. "Could I talk to you a minute in the back?"

Big Pat's eyes narrowed with concern—he had been aware of her eavesdropping—then he took her shoulders and coaxed her toward the back. When, at last, she turned, preparing to speak, he immediately interrupted her. "I know what you're thinkin' . . . that he looks safe enough. But, girlie, he's young and his eyesight's real good. You might be able to fool the old codgers with that floppy old hat and that boy's getup, but you ain't goin' to fool the likes of Brett McCallum."

"If he figures out that I'm a girl, that's the chance I have to take. I have a gun and I wouldn't hesitate to use it. I want Mr. McCallum to take me to, ummm, my father." She had lied to Big Pat about Millburn's relationship to her; guilt rushed upon her cheeks in a crimson tide.

Big Pat sighed wearily. There was no arguing with a cantankerous woman. "Let me check him out first."

Paulina shrugged delicately, the oversize shirt dragging at her slim shoulders. "You do what you want, but you get him for me, Big Pat. I've got to find my pa or I'm going to lose the little bit of property our family owns in Utah." A partial lie; would there be any salvation when she ultimately met her maker? But wasn't half a lie better than a full-blown one?

Big Pat's wide smile made crimson balls of his cheeks. "Now, you get on back to your room and I'll fetch you a tray of food and drink. The less you're seen, the better chance you have of getting away with"—his hand moved with dramatic flourish, emphasizing her masculine attire—"this."

Paulina did as she was told. While Big Pat responded to the bellowing of thirsty patrons, she dropped gently to the cot in what the friendly proprietor had called "the best room in the house," a room that, back home, she would probably have used for storage.

She felt a confidence she had not felt in two long months. While she remained determined to bring Millburn back to Turkey Gulch, she harbored doubts about her ability to find him. Alaska was, after all, a mighty big place, and Millburn's wanderings could not be tracked with any degree of certainty. But with a guide like Brett McCallum, she tried to feel confident that she would find him and they would return together to Turkey Gulch to stand before the city council, where Paulina would get the last laugh. Paulina allowed herself the indulgence of a smile. Brett McCallum was everything she had sworn not to seek in a guide. He was young and virile, and when he discovered that she had no money to pay him, his long, slender legs might easily be able to overpower her if she made a run for safety. Safety? In the vast, wild lands of Alaska? A gentle chuckle rose in her throat. She imagined, also, that Brett McCallum might have good eyesight . . . would he immediately recognize her feminine softness beneath her rough disguise? No . . . no, she refused to believe that he would.

Brett McCallum . . . she liked the sound of his name. Resting back against the single feather pillow, Paulina closed her eyes. Within moments, a tall male figure emerged from the smoky darkness behind her eyelids . . . a man who, if everything went as planned, she would be required to trust and to deceive in the same breath.

Two

Turkey Gulch, Utah

A warm April breeze wafted through the open windows of the apartment above the mercantile. Even at this early hour, Main Street was a-bustle with men in their stuffy suits and fancy carriages heading for their jobs in Salt Lake City, only four miles away. Buggies bumped along the rutted road and an occasional screech could be heard from children already beginning to fill the wide avenue comprising what there was of Turkey Gulch.

Lillian Winthrop arose from her high tester bed in an unusually good mood. She hurried around her apartment, straightening the bed, dusting the furniture, smoothing a doily beneath a precariously perched lamp badly in need of repair. Then she surveyed her own finished appearance in the cheval mirror she had neglected to clean in her nervous frenzy; her image was faintly enshrouded in a fog of dust to match that drifting through the street. The tar pits of Mr. Perrot's lumberyard half a mile away had already turned the morning-blue skies to a somber gray in the normally peaceful village.

But that did not matter. In just three days her mother,

whom she had not seen for almost seven years, would arrive from New York for an extended visit. Oh, if only Paulina were here rather than traipsing across Alaska in search of that old rascal Millburn Hanks.

Lillian shrugged delicately. Regardless of the family problems that had plagued them of late, she felt happy and alive, and she wanted only to descend the narrow stairs to the mercantile and open up for business as usual.

As she stood before the mirror, flicking at an annoying wisp of honey-colored hair refusing to be secured beneath a pin, she thought how good life had been to her. She and Paulina owned the mercantile and property her late father had left them. Free of debt, the business brought in enough money to pay the bills, with a little left over for a frivolity or luxury every now and then. She had her dear uncle, William Winthrop, who, despite being confined to a wheelchair, helped her in the mercantile, and the young orphan boy who lived in the back of the store and whose job was to stock the shelves when new goods arrived from their shippers.

As she continued to pick at the unruly curl, Lillian's golden eyes darkened to the color of onyx, and her mouth pinched into a thin line. Unfortunately there existed one rather rude kink in her otherwise perfect life—Earl Bartlett, one of the deputy marshals of Turkey Gulch who was a pompous, egotistical, boasting, loud-mouthed bully intent on making the lives of her family miserable until they sold their property to his brother, Lester. The elder Bartlett had been contracted by easterners wishing to construct overpriced town houses within driving distance of Salt Lake City for those wealthy slobs wishing to have easy access to town without actually having to live there. Earl and Lester, with the effective help of the town council—silly little men bullied into submission—had succeeded in running Paulina out of town on a wild chase that had no chance of success. And Lillian, only nineteen, was left with the thankless chore of keeping the mob at bay. If the Winthrops did not sell the land to Lester by the end of the year, the deal would be withdrawn and Lester, who had invested down to his last penny to buy the other sixteen small businesses, would lose a fortune.

Both of the Bartletts were handsome men, with coal-black hair, dark, piercing eyes, and charming ways at selective times. Those charms, along with unending supplies of ill-gotten wealth, had put them in the top notch of society. Unfortunately, both men had nurtured skills of small-time larceny and womanizing to perfection. Earl had once asked Paulina to marry him and, in the presence of a dozen of his friends, she had not only staunchly refused, but had laughed in his face. Thus, not only did her older sister have to deal with the pressures of Lester Bartlett to sell her father's business, she also had to deal with Earl's biting intimidations as he tried to get even for what he considered her past wrongs against him.

Enough of early morning depressions, Lillian thought, flinging back her hair with a refreshing vitality. A new shipment of ladies' fashions had arrived the week before from the East and Lillian, in anticipation of her mother's visit, had chosen a few of the dresses for herself. She wore her favorite that morning—a high-necked emerald green and white cotton print with pouffed sleeves tightening just below the elbows and tapering snugly at her wrists. A row of gathered ruffles half covered her slim white hands. The bustle was small but fashionable, and she tried to flatten it a bit more so that her bottom would not look so full. Why couldn't she have been as slim and perfectly formed as Paulina? Life could be so unjust! Then she decided to redo her unruly hair, French-braiding it and allowing the braid to hang loosely down her back to her waist. Garnishing it with a small emerald-colored bow at the crown of the braid, she then moved toward the stairs and the mercantile, where the boy, Matt, stoked the coals in the Franklin stove. He had probably put on a pot of coffee, and when either she or Uncle Will arrived, would rush off to the bakery for blueberry tarts and sugared pastries which Lillian kept on hand for her regular patrons. She imagined that she might be in part responsible for the wide girth of Mrs. McWhirter, owner of a nearby boarding-house and, in Paulina's absence, her very dearest female friend. Lucille McWhirter and her uncle Will were rumored to be romantically linked, but thus far her uncle had kept the marrying preacher tucked into his niche at the local Presbyterian church.

A mantel clock in the mercantile chimed eight musical notes as she descended the stairs. Matt had put the coffee on and the aroma filled the dimly lit room. "That coffee sure smells inviting," she greeted the slim boy, at which he turned, a grin stretching the width of his face.

"I'll be off to the bakery now, Miss Winthrop?" he inquired.

Just at that moment, a coal popped from the stove, whose door had not been properly secured, and landed in the center of the newspapers. A small fire immediately flared, catching a river of oil that had leaked from a defective lamp. Had it not been for Lillian's quick thinking, and the hastily grabbed blanket with which she doused the fire, the brittle wood of the mercantile, and its array of merchandise, might have gone up in flames.

It had happened so quickly that neither of them had found a moment to comment. Now, as Uncle Will pushed his wheelchair into the store area, a trembling

Lillian quickly explained, "A coal popped from the stove and caught the papers on fire. Matt will not allow it to happen again. Will you, Matt?" Her reproachful gaze cut to him. "Take a little money from the cash box and make your trip to the bakery." Closing a few coins inside his fist, Matt hastily exited the mercantile.

"Didn't hurt yourself, did you, girl?" Uncle Will asked.

"I don't think so." Sitting back on her knees, Lillian studied a singed ruffle at her elbow. "But I can't say the same thing for my dress." Drawing herself gracefully to her feet, she wiped her hands on a damp rag as she continued. "I believe this little incident should give me the incentive to see Mr. Tilford this morning—"

"That blasted insurance man? Hell, what'll you be wanting with him?" There were three kinds of human creatures Will Winthrop found intolerable—insurance men, lawyers, and preachers. Make that four—to include the Bartlett brothers, though considering them members of the species was stretching it a bit.

"You watch your vulgar tongue in front of the customers," Lillian lovingly admonished him. "Before she left, Paulina said I should take out a policy on the store. So I'll waste no more time. Paulina and I should have done it when we first returned for father's funeral and decided to stay."

"A waste of money," Uncle Will mumbled, "if you ask me. We're the only ones left on the block. Bartlett ain't goin' to let up till you sell. Hell . . . my brother should never have died and put this pressure on you."

"He didn't just die," Lillian argued. "Either Earl or Lester killed him . . . and you know it!"

"Don't know any such a thing."

Lillian took a moment to study her cynical but loving uncle. He had once been a strapping stagecoach driver, but an accident just outside Coffeeville, Kansas, five years before, had left his legs paralyzed. At times he refused to acknowledge his limitations and it had not been without great battle that she'd assigned tasks to Matt that Will would have preferred to do himself. His enormous bulbous nose and bloodshot eyes were easily recognized signs of his heavy indulgence in whiskey, and he often slurred his speech so thickly that not a single lucid word could be caught in conversation. But never once had he said anything to Lillian for which an apology would have been called for. He had once told her she was at the top of his list of good things in his life, though he had recently added Lucille McWhirter to that list.

A sadness was reflected in Lillian's eyes as she held her uncle's gaze. When at last, he growled, "That blasted insurance man is waiting. I'll watch the store till the boy gets back," she retrieved the black shawl she had left in the mercantile and moved toward the door.

"If Lucille comes, tell her I've gone to see Mr. Tilford, you grumbling old pup, and that I'll be back in a little while!"

Her affectionate tone elicited a toothy grin. "Paulina had that highfalutin gadget put in—" he reminded her, pointing to the large wood-cased telephone on the wall, "so why don't you ring up Mr. Swindler before you leave?"

"Uncle Will! Mr. Tilford is not a swindler! Do be kind and—" A coy smile creased her pale, ivory features. "I don't like talking to a voice without a body."

As she exited onto the boardwalk, Uncle Will mumbled, "Then why'd you encourage your sister to buy the contraption?" and poured himself a cup of coffee.

Out of doors, a warm April sun shone upon Lillian's features. She enjoyed the summerlike warmth as she watched a flock of migratory geese move with the breeze far across the horizon. She passed a young mother pushing a fringed-top baby carriage and stopped to admire the dimple-cheeked child, wondering if she would ever have one of her own. All along the street she greeted friends and acquaintances, pausing as she reached an empty lot to throw a wayward ball to a group of boys.

Momentarily, she ducked into Mr. Tilford's office and greeted his secretary, a disagreeable fellow she knew only as Gower, though she did not know if it was his first or his second name. "How are you today, Miss Winthrop?" he greeted her, peering at her from atop his spectacles.

"Fine and enjoying the weather, thank you," she replied.

"Don't thank me. I had nothing to do with the weather."

Pressing her mouth into a firm line for a moment, then drawing her shawl farther about her arms, she asked, "Are you always so rude, Gower?"

He looked down at the morning mail beneath his palm. "Didn't know I was being rude," he replied matter-of-factly, lifting a pencil-thin eyebrow as he forced himself to meet her gaze once again.

Mr. Tilford entered from the boardwalk, looking very much the Englishman in his bowler hat, an umbrella dangling from the crook of his arm and a monocle perched precariously in the wrinkles of his right eye. "Miss Winthrop"—the crisp accent cut the strangled atmosphere of the office—"don't tell me you and that sister of yours are finally going to insure your business? It's a little late now, with Bartlett pressuring you to sell."

"He can pressure all he wants. And"—she smiled sweetly—"he can build his town houses around my store. I'm not selling."

Theron Tilford was well aware that the pressure was

on and that the Bartletts' Eastern investors would take all the property, or they would take none of it. How the young sisters held out he would never know. Apparently, they were much stronger than they appeared. "How is your uncle?" he asked by way of changing the subject. "Is he getting along?"

"Fine, yes—" She answered each of his questions.

"And Millburn? Heard from him since he scatted out of town?"

Lillian instantly guessed he might be digging for information to pass on to the Bartletts. Casually, she replied, "If I had heard from him, I wouldn't tell anyone. You know that."

"And has he struck it rich yet?"

Lillian lifted a pale eyebrow. "I don't know what you mean."

"Rumor has it that he hightailed it to Alaska. Is that where your sister is headed?"

"As I said," Lillian replied, remaining deliberately calm, "I don't know what you're talking about. Paulina had business in the East."

Theron Tilford deposited his hat and umbrella on a gaudy piece of furniture constructed of Texas steer horns, then stretched out his arm. "I gather you have come to see me, and not Gower?"

A frenzied bull wouldn't purposely seek out Gower, she thought, replying instead, "I did, indeed, come to see you, Mr. Tilford."

When Lillian Winthrop exited the insurance office some minutes later, she had in her hand a receipt for payment of premiums for the first three months, and a handwritten policy covering her mercantile for the sum of two thousand dollars. Concentrating on tucking the items into her handbag, she did not see Earl Bartlett until she had collided with him on the boardwalk.

"Little lady," he chuckled in his deep, resonant, and very sarcastic voice, "better watch where you're going."

Righting herself, she looked upward, past Earl's barrel chest to his dark eyes beneath the brim of his soiled hat. He was a foreboding figure. "I'm sure you saw me in plenty of time, Earl Bartlett," she snapped harshly, "to realize that I was preoccupied."

Tucking his thumbs into the waist of his breeches, Earl stood with his feet apart, his oversize chest puffed like an amorous rooster as if he wished to display the tin star pinned to his shirt. "Old Will said you'd come this way. Thought you'd like to duck into the drugstore and have a sars'parilla, maybe talk about selling out."

"I've never known you to drink anything but whiskey, Earl Bartlett, and my sister and I have no intention of selling out. Excuse me"—she attempted to step around him on the boardwalk—"but I've got to get back to the store."

Earl's large body lumbered into her path, halting her. "You ladies need to get rid of that place, Miss Lillian. Ain't natural for women as handsome as you two not to get married and settle down. What are you now . . . eighteen, nineteen? I'd make a good husband."

She mustered a moment of tolerance. "Your specially ordered Levi's came in yesterday afternoon, Earl. You can collect them whenever you like."

When she started to walk off, Earl Bartlett grabbed her arm and held it fast. She winced from the pain. "You act high and mighty with me, little lady, but you're going to sell out. Or I'll—"

"Or you'll what, Earl?" Fury erased the morning gold of her eyes. "You've already intimidated our customers. Most are afraid to come anywhere near the store. As for

34

getting married and settling down, it certainly wouldn't be to a drag like you. I'd as soon marry Gower! And now, Earl Bartlett—" Prying his fingers loose from her arm, her look almost lethal as she did so, Lillian Winthrop flung herself around the great bulk of his body. Then she turned back, her eyes spitting uncontrolled fire, and hissed, "Don't you mess with me, Earl, or with my uncle or anyone in my employ. I won't put up with your shenanigans any longer! As soon as Paulina—"

Her threat halted abruptly, her eyes widening in surprise that she had almost spilled the beans, so to speak. As far as she knew, Earl and Lester knew nothing of the town council's challenge to Paulina and how, accomplished, it might change the face of life in Turkey Gulch and put the Bartletts where they belonged—in prison. Her chin lifting in a haughty air as she mulled her near blunder, she resumed her short walk to the mercantile.

Gower had heard the mention of his name from his desk in the insurance office. Lillian's patterned skirts had just disappeared around the corner when he stepped out to the boardwalk. "What was that about?" he asked Earl Bartlett.

A furious, red-faced Earl flicked his hat back from his forehead. "The woman needs tamin', that's all. What was she in Tilford's office for?"

"Purchased a policy on the mercantile."

Damn! he thought. Sounded like little sister was settling in permanently. "For how much?"

"Two thousand dollars." Gower could be as devious and conniving as the Bartletts. The physically unattractive man had a rather strange and defensive aversity to beautiful women . . . women like Paulina and Lillian Winthrop. "You know, you might use this to your advantage. Ever hear of insurance fraud?"

35

A grin stretched the width of Earl's face. "See you around, Gower," he said, departing.

As Lillian entered the mercantile, she called "I'm back" with surprising calm. But when Will, having immediately noticed the flushed shade of her usually pale cheeks, gave her a dubious look, she sighed. "It's that Earl Bartlett, Uncle Will. I wish he would leave us alone. I cannot even step around the corner without him needling me about selling out."

Scarcely had she completed her statement before Will retrieved his shotgun from behind the counter. "Blast! I shouldn't have told him where you'd gone. If he's bothering you, Lillian, I'll take care of him."

Matt entered the mercantile, his hands filled with pastries wrapped in brown paper. Seeing the shotgun across Will's lap, and a wide-eyed Lillian Winthrop blocking his path to the door, he asked, "What's going on here?" and deposited the pastries on a stool beside the Franklin stove.

"Uncle Will is going to shoot Earl Bartlett." Lillian spoke crisply, drawing her hands to her narrow hips. "What do you think about such foolishness, Matt?"

The boy scratched his head. "Well, I figure Mr. Bartlett would pop off the first round an' Uncle Will'd be 'bout as dead as a slow-movin' possum with wagon-wheel tracks cros't its backside."

Will could see that his stubborn niece was certainly not going to give an inch. She was so much like her older sister that it was sometimes hard to tell them apart. His dark eyes piercing the expanse of space separating him from the boy, he mumbled, "One of your kin, eh, boy, got run over by that wagon?"

Matt broke out in laughter, followed closely by Lillian,

despite trying so hard to concentrate on the severity of her uncle's objective. Then the plump Lucille McWhirter, wearing a very troubled frown, entered, cutting her gaze between the man she loved and the girl who was her closest friend. Lillian, tucking her arm through her older friend's, gently coaxed her to the coffeepot and fresh pastries, which Lucille politely declined. Across the bridge of her pert nose; a relieved Lillian watched Uncle Will return the shotgun to its usual resting place. If he took action every time he was prickled, there wouldn't be a single man left in Turkey Gulch, including the preacher.

Will poured another cup of coffee, staring off into the distance beyond the large store-front window as the two women chatted. Suddenly, the stillness of the mercantile was interrupted by Lillian's pained cry. He looked around. Lucille McWhirter was sobbing into a large handkerchief and before another minute could pass had fled past Will toward the boardwalk.

Lillian stamped her foot and pressed her fingers to her temples. "Damn . . . damn!" she exploded, turning imploring eyes toward her uncle. Hastening across the room, she fell to her knees and her fingers linked across his crippled legs. "Did you know that Lucille cannot come to the store anymore? Did you know that Earl and Lester pistol-whipped one of her boarders last night and threatened to do so again if she continued to make purchases here? Uncle Will, what am I going to do?"

"Lucy said nothing to me about it. But I did notice she was actin' funny this morning at breakfast." William Winthrop sighed deeply. "You'll have to sell, Lillian. It's just not worth the risk you and your sister are taking."

She shot to her feet and turned away, stamping her foot in a dramatic display of defiance. "Never! I will never sell to Lester Bartlett! Paulina will bring Millburn back. She swore she would, Uncle Will. And then the Bartletts will get their just deserts!''

The last of the afternoon trickle of patrons had just departed Winthrop's Mercantile when the messenger arrived with a telegram for Lillian. Because dismal news was usually sent by telegram, Lillian's heart quickened its beat as she held the missive, and her knees felt flaccid and weak. Uncle Will had departed an hour earlier for his afternoon nap, and the boy was taking the custom-made jeans to Earl Bartlett's office, her own ploy to keep him away from the mercantile. Sitting on an empty keg, Lillian slowly unfolded the telegram with trembling fingers. She began to read: DARLING LILLIAN. STOP. MUST JOURNEY TO ENGLAND AT WEEK'S END. STOP. WILL VISIT AFTER PAULINA RETURNS. STOP. SEND WIRE TO PALMEROY AT BRIGHTON WHEN SHE'S HOME. STOP. SENDING MY REGRETS. STOP. LOVE, MOTHER.

A feeling of disappointment immediately settled within Lillian. She read and reread the telegram, hoping that the words might transgress possibility and transform into a more acceptable message. Then she became angry. If it had been the other way around . . . if she was gone rather than Paulina, her mother would still have visited. She'd always favored Paulina and had not been discreet about it. Seven years had passed since Laura Roxbury Winthrop had felt smothered by her wifely duties to a merchant from Turkey Gulch and her duties as a mother . . . seven years since she had fled eastward to her snooty family on Staten Island and the mink muffs of New York society.

She *had* to journey to England? A fashion show? The christening of a royal yacht? Tea with the queen?

Well . . . damn her! Why couldn't her daughter come first in her life just this one time?

A mood that had inexplicably brightened in the hours following her confrontation with Earl Bartlett now turned ugly. Raking her knuckles across her cheek, Lillian attempted to remove a lock of recalcitrant hair she was sure was clinging there. Why had her mother disappointed her? Seven years was a very long time. Was Laura Winthrop still beautiful, with expressive brown eyes and silky auburn hair? Was she still slim? Did she still have the loveliest hands in the world? Was her voice still soft and sticky-sweet?

And did Laura care how Paulina and Lillian might have changed? Certainly, they weren't the gangly teenager and twelve-year-old they had been standing tearfully on the train platform. Had she seen the change in the photographs she had received over the years? Had she decided that Paulina and Lillian looked more like her, or like their father? Had she shown the photographs to family and friends and boasted about how her daughters had grown?

Lillian didn't think so. She remembered the many years ago when her mother had spent hours on her own hair and dress for something as mundane as morning church services, then had thrown any old garments on her daughters and dragged back their pale, unbrushed hair. She had been terribly vain and had frequently watched other people's faces for reaction to her loveliness. Had the women been envious, or simply piteous that a woman had no life outside of self-assessment, the men dreaming, wishing their own wives were as lovely? Lillian had always prided herself on her lack of vanity. That was one part of her mother's personality she had not wanted to exhibit. And Paulina, too, had shunned it.

39

She could not sit and brood all day. When an uncharacteristically sullen Matt returned much later than she had expected, she said, "Let me have the money for the jeans, Matt, and we'll close up early today."

Matt's eyes were red, as if he'd been crying. "Mr. Earl wouldn't give me the money, Miss Lillian."

"Oh, he wouldn't, would he?" Fury bubbled within her. "Well, you stay and watch the store. I'll have a little talk with Earl Bartlett."

When she charged into the marshal's office fifteen minutes later, her honey-pale locks half escaping from their French braid and bouncing the length of her back, Earl Bartlett rested back in a straight chair, his booted feet perched upon a cluttered desk and a cigar protruding from his ample mouth. He was wearing one of the new pairs of jeans Matt had delivered. "I want my money, Earl Bartlett," she snapped. "Twelve fifty due and owing for five pairs of jeans. I've given you credit for your deposit."

The chair hit the floor with a dull thud. "What you talkin' about, little lady? I ain't got no jeans from your store."

Her mouth twisted. "Then what are you wearing?"

"These old things?" Laughter erupted in his voice as his palm slapped the brand-new denims. "Had 'em for months. Look—" Earl shook his finger in her face. "You have a complaint, tell it to the marshal. Hey, Marshal . . ." Earl yelled toward the jail area at the back of the office. A cocky, swaggering Lester Bartlett emerged from the darkness beyond a heavy wood door.

"What are you doing here?" Lillian shrieked indignantly.

"Didn't I tell you?" Standing, Earl sauntered toward her, his cigar flopping between his lips. "City council

40

decided to appoint Lester marshal until the elections are held."

Lester muttered, "Like Earl said, if you have a complaint, take it to the marshal," then choked into taunting laughter.

Lillian was definitely up against a brick wall. She looked from one man to the other and quietly said, "All right, Earl, you've got the upper hand this time. May those pants split up between your legs and sever the only brain you think you've got. To hell with you. To hell with you both!"

Scarcely able to restrain the fury of emotions within her, Lillian turned and half ran from the office, the vicious play of their laughter following her along the boardwalk.

Out of hearing range, Lester Bartlett ordered, "I want the women out, Earl. I've got to have that property by the end of the year."

"I'll have her out. Don't you worry none about that," Earl promised. "First of all, I better find out where little Miss Paulina took off to."

"Thought she went east to visit their mother."

Earl drew himself up. "I don't think so, Lester."

Lillian had harbored the notion of going to the office of the United States marshal in Salt Lake City to file a complaint against the Bartletts. But how would she explain such a fuss over five pairs of jeans? And she had no proof of the intimidations by the Bartletts, who wanted the Winthrops out of Turkey Gulch. So instead, she simply hastened back to the mercantile and attempted to settle her nerves.

As the hour of six o'clock approached and no other customers had arrived, Lillian began to close down the store, dousing the embers in the stove, cleaning out the cash drawer, and writing up her meager bank deposit, which she would make first thing the next morning. Giving last-minute instructions to Matt and making arrangements with Mr. Pitney at the restaurant to deliver Uncle Will's favorite meals to him the following day, in celebration of his birthday, she saw the end to her daily regimen. All that was left to be done now was lock the door, turn on the one gas light kept burning for security, and traverse the steps, once again, that would take her to her small, neatly furnished apartment.

For the following week and a half, though she had sworn not to, she brooded miserably over her mother's lack of familial bonding, the intimidations of the Bartletts, and her mounting loneliness for Paulina. She wasn't sure why she held on to the mercantile. The local schoolmaster, fearful of retribution by the Bartletts, had canceled a shipment of McGuffey Readers for which she'd had to pay cash up front, and hardly three customers a day now patronized the store. When she closed up that Friday night and retired to her apartment, she wanted only to slip into her soft, clean bed and put all her worries behind her.

Earl Bartlett hadn't been around in three days, and both Uncle Will and Matt seemed to have been in better moods because of it.

Lillian, though, was suspicious. Earl had managed to encounter her at least once a day since his brother had started buying up the properties, and his recent absences had compelled her to watch more closely at her back. She didn't trust him for a minute; there was nothing he wouldn't do to enrich the bank accounts of the Bartletts. And she worried about the city council too. Shoved up against a wall by the powerful hand of the Bartletts, would they confess what they—and Paulina—were up to?

As she prepared for bed just past eight o'clock that evening, the sight of a glass upon the bedside table caused a chill to travel the length of her spine. She was sure she had washed all the dishes that morning before opening up the mercantile. How had she missed that one? And her bed seemed crumpled, as if someone had lain upon it.

Lillian, you're being ridiculous! she scolded herself inwardly. *No one has lain upon the bed, nor taken a drink from one of your glasses.* To pacify her sudden apprehensions, she sat at the dressing table and began brushing her waist-length hair, parting it in the back and drawing it across both shoulders. When her brush eventually moved, unobstructed, through the silky locks, she braided them, then rose and pulled back the covers of her bed.

The streets were quiet, as they had been for the four months since the block of businesses had been emptied of human occupation. Lillian felt alone in the world. Her mother didn't care enough about her to keep a promise and her sister was off on an impossible mission. If it weren't for Matt and Uncle Will, she might follow a dream of her own, though she knew not where her heart would carry her.

Despite the influx of worries, sleep easily came upon her. The few sounds of the night slowly drifted off, leaving a peaceful vortex in which dreams could grow.

Everything would work out. She just knew it would.

Mrs. McWhirter stifled personal conviction that Friday evening to allow one of the guests to bring a beer dispenser into the parlor of her boardinghouse. The men gathered around, waiting to fill ceramic mugs put out on the table.

Despite his propensity, Will Winthrop was almost too worried to await his turn at the draft, his façade of strength quickly waning in the invisible shadows of the Bartlett brothers. He often felt that he'd lost his inner strength the day he'd lost the use of his legs. He had buried himself in liquor and had disappointed the two people who loved him most. Paulina and Lillian deserved better, and from this moment on he'd do whatever was necessary to make their lives easier. He wanted Paulina back in Turkey Gulch, where she belonged.

The first thing he had to do was to turn his back on the liquor and stabilize his life. His nieces had better things to do than constantly worry about him. With only the slightest hesitation he returned the mug to the table, where Lucille McWhirter had put it.

"Are you all right, Will?" she asked.

"Lucille—" He gave her a sly grin. "Ain't never been better in my life. How about you and me callin' that preacher you been keepin' on the back burner?"

In a room suddenly filled with masculine whoops, Lucille McWhirter wrapped her plump arms around Will Winthrop's neck. "You old gazebo! Do you mean it?"

"That I do, Lucy girl. That I do."

The revelry and celebration extended well past the hour of ten. Amid the gaiety of the occasion, scarcely a man perked his head when the clang of fire bells resounded into the night. But the cries of "Fire! Fire!" from the street below drew every head to the windows.

Flames leapt at the horizon, and as firemen dove for the cover of wagons and alleyways, the splinters of the exploding mercantile so carefully closed up that night filled the glowing air.

Within moments the entire block of empty businesses added to the fiery carnage.

Three

Paulina sat back on her ankles and thought an expletive, hesitating to form it on her lips in light of her position as a lady of some breeding. Was it really worth the trouble to trek all this distance to find Millburn, she wondered, tugging at a lock—the only evidence as to the true length of her hair—fallen loose from her hat. *Bringing Millburn back will not give Father back his life,* she continued thinking. *And it might even cost poor Millburn his own.*

Paulina had slid the bolt on the door of her room at Big Pat's, removed her denims and baggy shirt, and now rose to her knees in her chemise and lace-edged bloomers. Having dragged the hat up from the pile of discarded clothing, she now tossed it off once again, her thick, wavy hair cascading the length of her back to settle its tips upon the planked floor.

Paulina sighed, dropping the backs of her hands upon her thighs as she did so. The small mirror she'd placed before her on the floor and angled upward reflected her pensive expression. What had happened to the good life she'd enjoyed before her father's death? She and her younger sister, Lillian, had journeyed to the East just after Christmas. They had hoped to see their mother,

46

only to find that she'd skipped off to Europe the week before. When the two disappointed sisters had returned to Turkey Gulch, they'd found their dear father, Sabin Winthrop, the town's marshal for twenty years as well as a merchant, lying in his coffin in the parlor of Lucille McWhirter's boardinghouse. Ambushed in the dead of night, he'd not even had the chance to clear his sidearm from its holster to defend himself. Death had come quickly—a revelation Lucille had thought would comfort Sabin's daughters—but the fact that death had come at all, and in such a hideous, cowardly manner, had sent Paulina immediately to the city council. She shuddered to recall their stern looks . . . Mr. Jeconiah's beady little eyes rolling beneath shaggy white brows; Mr. Roper's fingers linked and his thumbs circling each other; Mr. Logan clearing his throat every time she made a dramatic point. They had humored her, patronized her, outraged her, challenged her—and she had walked away, not really knowing if she had won or lost her case. She wondered now if their offer had been a serious one . . . or if they had just wanted to be rid of her.

Again she sighed, this time with the faintest hint of emotion lodging in her throat and moistening her eyes. She had been in Skagway for a whole week, her only friend the amiable Big Pat, and her only goal to find a suitable guide into the interior. She hoped she might have found him in the handsome, dark-haired Brett McCallum, though Big Pat was still voicing his distrust and trying to sway her otherwise. But she didn't want to travel for days, even weeks or months, gagging on the stench of a grizzled old bear who hadn't bathed in half a year. Even with the distance of twenty feet and the darkness parting them, Paulina had imagined she detected the pleasant scent of musk . . . her eyes had gazed with awe into dark, brooding features that had appeared trustworthy. Big Pat had promised to seek him out early that morning and now, way past the hour of ten, he had yet to report back to her.

In a rush of garbled thoughts she suddenly remembered that she hadn't sent a wire to Lillian as she had promised to do as soon as she reached Alaska. She climbed up from her knees, dragged on her denims and the oversize shirt, and began tucking her hair beneath the clumsy hat. Though she'd promised Big Pat to stay put until he returned, she gave the promise little thought as she crept out a back entrance.

Brett exited the tent restaurant and dragged in a long, deep breath of the morning. His hands covering his hips for a moment, he arched his back against the stiffness of two hours in the straight-back chair, his eyes moving fluidly along the street. He grinned. Now, there was a sight for sore eyes . . . a girl dressed like a boy, moving with a confidence that hinted she might really believe her disguise was working. He watched her intently, the baggy male clothing hiding an obviously slender female form, the bulge of the felt hat she wore straining against the weight of thick, lustrous hair . . . her pale oval features as pretty as any he'd ever seen. He wished he could see her eyes, but she kept them turned away from him. Her hands were exposed, as pale and slim as the rest of her, with long, tapered, unpolished nails that would give away her true gender if she didn't immediately conceal them. She must have read his thoughts, for suddenly her hands dropped into the deep pockets of her denims.

Brett decided to follow discreetly along, to see where she was going and what she was up to, donning such a ridiculous disguise. The forty-five-caliber sidearm on

48

her right hip looked large enough to topple her into the roadway. He would like to be there to catch her if it did.

Paulina knew he was following her. She kept her eyes turned away and stepped up her pace. The telegraph office was only a hundred yards or so ahead on the boardwalk, though it seemed more like a million miles as she waded through loitering men who seemed to grow in numbers even as she moved along. She was sure the sign above the entrance to the telegraph office was becoming smaller with distance; she wished she could reach out and halt its retreat. Oh, please, please, let me get there before he catches up to me, she thought, crossing her arms against her waistline.

The distance closed. She breathed a sigh of relief, seeing him, from the corner of her eye, halt across the muddy roadway and lean against a building. He still watched her, but he was no longer closing the distance. Then, as she turned to enter the telegraph office, the full-bearded, lecherously grinning Soapy Smith was blocking her path.

"Where you goin', boy? Don't tell me you got money to send a telegraph message."

Halting, then taking a precarious step backward, Paulina pulled her hat low to her forehead. In a voice straining to deepen convincingly, she warned, "Get out of my way, Smith," but he merely laughed. Her eyes widening, skirting the roadway, she saw two of his henchmen exit Clancy's Saloon.

Around Soapy's left wrist was coiled a thick, ugly, discolored bull whip. Suddenly loosening it, grabbing the handle in his right hand, he popped it scarcely half an inch from the toe of Paulina's boot. "Think I'll teach you to respect your elders, boy," he threatened.

Immediately Paulina's hand darted down and struggled to drag the forty-five from its heavy leather holster. As she gripped the weapon between her two slender hands, it wavered menacingly before Soapy Smith. "Don't you come no closer, or I'll put a hole in you for sure!" Her voice had lost its forced masculine depth; the high-pitched warning might just as well have been that of a prepubescent boy . . . if her disguise still held up.

Soapy merely stepped down to the roadway and motioned for his men to approach. The only thing on his mind was having a little fun and entertaining the gathering audience.

Brett suddenly realized that he was in the direct path of the woman's shaky aim. He saw Soapy's henchmen approaching from the saloon and knew he had to help somehow. His hand drawing up to find the sidearm on his right hip, he was just about to cross the roadway when a single shot rang out.

A fiery path ripped through his left thigh. Gritting his teeth, he stood there for a moment, his eyes shutting, then opening again. As Soapy and his men scattered for the cover of Clancy's Saloon, most of Skagway's other residents emerged onto the roadway to see who might be the latest casualty of the settlement's lawlessness. The blasted girl in men's clothing had dropped to her knees on the boardwalk outside the telegraph office and a boy of about fourteen had snatched the weapon from Paulina's trembling hands.

Brett could feel the warmth of blood covering his thigh and soaking the leg of his denims. Still, his main concern was reaching the girl before someone put a hole in her big enough to drive a cannon through.

As he dropped, grimacing, to his good leg and his

hands covered Paulina's shoulders, his eyes warned the others away. "Blast it, girl, you shot me!" he snapped, shaking her in spite of his resolve to offer her some comfort. "You should be careful with that thing!"

Tears flooded Paulina's eyes. She could not remember firing the weapon, and had not felt the impact of it. If she didn't know better—and if the man now gripping her shoulders were not bleeding—she'd have sworn that her gun had not been fired. And if she had not quickly recognized Brett's voice from his conversation the evening before with Big Pat, she'd have had no idea whose hands shook her shoulders. "I—I—" she stammered, unable to form words. Then another familiar voice approached.

"Damn, Pau-Paulie," came Big Pat's harsh tone. "You just shot the man you was aimin' to hire!"

"I—I don't think I—"

Brett cut her off. "*This* wisp of a girl is the *boy* who's wanting to find his pa on the Yukon River?"

Big Pat shrugged apologetically, then immediately began shooing off the bystanders. "Ain't nothin' goin' on here," he grumbled. "Go on about your business."

As Paulina dramatically sniffed back her tears, her thick, golden tresses tumbled from the cover of her hat. The velvety softness of it against his hands almost made Brett forget the throbbing bullet wound.

"Let's take care of that leg," said Big Pat, reminding Brett of his misfortune. Then, in a harsher tone to Paulina, "Where the hell do you think you were going?"

She looked up, avoiding Brett's searching eyes. "I—I was going to send a telegram to my sister."

"Hell—" Big Pat exclaimed, dragging his hand across his bald head. "Ain't no telegraph lines in Alaska. Ol' Soapy set up this operation just to get your five dollars.

You'd have got a message in reply, aw'right, but ol' Soapy, he'd of made it up."

"Oh, why am I alive?" Paulina said in a scarcely audible voice. "And what am I doing here?" Brett continued to hold her shoulders, but now he did so for support. As Paulina became aware of his need, her composure returned in one swift move, and she stared with horror at the blood spreading down Brett's thigh. "Dear Lord, what have I done?"

Big Pat's arm moved beneath Brett's in an effort to get him up. When at last he leaned heavily against the large bartender, his senses hanging on by a thread, Paulina was immediately on her feet, tucking herself beneath Brett's other arm. Before either took a step, Big Pat extended his hand and waited for the fresh-faced boy who'd taken Paulina's gun to surrender it to him. He did so without hesitation.

As Big Pat dragged Brett along, and Paulina struggled to keep pace and support the tall, muscular man she'd shot, bystanders eased aside. In moments, Brett was rather rudely dropped onto Paulina's bed in the back room at Big Pat's Saloon.

He was still and ashen, nary a twitch to his sharp good looks to indicate he was even alive. After soaking a cloth in the basin, Paulina rushed back to bathe Brett's forehead. "Do you think I've killed him?" she asked worriedly, watching as Big Pat cut away the denim to survey the damage she'd done. Then she drew back, caught her trembling lip between her teeth, and chewed lightly on it, deep in thought. After a moment she softly said, "I'm just bad luck, Big Pat, and I shouldn't be here. Tomorrow morning I'm heading home."

Big Pat was about to say *But what about your pa up north on the river*—when Brett's hand darted out, found the small one belonging to the trembling Paulina, and brought it down to his chest. Were she to try—and she didn't really feel an immediate need—she was sure she wouldn't be able to free it from his firm grip. "Don't go, pretty lady," he mumbled, his eyes closed. "Do you want to get married?"

She paused very briefly, almost unnoticeably. Then, jerking her hand free, she choked, "Oh, you . . . you . . . you slave to your loins . . . I'd as soon marry Soapy Smith!" Fury pressed firmly to her brows, darkening her eyes and stirring a most becoming state of embarrassment in her pale cheeks. Ignoring Big Pat's grin, she folded herself back into the chair, drew her legs up, and gently wrapped her arms around them. Mumbling to the half-conscious Brett "You deserve to bleed to death," she then turned her head and pouted prettily.

Big Pat chuckled. "Don't be too hard on him, Paulina. You gotta remember ain't much to the north of here but Lapps and Eskimos . . . maybe a few outlaws runnin' from badges. Fella didn't mean no insult."

"And you men! Always sticking up for each other."

Brett mumbled, "I'll file . . . attempted murder charges, sweet thing . . . if you don't . . . want to get married—"

Paulina shot from the chair, her hands lifting to cover her slim hips. "Can he do that, Big Pat? Can he . . . blackmail me?"

"Hell . . . pardon, Miss, you kill a man outright in Skagway, and Soapy's law'll hang ya faster'n ya can skedaddle . . . this here fella, I reckon it's up to him—" Taking a sheet off a tall, narrow shelf, Big Pat threw it to Paulina. "Tear some long strips off this, will ya?"

Paulina mentally slumped, even as her body grew rigid with disbelief. "You mean . . . *he*—that snake of a man—holds my fate in his hands?"

Big Pat merely shrugged, as if he regretted the whole affair.

Brett had drifted into unconsciousness. Over the next few minutes Big Pat brought the bleeding under control and determined that the bullet had exited the back of his thigh, and that no artery had been severed.

"Perhaps he was just funnin' with ya," Big Pat attempted to assure a now-silent tearful Paulina. "Ya know how men are?" When she did not respond, he continued. "Don't ya?"

"I know how *decent* men are," she said after a moment. "I don't know about . . . about creatures like him!"

Big Pat completed his ministrations, wrapped the wounded leg with the strips of white cotton Paulina had absently torn, then washed his bloodied hands in the basin. "I wish I could hide ya out, Paulina, until we see what ol' Soapy's goin' to do, but I need ya to take care of McCallum—"

"Me! Why me? I'd as soon breathe air into a snake!"

"Ya shot 'im . . . ya take care of 'im. I got a saloon to run and can't expect Rusty to work twenty-four hours a day."

"And what if Soapy sends that deputy marshal he installed to take me into custody?"

"If he does, we'll send to Dyea for a judge. Take care of McCallum. Let me know when he comes to."

"You can't just leave me alone with him!" Paulina smarted, her hand rising to clamp with some effort over Big Pat's thick shoulder. "Why, if he starts that marrying rubbish again, I'm liable to smother him!"

Big Pat shrugged again, as if it didn't make any difference to him one way or the other.

Soapy Smith was fit to be tied. He didn't like being backed down in the street and forced to run by a damn greenhorn boy, but when the boy turned out to be a girl, that made it even worse. On top of that, he had learned upon reaching Clancy's Saloon that one of his own men had fired the shot that had struck the bystander, and not the blasted girl.

"You"—he spoke to a couple of his men—"get over to Big Pat's place and get the gun that girl was wielding before somebody discovers it wasn't fired."

The opium-addicted Syd Dixon and Soapy's body-guard Yeah Mow Hopkins immediately moved toward the door.

By the time they reached the big man's saloon a few minutes later, the offending weapon was making the rounds of the patrons. On the boardwalk outside the door, the two henchmen heard Big Pat exclaiming, "It ain't been fired, has it, boys?" and two dozen men were mumbling their agreement.

As Soapy's men entered the saloon and stood there, beady, threatening eyes making a fluid sweep of the place, the mumbling died into silence. His boots clicking on the planked floorboards, Syd Dixon ambled toward a bearded man sitting at a table with four others and carefully removed the forty-five from his hand. "I'll take that, fella."

His features fearless and unmoving, Big Pat warned, "Fellas here know it ain't been fired, Dixon. You tell ol' Soapy, he'd better not make no trouble . . . an' he knows what I mean."

The two bastards who mopped up after Soapy had been warned about the bold bartender. His days were numbered. Like oiled-down lizards, the men slithered from the bar, quickly making their way back to Clancy's, where Soapy awaited them.

Big Pat was talking with one of the patrons when he heard from the darkness behind the tattered curtain,

"Psssst!" He turned, only the gleam of Paulina's sea-green eyes visible to him. "What do you think will happen?" she asked, her long, slender fingers closing over his arm as he neared.

Despite his large, bulky frame, Big Pat was gentle. The touch of his thick fingers closing over her own slim ones almost could not be felt. "I don't think you'll be having any more trouble with Soapy and his gang. He'll not be wanting any questions asked about where that bullet really came from . . . the one that tore through McCallum's leg."

"What do you mean . . . where the bullet really came from? Didn't it come from my gun?"

Big Pat grinned amiably. "Heck, no, little lady. Your gun weren't even fired. Reckon that's why Soapy sent a couple of his men over to get it."

"But—" Worry settled upon Paulina's pale brow. "They'll fire it, and they'll say I *did* shoot McCallum."

"An' you got two dozen witnesses in here who'll say you didn't."

"If they're not too afraid to testify to that!" Paulina's pretty mouth pressed into a defiant line as she cast a look across her shoulder. "Well, at least I won't have to marry that blackmailing rogue!" Actually, the idea wasn't altogether distasteful to her, if she was in a mind to marry, and she was superficial enough to consider looks somewhat important in the selection. Brett McCallum was a devil and a dog, but he made her heart beat quickly. She hated her body's reaction to him.

"You go on back and look after him."

She jumped, so lost in her thoughts that she'd forgotten Big Pat's presence. "Oh, yes . . . yes, I guess that's the least I can do." When the bartender turned away, Paulina called his name, halting him. "How long do you think he'll be laid up?"

"Couple of weeks, I reckon—"

"A couple of weeks! I can't wait that long!"

"Don't go to frettin', little lady. Two weeks pass real fast here in Skagway. Of course, if you've a mind to find someone else—"

Her chin lifted; she was about to dart back that perhaps she would . . . but something inside halted any such declaration. She wasn't sure what it was, but it was strong and undeniable, like the heartbeat of an ox. Entering her room, she gently closed the door and did not hear Big Pat's throaty chuckle.

Paulina plopped herself into the chair, dug one of her elbows into the mattress, and rested her cheek against her open palm. She watched the unconscious man for some sign of life, almost hoping she would see none. Men like that cared about nothing but sating their lusts in bawdy houses and losing their money at gambling halls. There was probably not one single redeemable bone in his tall, worthless body. "I hate you, Brett McCallum," she mumbled, narrowing her eyes to study the scar at his right temple. She half expected him to come out of his unconsciousness with a wicked sleight-of-hand to rob her of her money. "You should be one of Soapy's men," she continued her insults. "You've got all the qualifications for it." With a deep, weary sigh, she confessed in a quieter tone, "But—idiotic me—I want *you* to take me to the Yukon River to find Millburn Hanks. I've got to find him . . . everything I am and want to be . . . my whole family is depending on Millburn returning to Utah with me. As for you, you worthless male, I'll use my feminine wiles to get you to take me . . . because I don't have enough money to pay you, though you won't find out until it's too late to turn back. How dare you suggest that I marry you . . . you'll get your comeuppance, and I'm just the woman to give it to you."

When she dragged herself up and turned away, Brett McCallum's right eye slowly opened and a grin slid across his bronze features. Yup. This was the woman he wanted to take back to Gruff, to make his last year the happiest of his life. She had guts, and he imagined that she might also have the necessary stamina to reach their settlement near Nuklukayet and still be strong enough to fulfill Gruff's pleasures before a cold grave claimed his mortal remains.

As Paulina swung around, he quickly closed his eye and erased the grin from his mouth. Feigning unconsciousness had gotten him an earful just moments ago; he wondered what else she had to say. The very idea that she'd think *he* wanted to marry her kept the grin alive inside of him, and it was all he could do to keep it off his face. The very idea, indeed! He'd go to his grave a bachelor. No woman could lay a claim to him! He enjoyed satisfying his loins with a good woman now and then, but he certainly didn't want one clinging permanently to his coattails.

Paulina was almost sure the expression on Brett McCallum's face had changed somewhat. She took a small step toward the bed, then bent low to get a better look. A single lock of chestnut-colored hair rested on his forehead. When her fingers rose to lightly brush it back, she felt the warmth of fever upon his brow. So, feeling sorry for him once again, she sat down, settled back, and crossed her arms beneath her supple breasts and the yards of cotton wrapping tightly confining them.

He knew he was a dog. How could he not? Her insulting thoughts of him rushed through her, warming and cooling her, infuriating and calming her, all at the same time. She wondered how old he was, guessing that he was probably in his mid-thirties. The freshness of youth was long gone from his features, and the expressive little lines of aging had, for the time being, been held at bay. The rugged outdoors darkened his skin; she admired the healthy glow of it. His eyebrows were dark, eyelashes thick, only a gray hair or two clinging to the thick mass of hair at his temples and across his ears. His chest rippled with well-nurtured muscles; she could see the vague shadow of dark, curly hair straining against the fabric of his shirt. She imagined that if she ventured to touch him, he would be lean and iron-hard. Her gaze moved fluidly, along the crisscrossed ties holding the V of his shirt together, across the flat plane of his belly, fleeting across him . . . there . . . and plying a deliberate course down one of his thickly muscled legs and returning up the other, lingering on the tear in his trousers and the cotton dressing that was soaked with his blood.

With instinctive curiosity her gaze returned to the bulge of his manhood . . . either he was very well endowed, or he had vainly padded himself to impress the ladies—

"Want some candy, little girl?"

With a startled "Ooooh!" Paulina jumped from her chair, knocking it over in her speed to put distance between herself and Brett McCallum. "I didn't know you were awake!" she spat out at him, the pink in her cheeks slowly darkening. "Why didn't you tell me you were awake?"

"I was hoping those little fingers of yours would get as curious as those pretty green eyes."

"In your dreams!" she snipped, turning sharply, so sure was she that he could see her heart pounding fiercely against the threads of her oversize shirt. "Well, I'll tell you one thing, *Mister* Brett McCallum, I'll bloody well find someone else to take me to the Yukon!"

"Tsk . . . tsk . . . I know you don't have any money,"

he said in a sarcastic tone. "And I really don't think those feminine wiles are going to pay your ticket—"

"You bastard!" Paulina wanted to spring and kill, so angry was she at his unconscionable pretense. "You heard everything I said? You weren't unconscious! Why . . . why—"

Again his tone became softly mocking. "Don't you remember? You're just the woman to give me my come-uppance!"

If Big Pat hadn't made an appearance at just that moment, Paulina was sure she would have acted on impulse. When she met the questioning gaze of the man she had befriended, he said, "What the hell's going on in here! Suppose I need to call in a referee?"

Paulina balled up her fists and took several swings at the air. "You better hold me back, or I'm going to punch McCallum into obscurity." And when she made a dash for the bed, Big Pat's burly arm circled her waist and lifted her off the floor. While her arms flailed and her feet kicked at the air, Pat threw his head back and laughed. "What'd ya do to her, McCallum? She's mad-der'n a wet hen and just as noisy!"

A cockeyed smile twisted Brett's mouth, innocence springing into his rich blue eyes. "Just offered the little gal some candy," he responded, using his hands to push himself into a seated position. Then he pulled a small brown paper sack from his trousers pocket and popped a piece of rock candy into his mouth. With an eyebrow cocked he held the bag out to Paulina.

She had stopped twisting. Her breathing was still hard and labored but not heaving with anger, so Big Pat lowered her. In an even, controlled tone, she asked Pat, "What are my chances of getting a man to take me to the north Yukon for less than a hundred and nineteen dollars?"

"About the same as squeezing gold out of a goose egg," came Big Pat's immediate reply.

"I'll take you," offered Brett, the candy bunched up in his left jaw. "And the only fee I'll ask for is a visit to the preacher when we reach Nuklukayet."

"I hate you."

"Don't pick on the gal," said Big Pat, bemused, wondering what Paulina would do if Syd Dixon hadn't taken her gun. Then he glanced toward the pair of Colts hanging on the bedstead. Surely, she wouldn't shoot the man with one of his own guns? Pat gave her a sideways glance. Nah, she wouldn't.

If Paulina had known what he was thinking, she'd have quickly begged to differ. She had eyed one of those Colts herself, and the temptation was very strong. But, blast it, she needed Brett McCallum, at least for the time being, and killing the egotistical ass wasn't in her best interest. As Big Pat once again left the two alone, Paulina sank with the grace of a lady into the straight-back chair. Crossing her arms, she gave Brett McCallum a long, thoughtful look. He wanted a wife . . . and she wanted to find Millburn Hanks. He wanted to return to his place near Nuklukayet and she wanted to return to Turkey Gulch and claim her prize. Well, they couldn't both be winners.

"Very well—" she said after a moment. "You help me find Millburn Hanks and I'll willingly pay a visit to that preacher." Of course, she had no intention of marrying him, but she would let him think that she would. When he hesitated to respond, she prompted him with a curt "Well?"

"No fooling, little lady?" asked Brett, again scooting the candy into his jaw. Was this the time to tell her that the marrying wasn't with him, but with his terminally ill friend, Gruff? He mentally shrugged; no, that could wait until they reached Nuklukayet. "You got yourself a deal."

Paulina stood and offered her hand. "We'll shake on it!" *That'll convince him,* she thought. *Never did put much stock in a handshake myself.* It was a male thing; surely, *she* wouldn't be expected to honor it.

Though he was suspicious that she'd accepted his terms so easily, Brett took her slender hand and held it, even as she attempted to extract it from his grip. When she began to pull really hard, he let it go, and in the force of her own struggles she spun on the heel of her boot and landed clumsily in the chair. Collecting herself, in a sultry, sarcastic voice she said, "You know, Brett McCallum, I was raised to be a lady—" and with a smile strangled over clenched teeth, "but you sure know how to make me forget that."

Four

Paulina was dreadfully bored. In the five days since Brett McCallum had gotten himself shot outside the phantom telegraph office, she'd seen little more than the walls of the small back room in which she was imprisoned with the rascal. Had he not already ruffled her feathers, she would have found him a likable man, though infuriating at times. She kept herself on guard so that she would not fall victim to his masculine charms and the dramatic hurt-little-boy innocence he exhibited with the talents of an Oscar Wilde.

He had patiently written out, then had her sign, an agreement to marry upon reaching Nuklukayet. An oddly composed document, it had not contained Brett's name, though it had mentioned Paulina's numerous times. She would play his silly little game, because she had absolutely no intention of marrying him and hadn't felt the least pang of conscience when she had signed his ridiculous good-faith document.

"Paulina honey?"

She hated it when he called her *honey*. Spinning away from the dresser where she'd placed the alcohol and gauze, her eyes narrowed with lethal glow. "I am not your honey!'' she growled for the umpteenth time. "What do you want now, Brett McCallum? My soul?''

Brett grinned, his eyes raking her slim form, now covered by a simple white cotton gown whose bodice hugged her becomingly. "My shirt's gotten twisted. Could you help me straighten myself?''

"Ohhhh . . . I don't think you're nearly as helpless''—she fussed with indignation—"as you would have me believe. I do declare''—her slim hands scooted beneath the lapels of his shirt and tugged him forward—"you're just a big old baby, Brett McCallum. I just don't know what—'' Her gaze met his own, which immediately silenced her, immediately stilled her movements. Her mouth remained parted, now imperceptibly trembling, and she was much too surprised by the twinkling depths of his blue gaze and the lack of humor upon his features to bite her lip, as was her usual habit.

At the moment Brett felt anything but humor. Her long, rich tresses had fallen across her shoulder, and rested softly upon his forearm, the delicate scent of lavender clung to her youthful skin, and her fresh-faced loveliness left him unable to move. She was like a goddess suddenly turned to stone, no movement at all as she held her stand, her features mere inches away from his own, pale and porcelainlike. He'd never wanted anything in all his life as he wanted to taste the sweetness of her kiss, to feel the velvety smoothness of her body against his own . . . as he wanted to feel the warmth of her breath against his cheek and her tenderly spoken endearments against his hairline. He was arush with the sensual beauty of her, the alluring sexuality of her. . . .

And without first thinking and carefully assessing the consequences, his hands rose, circled her arms, and drew her close. At first his mouth only brushed hers, so lightly that it might not have been touched at all. Then the capture became deep, his mouth imprisoning her own, his right hand moving up to cradle her head, to draw her even closer. As his senses rushed back and he realized that she was responding, he pulled her slim body across his own, caring not that a momentary pain touched the injured leg.

Paulina lost herself in the stolen kiss—forgetting her determination not to fall victim to his charms—her dizzy mind rationalizing that because he'd been so bored remaining abed for the past week with only the curt temperance she'd shown to him, he deserved her attentions now. But who was she kidding? She loved the way his mouth felt upon hers, loved the musky, manly scent of him, loved the way his hand roughly caressed her neck beneath the masses of her hair. His breath was warm and sweet against her cheek, and the way his chest burned against the womanly curves of her made her wish that the threads of their clothing did not so rudely separate them. She wanted to lie with him, unclothed and uninhibited, to feel his muscular legs lying against her own smooth ones, to enjoy his gentle masculine hands arousing her in a way that she had never before been aroused but had dreamed of a thousand—no, a hundred thousand—times!

But when Brett McCallum, in that undertone of humor she hated so much, whispered huskily, "Hey, Paulina honey, let's get naked—" she pulled back from him so swiftly that she might have been dealt a painful blow to the jaw. Her eyes narrowed venomously, and as she jerked her arms free of him and her feet once again touched the planked floor, she knew, at that moment, that she could spring and kill, and he would be powerless against her strength.

"Oh . . . you!" was the best she could manage when

she groped for an insult, her trembling hands drawing up to cover her slim hips. "How dare you kiss me like that!"

Brett chuckled. "You were doing a fair share of that kissing yourself, honey—"

"I was not!"

"You was too!" He laughed back at her, his arm easing up to ward off a halfhearted attack. Catching her wrist, he drew her close, his tone softening as he said, "You don't have to worry, honey, I would be gentle with you. I know you are inexperienced—"

Paulina gasped. How dare he assume she had no experience with men. How dare he assume—and he was, surely!—that she was a virgin. How dare he assume that he knew her well enough to make any assumption at all! She was furious, more furious than if he'd accused her of being a wanton hussy! "I'll have you know, Brett McCallum," she grated between tightly clenched teeth as she once again tore herself free of him, "that I've been with many men, hundreds of men . . . certainly better men than you! If you wanted a virgin wife, well . . . I'm sorry to disappoint you!"

A half-grin slid onto Brett's mouth. "Hundreds, huh? Then what're you being so up in the air about now? Playing the highfalutin lady that's been insulted. Hell, if you've been with hundreds, then why are you making such a big deal out of pleasing me. You can make it a hundred and one, honey. One more notch on your—" He grinned, catching his little rhyme in mid-verse as he quietly said, "Gun."

"How dare you!" Paulina was prepared to sling her denials, to confess her lie regarding her state of chastity and viciously berate him for believing it. But on second thought, what harm would it do for him to believe she was anything less than a virgin? If he thought she'd been with a hundred men, perhaps he wouldn't find the prospect of marrying her so inviting. Perhaps he would take her to the Yukon to find Millburn Hanks, and decide that he'd rather hold out for a virtuous woman. And with that thought in mind, Paulina lifted a haughty chin, looked down her nose at him as one might look at chicken droppings and coolly said, "If I add another notch to my . . . gun, *Mister* McCallum, it'll be with a better man than you."

As she turned her back to him, crossed her arms, and tapped her foot, Brett said with that boyish innocence, "But Paulina honey, there is no better man than me . . . at least not in Skagway."

"I doubt that—" She pivoted back, a smirk playing on her mouth. "What about Soapy Smith?"

"Be my guest, ladybug. He probably likes his wenches well broken in—" He hadn't a single moment to prepare for an attack before Paulina lunged for him, her slim body covering his own and her fingers wrapping around his thick neck. Her vain efforts to throttle him merely added fuel to his laughter. But when he realized that she was sobbing uncontrollably, the laughter ceased and Brett's arms wrapped firmly around her to hold her close. "Why are you crying, Paulina?" he soothed her. "I was only teasing you."

Suddenly Paulina realized it wasn't his cruel teasing that had upset her. Missing her sister, and her uncle, and her little friend Matt . . . her father's death . . . her socialite mother's indifference to her daughters, the months since she'd left Utah . . . the challenge of the city council and the intimidations of certain sleazy malcontents back in Turkey Gulch—it had all built up to this emotional state. She could blame Brett because he was handy, but it really wasn't his fault. Actually, she enjoyed

67

the banterings, even when they got a little rough . . . because it made her forget all her troubles.

So, finding him receptive and caring, she sobbed away all her worries, dampening his shirt with her tears, and enjoyed the gentleness of his hands massaging her back and shoulders. Soon she lay very quietly against him, sniffing every now and then, her knuckles drawn up and pressed to her teeth.

"Brett?" The only response was his hand tightening against her back. "I really haven't been with a hundred men. I'm a virgin."

"I know—"

Her cheek shifted slightly against the coarse texture of his chest. "How do you know?"

Silence. Brett's eyebrows furrowed. "Because you're wearing a white dress . . . and everybody knows only virgins wear white dresses."

Her head snapped up. Through the blur of her tears she could not discern if he was teasing or if he'd been so long in the isolated interior of Alaska that he could honestly believe such nonsense. Then she again dropped her eyes from his view, buried her face against the sleeve of her dress, and tried not to snicker. But that was simply not possible.

"Are you laughing at me?" asked Brett McCallum, drawing slightly back in an effort to get a better view of her.

Pressing her mouth more firmly to the material of her dress, she mumbled, "N-no, I . . . of course . . . I wouldn't laugh at you."

But he could feel the movement of her suppressed laughter through the fabric of his shirt, and he suddenly perched over her with mock severity upon his dark good looks. "You *are* making fun of me, Paulina Winthrop. What did I say that was so amusing?" How pretty she was when she'd been weeping . . . the tip of her nose as rosy as her cheeks, her eyes glistening like dawn's dew . . . her mouth slightly trembling, yet still in control . . . an innocence molding her features like a child not yet fully awake. Guilt grabbed Brett within. He planned to take this lovely flower to the Yukon and bind her over in marriage to his dying friend. Surely, she had a life of her own, a family somewhere who cared very deeply for her. How selfish he was to want to take all that from her.

Paulina noticed the darkening of his features, the way his lips pressed together, the way his eyes narrowed. A hardness grew on his face, taking away the playfulness they had shared and the sorrow he'd felt for upsetting her, and she couldn't help wondering what he was thinking that overshadowed his prior mood.

Brett slid back onto his pillow, his fingers loosening then withdrawing from her shoulder, his gaze picking absently over the unpainted ceiling. So he would make her Gruff's wife . . . but it would be for so short a while and then she could return to her own life. Gruff was his friend, and he had made a promise, a promise he simply had to keep.

Paulina closed her eyes. Whatever he was thinking really didn't matter. Even though she loathed him sometimes, she enjoyed the warmth she felt against him now. Tomorrow she might be slinging degradations and insults at him, and bearing the brunt of his sarcasm and humiliation in return, but for now she just wanted to feel safe and secure, and to know that he would protect her when they left for the Yukon. She would find Millburn Hanks, and perhaps he would help her to get around the ridiculous marriage document Brett had made her sign. She knew only that she had no desire to remain in Alaska, or to marry Brett McCallum.

Brett had seen a lot of mystery in the woman from

Turkey Gulch, Utah, this past week. She claimed to want a guide to the interior, so that she could find her pa, but nine out of ten times she'd referred to Millburn Hanks as Millburn, had never explained the differences in their last names, but had shrugged off his inquiries, and the few times she had referred to him as "Pa" she had done so hesitatingly. She had even remarked once in conversation that "since her pa died—" then had immediately claimed the reference was to a stepfather. What was she hiding? And why was it so important to her to return Millburn to Turkey Gulch? Brett's curiosity was quickly piquing to painful heights.

But for now he was content to be Paulina's comforter and to feel the soft warmth of her lying ever so slightly against him. Glancing downward, he could see the rapid darting of her eyes beneath translucent lids, a pinching of her mouth to keep it from trembling, the fingers of her left hand lightly clenching and unclenching, frequently burying her long, tapered nails into the tender skin of her palm. What was the burden this lovely woman carried, and how could he help her?

Brett drew in an imperceptible sigh. Help her with her burden, indeed! He had already planned to add to it. He would take her back to Nuklukayet and marry her off to the dying Gruff. What an unconscionable bastard he was!

Will Winthrop kept close to his room at Lucille's boardinghouse. Since the fire that had destroyed the mercantile and half the row of closed-down businesses, he had remained in hiding, his errands done by the boy, Matt. When Lillian's body had not been found in the rubbish, Lester Bartlett had promptly filed arson and insurance fraud charges against her and, outrageously, a reward poster bearing her photograph had been circulated throughout the territory. At scarcely the age of nineteen, Lillian Winthrop was, in effect, a wanted criminal.

There were very few secrets kept in Turkey Gulch from the Bartlett brothers, but one of them existed right there in Lucille's boardinghouse. Her first husband, a much older man she'd married at the age of sixteen, had been sympathetic toward the Union deserters and, with the construction of the boardinghouse in progress, had written into the plans an inner room accessible through a panel in the upstairs parlor. With it disguised to look like part of the east wall, there was no one left in Turkey Gulch who knew the entrance existed. There, Lucille's first husband had hidden the deserters from army patrols, and had once hidden a boy falsely accused of murder in Salt Lake City for the better part of a year until the real culprit had confessed, then been promptly hanged.

It was there that Lillian Winthrop had been hiding for the past two weeks.

She was bored to tears. Lucille kept her up-to-date on the antics of the Bartletts, and she kept a copy of the reward poster tacked above her bed to remind her constantly of their treachery. She'd had nothing to do with the fire that had destroyed the mercantile; indeed, she'd almost been a victim of it herself. Piecing together the night of the fire, and remembering the little clues that someone had been in her apartment, she strongly suspected that the Bartletts had rigged the building to burn. But she had no proof of that, just as she had no proof of her innocence. The very fact that she'd appeared to flee had cast suspicion upon her, but Will and Lucille had been adamant that she would not be condemned to the confinement of the town jail, and the unquestionable barbarity of the Bartletts.

For a moment Lillian willed herself to hate Paulina. She was safely away, chasing her ghosts, though for the benefit of the family—and the silly little town of Turkey Gulch. She had heard that Alaska was beautiful this time of year, and Lillian envied Paulina's mission that had taken her there. Oh, to be away from Turkey Gulch and the Bartletts and the council of silly old men who thought they—and not the unscrupulous brothers—were running the town.

"Paulina . . . Paulina—" Lillian threw herself upon the bed and linked her fingers beneath her pert chin. "I wish I had gone with you. I wish I—"

Her softly spoken words ended with thoughts . . . one, two, three . . . from which she chose the best finish for the scatterings of her mind. *I wish I were with you. I wish I had gone to Europe to find Mother. I wish I weren't such a foolish girl!*

Turning over, throwing out her slender arms, Lillian drew up her legs, caring not that her skirts eased downward toward her thighs, exposing her lacy underthings. She was alone . . . what did it matter if she was indecent? Sighing deeply, Lillian closed her eyes and imagined what Alaska might be like in April. . . .

Paulina awoke with a start, immediately aware of Brett McCallum's eyes resting lazily on her features. Her palm digging into his chest, she pushed herself away.

"Ouch." Rubbing the area of abuse for a moment, Brett reached out and caught Paulina's wrist. "Where are you going?"

She used very little effort to twist herself from his light grip. "How long have we been asleep?"

"Oh, 'bout—" Feigned concentration sketched into his rough good looks. "A couple of hours or so. You in a hurry to go somewhere?"

Paulina gathered her thoughts for a resounding retort but instantly realized she wasn't in a mood to banter their usual insults and degradations. He had made her cry, but she wasn't embarrassed, and he had insulted her, but she wasn't angry. Though she hated to admit it, she liked the easygoing rogue, though she loathed to realize that she needed him as much as she did. Paulina Winthrop had prided herself on *never* needing anyone, but now it didn't seem so important to maintain her independence. Besides, her father had always said that honey attracted better than vinegar.

But what was she trying to attract?

So with a renewed tad of cynicism in her voice, Paulina turned full to the bedridden Brett McCallum and demanded, "When are we getting out of Skagway, McCallum? That leg looks half healed to me."

Dark eyebrows scooted low. Crossing his arms, he remarked, "Half healed . . . yes. But what about the other half? Don't I deserve another week of recuperation?"

"Surely, you've got a horse . . . it's not as if you'll have to walk back—"

"I walked in . . . I have every intention of walking back."

Paulina instantly remembered her lack of comfortable footwear. "Well, I don't intend to walk. We'll just have to find a suitable horse that's within my budget."

"Within your budget would be old and half dead."

Paulina, too, crossed her arms, her foot tapping the planked floor. She would not be outdone by the Alaskan. "Then a sled and a good pack of dogs—"

Brett threw his head back and laughed. "You've got a

hundred and nineteen dollars. You couldn't buy a broken-down sled and *one* good dog for that!"

Dropping her hands, Paulina turned away, hoping to hide from him the anger refreshing itself in her eyes. Then she grabbed her jacket from the back of a chair and moved toward the door. "I'm going out."

"Where are you going?"

She turned, her gaze locking to his own. "Out. Shall I spell it for you?"

He grinned devilishly. "Can you?"

She wouldn't give him the satisfaction. Exiting the room, she soon entered the saloon area behind the counter, where Big Pat rubbed glasses. "Where you going, Paulina?"

"Oh, you men! Can't I go out without you wanting to know the ins and outs of the cat's behind!"

With her skirts dancing at her heels, the swinging doors closed off her view of the big man's surprised features. "Women! Who can understand them?"

Paulina moved at a quick pace. She had stopped hiding her gender since the incident with Soapy, and now found herself the subject of masculine calls and wolf whistles. Turning a deaf ear, she quickly closed the distance between Big Pat's and the ticket office at the Skagway pier. Her first inquiry when she faced a bespectacled ticket agent was "Does Soapy Smith own this place?"

She immediately received a resounding "No, indeed!"

"Good! How far can two people get on one of your ships for a hundred and nineteen dollars?"

"In which direction, Miss?"

"Toward Nome."

The man relied on a large board behind him. "Well . . ." he mused. "Second-class fare to Nome is seventy-three

74

apiece, but I could get you to St. Michael for fifty-eight . . . second-class, of course—"

Paulina hastily figured, "A hundred and sixteen dollars," aloud, then to herself, *That leaves three dollars.* "How far is St. Michael from Nome?"

"Across the bay, less than a hundred and fifty miles."

"When is the next departure?"

"In the morning at six-thirty. Boarding begins at five-thirty—"

Paulina's hand left her pocket with the bundle of American notes. "I'll take two tickets—second-class," she said, peeling away the three dollars she would be allowed to keep. "How long will the trip take?"

Again the ticket agent referred to his schedule. "With overnight layovers at Valdez, Kodiak, and St. George, and layovers of shorter duration in between, the trip will take seventeen days."

"Do you know how far Nuklukayet is from St. Michael?"

Small, dark eyes peered across the rim of round spectacles as the man gave an exasperated sigh. "Madam, I did not lay out the settlements of Alaska. I am merely a ticket agent. You might refer to a map with a milage chart—"

"You needn't be go nasty," mumbled Paulina, accepting the tickets he now eased across the counter in exchange for her money. "Good day."

Turning crisply on her heel, Paulina wasted no time in returning to the room at Big Pat's and throwing the tickets atop Brett McCallum's chest. "There . . . tickets to St. Michael. We don't need dogs or horses or sleds." Turning from his smiling gaze, she began to dig among her things for the map she'd brought with her from Turkey Gulch . . . a map that Millburn himself had sent to her. Unfolding and scanning it for a second or two, she again pivoted, exclaiming, "Ah-ha! It appears to be about two hundred miles to your silly Nuklukayet . . . what kind of name is that, anyway . . . and Millburn . . . I mean Pa is on the Yukon somewhere near here—" Approaching to sit on the bed, Paulina turned the map to Brett's view and again pointed out the area near Fort Yukon where Millburn was supposed to be living.

Brett, however, had not taken his gaze off Paulina's slightly flushed, wind-cooled features to look at her map. "And how much did these blasted tickets cost? And did you use the money you were reserving for my fee?"

Digging into the pocket of her coat, Paulina tossed the three dollars onto his chest. "That's all there is . . . three dollars." When she thought he would protest, she blurted out, "Well, what are you complaining about? You're getting a wife out of the deal, aren't you? Didn't I sign your silly old document?"

He nodded, a smile turning up the corners of his mouth. "And how do you suppose we're going to purchase supplies for the trip between St. Michael and the Yukon? Nuklukayet is almost three hundred miles, and I would guess it's going to take the better part of a month on foot."

Paulina bounced to her feet. "And what about these long months of night? Have you accounted for that, Brett McCallum? Whoever heard of six months of night! Why, good heavens, why would any sensible man want to live in such a topsy-turvy place?"

Brett chuckled, reaching out to take her hand. "That is behind us, Paulina. The days will grow steadily longer and longer, and between June and August there will be little more than two or three hours of twilight between sunset and sunrise. Don't worry . . . you won't have to spend long, endless nights with the big, bad bogeyman—"

"Oh, pooh." Approaching, she began to fumble

about, checking his bandages, plumping pillows, and pulling up the single sheet. "I want you to know, Brett McCallum, that I'm not the least bit afraid of you. You're all huff and puff and I can think of a lot worse things to be fearful of. Polar bears and mad walruses and wolves and a few charging mooses—"

"That's *moose* . . . charging *moose*—"

"Well—" Paulina pouted attractively. "I was talking about more than one."

"It's *moose* whether it's one or a thousand. *Moose!*"

"Oh, all right! You don't have to be so precise. What difference does it make anyway?"

His arms easing around her waistline, he pulled her down to him. When at last her annoyance-laced eyes turned to hold him full, he said huskily, "How am I supposed to get aboard ship, pretty lady? I'm just a poor man with a big ol' mean bullet hole in his leg, and I do declare"—she hated it when he mimicked her favorite phrases—"I think I'm stuck to this bed until recovery is complete—"

Raising a pretty, pale eyebrow, Paulina reminded him, "There are things a man must take care of that would take him out of this bed . . . and I haven't seen any evidence that those duties were performed here. I certainly haven't had to change the sheets—"

Brett was well aware that his cockeyed grin almost made her smile. "All right . . . you've got me. But I'm still sore, and it's hard to walk." The grin widening, he asked, "You do feel sorry for me, don't you?"

"Feel sorry for you, indeed! I feel sorry for the poor lady who gave birth to you, and had to raise you. I imagine you were a hellion!" Plopping herself on the edge of the bed, she asked, "Where are your parents, Brett?"

"My mother operates a boardinghouse in San Francisco, and my father's buried at the base of Denali—"

"I'm sorry."

"No need. He died the way he lived. Playing out an adventure. He was mauled to death by a grizzly . . . the same grizzly, by the way, that took a few inches of flesh off the side of my head." Turning, Brett showed her the scars disappearing into his dark hairline. "One day I'm going to bring down that killer."

"If it doesn't bring you down first. I'd imagine that all grizzlies look alike. How will you know which one to go after?"

Brett nodded his head. "I'll know him. He has six toes on each of his front paws and a patch of fur as big as a hat missing from a rear haunch."

"Fur grows back."

"The beast fell on the campfire while he was killing my father. No . . . he's scarred for life."

Silence. Paulina saw conviction in his face. It was rather an odd emotion, since she'd seen nothing there but humor, child's play, and cynicism. But when he spoke of the bear and his father and his own maiming, he spoke like a man possessed. Hoping to change the subject, Paulina hopped up, exclaiming, "I'm famished! Shall I order in an early supper? We'll have some packing to do."

"Oh?" The lightness returned to his voice. "What have you got to pack, my lady? A couple of dresses Big Pat bought for you, an oversize hat, and a gangly boy's shirt and denims?"

"Well—" She managed a small smile. "I thought that since you're so grievously bedridden, I'd have to pack for you too."

"I'm all packed," Brett replied immediately, pointing an index finger toward the corner of the room. "When Big Pat brought my things over, I left everything packed. Ain't no need to do a thing for me." Puckering his mouth, an again-playful Brett continued outrageously. "But if you want to do something for me, why don't you plant those purty lips right here." The index finger made a slow sweep toward his mouth.

"I'll do no such thing," she responded, undaunted by his teasing. "I'll see if I can do anything for Big Pat. His bartender didn't show up today."

The index finger remained lightly pressed to the corner of his mouth. "But . . . it hurts."

"Then I'll put some salve on it."

"No kiss?"

Paulina managed a half-cocked smile, her eyes expressing little emotion. "A kiss, Brett McCallum? Only when man flies to the moon and back."

When she moved toward the door, Brett outswept his hands, the chuckle in his voice causing her to halt. "Hey, Paulina honey . . . it could happen, you know."

Her gaze connected to his own in disbelief. "Sure, and I believe in fairies too."

Then she swept from the room like a breath of fresh air.

And the lingering fragrance of lilacs kept Brett company . . . and longing for her return.

Five

Paulina had one more important mission that Thursday afternoon. Sneaking out a rear entrance and into an alleyway, she moved on a confident course toward Clancy's Saloon. When she entered the large, dimly lit room with its nauseating swirls of cigar smoke, and odors of unwashed bodies and rank perfumes worn by the gaudily clad women, she stood for a moment, steadying herself, her green eyes scanning the patrons—cheap women and dark-clothed outlaws reeking of gin and filth. Spotting Soapy Smith at a table with Syd Dixon and some of his other henchmen, she began to move through the tables of gambling men and cackling women.

A hush fell over the crowd, a hush so sudden that Soapy looked up, at the same moment his hand moving toward his gun. One of the saloon girls yelled at Paulina, "Out of your element, ain't ya, honey?"

Then Soapy saw the slim form of Paulina Winthrop easing toward him. A grin spread across his face and saliva dripped from the left corner of his mouth.

Before Soapy could sarcastically comment on how fine she looked, Paulina demanded, "I want my gun back."

Leaning back, Soapy mumbled, "That gun shot a man, little lady."

"I want it back. It was my father's and I want it back."

Actually, Soapy was wearing the gun—a fine weapon identical to one he'd seen on the hip of Wyatt Earp a year or so before—and he didn't want to give it up. But he also didn't want to shoot the girl with so many witnesses lingering about. He might have the deputy marshal in his back pocket, but he'd seen a growing intolerance for his form of justice among Skagway's residents, and he didn't want to make too many waves.

Paulina stood her ground, her hands at her sides clenching and unclenching. When Soapy's hand eased again toward his sidearm, she was almost certain she was enjoying the last moments of her life. But as she felt the instinct to flee, he merely brought the weapon up, turned it safely toward her, and held his hand out. "This what you want, little lady?"

Hesitantly, Paulina approached, thinking that he might suddenly turn the gun, position his finger on the trigger, and shoot her dead. Her knees felt like jelly, and beads of perspiration dotted her forehead and neck. But she could not—would not—give him the satisfaction of seeing her fear. Thus, when she got within touching distance of her father's gun, her eyes narrowed ever so slightly, a pretense, she thought on the spur of the moment, to make him believe she could be fierce, if it came to that. "Why are you giving it back without a struggle?" she asked, her voice so strained, it surprised, and embarrassed her.

Soapy repositioned a wad of chewing tobacco in his right jaw and grinned, betraying the remnants of teeth stained a disgusting brown. "There's some real good men here in Skagway that sidesteps me out of fear, little lady. But if you want the truth—and you think I'm capable of it—I really admire your spunk. You need a good kick in the britches, but ain't no man goin' to do it while you're here in Skagway. I'll see to it. Now—" His arm, feeling the strain of the heavy weapon, jerked toward her. "Take your father's gun and be on your way."

After only a fleeting moment of apprehension, Paulina grabbed the gun, tucked it close to her, then turned and fled from Clancy's Saloon. She did not hear what Soapy had said to bring down the house in laughter, but she was glad to be out of his sight. Turning toward Big Pat's, she beat a hasty retreat before Soapy could change his mind about the gun . . . and shoot her down just for the heck of it.

His mood instantly clashed with the laughter that his face-saving joke had caused. Soapy leaned toward his man, Buckeye Puckett, across the table from him. "To-night you pay a visit to the little lady, take back that blasted Colt, and put a hole bigger'n a caboose in the back of her head. You do it, or tomorrow you'll be the one twelve hours dead."

"Sure, Soapy . . . I ain't let ya down yet, have I?"

Big Pat was blocking the door, his burly arms crossed and his booted feet firmly planted apart, when Paulina attempted to sneak back in through the rear door. She mentally slumped, wondering if it showed on the outside. "Big Pat, what are you—"

"What are *you* doing out?" he asked, cutting her off, his voice more graveled than usual. "I told ya not to leave. An' poor ol' McCallum back there, he's been in a heap of pain an' no one to see to his needs—"

"Pain, pooh!" retorted Paulina, dashing beneath the

arm Big Pat stretched out to add emphasis. "He's just a big old baby who likes to be pampered."

"I am not!" Actually, he was, but the manly part of him would not allow the confession.

Paulina immediately faced Brett McCallum, supporting himself on one leg, a makeshift crutch beneath his arm. "You are too!" she snapped just as sharply, a smile curling her luscious mouth as she held up her father's Colt. "Look what Soapy just gave me."

Brett almost toppled in his haste to grab the weapon. "Blast it, woman! Did you confront that snake on your own?"

A shapely eyebrow almost became airborne. "Well, do tell me that you care about me, Brett McCallum. I've grown accustomed to your lies—"

"Blast it, I do care," he shot back, turning to drop into a chair before he crumpled. The pain shot through his hip and his body in ricochets, and he could almost feel it at the top of his head. He was that annoyed with the lovely woman from Utah. Then his hand went out and he was a little surprised when hers, without hesitation, slipped between his fingers. "Why would you put yourself in that kind of danger?"

She shrugged, her eyes dropping like a scolded child's. "I wanted my father's gun back."

"Why? Don't you think he has another one by now?"

"Don't be ridiculous. You know that he's—" She'd been about to say "dead." But she was beginning to forget which lies she had told and when; unknowingly, she might contradict herself . . . again. Thus she ended quietly, "He's particularly fond of this one." Gently wresting her hand away from him, she turned, throwing herself across the bed he had vacated. "Brett McCallum, let's call a truce. No more bickering . . . no more fights . . . no more insults. What do you think?"

"Sounds rather boring," he remarked, drawing his fingers to his clean-shaven chin . . . a shaving he had performed just moments before. "Why would you want to get along? You have as much fun with our disagreements as I do."

"That may be true," she reflected quietly, her eyes holding his in a moment of humor. "But we have a long, long way to travel together, and we might as well get along. We might even grow to like each other . . . just a little bit."

" 'Little bit' is redundant, Paulina Winthrop."

"Oh, pooh . . . I know that. But everyone says 'little bit,' don't they?"

"We're arguing," he pointed out, grinning.

"Merely discussing," she countered politely, turning on her back and stretching out her arms. Her head tipped over the edge of the bed, and when she met his gaze, she smiled brightly. "Now, aren't we? Besides, where did a backwoods boy from the interior of Alaska hear a word like redundant?"

Was this the time to admit that he had been educated at Yale in Connecticut, had served a stint in the United States cavalry as a captain, and that he had a degree in law? "Picked it up," he replied after a moment, "from an educated sourdough some years back. I've just been waiting for the moment to use it in conversation."

Rolling again to her stomach, Paulina tucked her hands beneath her chin. "You're a silly man, Brett McCallum." She spoke lightly, without feeling. "Have you ever made love to a woman?"

Brett almost fell off the chair. "Hell . . . what kind of a question is that?"

"Well? Have you?"

"I'm thirty-five years old, Paulina, and I'm a normal, red-blooded Alaskan male. What do you think?"

"You've probably been around. So . . . why haven't you gotten married?"

Darkness suddenly invaded his brow. "I was married once."

Now, this was a surprise. "Oh? What happened? She didn't like Alaska?"

"I met and married her in Virginia. The week after our wedding, she was thrown from a horse and instantly killed."

Her frivolous mood instantly changed. Dropping her gaze, she remarked, "I am very sorry. Were you young?"

"I was twenty-four."

"My age," she reflected quietly. "Did you love her?"

Brett hadn't thought about Kathleen in a long, long time. He wasn't sure if he had loved her the way a man should love a woman he has made his wife, but he liked to think that he had. She was vivacious and happy and fun to be with. And she was beautiful, a true belle of Virginia, and heatedly adamant that she would *never* live in his world . . . his Alaska. That was a confession she had not made, however, until after they exchanged their wedding vows and signed the marriage certificate.

"Did you love her, Brett?"

His thoughts snapped instantly from those warm spring days on the Virginia horse farm, the wealthy estate of her grandparents, where they had honeymooned and where the fatal accident had occurred. "Of course I loved her," he responded, and really wasn't sure if he'd responded from the heart. He had intended to be a good husband, and to take care of her, for better, for worse, for richer, for poorer . . . and that was all that really mattered. Wasn't it?

Paulina thought he hadn't sounded very convincing. "What shall we do this afternoon, Brett McCallum?" she asked, changing the subject. She wasn't at all in the mood for dismal conversation. Besides, if she questioned his past, he might feel obligated to question her own, and there were things she could not—would not—tell him. And she suspected there were things in his past he wouldn't wish to divulge, even to a woman he would take, against her will, as a wife.

"I think we'll just rest up and be ready for our journey in the morning. I don't like traveling on ships. They tend to sink—"

"And trains wreck, wagons overturn, and horses buck. That's life, isn't it, Brett McCallum?"

How precocious she looked all of a sudden . . . the waves of her sun-colored hair hanging down the side of the bed, touching the floor, her eyes darkening to the color of emeralds in the half-light, the shadows of a tree wavering outside the single window casting specks of dark and light across her rosy features. She looked both luminous and shrouded in mystery, both youthful in her beauty and mature in her wisdom. Brett imagined that there was more to Miss Paulina Winthrop than met the eye, and that she would choose to die rather than back down from any challenge. "Tell me about yourself, Paulina."

Paulina looked toward the tall, bronze-skinned Alaskan. He was such a mystery. He would have her believe he was just a simple man from the interior of Alaska, who neither knew nor cared about much outside his own rugged life and personal challenges. But she imagined that he was a man of many faces, educated and not just intelligent, witty rather than insulting, and gentle of heart, though he would have her believe just the opposite. When it came right down to it, Paulina didn't believe for a minute that he'd make her become his wife if it wasn't what she wanted. "About me?" she eventually responded. "I'm just a small-town girl with a lot of woes,

Brett McCallum. That's why I'm here, in your Alaska, hoping beyond hope that I might unload two skinny shoulders weighted down by problems." When she sighed wearily, Brett climbed to his feet and, without the crutch, hobbled the few feet across the floor toward Paulina. Sitting on the edge of the bed, his right hand closed lightly over her shoulder. Loving the caress of his fingers but not wanting him to know, she blurted out, "See? What did I tell you? Skin and bones!"

Rather than respond, Brett gently turned her to him. She was a little surprised, both by the darkening of his eyes as they gazed at her features and by the soft caresses of his hands upon her shoulders. Her mouth parted, trembling, the tip of her tongue attempting to relieve the sudden dryness of her lips, her hands clenching at her sides, so instinctively did she want to touch him, to draw him close and taste his mouth against her own, to feel the iron hardness of his body against her pale, slim one. If his wound pained him, it did not reflect in his eyes . . . if he were angry with her, there was no flash there to indicate it.

"Do you know what I wish?"

His words visibly startled her. "What, Brett?"

"I wish I were with you—"

Her eyes narrowed. "You are with me."

"No—" A husky emotion affected his voice. "I mean *with* you, Paulina. No barriers, no inhibitions . . . just you and me, alone in a world with so little love . . . caring for each other . . . being with each other"—he hesitated to continue—"loving each other—" Then the fingers of his right hand dipped lightly into her bodice and caressed the tender flesh there without going any farther.

She wished she could be angry with him, could tell him what she thought of him and of his softly spoken wish. But if she spoke her heart, there would be no stopping him, nor would she want to. If she spoke her heart, they would be together, without the restrictions of clothing, in each other's arms, her own passions rapidly awakening as she gave herself fully to him. She had never been with a man, and though she had always wondered what it would be like, she had never met anyone she wanted to be with in that way—until then.

Brett McCallum was the man she wanted . . . and Brett McCallum was the man she knew she could not have.

Family came first . . . a sister, an uncle . . . a father's honor . . . and she almost hated them for it.

So Paulina forced her body to grow rigid beneath him, her mouth to press into a thin line for a moment, and an edge of sarcasm to ease into her voice. "Oh . . . I forgot to tell you, Brett McCallum . . . I hate men. I think they're useless, vile creatures to be kept around only to do chores. I would rather die than have one touch me, even one as brawny and as good-looking as you. In fact, you are the kind of man I loathe the most. The kind who knows women are attracted to him, and the kind who takes advantage of it. You will grow to realize I am not your normal, run-of-the-mill woman. I have more important things on my mind than making love . . . and making conquests." Paulina had once enjoyed a forbidden novel, a licentious thing her father would have taken a strap to her for reading, that had said a man most wanted a woman who did not want him. Thus, to make herself less appealing to Brett, she continued with haste. "But of course, if you want to make love to me and get it out of your system—so that we can get on with business—then be my guest." There, that would surely quell his desires. . . .

Brett quietly assessed her words, and her cynicism, as

88

it was matter-of-factly dealt to him. She was challenging him, and denying her own desires for him. And, blast it, he was up to a good challenge, and knew just how to handle this one. "Very well . . ." He sat up and began unbuttoning his shirt. "Let's get out of these clothes, have a quick go, and get on to that more important business—"

"What?" Paulina drew herself up, supporting her slim weight on her elbows. Any color remaining in her features suddenly drained. "What do you think you're doing?"

Brett pulled the shirt down his arms, betraying hard muscles and the wide, hair-covered expanse of his chest. Reaching down to unbuckle his belt, he gave Paulina a narrow look. "What do you mean? Wasn't this your idea? To make love?"

"Don't be preposterous!"

Cocking his head slightly, Brett forced an air of innocence upon his dark features. "Oh . . . would you rather I slipped the bolt so we won't be disturbed. Are you modest, honey?" Rising unsteadily to his feet, he said, "No problem there," and moved toward the door.

If he'd turned just then, he'd have seen suppressed rage causing a slight tick beneath her left eye, a clamping in her jaw that caused her pain, hands clenched so tightly that her knuckles were as white as the snows on Denali. He did not turn when he became aware of her sudden movement, though he did mentally prepare for an attack. But when the doorway exiting onto the alley was jerked open, and Paulina yelled, "You there . . . yes, you in the red dress . . . will you pleasure this man in here for three dollars?" Brett pivoted so swiftly that he lost his footing and landed heavily in the straight-back chair, nearly toppling it.

Paulina was now out of his sight, and female muttering drifted to him from the alleyway. Presently, she returned, stood in the doorway, and drew her hands to her slim hips. "This, ummm, lady out here says she'll do anything you want for three dollars."

Brett drew in his breath and held it for a moment. He saw the woman in question through the gauze-covered window, and though she wasn't totally unattractive, she wasn't the kind of woman he preferred. *So, this is the way Miss Paulina Winthrop wants it . . . or does she?* "Ask her if she's got the clap—"

Paulina didn't have to. A resounding "No!" from the prostitute quickly reached his ear, followed closely by "Does he?"

"Tell her no. Tell her to make it a buck and a half and she's got herself a man for the afternoon."

Paulina gave him one of those looks . . . half-disbelief . . . half-revulsion. Again she slipped from view; again the exchange . . . again she returned to the doorway. "She said two dollars and one hour—"

"Okay—"

Paulina was sure he was merely bantering with her and that he really wasn't serious. "Enough, Brett McCallum. You do want me to send her away, don't you?"

Brett stood, supported most of his weight on his good leg, and arched his back, the muscles of his arms expanding as he drew them back. "No . . . send her in and take a powder, Paulina. I don't need a blasted virgin lingering and pouting . . . pouting and lingering . . . because she missed a great opportunity to become a woman." As an afterthought he added, "And I wasn't going to charge you a cent for my service. Now, send her in and scat!"

Her mouth pressed into a defiant line. Lifting her chin, she gave him a cool, haughty look. "I am sure, Brett McCallum, that I wouldn't have gotten my penny's worth anyway." And with that she called in the plump, dark-haired "lady of the evening," and quickly departed for the saloon to give Big Pat a hand at the bar.

Tears burned in her eyes. She'd heard the bolt slip on the other side of the door immediately after her departure, and then the curtains snapped shut at the rear exit. She hated to think what Brett was doing with the hussy, and wished she could tear through that door and rip every last strand of dyed hair out of her head.

She had thought that Brett McCallum had scruples. She'd even thought he had some sense. But all he had to his name was her three dollars and a pitiful little brain below his waistline. Oh, how she hated him!

How she envied the woman who was with him!

With her there to help, Big Pat decided to run some errands. For an hour or so she cleaned bar glasses, dusted, straightened the bottles of whiskey and other liquors on the shelf against the wall, and waited for Brett McCallum to finish whatever he was doing behind that door. How should she react when again she faced him? Should she give him a good piece of her mind, or should she act indifferent and let him believe she didn't care one way or the other what he did with other women? After all, she had no claim on him except that she was going to be his wife, if he had his way about it. . . .

But, of course, that wasn't in her plans.

The bolt slipped. Paulina jerked to attention, though she did not look toward the short, dark corridor separating her from the room where *he* was with the whore. She wished Big Pat were there; she'd like to be free to charge into that room with a glass of whiskey and sling it in the rascal's face!

The door opened and Brett McCallum limped out,

tucking his shirt into his trousers. When he was separated from her by five feet he said, "I've got a dollar left. How much whiskey can I buy?"

"A quarter a shot. Add it up, McCallum."

He pretended to figure in his head, then replied, "That comes to five shots, doesn't it?"

Well, if he was that stupid! "No, McCallum—" The way she swirled the rag on the counter, pressing it firmly, she might have removed the varnish had there been any. "That buys you only three shots! Do you want them one at a time . . . or all at once? I suppose"—she hesitated—"that your entertainment back there is thirsty too?"

He approached, folded his hands over her shoulders, and leaned ever so close. "My *entertainment* has departed, Paulina. And now, I need you—"

"You aren't Hercules, Brett McCallum."

"I don't need you *that* way. I need you to change the bandages on my leg."

Oh! So that was all she was good for! Nursing services! No matter that she herself had contracted his time with the prostitute! Though she was furious, she forced a smile upon her lips. "Too much activity, hmmm?" Was she failing in her determination to portray indifference? If she could clearly discern the sarcasm in her tone, surely he could too. But then, he didn't even know how many quarters there were in a dollar! So, would he be able to tell the difference between sarcasm and pure mockery? She thought not.

A chuckle rested behind Brett's controlled tone. "You know what, Miss Paulina Winthrop? I think you're jealous."

"And I think you're delirious," came her instant retort, her shoulders jerking from the touch of his hands.

92

"By cracky, Brett McCallum, I think you're the most pitiful excuse for a human being I've ever met!"

Drawing back with feigned indignation, Brett drew his hands to his hips. "Now . . . what brought that on?"

One of the men within hearing range yelled out, "The little lady wants you, McCallum."

And Brett looked into the smoke-filled interior to see old Obadiah moving toward him. "How 'bout one of them whiskies ye'r about to throw down that dollar for?"

"Sure, Obadiah. You go on over to that corner table and let me finish my business with the little lady." The old man turned and walked off to await the promised nourishment. When Brett was again alone with Paulina, he took her arm and pulled her into the semi-darkness of the small corridor. Opening her hand, he pressed a wad of bills into it. "Now, this is all your hundred and nineteen dollars, Paulina. Since you've agreed to become a wife, I feel that *I* should finance the trip."

"But—" Pretty green eyes widened in surprise. "I thought you didn't have any money. I thought you came to Skagway to pick up sourdoughs to finance your return to Nuklukayet. I thought—"

"It doesn't matter what you thought. What I do care about is that you would think I'd let *you* pay for *my* bed pleasures. Now"—he released her arm as though he'd instantly found her repulsive to his touch—"I've got a friend to collect just out of town. I can't board ship without him."

"What? You never said you had a friend who would—"

"I don't tell you everything, Paulina." Silence. Their gazes met and held, transfixed, a mutual stirring of rebellion and distrust and . . . something else . . . there was no denying the attraction . . . and Paulina's was just

93

as strong . . . just as tangible . . . just as destined for culmination. . . .

Dropping her gaze and instantly hating herself for what he might consider a surrender, Paulina said, "Well, go and collect this friend, whoever he is. But"—her eyes lifted, again rebellious, again flashing the green fire of hostility—"you will pay his passage."

Obadiah called across the saloon, "I'm waitin' fer that drink, Cap'n."

And Brett called, "It's on the way." Slapping a five-dollar bill down on the bar, he continued. "This will pay for a bottle," he declared, and snatched one from across Paulina's shoulder, leaving a clean circle on an otherwise dusty counter. "You missed a spot!"

Scarcely had Brett and his makeshift crutch hobbled across the room before Big Pat returned. "I think there's trouble brewin', Paulina," he said. "Soapy's up to something."

"I can't worry about that. I'll be leaving in the morning with that rascal of a guide." Her gaze cut to him, but he was engaged in conversation with Obadiah. "Soapy can do anything he pleases."

"Just promise you'll be extra special careful until the morning."

She only halfheartedly responded, "Sure, Pat. I'll do that," and retreated toward the room she had shared with Brett McCallum.

A friend, she was thinking, angry again. *Brett McCallum had left a friend outside of town?* Tossing herself upon the bed, she tried to nurture her mood to something far beyond anger . . . fury, perhaps, even rage . . . maybe even a temper tantrum such as she'd performed to perfection as a small girl. But in the threads of the bedcoverings lingered the manly smell of the rascal who would be her guide . . . and she wanted him

94

here, with her, touching her, awakening her passions, whispering words of adoration against her hairline. When she was near Brett McCallum, he was all she wanted. Nothing else in her life seemed important— the challenge of the town council drifted off into a netherworld . . . her compelling need to defeat the Bartlett brothers was as remote as the great Denali Brett had spoken so fondly of. She wanted only to be with Brett, to see his world in the interior of Alaska, to meet the people who were his friends, to witness the excitement of the life he had chosen for himself.

But then she grew angry with herself and with the traitorous thoughts scattering through her brain like a rampant wind. She had a duty to her family . . . and to the memory of her dead father. She had made a promise to bring Millburn Hanks back. She had made a promise to clean up Turkey Gulch, and if she successfully met the challenge of the city council, the town would be renamed Winthrop, in honor of her father. And they would have to fulfill yet another promise to her. That was all that mattered.

She had to forget about Brett McCallum.

She had to forget how she felt about him.

She had to forget that for the first time in her life, a man had been able to awaken the passions she had so long denied.

She had to forget that she was a woman and he was a man.

She had a mission.

And Brett McCallum was nothing more than the guide she had chosen to take her to a land with which she was unfamiliar . . . a land that was as treacherous as it was beautiful . . . and a land hiding in its vast interior the one man who could make things right in Turkey Gulch, Utah.

I will bring you back, Millburn. You can bank on that!

And Brett McCallum . . . you have touched me for the last time!

Six

That evening Paulina tucked herself beneath the covers of the cot where she'd slept for the past week. She was only too aware of Brett McCallum across the small room, of his rhythmic breathing, the smell of him, the outline of his body against the pale light of the single window. What a strange man he was . . . and what an enigma he was proving to be! Though he had told her of a wife who'd died young, of his days in the United States cavalry, and bits and pieces of tales of his life with a father who'd been killed by a rogue bear, there was still something, hanging just out of reach, that enshrouded him in mystery. There was something that compelled her to care for him when everything he did seemed designed to make her hate him. But she couldn't hate him; and she despised the way she felt inside. Where would it all lead?

Though she was loathe to admit it, she had wanted to travel alone with him to the Yukon River. But now he had a friend who would tag along . . . a friend Obadiah had promised to have at the dock in the morning before departure . . . a friend Brett would tell her nothing about except that "he doesn't talk much, just sits and looks at you with big, moping eyes." Was she going to have to play nursemaid to a prepubescent boy so unruly that Brett McCallum had refused to bring him into town?

She really didn't have the time, or the patience!

A creak in the corridor just outside made her fully alert. Pushing herself onto her elbow, she looked across toward Brett, who stirred slightly, only to gain more comfort upon the mattress. Then a light rapping sounded at the door, and she whispered, "Who is it?"

Big Pat replied in a suppressed tone, "I'm sittin' up the night, Paulie. Somethin' don't feel right."

"All right," she whispered in return. "Shall I keep an eye open?"

"I'll do it for you," came his reply.

Massive footsteps retreated from the door and momentarily Paulina heard him drop into a chair. A dull thud on the floor was that of a rifle being placed down, and she again tucked her arm beneath her head. What could be worrying Big Pat that he would deny himself a night of sleep when it was all, by his own confession, that he looked forward to after a day at the bar?

Again she looked toward Brett, sleeping soundly and stirring not a muscle. He didn't have a care in the world except getting his beauty sleep! How selfish he was!

Brett had heard the exchange of words between Paulina and Big Pat. But even before that, he'd kept an eye open and his sidearm was beneath the covers with his index finger resting on the trigger. He, too, had heard murmurings through the afternoon that hinted at trouble, and he was prepared to deal with it.

He could hear the occasional creak of the chair Big Pat was occupying outside the door, a large, booted foot shuffling across the floor every now and then, and farther, past the hastily constructed walls, the familiar sounds of the saloons, of arguing men, enticing women, the sporadic explosion of gunfire, the haunting echo of a dog baying at the moon. Sounds that distinguished themselves, and yet commingled, threatened, and soothed—sounds that were eerie, and somehow peaceful. Brett found himself questioning his sanity . . . found himself watching the darkness for the movement of Paulina, only a few feet distant from him. He wanted her with him, against him, protected by him, and yet he felt trapped by his need to be her champion. He had always held himself aloof from female charms and seductions, but Paulina seemed to be the exception to that rule. He wanted her for himself, not for his dying friend, Gruff.

What did he know of Gruff anyway? Until seven years ago he hadn't even known he existed. He had shown up in Nuklukayet, wanting a guide to the gold fields of the Yukon, and Brett had happened to be free at the moment. A friendship had developed. Each man had saved the other's life on at least one occasion, and they'd suffered together through the insurmountable hardships of the Yukon. Hell, Brett didn't even know Gruff's real name, didn't even know if he had one. He'd never asked. Had never wanted to.

Still, a lifetime friendship had developed between the two men, and Brett intended to fulfill Gruff's final wish, a wish for a wife, a wish that Brett would bring to fruition by bringing Paulina Winthrop to him as an offering.

But he hadn't expected that decision to hurt so much, and as he continued to gaze across the darkness and into the pale aura of light now illuminating Paulina's breathtaking features, guilt grabbed him within and made him wish that he were dead.

Her eyes were closed, the fingers of her left hand tucked beneath her cheek, her mouth slightly trembling.

If she slept, what did she dream? If she was awake, what was she thinking? He wanted to know if she dreamed of him . . . if her thoughts were of him . . . as his were of her.

Paulina . . . Paulina . . . the echo of her name warmed his thoughts and flooded his body with want of her.

A shuffle in the alleyway impaled Brett with a sense of foreboding. His finger easing again onto the trigger of the weapon at his side, he felt his breathing suddenly cease. Across the pale form of Paulina Winthrop, against the half-light of the window behind her moved the vagueness of shadow, a shadow formed like a man . . . and a shadow armed, the gun clutched in the hand as sharp and clear as the fear he so strongly felt. He waited, silent, breath caught, body rigid, the only movement his eyes following the threat. The door to the alleyway creaked open—damn! Why hadn't Big Pat installed a bolt? And the arm and the gun slowly descended toward the sleeping Paulina.

Instantly Brett was out of the bed, his good knee hitting the floor with a thud, and his own weapon discharging in rapid fire. Buckeye Puckett, instantly killed by the first of Brett's bullets, crashed through the door and fell full upon Paulina Winthrop. In that moment the bolt of another shot, muffled by Paulina's slender form, ricocheted through the room like a volley of cannons.

Paulina felt a moment of pain, then a darkness began to enfold her. But almost in the same instant the darkness began to withdraw and the pain was gone. She knew she had somehow been assaulted, though not by whom.

Rudely jarred to full wakefulness, Paulina saw Big Pat break through the inside door, rifle wavering menacingly before him, and his small eyes sweeping the dimly lit room.

"Ya killed the bastard, McCallum!" he yelled hoarsely, and before Brett could find his footing, he was across the room, yanking the weight of the dead man off Paulina.

Paulina was shocked and horrified. Warm, sticky blood was upon both her palms and staining the bodice of the gown she had worn to bed. She could not move, even when the weight of the dead man was removed from her, and she thought some alien thing had crawled into her throat and stolen her voice. No sound was forthcoming, not a scream, not a sob . . . not anything. If her heart was beating, she couldn't feel it . . . if she was still alive, she had no breath to betray it.

By the time Big Pat had dragged the dead man into the alley, Brett was beside Paulina, drawing her into his arms. When she made no response to his nearness, he took her by the shoulders and shook her gently. "Paulina, speak to me." *God!* he thought. *Did one of my bullets strike her too?* When she still failed to respond, the shaking became harsher, as did his words. "Dammit, girl, tell me you're all right!" Of course, she was female, and he expected hysterics. Mentally preparing himself, he shook her again.

A pain eased through her shoulders like a slow tide, invading her head which bobbed against the strength of his attack. Then her fingers closed over the thick muscles of his arms and her gaze made a fluid sweep upward, connecting almost immediately to his own dark, hooded one. Quietly, she said, "I'm all right. It happened so suddenly—"

What? No hysterics, no thrashing of slim arms and legs? Shouldn't he now be crushing her to his chest to still her sobs? Brett's blue eyes narrowed suspiciously.

"What do you mean? You're all right? Of course you're not all right!"

She was a bit surprised by his curtness and drew slightly back. "I am too all right. What did you expect? Hysterics?" The ever so slight widening of his eyes indicated that he had, indeed. "Well—" Slowly, methodically, she peeled herself from his arms. "I am so sorry to disappoint you, Brett McCallum. No hysterics here! Of course, if *you'd* like to exhibit hysterics, I'll be more than happy to offer a comforting shoulder!" She had now leaned back on her elbows for support, her palms pressed firmly to the mattress. When he, too, drew back, a shady smirk played at the corners of her mouth. "Well? Show me those hysterics. Paulina will soothe poor baby McCallum!"

If Brett was aware of Big Pat out in the alley, explaining to the gathering crowd what had happened, he made no indication of it. Without prelude he pulled Paulina firmly to him and his mouth roughly captured her own. She was much too stunned at first to react, but then her senses came flooding back and she attempted to break away from the bruising assault. How dare he molest her! Did he think she was so frightened by her brush with death that she would welcome the taste of his kiss? Oh, what an animal he was! And how she would make him suffer later!

But for now she could not find the strength to end the assault. His breath was hot and sweet against her cheek, his hands circling her upper arms and brushing her breasts, lingering—oh, the rogue!—against the softness of her there. She gasped for air, attempting to will her mouth into a thin line but finding it impossible. . . .

Brett couldn't have cared less about the crowd gathering outside. All he knew was that Paulina's mouth was soft and willing against his own and her body was slowly closing the short expanse of space between them. Damn, she was willing! If only they were alone!

He could not remember feeling her arm wrench away from him, but now he was painfully aware of a slim palm bristling back and striking his cheek very hard. He reeled from the blow, then sat back, rubbing the stinging flesh and looking at her as if she'd suddenly lost her senses.

"What was that for?"

"You were assaulting me!"

Her eyes were like emeralds on fire. Unconsciously, Brett again drew back, preparing for another stinging slap. "*I* assaulted *you!* I think you've got it backwards!"

She scrambled from the bed, catching her leg in the bedcovers and immediately attempting to fight them off. When Brett chuckled, she snarled, "Help me, Brett McCallum! Don't you laugh at me!" Seeing the direction of his eyes, she folded her arms across the bodice of her modest bedgown. "And don't you look at me like that!"

Stretching out his arms, he responded, "Like what?"

"Don't you give me that innocent, little-boy-accused look. Like what, indeed!"

Big Pat looked in the door. "McCallum, the marshal's out here. Wants your account of what happened."

Absently, his eyes remaining upon the flustered Paulina, Brett replied, "Be right there." Then to Paulina, with a finger shaking in her face, he said, "And don't you go anywhere, Paulina Winthrop! Do you hear?"

She sniffed impudently. "I'll go anywhere I please!"

He grinned, again dragging his hand to the assaulted cheek. "Blast, woman . . . you strike a mighty blow."

103

Then he moved into the alley . . . and Paulina immediately wished she weren't alone.

After the excitement died down and the body was taken away for burial, some degree of normalcy returned to Big Pat's Saloon and the small room to which a man and a woman were condemned together. At least, that was how Paulina looked at it. Thankfully, the togetherness would end when they boarded ship in the morning; she would be lodged in the ladies' quarters, and he with the second-class gentlemen.

What Paulina did not know was that Brett **had asked** Big Pat to take their second-class tickets back to the ticket office and trade them in for first-class accommodations . . . for a husband and his wife, which meant a shared cabin. If she had known that then, in the predawn hours with him sleeping innocently in the bed across the room, she was reasonably certain he would not have lived out the night.

The hour had passed midnight when Big Pat returned to the saloon to relieve his night bartender. Through the veneer-thin walls she could hear the clink of glasses, of cards being shuffled, the mutterings of men and, occasionally, a scuffle and loud male voices. Paulina could not sleep and the ache of boredom crawled through her back and shoulders. So she scooted silently from the bed, her gaze steadily upon Brett McCallum as she assured herself that he was asleep. Then she turned her back to him. As her hand eased down the length of her thigh and toward the hem of her bedgown, she took one final glance at Brett across her shoulder and peeled the garment from her slim form.

* * *

Brett had never seen such a perfect feminine form . . . her hips curved, her buttocks firm, her waist so small he was sure he could span it with his hands. Her legs were long and slender, her shoulders narrow, and her back—God, he wished he could see it, but her golden tresses barred his view. Her skin was like porcelain and the full image of her caused a cruel lust to crawl viciously through his body. How could she tease him so! Ah, but of course, she thought he was asleep!

Paulina dropped the bedgown and hastily grabbed the gray wool dress she would wear aboard ship that morning. She pulled it quickly over her slim, nude form, her eyes turning quickly to Brett McCallum. She had no idea that he'd had to just as quickly close his eyes so that she would not know he'd been spying on her.

In the pale moonlight permeating the room, Paulina quickly drew a brush through her hair, then pulled it back and tied it with a length of black velvet ribbon. With one last look, and quite a venomous one at that, in Brett's direction, she slipped from the room and crossed the distance to the saloon just beyond the dark corridor.

"What you doin' out here, Paulie?" asked Big Pat.

"Couldn't sleep," came her response. "I thought you could use a little help."

"Ain't much goin' on. Thought I'd close up in about an hour. Most of the fellas're over at Clancy's. I 'spect Soapy's real mad about ol' Buckeye."

"Think he'll try again?"

He shrugged one shoulder. "Don't reckon. He knows we'll be watchin' out for him now."

Paulina took a bottle of whiskey from the back bar. "Could I have some of this?" she asked.

Big Pat gave a low chuckle. "Sure, if you want a drink—"

"Not a drink," came her instant response. "I'm going to drink the whole bottle."

"What fer, Paulie?"

"Just so I'll know what it's like to be falling-down drunk on my behind."

Again Big Pat laughed, his hand sweeping across his bald head. "It ain't a purty sight for a man, an' it sure ain't a purty sight for a lady."

"Oh, Pat—" Paulina moaned with the innocence of a child. "I'm so restless. I thought a shot or two might put me to sleep."

"Hey, little gal—" One of the patrons, a tall, full-bearded fellow off in a corner, spat tobacco juice into a nearby spittoon. "I got somethin' here—" he continued, pulling at his crotch, "that'll put ya right off to sleep."

A silent, wide-eyed Paulina watched Big Pat slowly amble around the end of the bar and flip a small towel across his shoulder. When he stood before the offensive patron, he asked, "Now, what was that ya said to Miss Paulina?"

"I said," the man responded boldly, "that I got somethin' here the little gal can sleep off."

Scarcely had he uttered the last word before Big Pat's fist shot out from his side and caught the man full in the face. When he crashed into an unconscious heap in the corner, knocking the spittoon and its vile contents across his chest Big Pat said, "There, sleep *that* off, Mister," and quietly returned to the bar. "Now"—admonishment edged into his voice—"you drink a couple shots of that whiskey an' you go on back and get some sleep. You'll be risin' in a few hours."

"All right, my friend," she replied, dropping to Big Pat's stool behind the bar. When he took the bottle and poured her a shot, handing it to her, she touched the liquid to her lips, shuddering as she did so. "I don't think I'll ever be a good drunk," she said quietly. "This tastes like kerosene." Then, closing her eyes, she quickly gulped it down and held the small glass out for another.

"You sure, Paulie?"

"Hit me, Big Pat," she replied, her mouth twisting into a comical smile. "Lord, that's awful." Paulina felt a sudden compulsion to twist her fingers into the fire at her midriff. How could men drink this stuff and continue to live? Surely, enough of it would rot the gut!

Big Pat was getting a big kick out of Paulina's reaction to the whiskey. He suppressed his own grin while he filled her glass to the rim, then pretended to go about his other duties. But all the while his eyes held her slim form, sitting upon the stool, and her pretty, sea-green eyes watching the whiskey swirl in the glass as she contemplated drinking it. Finally, he asked, "You goin' to drink that, or you goin' to play with it?"

Silence. She hesitated, cutting a quick glance to him and easily recognizing his suppressed humor. "You don't think I'll drink it, do you?"

"Hell, I think the first one's got your eyeballs to spinning."

Though they were, indeed, Paulina would die before admitting it. "Why, I'll have you know I might as well have drunk milk for all the effect it has had on me."

"Sure," said Big Pat. "Then why ain't ya swallowing that?"

"I am." She gently shrugged. "Just give me time."

"Sissy," he said beneath his breath, and when she shot him a look of pure venom, he said, "What? What did I say?"

"You called me a"—Paulina lifted the glass and swallowed the whiskey in one gulp—"sissy." Immediately, she felt sick, and her head was spinning, just like the time, seven years ago, when her father had taken her and Lillian to the county fair and they'd gone on the merry-go-round. The very young operator had taken a fancy to her and the ride had lasted almost an hour. When her feet again touched the ground, she'd almost toppled over. Lillian, only twelve at the time, had gotten sick to her stomach, then blamed her sister's shameless flirtations, and their aggravated father had taken them both home before the end of the day.

"What's wrong, Paulie?"

Her head snapped up, her hand immediately snatching for the bar to steady herself. "Nothing. Just thinking about going back to bed."

"Can you walk?"

Impudent defiance pressed upon her mouth. "Of course I can." But she really didn't know for sure that she could. Only determination would aid her in finding her footing and her way back to the room where Brett McCallum slept. Slowly, she slipped down from the stool, again steadied herself, said a perfunctory good night, and eased along the bar toward the corridor. Her head was spinning, the room was spinning, and her knees had no bones running through them to hold her up. How she got to the room, and how she refrained from reacting to Big Pat's laughter, and the laughter of the men in the bar, she would never know.

The darkness of the room swirled, foglike and indistinct, the moonlight touching her eyelids like invading monsters . . . a warmth suddenly drifting through her body from head to toe . . . or vice versa . . . she really wasn't sure which. She knew only that she had to get out of her dress before she exploded, before she became a million tiny fragments of human flesh clinging to the walls of the midnight-darkened room.

Even across the few feet Brett got the strong whiff of whiskey. She hadn't been gone long enough to drink very much, and the way she swayed to and fro as she fought the dress almost made him laugh out loud. But then she stood naked before him, her back to him, and she seemed to be trying to gain some sense of direction. And as he watched, she turned slowly, her hands out-stretched for balance. She moved across the floor toward him, and as the ribbon tumbled from her hair, crawled beneath the covers and tucked herself gently against him.

"Good night," she mumbled, and instantly fell asleep.

Brett was in a quandary; should he wake her and make her aware of her folly, or should he simply allow her to sleep beside him? But could he do that without wanting to touch her, to feel the velvety smoothness of her un-clothed flesh, to feel the soft curves of her molding so perfectly to his own body?

Blast! The single expletive ricocheted through his brain. He would let her sleep and . . . dammit, he would be a gentleman . . . for as long as humanly possible. What a dilemma she was to him . . . and what a trial! He would learn now just how much control he had!

Paulina knew only that she was warm and comfortable and that she felt secure. Her sleep instantly thrust her into a wonderful world of dreams and happy memories, and the fog swirling about her thrust her along on a journey that would not be soon forgotten.

Into a netherworld she was destined to travel . . . into

a world of excitement and adventure, with the man who lay at her side . . . the man whose musky manliness and nearness was all she wanted.

Part Two

The pools of fantasy and lore run deep
In the shady dell of the dreamer's sleep

Seven

Brett McCallum might as well have sounded a fire alarm, so piercingly painful was his crude bark at just after five o'clock that morning. Paulina, rudely awakened, wanted to pounce on him with all her might and make her fury known loud and clear. But then, in the darkness lit only by a single candle, she saw his smile as he looked down upon her, and it somehow managed to quell her moment of ire.

"Arise and shine, honey. We've got a ship to board in half an hour."

With a low, guttural groan, Paulina threw the covers over her head. "Leave me alone, Brett McCallum. I just want to sleep."

"Have a hangover, love?" The blanket was rudely yanked back, exposing translucent eyelids and painfully pounding eyes to the glare of the modest circle of light.

Paulina had very little recollection of the night before and could not remember pulling on the bedgown covering her slim form. And now that she thought about it . . . whose bed had she crawled into last evening? She had a very vague image of nestling against a warm masculine body.

Oh, well . . . enough to worry about without what may

or may not have happened last night. At least she felt reasonably sure her virtue was still intact. When Brett McCallum was gentleman enough to give her some privacy, Paulina arose, dressed, and put herself in some semblance of order. With her modest canvas bag packed and taken to the saloon area, she soon joined Brett and Big Pat, chatting over steaming cups of coffee.

"Pull up a chair, gal," said Big Pat, arising and taking the pot from the stove behind the bar and pouring her a cup of coffee.

"Thanks, Big Pat." As Paulina sat at the small table between them, nursing the strong brew between her fingers, she felt a sudden compulsion to cry. To her left sat the kind, amiable man who had befriended her when she'd stumbled into his saloon looking for a guide, and to her right sat the rogue who would be her companion for the next month or so . . . and her companion in marriage, if he had his way about it. She would like to boot the sarcastically smirking rogue all the way to kingdom come, but she felt certain that the good Lord would boot him right back. Why accept a troublemaker beyond the pearly gates until it was absolutely necessary?

Brett McCallum climbed to his feet. "Well, honey, we need to be going."

Without looking up, Paulina retorted, "Don't call me honey. Go out on the walkway and smoke a cigar or something. I would like a few minutes alone with Big Pat."

"I don't smoke. Turns the lungs black."

"You don't know that," she quipped with a note of exasperation. "Are you going to give me a moment to speak in private with a friend?"

Brett darted a look between Big Pat and Paulina, then shrugged his shoulders as if it didn't matter one way or another. Picking up both their bags from the floor where he'd deposited them, he ambled toward the door leading out onto the main street of Skagway.

Before Paulina could speak, Big Pat cut her off. "Got somethin' to tell ya, Miss Paulie."

"What is that?" She had not looked up, but kept her tear-filled eyes upon her linked fingers and the checkered cloth covering the small table.

"Ya got to promise not to say anything to him about you knowing."

"About what?," she replied halfheartedly.

"About this marryin' proposal McCallum made ya sign—"

Still, she did not look up. "Oh? What about it?"

"He confided in me that it ain't him he'll be wantin' ya to marry. He's got a friend up there near Nuklukayet who's dyin'—"

Paulina felt that she'd suddenly been impaled by dozens of arrows. Her body straightened so quickly that a muscle caught over her heart and became a painful ball. Instantly, her hand moved to massage the twisted muscle. "What do you mean? He wants me to marry a dying man?"

"I'm tellin' you this to make you feel better, Paulina. Chances are by the time you get there the fella will be cold an' in his grave. Can't marry a dead man, can you, Paulie?"

The anger she'd felt suddenly subsided. Of course, Big Pat was right. She could accomplish her purpose, find Millburn Hanks, and convince him to return to Utah with her, and she wouldn't have to marry Brett's unfortunate friend. "Thanks for telling me, Big Pat. Don't worry. I won't say anything to him about our talk."

"An' you don't worry about that marryin' he'd have you do. Just don't reckon it's goin' to happen."

Paulina's hand eased across the table and covered only half of Big Pat's large one. "We have a secret, Big Pat. And, by George, we'll get the best of that rascal McCallum yet, won't we?"

A wide, toothy grin broadened the big man's face. "You bet we do! Paulie. Now, you go on out and let McCallum think he's got one over on you."

Paulina stood and Big Pat, too, pushed himself up from his chair. When his arms spread out, Paulina moved into them and allowed herself to be roughly hugged. "Thank you for being my friend, Big Pat."

"Anytime, little lady. You just come back safe and sound, ya hear?" Despite her resolve, tears gathered on her lower lids and trickled onto her cheeks. "Don't cry, Paulie—"

"They aren't tears, Big Pat. They're little memories gathering, so that when things seem their worst, I'll remember you and be happy again."

"Aw, Paulie—" A lump as big as Denali gathered in Big Pat's throat, taking away his words. Roughly putting Paulina away from him, he turned and quickly disappeared into the darkness beyond the bar where, in a few hours, he would again tend to the business of the day.

A tearful Paulina joined Brett McCallum on the walkway outside the saloon. The street in the predawn darkness was quiet, only a window or two gently lighted beyond ragged gauze curtains. "Are you ready?" asked Brett, politely turning his eyes from her tears.

Paulina assumed a façade of strength, the gathering of anger for this rogue Alaskan held within and unexhibited. "Let's go."

Scarcely had the two of them taken more than a dozen steps before gunfire erupted from the vicinity of Big Pat's Saloon. Both turned simultaneously, just as the shadow of a fast-moving man shot from the saloon and disappeared into an alley across the road. With horror darkening her features, Paulina watched Big Pat stumble through the swinging doors, the moonlight catching the glistening of blood upon his shirt and oozing between fingers clutching at his chest. With a strangled scream Paulina rushed to him just as he collapsed onto the planked boardwalk.

Stunned and yet still sensible, she dropped to her knees and eased his head onto her lap. He looked at her, smiled . . . and gently died.

That was when she lost all sense of reason. Scarcely was she aware of Brett McCallum, his own features horrified and ashen, jerking her up and into his arms, to rush along the boardwalk. Both of their meager belongings contained in canvas bags were left behind.

At that point some semblance of sensibility rushed back to claim her, and she began to fight Brett, her arms flailing at the broad expanse of his chest and her feet kicking out in an attempt to disengage herself from him. "Let me go! Let me go! We have to help Big Pat!"

Her efforts threw him against the wall. When her feet touched the boardwalk and she attempted to pull free, he drew her ever closer, refusing to yield freedom to her. "No . . . no, Paulina. Big Pat is dead. And you will be, too, if you return! You must know that Soapy's responsible for this. He swore to kill Big Pat . . . and he swore to kill you too. Be sensible. Dammit, be sensible for the first time in your life!"

Of course, he was right. But even as she allowed herself to be dragged along, she still felt that she was turning her back on a friend. And that was something she absolutely never did!

If anything . . . she was loyal.

Two days later

The sea was choppy; a cold wind blew across the bow of the ship and found Paulina's sanctuary, the wide, spa-

117

cious cabin she only sporadically shared with Brett McCallum and the wolf dog named Alujian that Obadiah had taken to the dock to await them. It was a great black, grumpy, growling, threatening creature that Paulina had taken an instant dislike to, but that Brett shared a special bond with. She refused, though, to let the aggravating thing get the best of her.

Most of these past forty-eight hours she had spent sleeping, as if she could not quite rest enough. She was much too distraught over Big Pat's death to care about the strange things she'd noticed since leaving Skagway . . . the black ship, *Crown Prince of Talantia*, whose crisp white sails seemed to fill with wind even when the air was still . . . the fact that she and Brett were the only passengers . . . and the almost eerie resemblance among the sparse crew . . . all tall, blue-eyed and sable-haired—

Like Brett.

Paulina touched her fingers to the silken bedgown she wore, an exotic, full-skirted garment like the many others in the elaborate hand-carved chifforobe across the mirrored and balustraded cabin. This one was so pale a shade of pink, it hardly had color at all. Braided multihued chiffon hugged her waistline and cascaded down the back of the skirts. She wasn't sure where the clothing had come from, or why it had been offered to her, but she was flattered by the garments that seemed to have been made especially for her.

Out on the deck she could hear muted male exchanges. Sitting forward, she tried to catch a word or two between Brett McCallum and the unknown man to whom he spoke. Then two words in particular caught her attention and her breath caught. When the murmuring abruptly ceased and a light rap echoed at the door, she eased back onto the mound of silken pillows and called, "Come in."

The black-clothed Brett—the dog at his side—entered the chamber and dropped into a plush chair. When the dog took its place beside him, Brett rubbed his head almost absently. "How are you feeling this morning?" he asked.

"Did I just hear a man refer to you as 'my prince'?"

A nervous chuckle echoed toward her. "Don't be ridiculous. The captain and I were discussing the ship. He refers to it with strong affection, since he's been captain for a hun—for many, many years."

"Why have you been avoiding me?"

His fingers linked and drew up beneath his chin. "I haven't been avoiding you. In fact, I have been checking on you every few hours, and making sure your meals were to your liking."

"Then where have you been sleeping at night?"

"In another cabin. I thought you wanted your privacy."

Paulina disengaged a lock of her hair that had caught against her arm and swung it back. Then her fingers gently caressed the full chiffon sleeve of the gown she wore. "And these garments? Why am I allowed to wear them?"

Silence. Brett's dark eyebrows met in a thoughtful frown, his full mouth pinching into a line. "They were left aboard by another passenger. Why shouldn't you wear them? The captain would have had to discard them otherwise."

"Passengers do not leave such expensive garments aboard a ship. No, there is something strange going on here. I—" Her voice caught, as though she strangled on her own thoughts. "I believe something sinister is in the works—"

"Sinister!" Brett snapped to his feet and his palms struck flatly against his thick thighs. "I've been accused

119

of all manner of atrocity in my lifetime . . . but certainly nothing sinister!"

Paulina noticed something different in his almost-hostile move. Upon the little finger of his left hand gleamed what appeared to be a stunning diamond. "Where did you get that?"

Instantly, Brett tried to tuck his hand away. "Get what? Oh, the ring—" Holding his hand at the level of his waist, he pretended to study the piece of jewelry. "It's nothing. Crystal and gold . . . a mere pittance in value."

"May I see?"

He seemed reluctant and started to tuck his hand back into his pocket. Then with an authoritative "Stay, Alujian!" he began to move slowly toward Paulina. Extending his hand, he said, "See? What did I tell you . . . a gaudy bauble with a crystal trying to convince a very pretty lady that it is a diamond."

When Paulina took his hand, she thought it seemed overly warm. But her concentration was on the ring, which depicted a beguiling pair of young lovers with the very large stone between them. An opaque enamel had been used for the hands and faces of the tiny figures, and translucent blue enamel for their garments. It was, perhaps, the most beautiful piece of jewelry she had ever seen. Quietly, she looked up, her gaze holding Brett's own with wonder. "If you think I'll believe that is a crystal, Brett McCallum, then you must think I am as dumb as dirt."

Brett slowly withdrew his hand. "Then I guess, princess, that you are dumb as dirt."

"Princess! Well now, that is a new title . . . and one preferable to honey."

A rap echoed from the door. Brett called, "Yes, what is it?" and the door came open.

The captain, a man who appeared to be about fifty,

with snow-white hair and a neatly trimmed beard, looked in on the two. "May I have a word with you—" He hesitated to add, "Sir."

Brett nodded, the captain left, and he looked back toward Paulina. "Is there anything I can get for you?"

"A big slice of chocolate cake," came her instant reply.

He grinned, but it was different somehow, free of the sarcasm she had grown so accustomed to. "We can't have you getting fat, can we?"

"Why not? I feel that human sacrifices for the marriage altar should be plumped up. Don't you?"

"No," came his curt reply, and he instantly began his withdrawal from the chamber. "Stay with her, Alujian."

Hearing their voices outside, Paulina waited for the dog to move toward a dark corner and lie down. Then she slipped from the massive gossamer-enshrouded bed and eased across the plush carpeting. With an ear pressed to the door she listened to the bizarre and frightening conversation between the two men.

"Does she suspect, my prince?"

"No," Brett replied. "Are you steadily on course for Talantia?"

"We are, but our forecasters have signaled that a gale is forming just north of the Pribilof Islands. It is bearing down directly on our course."

Forecasters? Signaled from where? Who were these people? Paulina caught her breath, wanting to flee from her moment of eavesdropping, but much too curious. Again she pressed her ear to the door.

"Captain, you must understand how imperative it is that we reach Talantia before the sun is at its zenith in the northern sky. My brother cannot be crowned without a queen . . . and if he is not crowned by evening twilight of the zenith, then the law prescribes that he die."

"You needn't remind me, my prince. I am your humble servant and will fulfill my duty to you and to Talantia . . . or I myself will die. This I promise you."

Paulina drew back so quickly from this declaration that her first footstep caught in the hem of the exotic gown, causing her to lose her balance. When the men's voices abruptly halted, she gained her footing and dove for the bed, tucking herself in just as Brett snapped the door open. Managing the smallest of smiles, she asked, "Have you brought my chocolate cake?"

His look was wary, filled with suspicion, and darkening his features even as she gazed upon them. "I'll have some fruit brought to you if you wish. It is more nutritious—"

"I don't want nutritious, Brett. I want yum-yum." A dark eyebrow arched and disapproval pinched his mouth. When he began to withdraw, she asked, "I heard the word *gale*. Are we heading for bad weather, or is that simply the name of one of your lady friends?" He seemed different, somehow, from the Brett she had known in Skagway, not as quick to smile, and hesitating, almost as if he revered her, to tease and taunt her. She didn't like it at all.

In a bland tone he replied, "The ship can take bad weather. You needn't worry about it, princess."

"Don't call me princess. It's ridiculous."

Brett withdrew without comment. On the deck once more he confessed to the captain, "You must know that I want the woman. If I touch her, I am to be punished. She *must* be a virgin when she is presented to my brother. If he discovers she is not, he will be dishonored—"

"Yes, my prince," came the captain's grim reply. "And the repercussions will be severe."

* * *

Paulina felt that she'd either been caught in a nightmare, or that Brett was pulling a very realistic hoax on her. After pinching herself and feeling the stinging pain, she felt it must be the latter. That must be it; Brett McCallum was playing a game with her, and from the looks of her surroundings, a very expensive one.

All this talk of princes and forecasters and sacrifices was being staged. Brett knew that she was a little nosy and that she might eavesdrop, and he was trying to see how far he could carry the hoax before she called him down on it.

Well, he'd see that she could play the game just as well as he could. He would admire her talent as an actress.

So Paulina drew herself from her somber mood and bouts of tears and chose one of the lovely gowns from the chifforobe bolted to the wall with brass fittings.

A sound nearby startled her, and she caught her breath, seeing a dark movement in the far corner. She had forgotten that the wolf dog was sleeping there, but now he made his presence known by emerging from the corner and growling, low and threatening, his eyes dark and hypnotic as she dared to cut her gaze and nervously hold his own.

Quickly, Paulina chose a dress, one that was much too elaborate for the occasion, but still the most modest dress in the chifforobe. The rich red fabric was edged by gold lace, and a sweeping underskirt reflected the opulence of the Renaissance. She assumed the opal and diamond accents of the lace bodice were paste, because if they weren't, the gown would be regal enough for a coronation.

Ah, so that was it! Brett had planted the appropriate clothing to pull off his elaborate hoax. All right . . . if he wanted opulence, then he would have it!

* * *

Brett had not spied on her while she had dressed, though he had wanted to, but now watched her through the close grillwork of the small concealed opening connecting her cabin to his own. He saw her joyful eyes, her regal profile and delicate lips, poised, he thought, for some future mischief, and his heart swelled from the vision of her loveliness.

Why, he asked himself for the hundredth time, had he chosen her to marry his brother, the crown prince, when he wanted her for himself?

He had mentally kicked himself in the britches as many times as he had cursed his brother's good luck.

Now he watched her sweep her hair back and tie it with a length of golden brocade she had taken from the chifforobe. How lovely she was in the bold shade of crimson . . . and, God, how he could envision the crown of precious gems that would be placed upon her head, a crown that would identify her as his brother's bride, his brother's wife, his brother's queen.

Brett curled his fist and pressed it to his mouth, wanting to pound the wall in his rage but knowing he could not. The captain, his protector, was already suspicious, and he could not add to that suspicion by displaying anger that he could not explain.

But he was not only enraged by the idea of having to pledge her to his brother, he was also enraged that he'd had to lie to her, to make her believe that he would take her to find the man, Millburn Hanks, who was so important to her. She would never see Millburn Hanks. He owed it to his country to see to that. She was the only thing that could save his world, his brother's life, and ensure the future prosperity of Talantia.

And she would never again see her own world . . . or

reunite with the sister and the uncle and the little friend, Matt, whom she had spoken so fondly of.

He hated himself for that.

And he hated himself for loving Paulina . . . yes, he had to admit it . . . he was in love with the beautiful flaxen-haired woman from Turkey Gulch, Utah, who couldn't keep her many lies straight in her head.

She would make a regal queen for Talantia.

His brother, the crown prince, would be pleased.

Paulina wandered out on deck and watched the sea roll out from beneath the bow of the *Crown Prince of Talantia*. She was a fine, full-masted vessel, her timbers as smooth and black as teak, her sails as white as a virgin's sleeping attire.

The sky was like a pane of burnt umber—Paulina felt almost as if with a slightly keener eye she could see the universe beyond and discern its individual characteristics—the far horizon of the sea separated from the sky by a thin scattering of violet and pink, like angry brushes' work a painter's canvas. It was like no sky she had ever seen, sinister and yet compelling, a fantasy, and yet familiar in its distinctions . . . like carefully phrased descriptions within the pages of a well-written novel, of a world that no living being had ever seen—

"What are you thinking?"

She was startled, her hand rising to clutch her throat in her moment of alarm. She did not look into Brett's features, but felt the heavy gaze of his eyes upon her profile. "I was thinking how beautiful the day is . . . how beautiful this ship. I cannot imagine that a gale could interrupt this serenity."

"I told you not to worry about such things." There was an abrupt reprimand in his voice, so unlike the character he had exhibited prior to boarding this strange vessel. "We are making good time."

"Oh? Is that what the mysterious Captain Ahab says?"

"Captain Ahab?" Silence. Brett gave her a look of perplexity before his features registered some semblance of understanding. "Ah, yes, *Moby Dick* by Mr. Herman Melville. The captain of the *Crown Prince* does not chase white whales."

"Oh?" She tried to sound somewhat disinterested. "He should, perhaps. It might add a little excitement to the trip."

"Captain Pericles tries to avoid adventure. You might say he's a rather dull fellow."

"Oh? And you knew him before? Or do you impulsively judge all people you meet?"

Ignoring her inquiry, he remarked, "Might I say that you look lovely?"

"I'm a bit overdressed, don't you think?"

"You look like a princess."

"I am a princess." When he gave her another of those strangely quizzical looks, she hastily added, "How can I not feel like a princess when I am so elegantly dressed?"

"You should always dress elegantly. You are a beautiful woman—"

"Pooh, Brett McCallum. If I could find the gray wool dress I wore aboard ship, I would much prefer it."

"I believe it was thrown overboard."

"That wasn't nice." She'd spoken as if the fate of the dress really didn't matter one way or the other. A crisp flapping in the breeze overhead caught her attention, and she looked up to see the gentle unfurling of the banner topping the main mast. "That is a very strange flag. Why is the sun below the line of the mountains?"

Brett, too, looked upward, feeling a moment of pride as he beheld the crisp red and gold banner of Talantia.

126

"Because the sun is the core of life, and all around it . . . the mountains, the sea, the air, the plains and the fields, the meadows and the glens and forests . . . they emanate from the thread of life, from the sun . . . from the core of the earth where life began."

Paulina's gaze was one of disbelief. "Why, Brett McCallum, you're not a simple backwoods boy at all, you're a philosopher." Yes, she would play his game . . . and believe in his Talantia, and the core of the earth being like the sun, the eternal spring of life and all that it encompassed. "So, what's for supper?"

"Is eating all you think about?"

For the first time in two days she detected a tone of humor in his voice. "Well, it is when you've got a companion who feeds you apples, plums, and Brazil nuts—"

"Now, that isn't true. Didn't you have a fine cut of caribou last evening, and smoked salmon for your noonday meal?"

A thought came to her, one she was surprised hadn't occurred before. "By the way, where does one get fresh fruit out of season?"

Out of season? In Talantia, the trees yielded fruit year round. "Proper storage is the key," he replied after a moment, drawing himself up as he prepared to excuse himself. "Now, why don't you find a way to entertain yourself while I talk to the captain about this gale you're so worried about."

"Is it all right if I snoop about?"

"I am sure that the captain will not mind, as long as you are discreet."

One of the crew, naked to the waist and barefoot, approached, bowed slightly, then continued his journey past them. "Goodness," said Paulina. "The respect of these men makes me feel like a princess—"

"You *are* a princess," he said a little more curtly than

127

he'd intended, immediately softening his voice. "And don't ever forget it."

With that, Brett McCallum departed from her, and she looked first in one direction, and then in the other, wondering where to begin her snooping.

She was having such fun with his little game.

Eight

Paulina did not like the way Brett watched the darkening of the northern sky. Even the great dog stood bristling in alarm at his side, and the two of them there, together, filled her with such a sense of fear and foreboding that she felt her life might be very near its end. She had pressed herself against the outer door of her cabin, watching him across this short distance, the rising wind crossing the bow and sweeping her skirts all about her.

Men rushed to and fro, dragging at the riggings, climbing the ratlines and masts to release the sails. As they were brought down from their heights, the large black ship turned slowly in the direction of the approaching storm to meet it head-on.

The wind lofted, strengthened, snapping at Paulina's voluminous skirts and attempting to drag her from the safety of the recessed doorway. The sky billowed in massive rages of gray and black, tumbling ever closer and enshrouding them in the blackest of threats.

She had done nothing to make her presence known, but suddenly, Brett turned toward her, almost as if he sensed her presence, his eyes as dark as the descending sky. He had changed into a shirt of purple silk, with wide, billowing sleeves and tight cuffs. He might easily have passed as a pirate, and he gave the easy impression of being fully in charge, just as if the ship belonged to him.

"What are you doing out, Paulina? Go into your cabin."

Even above the omnipresent howl of the wind, his tone startled her. "But I—" She really wasn't sure why she felt the need to argue. "I don't want to be alone."

"Don't be a baby!" came his instant reproach. "Do as you're told!"

A sudden draft of wind caught the bow of the ship and tipped it to starboard, pulling Paulina out of the narrow recess. She might have tumbled across the deck if Brett's hand had not closed over her arm just above the elbow. The grip was painful, though she didn't believe he'd intended to hurt her. "All right. I should go to my cabin," she conceded, her fingers easing beneath his own to pry them loose. "I will be safer there."

Though he had trouble maintaining his own footing, he saw her safely to the door and waited until her slim fingers closed over the handle. She had never seen him like this, protective, like a warrior, staid and dignified, like royalty, fearful, and yet deliberately suppressing it. Her feelings toward him were different from those that had nestled within her in Skagway . . . no loathing, no annoyance as she remembered his light moments of teasing and taunting.

"Go inside."

Only then, with his eyes glaring at her, did Paulina remember the danger. Her thoughts scattered into fragments as her gaze lifted for a final glimpse of his own dark, hooded one. Then she closed herself in the cabin, wishing he were with her.

A ship's lantern against the wall gave off the faintest glow, and even that dimmed as the midmorning light outside the one small porthole darkened to the color of ebony. The sky was speaking now, low grumbles nearby gaining in clarity and frequency, and far away, the echo of lightning cracking wildly against land masses . . . or against the waves beginning to pitch and gain in height and depth. The slow, methodical rocking of the *Crown Prince* quickly became hard and turbulent, and as Paulina settled upon the bed, she felt her fingers digging into the mattress for mere support.

All the while her wide emerald eyes held the single door, waiting for the appearance of Brett McCallum, the one man in all the world she felt could be a calming influence in her life. The voices of the crew, almost a dutiful drone before, now pitched to the same degree of alarm and intensity as the sea. Harder and harder the bow hit upon the thrashing waves, and Paulina felt the illness of blind fear grabbing her within.

Just then she heard a cry . . . a familiar voice that almost squeezed the life out of her. Thinking only of Brett being in danger, she rushed toward the door, jerked it open, and saw him . . . dear God, saw him at the rail of the *Crown Prince of Talantia,* holding on for dear life. Just at that moment an invisible hand reached into the recess of the doorway and pulled her out, and she felt herself tumbling . . . tumbling, into the deep black depths of the sea.

But not only did the sea hold her in its deathly grip . . . for she felt the fingers of a familiar hand firmly entwine among her own, and together they plummeted into the icy depths of purgatory. . . .

Turkey Gulch, Utah, that morning

Four aging gentlemen huddled together in a circle of secrecy, conspiracy, and fear. At sixty-three, Thurman

Roper was the youngest member of the group, and at eighty-two, Izzy Jeconiah was the oldest. At the middle of the argument and controversy were Kermit and Warren Logan, seventy-two-year-old twin brothers who were as different in appearance as maple syrup and manure. The four of them, since the death of fifth member John Wynn, comprised what was left of the city council.

"I'll tell you again," snapped Thurman Roper, "that we were wrong to send that little gal off on a wildgoose chase. Millburn fled Turkey Gulch because he was afraid of Lester and Earl, and he won't be making himself easy to find. We're going to have to take care of the problem and send for that little gal to come home. Dammit, she's shown some real spunk, and I say we get rid of the Bartletts ourselves and give the gal the job—"

"I agree," interrupted Izzy Jeconiah, a short, heavyset man who wheezed when he spoke. "We took the easy way out and, certainly, we took advantage of Miss Winthrop at a most vulnerable moment, after her father had been killed. I say we take care of our problem and get back to making Turkey Gulch a fine little town—"

"Lynch mob!" growled Kermit Logan.

And his brother echoed "Lynch mob," quickly adding his own thought. "We'll make barbarians out of ourselves. We've got to uphold the law!"

"The law has let us down," Thurman Roper responded quietly, taking a moment to drag on a good Cuban cigar. "Wherever Miss Lillian is hiding, she won't come out as long as the Bartletts are waiting to clamp irons on her wrists."

"She broke the law," growled Kermit.

"She did not!" countered Thurman. "And you know it! She had nothing to do with the fire."

"But the insurance policy—" Warren had spoken out of loyalty to the stand his brother had taken. Kermit had always been one shade smarter and two shades more dubious. Warren agreed with Thurman and Izzy that Lillian was innocent of all wrongdoing, but Kermit had ordered him to keep his opinion behind the closed doors of the large white house the bachelor brothers shared at the end of the street.

"I say we vote on the issue," challenged Thurman, exhausted after the two hours the council had been arguing.

"You want to vote on a lynch mob," pointed out Kermit for the hundredth time. "You know that my brother and I will vote against it, and you and Izzy will vote for it. We're at a standstill."

"I don't think so." The familiar voice at the doorway caused each man to pivot. No one had heard them enter, but now Will Winthrop leaned forward in his wheelchair. Behind him, Lucille McWhirter put a comforting hand upon his shoulder.

"This is a closed meeting," said Kermit Logan.

And Warren mimicked, "This is a closed meeting," without intending to be rude to his brother.

Will Winthrop's hand came up from the pocket of his jacket. "I have here the deciding vote. John Wynn wrote it out the day before he died."

Thurman Roper and Izzy Jeconiah shared the opinion that the announcement of this meeting, and the issue of dealing with the Bartletts, had caused John's fatal heart attack. They had both thought that because of his poor health, John would have made a written account of his vote, just in case. But until now no one had come forward. "If that is John's vote," asked Izzy Jeconiah, "how did you come by it?"

"Martha brought it to me only this morning."

Martha was John's widow. Yesterday, when Kermit had paid his respects, she had denied any knowledge of

John's casting his vote or intending to have it counted posthumously. Thurman smiled to himself; he was pretty damn sure he knew why.

"I say we take our vote now," said Thurman. "All in favor of proposition one, cast your vote aye." In harmony with Izzy Jeconiah, Thurman said, "Aye."

"All against proposition one, cast your vote nay."

At which time the Logan brothers said, "Nay."

"Bring us John's vote," requested Thurman. Lucille took the folded document from Will's hand and brought it to Thurman. Slowly, he unfolded it, saw that it was signed by John, properly witnessed by two respected citizens and notarized by the only lawyer in Turkey Gulch. Then he looked at the faces of the three other members of the city council and quietly said, "John Wynn has cast his vote posthumously . . . aye to proposition one."

Kermit slammed his fist upon the tabletop. "I wash my hands of it. You do what you must!"

"You cannot wash your hands of it," argued Izzy. "You agreed that if a majority of the council voted aye, that you would do your part."

Kermit grumbled, "But under normal circumstances, a dead man's vote wouldn't count."

"These are not normal circumstances," Thurman pointed out.

Again Kermit grumbled, without saying a word, and Warren blew a quick burst of air between his thin lips.

Lester leaned back in the chair and linked his fingers behind his head. Earl had ridden out to the ranch a couple of hours before to meet with Gower, the clerk at Mr. Tillford's insurance office, and he was awaiting his return. Gower had claimed to have information the Bartletts would find valuable, and had not been willing to meet with either Lester or Earl within the corporate limits of Turkey Gulch.

The door slammed. Lester's chair hit the floor with a thud, and he hopped up, arching his back to relieve the stiffness. The way Earl grinned back at him when their gazes met gave Lester a pretty good indication that the information had been worth the hundred dollars Gower had demanded for it. Earl's fingers were curled around a large document rolled up and held with a length of rawhide.

"What you got there, Earl?"

"Floor plan of that damned boardinghouse the McWhirter woman operates. I got me a real good idea where the Winthrop gal is." Approaching the desk, Earl untied the length of rawhide and unrolled the plan. A thick, gnarled finger began tracing the straight blue lines of the draftsman's pen. "Look here . . . Gower did some snoopin' over in that shed behind the boarding- house and found these plans. See this block right here? An interior room without doors or windows. Gower got into the house yesterday morning . . . by claimin' he was lookin' over the place for the purpose of updatin' the insurance. He says there's a panel right about here—" The finger jabbed several times on a westerly wall. "An' I'll be willin' to lay my life on the line that the gal's holed up in there."

"Then let's go get her—"

"Can't. Law says we gotta have probable cause to think she's in there to get a search warrant. An' we ain't got that, Lester."

"To hell with warrants and probable cause. I say we go get her."

Earl really liked the idea of getting the little gal—and not just having her as a resident in the jail. Tucking his thumbs into his waistband beneath the expanse of his

135

belly, he grinned widely. "I say we wait till night, Lester. No sense in makin' the folks in town any madder'n they already are."

"Yeah," Lester conceded. "Those damn Winthrop women always were real popular with the folks here and about."

The grin remained. "Even Miss Laura. You reckon her girls will ever know the real reason she left town?"

"Not unless you tell 'em," came Lester's reply. "An' now that their old man's gone, I'm surprised you ain't already." Lester returned to the desk and resumed his lazy position, drawing his booted feet up to the clutter. "What do you reckon she did with that kid you gave her? Must be, what, almost seven years old now."

"Almost." Earl didn't like thinking about Laura. He'd always thought that if *he'd* won her hand instead of his rival's having done so, things might have been different for him. Maybe he wouldn't have been so mean. Maybe people around Turkey Gulch would have respected him rather than abhorred him. Perhaps—

But it didn't happen.

He'd been trying to find out about Laura for the past seven years, but none of her family would respond to his letters, and his one journey to the East, four years earlier, had been a journey head-on into a brick wall. Hell, he gave up—he'd returned to Turkey Gulch and had started a pattern of vengeance. He'd killed old man Winthrop, and now he'd burned their business . . . and tonight . . . yeah, tonight he'd have his way with the younger daughter, Lillian. And when Paulina got back— if she ever did—she'd get a bullet in her back just like her old man did.

"What you thinkin' Earl?" Lester's gaze had snapped up from its absent scrutiny of the floor plans of Lucille McWhirter's boardinghouse.

136

"Just thinkin' how I'm lookin' forward to tonight. You just remember"—a grin snaked across the younger Bartlett's swarthy features—"I git her first, Lester."

Lester chuckled his response. "You just make sure you leave some for me, Earl!"

Lillian threw down Bram Stoker's latest novel, *Dracula*, so fresh from the author's publishing house she could still feel the dampness of the ink. Even at mid-morning the descriptive scenes between the ivory-colored pages filled her with her own brand of terror. Why would Uncle Will send her such reading material, unless it was simply to keep her alert and on her toes. Yes . . . that was something he would do . . . a rather sadistic maneuver to protect her from the perils that might lurk across one's shoulder.

Rising, Lillian straightened the folds of her pale blue gown and untucked the row of cotton lace that had been untidied by her tosses upon the bed while she'd been reading. Then she went to the panel, the only mode of entry into the room, and looked through the narrow crack, hoping that she might see at least one human face.

But no one loitered about the parlor and she turned away, disappointed. Things had to get better, and get better fast, or she was going to go absolutely mad in her confinement. Boredom prickled through her shoulders, then dug its ugly fingers into her spine and slid all the way down into her hips and legs. She wondered if dancing might help, but felt much too ridiculous to do it alone. She needed some change . . . any change at all in her daily regimen if she were to survive another week.

But one thing remained unchanged in her small, prisonlike antechamber. Her hatred of the Bartletts.

They were like the terrifying Count Dracula she'd been reading about . . . sucking the very life out of the small village of Turkey Gulch and blending back into the night with ruthless calm.

With the exception of a vampire in her company, she was so bored that she'd welcome any change in her confinement.

Any change!

Night fell with deathly calm. The one saloon in town allowed to be open past eight in the evening because it was owned by Lester and Earl was loud and raucous, and occasional bursts of gunfire could be heard among the drunken patrons.

Lester was suspicious of the offered hospitality, but not too suspicious to accept the two bottles of whiskey Thurman Roper sent over to the table he shared with his brother.

"The old bastard's had a change of heart," murmured Earl. "Reckon if he can't fight us, he might as well join us." Clicking his fingers, Earl called Thurman over to the table. "Mighty kind of you, Thurman. How about a drink?"

"I can't." A nervous tick caught at the corner of the gentleman's right eye. "Wednesday evening prayer services. I promised my Bonnie I'd attend tonight."

"How is that little gal of yours, Thurman? How old is she now . . . 'bout twenty-eight . . . nine?"

"She's thirty-one," replied Thurman. "Now, you two enjoy your drinks—" He tipped his hat. "And I'll be on my way."

"Good evenin' to ya, Thurman," said Earl.

And when the older man was out of hearing range, Lester asked, "What do you think he's up to?"

"Nothing," laughed Earl, tipping one of the bottles to fill their empty glasses. "Those old men on the city council are a pack of scared rabbits."

They laughed, clinked their glasses, and drank until both bottles, and yet a third, were clean and empty.

Just past midnight Earl collected the day's earnings from the till behind the bar, stuffing the money into a brown leather bag he then tucked into an inside pocket of his jacket. When he and Lester left the saloon that night, they had one thing in mind—taking custody of Miss Lillian Winthrop when she least expected it.

As was their usual habit, and one the entire town was aware of, Lester and Earl took a shortcut through an alley toward the marshal's office. Lester wanted to deposit the money in the safe there before accomplishing the pleasant little job they'd decided to do that night.

The two men, each with an arm across the other's shoulder, laughed and joked about what they were going to do when Lillian was in their custody, and did not hear the crunch of boots when they were a good hundred yards into the alley.

Four simultaneous shots rang out, then male cries of surprise and pain. By the time the night was still again, Lester and Earl lay dead, facedown, in the dark alley.

Thurman, rifle in hand, edged a few wary steps toward the two men. Then approached Izzy Jeconiah, and lastly—and hesitatingly—Kermit and Warren Logan. Sharing a silent look among them, the four men then aimed and fired once more, two bullets into each of the Bartlett brothers' backs.

"It's done," said Thurman.

Quickly, with bootsteps fast approaching from Main Street in response to the shots, the four conspirators cut into a vacant building and then joined the men gathering around the dead bodies.

"Got ambushed," said the bartender from the Bartlett brothers' saloon.

Thurman Roper quietly added, "It was bound to happen."

By the afternoon of the following day, Lester and Earl were buried in the village cemetery, and Lillian, exonerated of all wrongdoing by the United States marshal's office in Salt Lake City, emerged from her place of hiding in Lucille's boardinghouse.

Lillian couldn't help but wonder how two men who had been so hated by the entire village of Turkey Gulch could now have so many redeeming qualities. Did the state of being dead expunge the character of the man, or did it merely expunge the memories of the living?

That evening Lillian also received confirmation that the insurance proceeds would be paid on the mercantile.

Now all that was left to be done was to get Paulina back home, where she belonged.

She had in her hand the last letter—actually, little more than a hastily written note in her sister's hand—that had arrived the week before from a place called Skagway. Paulina had said that if she needed to get in touch with her, that she could do so through a place called Big Pat's Saloon. So Lillian sat down to write her a letter, and found herself quietly mulling over where to begin.

Why not just come out with it? she thought, placing the tip of her pen to the smooth sheet of linen paper.

My dearest sister Paulina,
   Lester and Earl are dead and buried.
   The council met this morning and have agreed to give you the job.

*The mercantile burned several weeks ago, but Mr. Till-
ford has agreed to pay the insurance proceeds on the building. Uncle Will contacted Dewey Beauford, and he and
his crew will begin rebuilding tomorrow.*

*Mother didn't visit in April as she promised but will
await your return.*

Please come home at once.

> With affection,
> Lillian

Hastily, Lillian addressed the envelope to Miss Paulina
Winthrop, c/o Big Pat's Saloon, Skagway, Alaska, tucked
the letter inside, and glued a small gold seal to the flap.
Tomorrow she would ride to the post office in Salt Lake
City so that her summons could immediately begin its
journey to Skagway, and her dear sister.

It had been a hectic day, and one, certainly, that was
the beginning of a new, exciting and yet more tranquil
life for Turkey Gulch. The future, almost destroyed by
the Bartletts over the past twenty years, now looked
bright again. Paulina was a very vital part of that future,
and one who would return integrity to a population that
had all but lost it.

Now, the duty of the letter accomplished, Lillian
moved on to other things. One was to draw Uncle Will—
and Lucille McWhirter—out of their state of despon-
dency. She was not sure what had caused it, though she
felt it could not possibly be grief over the loss of the
Bartletts. Perhaps she would be able to cheer them up.

Lillian sent Matt to the bakery—which had escaped the
inferno—to order a cake. Tomorrow evening they would
gather together all their friends to toast the future of
Turkey Gulch and the future happiness of Will and Lucille, who would marry as soon as Paulina returned
home.

And, lastly, they would say a special prayer to God, to keep Paulina safe, wherever she was, and to see her safely returned to them.

Nine

Paulina felt the pain of a blinding light above her. She tried to open her eyes, but she felt as though her eyelids had been glued shut. Though she knew it was impossible, she could almost detect the familiar odors of the small backroom at Big Pat's Saloon; her mind's eye could see a worried Brett hovering over her; her mind's ear caught the murmurings of worry, and she could feel, almost, an overly warm hand covering her forehead. Then there was nothing more . . . just a darkness withdrawing into a long, long tunnel.

Brett dragged himself onto the sand, gagging on the seawater bursting up from his lungs. His hand touched a smooth, round boulder and he turned, dropping back and feeling the coolness of it through the tattered remains of his shirt. Ancient driftwood scattered at his feet was like the skeletal frame of a beached ship, and he extended his leg, feeling a bare foot come to rest against a smooth, weathered timber. What had happened to his boot and sock? He ventured a look down. Only one of the expensive boots he'd been wearing remained at the end of a painfully throbbing leg.

The wound in his thigh had started to bleed again, though the stain upon his trousers was diluted by the sea through which he'd dragged himself from certain death. Every breath he took burned his lungs, every movement racked his body with pain.

All at once he wondered if he was still alive . . . and worse, if he was lost in a perpetual dream—or nightmare—without beginning and without end. Had he only dreamed of Paulina Winthrop, the woman he had chosen to mate with his brother and become his queen? Was she a mere figment of his imagination? And was he a prince too, as all his memories told him he was? Or was that a delusion as well?

Hesitantly, Brett ventured a look down the debris-littered beach, hoping for a glimpse of the crimson gown he had last seen her wearing. But he saw nothing but driftwood, a keg half buried in the sand, and a plank torn asunder by the storm that had dragged him in from the sea.

Oh, though she was so very real to him, he knew he had merely imagined her existence—

"Brett?"

He spun rapidly, forgetting to guard the hurting leg, though the moment of pain did not reflect in his gaze. There she stood, the crimson gown tattered, a slim shoulder exposed through long, wet strands of wheat-colored hair, her full mouth attempting a smile but not quite able to accomplish it. "Paulina . . ." Slowly, he rose to his feet, remembered the one boot that had clung to him, and dragged it off. Then his hands were gently touching her shoulders and pulling her close. "God . . . I thought you were only a dream—"

"I was so worried for you. I tried to hold on to your hand, but the sea ripped us apart."

"I know," came his soft answer. "But you are safe . . . I am safe . . . and that's all that matters."

Paulina allowed herself to be held close, to be comforted by the strong hand now caressing her back. "Do you know where we are?"

"I've no earthly idea," he responded.

"Then how about a celestial one?"

Brett drew slightly back, his fingers now closing over her slender arms. Their gazes met, held, hers with the sheer joy of being with him, and his with guilt, guilt that all he could think about was being with her and wanting her, taking her as his woman and winning her love . . . ultimately, yes . . . ultimately making her his own bride. He hated his brother right then because he was bound by honor to turn Paulina over to him when they reached Talantia, if, indeed, they ever reached his homeland to the north.

So, without giving her an answer, he removed his hands from her and turned away, facing the sea with thoughts ricocheting through his head. He could not have Paulina for his own . . . he had known that from the very beginning.

Thus, when her hand touched gently upon his forearm, he wrenched it back, and the way his eyes narrowed as they met her gaze revealed an emotion strongly bordering on pure, unadulterated loathing. As tears gathered in Paulina's sea-green eyes, Brett took a precarious step, testing the strength of his crippled leg, then put several feet of sand between them. Without looking back he ordered brusquely, "Stay put. I'll walk around and see if I can spot the *Crown Prince* on the sea."

Paulina watched him walk away, tall, proud, deliberately attempting to suppress the limp, his shoulders strong and sturdy, his chestnut-colored hair darkened by the seawater and now being hastily dried by the brisk wind following after the storm. *Brett . . . Brett . . . what goes on in that deep, impenetrable heart of yours?*

The days grew longer, the nights, what there was of them, warmer. Since the disaster that had washed them ashore, debris had also drifted in which hinted strongly that the *Crown Prince* had not survived the storm. Wood the color of teak, splintered by the raging sea, lay scattered about on the beach . . . a keg half filled with the captain's favorite brandy . . . shredded white canvas . . . the bloated bodies of eight seamen, one each day since they'd arrived on the island, had been buried against a stand of bristly Sitka spruce.

On the ninth day of their captivity on the island, a trunk washed ashore from the *Crown Prince* . . . and inside, still dry, were tools from the captain's quarters: a saw and hammer, needles, thick twine, and yards and yards of canvas, iron nails, and a lathe.

So in the silent fury that had become Brett's character, without explanation to the woman who was trapped with him, he began to construct separate shelters for them among the thick trunks of hemlocks.

Paulina watched him, naked to the waist, his bronze skin glistening in the fading sun of the day, and performed her own mundane duty . . . cooking the trout he'd caught at a small freshwater lake he'd discovered half a mile inland. She watched the fire leap and sizzle against the cooking fish, remembering how he'd started it by repeatedly hitting the hammer against a rock until the remains of dryas had caught the dancing sparks. She had almost expected the fire to die right out, the way her heart was dying now.

Soon she removed the cooked fish from the fire and put it into the wooden bowls that had washed ashore.

Brett had made two roughly carved forks, and she now placed one upon each of their plates. She rose to stand behind him, quietly watching his labors, then hesitantly laid her hand on his shoulder. He pivoted sharply, his gaze dark with annoyance.

"Our supper is ready," she announced. When he dropped the tools and stared up at her, she asked hastily, "Why are you so angry with me?"

Again he pivoted, his gaze watching the far horizon and his hands rising slowly to cover his narrow hips. "Let's eat, Paulina. I have a lot to do before nightfall." Then he walked toward the cooking fire he had built on the beach.

Well, this just won't do! The declaration rushed through Paulina's head as she watched him put distance between them. Gathering up her tattered skirts, her bare feet broke into a run until she skirted him, then took a stand that caused his immediate halt. "You will tell me what I've done to deserve your disfavor, or I swear, Brett McCallum, I won't eat anything, and I won't drink anything. I'll let myself die, Brett McCallum, and let you explain that, if you can, when someone comes searching for us! Let's see how you'll explain my death!"

A smirk twisted his mouth. "I could lie like a dog, Paulina, because there will be no witnesses to contradict me. Poor little Paulina, couldn't survive the sea, washed up dead on the shore, and brokenhearted Brett McCallum had to bury her. What a pity!"

She certainly did not appreciate his sarcasm. Drawing her hands to her hips, she pressed her lips into a thin line. Then she quietly said, "I just don't understand you, Brett McCallum. When we were together in Skagway, you were teasing and taunting, and, I must admit, a most likable rogue. Aboard ship you were a totally different man . . . you were aloof and businesslike

147

and . . . and I didn't much like you then. And now . . . now you are even more deplorable. You treat me like an outcast, like some smelly little street urchin you'd like to swipe out of your path with a heavy hand. I just don't understand, Brett. What have I done to make you despise me so? Am I not the same woman you met in Skagway? Am I not the same woman you boarded ship with? Am I not the same woman who washed up on this lonely beach with you nine days ago? Dear Lord, won't you tell me—" Tears had now popped into her eyes, and she crossed her arms in an attempt to still her trembling. "Won't you tell me what I've done, so that I can try to make it right by you?"

Guilt and shame crawled through Brett's shoulders, even as he fought to remain hard and controlled in appearance, to show no response or emotion to her tearful plea. But suddenly, he couldn't think past the beauty of her standing there . . . the dying sun behind her casting a hauntingly soft glow upon her golden hair, her tears like diamonds trailing upon the pale rose of her cheeks . . . the luscious curves of her most womanly form racking against the fabric of her gown in her attempts to quell her emotions . . . damn, but he wanted her in his arms, in his heart.

Before he could reason within himself, before he could remember the repercussions, he had taken her in his arms and pressed her close, his mouth trailing upon her tear-dampened cheeks in the softest of caresses, the weight of her body dropping to the sand along with his own, and her mouth oh, so sweet and willing a mouth . . . accepting his kisses, her cheek his warm, assailing breath, and her body pressed to his own hard, traitorous one . . . a body that did not care that she was intended for his brother . . . a body that wanted to be sated and satisfied by the one woman in all the world who could enter his heart and stay there, permanently, because it was what he wanted.

Only a moment ago Paulina was tearfully exhausting herself with questions demanding answers, begging for explanations that would not be forthcoming, and hating him . . . hating him for making her life miserable when the confinement of the island was misery enough. Now she was in his arms, feeling the hardness of him against her thighs, feeling the wide expanse of his chest against the softness of her bodice, feeling the threads of her garments straining to be ripped away so that their flesh could touch and mingle without the rudeness of barriers. Her heart fluttered with want for this tall, moody rogue who was either a guide or a prince, and at the moment she didn't care which, and the coolness of the beach upon which they held each other surged with a heat created by their own entwined bodies. She wanted Brett to hold her in his arms so tightly that their bodies might fuse together and become one. Oh, she wanted him that badly . . . and if he withdrew from her now, she knew that the heated core of her heart would explode or she might pummel him with her fists until there was nothing left of him to be scraped up from the sand.

But he made no move to separate himself from her. Rather, he held her even closer, if it was at all possible, and his hands moved fluidly over her waist and the gentle curving of her hips. She was wondrously riveted to the masculine smell of him, to his kisses demanding her own, to his tongue tasting the sweetness of her mouth.

Brett lost himself in the erotic beauty of her, of her willingness to be in his arms and to enjoy the bold explorations of his hands. If he had a past, he could not remember it; if he had a future, it was as remote as the stars beginning to gather in the sky overhead. If he was hungry, he could not feel it . . . if he was thirsty, he would drink of her loveliness and be satisfied. Paulina was all that he wanted.

The tattered remnants of her gown clung tenuously to her youthful and yet womanly frame, and the search of his hands had half exposed her breasts so that he was able to cup his hands over them, with only his fingertips beneath the fabric. She did not withdraw from him, but pressed herself even closer, and he became aware of the slim column of her legs spreading across one of his hard, muscled ones, the folds of her gown easing upward to expose the silky softness of her flesh—and his groin ached with want of her—

Paulina had lost all reasoning, all fear. If she'd been angry with him just moments earlier, she didn't remember it. She felt only the shiver of her body as it anticipated his possession. She felt only the intensely wild desire swelling within her, begging him to take her, then and there . . . she wanted to see his maleness lowering to her, entering her, possessing her . . . oh, but she wanted to be free of the tattered remains of the horrid gown and feel the night upon her skin . . . the glow of moonlight around his thick hair, and see the gaze of lust darkening his eyes. She wanted to feel his slim, strong hands tunneling into the pale tresses of her hair and dragging her forward, to feel his mouth commandingly, demandingly, lovingly claiming her own. Her heart no longer beat its need for life, it raced painfully in anticipation of him . . . of this mysterious rogue who was her warden . . . and her prisoner—

Paulina could not recall the move, but now she was upon her back, with the cool sand beneath her. Brett's body covered her own and she felt her wanton abandon inspire a fierce need in him. She ached for his kisses, for the caresses of his strong hands, for the rush of his breath against her cheek. His mouth claimed her, possessed her, again and again and again, making her sighs part of his own . . . and her world was the island, her passion the sea . . . and Brett was the prince who would take her into his kingdom . . . and make her his own—

But then, without warning . . . he might as well have thrown a ladle of cold water in her face . . . he withdrew from her so quickly, she felt the immediate shock of her solitude. He had first jerked himself to his knees, and now, in one swift move, he was on his feet, his hands covering his hips and his eyes glaring, almost lethally, down at her.

She was both flustered and embarrassed by his unexpected departure from her, but not too embarrassed to demand, "What are you doing? Am I so repulsive to you?"

At the moment Brett would have liked to dive into a clear, icy pool and drown the fire consuming him. But since one was not immediately at hand, he drew in a cool breath and blew it out slowly and methodically. "I'm hungry, dammit," he said, turning away. Then Brett put distance between them, and soon sat down on a rock near the plates she had prepared.

He acted casual and indifferent as he picked up the plate with the smaller portion of food, but when he saw from the corner of his eye a tearful Paulina fleeing into the darkness in the opposite direction, he slowly put the plate down. He sat there, tears moistening his own eyes, his hands hanging limply over his drawn-up knees, and he cursed himself and the fate that had thrown them together.

Should he go after her? he wondered, remembering immediately his exploration of the island the day after they'd washed up. By his estimation, it was three miles long and one mile wide, give or take a yard or two, and uninhabited, except for a nest of gulls, a few walrus and seals, and a muskrat or two residing beside the small inland lake. No . . . she would be safe . . . she would come to her senses and realize that they were not destined to be together.

Perhaps she had felt rebuffed and had fled out of embarrassment.

Didn't the blasted woman know how much he wanted her?

Paulina didn't know where her feet were carrying her and she really didn't care. All she knew was that she wanted to be as far away from Brett McCallum as possible, and by the account he had given her, that wasn't nearly far enough. So she ran, and ran ever farther, over cool sand, through harsh underbrush that grabbed and snagged at her skin and clothing, over smooth white rocks and boulders that challenged the strength within her . . . until she stood, sobbing, at the entrance of a cave that was as black as any nightmare she'd ever suffered. A distinct echo of silence beckoned her and slowly her feet began to take precarious steps into the tunnel of darkness.

It had been cold on the beach and among the boulders, but this was a cold she had never imagined, penetrating all the way to the core of her heart. Fear leapt within her, but it was not strong enough to compel her to turn her feet around and rush from the core of the silent crypt eerily enveloping her. She wanted only to be as far away from Brett McCallum as time and distance could take her, and she could imagine nothing more suitable to accomplish that purpose than being swallowed up by the earth . . . for now her feet were carrying her downward, and frigid water trickled along the sides of the narrowing cavern, soaking its floor, and covering her tattered shoes and stockings.

Suddenly, the narrowing darkness emerged into a pale glow, and Paulina halted abruptly at what appeared to be a doorway into a wide cavern pulsating with light from all sides. The smooth floor gleamed like ice the color of amethyst, and the stalactites dotting the massive ceiling were like fire frozen in time. It was, perhaps, the loveliest sight she'd ever beheld, and she could only stand there in awe and wonder. Somewhere deep in the bowels of the earth a waterfall splashed into a lake-filled chamber, but otherwise, the silence rushed like a haunting wind. Momentarily, she forgot the cold, even as it prickled at her skin, and if her heart had continued its soft, rhythmic cadence, she couldn't feel it. All she knew was that she had entered a world of frozen beauty . . . a world that warmed her through and made her forget the ugliness outside.

Then, when she might have lost herself completely in the surrounding loveliness, she sensed a movement nearby that prickled her flesh with fear. She turned sharply to the left and there, merciful heavens, could it truly be . . . the great black wolf dog stood a silent guard at the entrance to still another cavern descending into the earth. Though a low growl emitted from the depths of its throat, it made no threatening move toward her.

"Alujian—" Paulina softly spoke his name, hoping that it might give him some small memory of her familiarity. "Alujian, how long have you been there? You must be starved." The quietness of her voice echoed all about her, bouncing off the walls of the massive cavern in which the two of them stood. Even as it held her attention, her gaze remained upon the dog.

The long, furry tail began to wag, the soft flesh of Alujian's mouth covered the bared teeth, and the dog

153

that hadn't much liked her aboard ship began moving slowly toward her. When he halted within touching distance of her, a still-fearful Paulina gently folded herself to her knees. Then the great head was resting upon her shoulder, a soft whine emitted from his throat, and Paulina, yet a little hesitant, wrapped her slim arms around the thick muscles of Alujian's neck. "So, now you want to be my friend?" she queried with a small laugh, and the laugh echoed around her like a blanket of song. "Or do you intend to sink those fangs into my throat when I least suspect it." When the dog's black-spotted tongue made a swipe at her cheek in friendly greeting, Pauline, a crinkle twisting her nose, said, "Thanks, Alujian . . . just the kind of kiss a girl needs."

With the dog at her side, Paulina moved toward a wide, flat rock and sat down, her eyes scanning the undulating cascades of flowstone that formed the walls of the great cavern. A small lake encircled by a crescent-shaped dam gleamed like a blue sapphire, hinting at immense depth, and farther beyond, translucent draperies hung from the ceilings, sunbursts and crystalline images, like flowers, spangling the walls. Everything about her glowed, like an immense palace lighted against a veil of enchanting darkness, in a land that existed only in the imagination.

Because she was able to forget the pain and the humiliation that had sent her fleeing into the night, at least for a little while, Paulina remembered her hunger. A gnawing inside her made her clutch her stomach, and she looked at the dog sitting quietly at her side. "What did you have for supper?" And as if he had understood her, his dark, soulful eyes turned to a mound of fish heads a dozen feet away. Again Paulina's nose crinkled. "Well . . . I think I'll pass. Raw fish was never my favorite nourishment."

154

So Paulina found a bed of straw and seaweed that had washed into the cave, made sure that no living creatures were inhabiting it, and stretched out for a long night of sleep. The dog curled up against the small of her back, and quite before she realized it, her eyes were closing, and the gentle hints that sleep was almost upon her penetrated her eyelids and her ears . . . the fading of the cave's natural glow . . . the silence of the underground streams that had rushed just moments before . . . the worries of a conscious mind . . . the coolness that evaporated when sleep washed over her—

And in her sleep she dreamed . . . and in her dream she slept peacefully . . . and in her sleep within her dream, yet another dream was in the making. . . .

Brett was frantic with worry. Paulina had been gone for two hours, and despite all his concentration he could not pick up the faintest hint of her anywhere. He could not hear the soft footfalls of her shoes upon the beach or the rocks . . . he could not see the tall, willowy form of her hiding among the spruce . . . he could not detect the soft aroma of her, or see the gold of her hair gleaming against the pale moonlight.

All manners of horror rushed through his brain. Had she wandered into the walruses wallowing on the beach? A seven-hundred-pound bull, startled by her appearance, would not hesitate to crush her with its massive weight. Had she climbed a boulder and fallen? Had she wandered into the sea and been swallowed up? Dear God, had he upset her so much that she would endanger her life simply to get back at him?

The trout she had cooked on the open fire remained untouched in the wooden plates. How could he possibly eat when he was sick with worry for her?

155

He stood for a moment and tried to decide where she might have gone. She would probably stay along the beachfront, because it was the part of the island with which she was most familiar. But where along the beach? There were between six and eight miles of it, and she could have traveled quite a long way in the span of two hours. So he moved off in the direction that he had seen her flee, the canvas on the end of a piece of driftwood flaming against the violet streaks of an otherwise blackened sky lighting his way.

As his bare feet moved over the cool sand, he called— "Pauuuuulina . . . Pauuuu-lina," grew quiet, moved another hundred yards or so, and called her name again, over and over . . . cupping his hand to his mouth so that the sound would carry farther.

By the time he had covered the distance of a mile, and no subtle sound of her had betrayed her existence, he began to feel amidst the frantic pounding of his heart that some horror had, indeed, befallen her. They could have made love and lain together in its exquisite aftermath, and she would be safe and secure in his arms. Now . . . dammit, now he wasn't sure of her fate. If anything happened to her, he didn't know what he would do. He wouldn't be able to live with himself.

He wouldn't want to.

A rustle in the bushy alders up the shore from him suddenly captured his attention. "Paulina?" He held up the burning timber but could see no farther than a half-dozen feet past its glow. Again he called her name. "Paulina?" And again, she did not answer.

Then he saw it—a great walrus bull charging toward him, its tusks, fully two feet in length, digging into the sand in its awkward rush. As he turned to run, losing the glowing driftwood that had lit his way, he could feel the great weight of the beast bearing down on him.

Brett, feeling again the ache of the wound, wasn't sure that he would break any records for human speed, but he was aware that he was outdistancing the walrus. He glanced behind him, seeing its sparsely haired skin forming great folds about its body as it tired and eventually dropped into the cool sand. Brett, too, halted, turned, and watched the lumberous beast, then took a step or two back in its direction. Had its exertion killed it? Was it an ancient mariner of its species that had enjoyed a final challenge?

Brett moved ever closer, curious now, and wanting to get a better look at the massive creature such as he had seen only from a distance.

The walrus watched the strange two-legged beast approach. He lay very still, his tremendously enlarged canine teeth sunk a depth of half a foot into the sand. The man-beast had made the fatal mistake of wandering too close to the cow, one of his many mates, that was giving birth up the shore. And for it the man-beast must die.

He wasn't sure what he was doing, but instinct told him that if he lay very still, the two-legged creature would believe he was no longer a threat.

He watched it move slowly, precariously, ever closer. . . .

And when the man-beast was within touching distance, he charged with full fury.

Ten

Brought from her sleep by the blinding glare of the luminescent, jewellike walls, Paulina rose from her bed of straw and seaweed. She contemplated returning to Brett with the news of her discovery, but immediately decided against it. So she began her explorations of the exquisite cavern and its many connections, giving little thought to the moody Brett McCallum. She was still angry with him and still felt the traitorous shades of crimson upon her cheeks as she remembered the way he had rebuffed her at a most awkward moment.

There was a warmth permeating the caverns that made her feel safe and secure. She hadn't eaten since the early afternoon of the previous day, but somehow she didn't feel the usual pangs of hunger. She felt empty, she felt that she could eat half a barbecued cow, but the emptiness did not hurt. Perhaps it was the excitement generated by the caverns and the delights they might contain.

The dog, still exhibiting his mood of friendliness, posed at her side, waiting to see which direction she would take. Dropping her hand gently to the patch of fur between his ears, she asked, "You won't let me get lost, will you, Alujian?"

A low whine was the only answer forthcoming. Drawing in a shallow breath, Paulina moved toward the nearest of the tunnels. Though it had appeared dark across the short expanse of space, she looked deeply in to see arched ceilings at least twenty feet high speckled with a gold and silver brilliance that seemed to have no energy source. The tunnel itself was the palest shade of lavender, and when she touched the side wall, she discovered that it was solid ice, its texture like hardened wax.

The sand beneath her feet was clean and white, glimmering, like the ceiling, with flecks of gold and silver that seemed to provide a natural light. She moved thirty feet or more into the tunnel, then paused, awe-struck. Here, from the walls of pitted ice, protruded quartz in shades varying from lavender to the deepest amethyst, some pieces as large as she was herself. And among all this she saw veins of gold and silver a foot wide in places . . . and emeralds . . . loose emeralds scattered upon the floors, emeralds embedded in the walls and ceilings . . . the loveliest sight she had ever witnessed, or even imagined in her wildest dreams. She couldn't help but be a little bewildered. If this had been Utah or Montana or Wyoming . . . or any of the mineral-rich sites in the United States, it would have been mined of its wealth and beauty years before. How, then, had it been left untouched by the greedy hands of humans?

She forced herself to move on, Alujian ever-present, and when she emerged into still another chamber, she felt the wonderful warmth of steam rising from a small, bubbling pond. Bending to her knees, she dragged her hand through the current. It was hot but not unpleasantly so. She tasted the water; it was clean and pure.

"A bath—" she murmured. "Finally, I'll be able to have a decent bath."

While the dog wandered off, Paulina shed her tattered

clothing. When she stood naked, she untied the ribbon from her hair and tossed it beside her dress. With a carefully placed toe she tested the water, felt the sand of the bottom, then moved with caution into the shallow edge of the pond.

Finally, she ventured into depths that covered her with delightfully warm water up to her shoulders. She dragged her hair through the currents, floated on her back, submerged her face, and finally dived beneath the water to see how deep it was.

Paulina guessed that at the deepest, she was twenty feet below the surface. Slowly, she propelled herself along the sandy bottom, studying the shells and rocks that had washed into the pond over the centuries. Then, in a moment of surprise that caused her to lose most of the air she had stored in her lungs, she picked up an exquisite vase carved with figures in cameo style. And she shot to the surface to study her new-found treasure.

After giving it close scrutiny, she carefully deposited the vase on the shore, then gathered air in her lungs and again went under. Time after time she came up, adding to her treasure trove, glass bowls and mosaic glass plates, free-blown vessels and flasks, ewers and goblets that were as perfect as they had been when, centuries past, they had washed into the lake. Near exhaustion, she came up with a miniature shoe, free-blown in amethyst glass, and an enamel-painted decanter. Then, as she floated on her stomach, contemplating an end to her search for treasure, she saw something else at a depth of twelve or fourteen feet through the clear, warm water and, taking in a lungful of air, made a final dive.

* * *

Brett entered the bathing chamber she had found just as she went under. He was angry, hungry, thirsty—he'd almost been squashed into an ugly mound of unrecognizable human flesh by what appeared to be a thousand pounds of blubber, and he was so tired he could hardly keep his eyes open. He'd spent the past nine hours looking for the beautiful emerald-eyed nymph now going down for a casual dive.

He hadn't realized she was naked until he saw her pile of discarded clothing at the edge of the pool. And he did not hesitate to stare deeply into the clear water to see her slim form gently treading water, her long, pale hair floating, mesmerizingly, all around her, her slim fingers digging into the sand. And—he caught a breath— a tiny waist, slim buttocks, long, tapered legs the color of peaches . . . so sensual was she, like the goddess of the sea . . . and so unaware that mortal man boldly looked down upon her.

Then he saw the treasures she had brought up: colorful flasks and vases with the goddess Aphrodite in cameo, lovely things from centuries past that had caught her eye and sent her plunging into the magical pond in search of more.

He smiled to himself. Should he wait boldly there until she surfaced, and let her attempt to hide her virginal nakedness, or should he discreetly disappear into one of the tunnels?

Considering the sleepless, aggravating night he'd had, the answer was simple.

With his feet apart in a careless stand, and his arms crossed against the expanse of his chest, he watched for her reappearance.

A stirring among rocks a dozen yards away caused him to spin and drop to his knees, his hand going for a sidearm that was not there. To Brett's surprise, and disbelief, there stood Alujian, wagging his tail so fiercely that his whole back end waved from side to side.

"Well, I'll be damned—" muttered Brett, coming to his feet and immediately being pounded upon by the dog. With Alujian's large paws draped across his shoulders, Brett roughly tousled the thick mane of fur around his neck. "Where the hell did you come from? I thought you'd gone down with the ship."

Alujian cocked his head against Brett's jaw so that he could feel the comforting movement of the words his master spoke.

Brett ended the reunion effectively, returning his attention to the pool where a beautiful, alluring Paulina swam. His gaze instantly returned to the spot he had last seen her, but she was not there. A quick search of the pool's bottom failed to yield sight of her, and Brett, thinking that she might have seen him and slipped from the water while he was greeting Alujian, began, with a worried gaze, to search the small cavern. But still he did not see her, and panic seized him inside.

Without a moment's hesitation Brett dived into the pool and immediately began to tread water toward the bottom. Perhaps a small boulder had loosened, trapping her against the steep cliff at the pond's far side, where she had been searching.

She couldn't have just disappeared.

Could she?

Paulina popped up in the interior chamber accessed through the underwater tunnel she had found, and drew in a long, steady breath of air. At some point far beyond the scattering of gothic arches, she could see light gently flooding the chamber and glistening upon the smooth surface of the pond.

She might not have found the tunnel and this quiet chamber if she'd not seen the dark form of Brett McCallum at the edge of the pond. She'd almost not recognized him, as he now sported a short, dark beard, until the moment she'd seen his misshapened form through the ripple of water. Then she had been so desperate to hide her nakedness from him that she'd begun a frantic search for an alcove where she might accomplish that purpose. Rather ridiculous, really, since she'd been only too willing to make love to him the previous night, and she'd certainly planned to do it without the barrier of clothing!

Paulina knew that when Brett did not see her in the pool he would come searching for her. In anticipation of that, she quickly climbed out of the pool and found a rock large enough to hide behind. Then she waited for the rogue to pop up from the glassy black surface.

She did not have long to wait. Scarcely had she settled there to drag the wet strands of her hair across her bare breasts before she heard a splash in the water. As Brett McCallum moved fluidly to the edge of the pond, Paulina called crossly, "Don't you dare come near me, Brett."

With his forearms resting along the smooth rock at the edge of the pond, Brett called back just as crossly, "You can't stay there for the rest of your life. You'll have to come out eventually."

"Well—" She took a moment to think. "You could give me your shirt. A gentleman would—"

"I'm no gentleman."

"I know that. You could make an exception."

"What's in it for me?"

For the first time in many days, Paulina recognized that all-too-familiar teasing in his voice, a teasing she had not heard since Skagway, and had dearly missed. "I'll let you live, Brett McCallum, that's what's in it for you. I swear, if you see me naked, I'll plunge a dagger into your back when you least expect it—"

Brett suppressed a small laugh as he responded, "What makes you think I have not already seen you naked? You were kind of pretty down there, digging in the sand for that blasted vase—"

"Brett . . . you didn't watch me! Say that you didn't!" She stopped to think a moment. He would be pleased if his watching horrified her. With only a small pause she continued. "Well, if you did, you did. I'm getting a little cold. Won't you please give me your shirt?"

"It's wet."

"Oh, do tell! You mean you couldn't have the decency to come through the water dry?"

"Your sarcasm is not appreciated."

The playful bantering did not diminish the severity of her state of undress. "Give me your shirt!"

Casually, Brett took off the shirt, balled it, and threw it to the rock where she hid. "There, take the blasted shirt. I can think of a lot of things I'd rather do than see you naked." Actually, he couldn't think of a single thing he'd prefer, but he kept the thought to himself. Rather, he continued. "Now, put it on and let's get out of here. I believe our agreement was that I—man—catch the food and you—woman—cook it."

"Don't harass me, Brett McCallum. I dislike you enough as it is. By the way"—Paulina stepped out from behind the rock, the purple silk shirt dragging fully to her knees—"is Brett McCallum your real name? Or is it Prince Albert or something?"

"Or something—" he responded, attempting to suppress his delight at the alluring loveliness of her. Using his palms, he pushed himself up from the pond in one swift move. "You look like a wet muskrat," he continued, sweeping back his hair that, as wet as it was, looked the color of onyx.

"Thank you," came her response. "Just what every girl likes to hear."

Brett prepared to tease her further, but then caught himself. No . . . no, he could not let her believe he had relaxed, that things could be different. He had to continue the façade of indifference toward her, because she had to be his brother's wife. He had been entrusted with this very special mission, and he had to accomplish it by any means. "Let's get out of here," he said gruffly. "I'm as hungry as a bear and I've got a line set. I don't want my fish to get poached by a four-legged creature."

Paulina did not like the tone of his voice—authoritative, commanding . . . superior. Lifting her pert chin, she argued, "I'm not ready to leave. I see a tunnel over there I'd like to check out." She started in that direction.

An exasperated Brett drew his hands to his hips and watched her for a moment, putting distance between them with carefully placed footsteps. When she disappeared into a dark tunnel, Brett, shrugging his shoulders with cool acceptance—she was, after all, a woman of the nineties, and a woman who did not want anyone telling her what to do—moved in her direction, though he did not attempt to catch up to her.

He could not see her, but he detected her movements in an indistinct display of lights and shadows in the arched corridor of massive stones twisting through the earth. He would let her get her explorations out of her blood, and then they could go on with what they had to do . . . survive . . . and hope for rescue.

Then he heard her scream, a high-pitched scream that ricocheted through the tunnel like a volley of gunfire. He took off in a run, thinking that she'd come face-to-face with a predator deep in the bowels of the earth. But when he emerged into the grandest cavern of all, its Corinthian beauty hand-carved by humans in the sheer face of a wall half a league high it seemed, he, too, felt an excitement that threatened to burst forth in a scream similar to hers.

But the excitement instantly became horror . . . as Brett's eyes swept the chamber . . . for here lay the engraved slab coverings of tombs, and in the center, deeply embedded in the sand, were the granite serpentine figures with catlike eyes, clustered against obelisks bearing the sacred carvings of the ancients of Talantia.

"Dear God—" Brett mumbled the two words so quietly that Paulina did not hear him. Here he stood, in the place most sacred to all Talantians . . . the Crypt of the Kings and Queens . . . the one place in all the world off-limits to all citizens with the exception of the high priest and the burial party who would travel here by ship to entomb the dead royalty. To be on the Island of the Royal Crypt was a crime punishable by death . . . and it mattered not who you were or what unfortunate circumstances had brought you to the island. If caught, a prince would be executed as quickly as a servant . . . a woman as quickly as a man . . . a castaway as quickly as a deliberate interloper—

Inside, Brett died, because he knew that he had broken a sacred trust, though it had been unavoidable. He was honor bound to tell his father that he had been on the island. He was honor bound to accept the consequences.

In reverence . . . in horror . . . he turned away, drawing his fingers up to press against his closed eyes. Why here, of all places? Why did the storm have to cast them upon the Island of the Royal Crypt?

Paulina rushed back to him. "Look, Brett! Isn't it beautiful? What is it? Who do you think built it?" When

166

he did not answer, she quipped, "Well, what is wrong with you? Still sulking because you're hungry?"

Suddenly, for Brett, life took on a new meaning. When he dragged his fingers away from his eyes, he saw Paulina in a different light, an interloper upon the Island of the Royal Crypt could never become a queen . . . and there was no reason in the world they could not be together . . . in every way.

With a strange gentleness Brett took her hand and held it, and his mouth eased up into a sad smile. "Let's get out of here, Paulina."

"But—" The sudden change in his mood piqued her curiosity, though she said nothing about it. "Don't you want to explore?" she asked. "To find out who is buried here? Why, we may have discovered an ancient burial ground that human eyes have not beheld for many hundreds of years—"

"I do not want to explore. I just want to get out of here, and for us to—"

"For us to what?" Annoyance sprang into her eyes. "For us to catch fish and cook them and fill our stomachs? Where is your sense of adventure?" But his mood remained so strange that it frightened her, and her resistance and her desire to rebel against him ebbed. Suddenly, she wanted only to be away from this very odd and ancient burial ground and to try to make some sense of Brett's preoccupation. So she took his hand and her bare feet began to move into the tunnel, back toward the black reflective pool.

When Paulina slipped into the water and made her dive, she did not think about her nakedness beneath the tattered purple shirt. It just didn't seem to matter. She wanted only to be away from the caverns, feeling the light of early morning upon her features, hearing Brett's cross tone and bearing the brunt of his argumentative ways.

Alujian was awaiting her when she surfaced from the heated pool. She hurriedly propelled herself from the water, snatched up her mound of clothing, and slipped behind a rock to dress. By the time Brett exited the pool, she was slinging the purple shirt across to him.

From her position she saw him turn and sit on the rock at the edge of the pond. When the dog approached, Brett dropped an arm across him for a moment and ruffled his fur, then began dragging the shirt on.

She hadn't known Brett for long, but still felt she'd grown to know what to expect of him. Now, though, he was as remote as the ancient wonder they had stumbled across just moments earlier. He was detached, uncommunicative, though not insultingly so, and his unexplained silence drew her like a magnet, where before it had repelled her.

When she'd dressed, she came around the rock and stood just behind him. "I'm ready. You two fellows ready to leave here?"

Brett snapped around as if she'd startled him. When he climbed to his feet, saying "Sure," Paulina's hand fell gently to his arm.

"What's wrong, Brett? You're frightening me."

He forced a smile. "What do you mean?"

A tremble settled upon her mouth. "There's something different about you. Something overwhelming, almost as if you have decided to give up on life—"

"Don't be preposterous." *God, had she read him so easily . . . so portentously?* He could not alarm her; immediately, he softened his voice. "I am just tired." Tucking an arm across her shoulder, he continued. "Just wait until I tell you about the adventure I had last night while I was out searching for you."

168

She drew away. "Wait . . . I want to take the things I brought up from the pond—"

"No!" He had not meant to speak the single word so sharply. "Perhaps they were offerings to those buried in the crypt. It would be a sacrilege—" he added gently.

"Do you think so?" A shiver crawled the length of her spine. "Perhaps you're right." Taking his hand, she pulled him into a half-run. "I am starving, Brett McCallum. Come, Alujian—"

After they ate their meager meal of fish in silence, Brett, complaining of exhaustion, lay down beneath his tarpaulin and immediately fell off to sleep. Paulina, a little disappointed to be left without company, sat beneath a Sitka spruce and began sewing those rips in her gown that she could get to without taking it off.

Now that she was alone and able to think, she tried to force herself to be angry that Brett had seen her naked in the pond, but somehow it didn't seem to matter. She had more important things to think about, and one of them was survival. She and Brett and the dog were stranded on an uninhabited island that some long-lost civilization had used as a burial ground. Was it still considered sacred? Was it taboo? Were she and Brett in danger just being there?

After a while she tired of her mending and dragged herself to her feet. Casually, for an hour or two or three— she really wasn't counting—she walked in the shallow currents washing across the beach, feeling the cool water against her bare feet and losing herself in far and distant memories. She had come to Alaska to find Millburn Hanks so that she could return to Turkey Gulch and see the Bartletts hang for what Millburn had witnessed two years ago, and now she was stranded on an island with a moody man who might or might not be a legitimate guide. And she had agreed to marry the man in return for his services. She almost felt like a whore—

A sound in the current behind her caused her to start, but it was merely the dog bounding after a fish that had swam into shallow water. She hadn't realized he'd been following her until his spirit of adventure had sent him in pursuit of a meal, but she was glad of the company.

Throughout the afternoon the island lay white and silent around her except for an occasional gull or a wave breaking against rocks. Once she almost thought she heard a human voice, but it was merely the wind. Soon she settled upon the smooth surface of a boulder and watched the flotsam drift in with the tide. Her gaze lifted and swept along the horizon as she wished for the appearance of tall masts and crisp white sails, or the telltale smoke of a steamer plying the sea. She wanted to be off this accursed island, accomplishing her mission and returning home to Utah and the people who loved her.

As she thought of her family, her throat constricted and moisture sheened her emerald eyes. Dropping her face into her palms, she gently wept.

When Brett saw that she was weeping, he moved off the beach and skirted the timberline until he was almost behind her. Should he interrupt her solitude and offer words of comfort, or should he allow her this time to vent her sorrow and frustration?

He'd just about decided to give her time alone, when she turned and their gazes met. The backs of her hands scraped along her cheeks, taking away the tears. She forced a smile. "You had a good rest?" she asked him, managing some semblance of a smile.

"A very good rest." Crawling up the boulder, he soon dropped beside her. "I'm sorry you had to spend the afternoon alone."

As if it were a natural thing to do, her palm rose to touch his jawline. "You shaved? How? Did you find a straight razor in that trunk?"

"No . . . I sharpened the knife." Instantly, his hand covered her own, trapping it against his cheek. "It's not a very smooth shave, is it?"

Withdrawing her hand, she timidly dropped her eyes. "You needn't have worried about me," she said by way of changing the subject. "I wasn't alone. Alujian stayed with me until he found a fish stranded in shallow water."

"Yes, I saw him, but he ignored me." After a short pause he looked skyward, his eyes reflective and worried. "I feel like a fish stranded in shallow water myself," Brett said casually. "Don't you sometimes?" She shrugged, failing to answer. "What's wrong, Paulina?"

A small musical laugh echoed. "What isn't wrong? We've been shipwrecked, and now we're trapped on an island and . . . God knows how long we will be here. It could be years. I could be an old woman when I see civilization again. I—we might never see civilization again, for that matter. Doesn't that bother you?"

How innocently frightened she was. Something inside him melted; it was his heart. Leaning slowly, lingeringly, forward, Brett captured Paulina's trembling lips in a warm, comforting kiss. When only a breath of space separated their mouths, he murmured huskily, "I am so sorry this has happened, Paulina. But . . . I swear, I will take care of you—"

Her arms slipped around his neck and she pulled herself ever so close to him. When at last his arms circled her waist, she whispered, "But why have you been so hateful? Why have you acted as though you hate me? Oh, Brett . . . Brett, don't you know how I care for you?" She felt the sensual pleasure of his touch, smelled the musky manliness of him, felt the freshly shaved face against her own soft one . . . and his hands, oh, so gently closing over her arms.

Life had ceased for him the moment he'd stood in the crypt of the Kings and Queens and realized that he'd broken an ancient law. Whenever he reached Talantia, he would have to die . . . but God, he knew he could not allow Paulina to meet such a fate. If it was the last thing he did, he would see her to the safety of her own people.

For now she was his. What time they had would be enjoyed on this island. "Come—" Standing upon the boulder, he took her hand and coaxed her up, pulling her into his embrace. "The night will fall soon, and we must return to our encampment."

With mellow enticement she murmured, "I hated the way you treated me last night, Brett. But I'm willing to give you another chance. Make love to me tonight, Brett. Make love to me as though these were our last moments and tomorrow will not exist—"

How ironic was her soft entreaty. Jumping down from the boulder, he lifted his hands and waited for her to ease into them.

As they moved across the warm sand, Brett dropped his arm across her shoulder. Midway to their encampment, Alujian fell in beside them, then again bounded off after a rustle among the alders.

A new sense of understanding and respect existed between Brett and Paulina now.

For Brett, certainty of the future motivated his change; for Paulina, it was the uncertainty.

Eleven

The great black wolf dog bounded up to Brett, carrying a large crab in his mouth. He seemed proud of his catch, but when one of the flailing pincers caught him full upon the nose, he began running and scraping the assaulted spot along the sand until the crab let go. As Brett and Paulina both laughed, Alujian, head cocked and ears perked, took a stand a safe distance from the crab and seemed to contemplate his next move and one, apparently, that would not result in a second attack.

"What do you think?" asked Brett, a grin crossing his dark features. "Supper?"

"The crab doesn't look willing," laughed Paulina. "What do you say we let it live a day or two longer?"

Brett said nothing, but snapped his fingers to call the dog to him.

The sky had begun to darken as they entered their encampment. Heaving a sigh, Paulina began to collect the wooden plates and forks from their noontime meal and, with a silent Brett looking on, moved toward the shallow water to wash them. But as she started to step around him, he took her arm and held it gently. "What is this, Paulina? One moment you are saying that you

173

want us to make love, and the next minute it is forgotten, and you are preparing to wash a few dishes."

She shrugged, her eyes downcast. "Last night you did not want me. Why would you want me tonight?" Again she sighed. "I was being impetuous . . . impulsive." A slim foot made one slow sweep upon the sand. "And foolish," she added as an afterthought.

"Last night—" His grip on her arm relaxed into a gentle caress. "Last night," he began again, "I was being a bastard. Things have changed, Paulina. I want you—"

Actually, last night's rejection had soured her. Perhaps she had said, just a few minutes before, that she wanted to be with him—that way—but now she was thinking more sensibly. Now she knew that more than likely he would repeat last night's insult and humiliating rejection, and she simply would not give him the chance. She relied on the old adage, Fool me once, shame on you. Fool me twice, shame on me. She calmly pulled her arm free and continued her journey to the water's edge.

Brett's piercing gaze followed after her. Her moods were titillating, and now he thought he understood how she felt, never knowing what to expect of him. Perhaps she was giving him back a little of what he had given her . . . and perhaps he deserved it.

But he would not allow the night to begin like this, and it certainly was not the end he had anticipated. So he sauntered toward her kneeling form, his larger footprints covered her own in the sand, where the water washed over her slender legs. Then he bent to his knees before her and waited for her captivatingly lovely eyes to lift to him in a moment of rebellion and pride. At that point he forced the dishes from her hand.

"Come and sit beneath the shelter with me, Paulina. We will talk."

She attempted to pry her hand loose from his strong

grip, but he merely took her other hand and held it too. "I must wash the dishes—"

"The dishes can wait." He straightened to his full height, then coaxed her up before him.

"And so can the talking," she said, the rebellion strong again. "Until the morning."

"Then will you simply let me hold you?" When her gaze lowered, his fingers eased beneath her chin to force eye contact. "Please . . . let me prove to you that I can be gentle, that I can be a comfort—"

"I don't need gentleness or comfort. I just need to survive."

"I don't believe that."

"Believe what you want. It is of no concern to me."

But he was relentless. Taking her hand, he pulled her from the water and she stalled, her slender feet dragging along in the sand behind him. When she growled "Ouf!" he turned, a dark eyebrow rising ever so slightly.

"Are we going to talk? Or are we going to get on each other's nerves?"

"I'd put my vote on the nerves!" she shot back, attempting to pry his fingers off her wrist. "But women can't vote in my country, so I guess we'll have to talk!"

She gathered up her wits, impudent and haughty, and kept pace with his longer strides. When he dropped to the canvas beneath the shelter he had constructed for her, she took a second rebellious stand, her arms crossed firmly against her waistline. His hand reached for her; she ignored it, though she did drop to her knees just out of touching distance of him.

"All right, do your talking," she sighed indulgently, "so that I can return to our simple plates before the tide washes them out to sea."

"What do you want to talk about?" came his soft reply.

A pale, fine eyebrow slightly arched. "The talking was your idea. I thought you had something in mind?"

"No, I didn't," he replied matter-of-factly. "You name the subject, and we'll discuss it."

Silence. A moment of thought took away the annoyance upon her pretty features. "All right . . . your homeland. Tell me about it."

"Nuklukayet?"

"No . . . Talantia."

He was token aback. His swarthy features drained of color as he realized she might, indeed, have eavesdropped aboard ship. "But—it is only the name of the ship," he lied unconvincingly. "What could I tell you about it?"

"Talantia is your homeland," she argued, the softness in her voice almost reverent. "It isn't just a ship. And you are not just a guide. So why don't you do something out of character? Why don't you tell me the truth for once?"

Again silence captured the moment. Brett's darkening gaze met Paulina's expectant emerald one. He thought again how exquisite was her loveliness, but how sad now her expression. Unconsciously, his gaze dropped, held by the smooth, supple contours above the tattered bodice of her gown. Then he saw her catch a breath and his gaze lifted, a mute apology briefly curling one side of his ample mouth. "Sorry . . . you are so lovely, Paulina—"

"I have asked a question, Brett."

"All right . . . I am from an isolated culture, and we call it Talantia, which is far to the north, far above Nuklukayet." He stopped short of telling her that he was taking her there to present to his brother as a future bride. She would hate him for that, and he wouldn't blame her.

"Then I was not to be the bride of a dying friend?"

176

A dark eyebrow arched. "Who told you that? Big Pat?"

"No—" she lied. "I overheard you talking to him that night Soapy's henchman was shot. You told him you had a friend named Gruff, who was dying, and who wanted only one thing . . . a bride . . . and that was a role that I was expected to fill."

"Well"—his broad shoulders shrugged lightly—"I lied."

"I know that. So, why were you taking me to Talantia?"

Brett contemplated an answer. He could not tell Paulina that the crown prince, to whom he was taking her to be his bride, was not allowed to leave Talantia to find his own wife . . . that it was destined to be his prison for as long as he lived. As second son, he alone was permitted to make journeys to the outside . . . he was rather like a royal errand boy . . . and it was a job he hated. No, he could not tell Paulina the ugly truth regarding his mission, so he had to depend on his ability to lie once again. "My brother suffers from a sickness within that prohibits him from leaving the confines of his house. He trembles, convulses . . . and eventually loses consciousness. I wanted to consult a doctor."

"But I am not a doctor."

Suddenly, a distinctive and familiar aroma wafted toward Paulina. Rising quickly to her feet, she turned in a circle, her arms outstretched. "Gardenias . . . do you smell them, Brett? Gardenias . . . my sister, Lillian, always smells like gardenias. It is her favorite flower."

"I smell nothing, he responded, glad the direction of their conversation had changed the subject. He took her fingers to still the movement of her hand. "Only the sea and the island—"

But her exuberance would not be contained. "No, it is distinctly gardenias. Oh, so familiar . . . Lillian?" She had spoken her sister's name softly, but now her voice rose to an almost desperate pitch. "Lillian? Lillian, where are you?" And she was sure that Lillian spoke her name. She'd heard it, like a distant rhythm blending with the wind.

Now Brett climbed to his feet. She was so lonely for home and family . . . and he felt the same emotion choke him within that now glazed her eyes like an emerald sea. Gathering her to him, he said soothingly, "Lillian is not here, but I am."

And suddenly, without further words, she was on her knees again, facing him, her trembling hand resting ever so gently upon his hair-matted chest. Her gaze had lowered, so that her long lashes blocked his view of the exquisite, multifaceted emeralds that were her eyes, but he knew they were moisture-sheened and hesitant to face him.

One moment she had been rebellious and proud, longing for a sister many miles away, and now . . . yes, now she was his . . . and he wasn't quite sure how it had happened. He knew only that the sheen of her eyes mirrored the desire he had seen the evening before . . . not a few minutes ago, when she'd been near tears, calling to her sister. He felt the soft caress of her fingers upon his chest, and they ceased to tremble, and in her gaze he saw that she wanted the same thing from the night . . . and from the moment . . . as he did. She no longer cared about Talantia . . . she cared only about being with him. And he wanted this moment to be wonderful for her, to be a lasting and loving memory of him after he was gone. When his hands rose to cover her slender shoulders, he drew her to him.

"You cannot know how much I have wanted this moment, Paulina," he whispered huskily, his hands now rising to sift through her pale hair. "I cannot bear the fear that trembles through your body—"

Her gaze lifted quickly to his own. "It isn't fear of you, Brett. True, I have never been with a man . . . like this . . . but, my fear . . . it is something that I cannot explain. Something that grabs me within and squeezes the very life out of me."

"Are you fearful that you will die, Paulina?"

Gently, she pressed her face to his chest and held him close. "No, I am fearful that *you* will die. There is something you are not telling me, and that is what frightens me."

Brett drew slightly back, his small laugh managing, somehow, to ease her apprehension and her foreboding. "Do you realize, my beautiful Paulina, how many men and women would give everything they have for what we have now? Two people who care very deeply for each other, together and alone on an exotic island. I can love you, Paulina, as no other man on this earth can love you . . . and there will be no rude interruptions."

"Love me . . . or make love *to* me?" she asked softly.

A gentle laugh tickled her hairline. "Both, princess. I have a lot of confidence in myself."

How tender were his words, soothing and yet enflaming, his eyes glistening with a wild desire that awakened and enraptured the very core of her being. An intense and wonderful desire grew within her as she wanted his nearness, wanted to feel the heat of his hands flowing along her soft, supple curves. Oh, but should she allow this? Was it love consuming her, or was it merely a shallow physical need that would be quelled once they had been together fully and completely? Her emotions defied logic. She had wanted only to accomplish her mission and return to Utah, but now . . . dear, merciful heaven . . . all she wanted now was to feel the strength of this strange, mysterious man against her. She wanted only to feel his kisses upon her mouth, his fingers gently and wondrously traveling along her passion-sensitive skin and awakening her all the way through to her heart. Yes . . . yes, that was what she wanted. Womanhood . . . and she wanted to experience it with Brett, without interference . . . and with full and complete abandon.

So, her logic . . . and the goals she had set yesterday . . . flew off with the wind now traveling across the sand. She wanted only to taste his kisses, to experience the ultimate joy of his touch, his strength and the gentle command of him. She wanted only sweet, full, exquisite surrender . . . she wanted to drown in the passion of him. . . .

Brett seemed to sense all that, for with a renewed fervor his gentleness worked its magic . . . his fingers caressing along her soft, vibrant skin, easing beneath the tattered fabric of her sleeves and slowly slipping them downward.

She felt an erotic burning in response to his manly movements, then Paulina felt the breeze cool her breasts; otherwise, she might not have noticed her bareness, for her loving gaze was upon his features . . . and the obsessive hunger consuming her was merely fueled by the way his head dipped, and his tongue traced a circle around each of her breasts. Then his hands were filled with her womanly curves, and a long, low moan grew deep within her.

"How beautiful you are," he whispered, kneading the supple white flesh and capturing each pale rosebud of her breasts in his mouth, to taste their sweetness.

A wondrous, alien, delirious ache crawled into Paulina's abdomen. She wanted only to be free of her garments, to experience the full, bold explorations of his hands. She did not understand the hunger consuming her within, for she had never before known it . . . she knew only that if her hunger were not satisfied . . .

and soon . . . that she would burst for want of this satisfaction.

Her fingers lifted with maddening desperation and entwined through his thick chestnut hair. Again and again she offered the sweetness of her breasts to his seeking mouth, and before she realized it, she was taking his hands to coax them beneath the waist of her gown. "Love me, Brett . . . love me as if there will be no tomorrow . . . love me as if I am precious to you—"

"You are precious to me," he responded with husky need, his hands now managing to loosen the stays holding the fabric tightly against her slim form. Then his hands were roving over her hips, the fabric was ripping, and she gently parted her knees upon the sand, expecting, enticing his explorations where she most wanted them.

As much as she wanted him, when one of his tanned fingers dipped into the well of her most womanly place, she gasped, immediately feeling his bold caress cease and the finger withdraw. "No . . . no, Brett, please . . . don't stop—" Though she was suddenly filled with fear and apprehension, a smoldering fire raged through her flesh. And when she felt his intimate reentry, she pulled herself fully against him. "I am not afraid—"

"I will not hurt you, Paulina—"

"Yes, you will," she immediately argued, her fingers weaving through the fine waves of his hair, "but it is necessary." Given that Paulina claimed to be a virgin, Brett was surprised by the adept explorations of her hands as they boldly scooted along the waist of his trousers and a long, slim finger dipped beneath the fabric. "Aren't you going to take these off?" she whispered, tugging at the waistline.

Putting a mere breath of space between them, he responded, "I thought"—teasing kisses again touched

181

upon her breasts, then traveled the slim column of her neck until his mouth was at her ear—"that you would like to undress me as I have undressed you."

"But I might hurt it . . . I mean, you—"

Dropping back on his knees, Brett gave her a humorous, disbelieving look, then laughed lightly as his hands recaptured her shoulders. "It will not break off, princess. I promise you—" When her gaze dropped in timid innocence, his fingers moved swiftly down to unfasten the buttons of his trousers. Then he again drew himself up and stretched them down his thighs, discarding them to the sand.

As his maleness met her shy gaze, Paulina clamped her eyes shut. Then she threw herself into his arms, almost knocking him over. "I lied . . . I lied—" she gasped. "I am afraid."

Though his need for this beautiful, desirable woman was overwhelming, her confession had the same effect on him as a bucket of cold water. Closing her within the confines of his embrace, he whispered, "Then we need not do anything that will hurt you, Paulina. I am content simply to hold you." Damn, that was a lie! Brett felt that if he did not satisfy his own need, he would explode into a million indistinguishable fragments.

Even as he had spoken, Paulina had felt the hardness of his groin expanding against the tender flesh of her thigh. Yes, she was afraid . . . but not so afraid that she would deny herself the all-consuming pleasure he obviously sought with her. So with renewed determination she folded herself gently to the canvas, stretched out her arms in unspoken invitation, and waited for him to drop into them.

As his tantalizing caresses again seared her flesh, Paulina was unsure of the role she was expected to play. Though her hands caressed the hard muscles of his back and shoulders, and her mouth accepted his rough, commanding kisses, she hesitated to touch him as intimately as he touched her.

A purple haze wafted across the far horizon. Moonlight touched her bright, passion-glazed eyes, and Brett felt the torment of her hesitation. But he would not force her; gently, he took her hand and touched it to his mouth, dragged it down the expanse of his chest, then tenderly positioned it upon the small of his back.

His eyes were as dark as sapphires; Paulina felt herself being consumed by their fiery depths. She did not know how to let him know that she was ready for him . . . as ready as she would ever be, without saying it outright. And she was too timid to do that. So, instinctively, her legs eased apart, her knees lifted and folded against his slim hips, and her tongue traced a circle around her parted mouth. Then she felt his own tongue in her mouth as he positioned himself against her below, made a partial penetration, and rested there for a moment, his right hand gently caressing the searing flesh of her inner thighs.

He moved against her, within her, the maleness of him flowing along the smooth walls of her most womanly place, and she tensed for the pain she anticipated and feared. Before she had expected it, she accepted his hard thrust and . . . she gasped in surprise and wonderment . . . there was no pain. She had expected to be seized by a horrendous tremor and there was none. And she couldn't understand why.

Brett had mistaken her gasp for one of pain and his mouth gently covered her own. "I am sorry. I did not mean to hurt you—"

"You didn't," she whispered in return. "Truly, you didn't."

The fullness she felt within her was an unknown sensation, wonderful, erotic, deliciously naughty, and she felt dizzy with happiness. Wrapping her arms around him, her hips rose to accept him fully, and the perfect rhythm and cadence they achieved together was like a song joining their souls.

Brett felt that every wish he'd ever wished had come true at that moment. The exquisite ecstasy of their union corded within him, thundering through him like a storm approaching a serene horizon. He had desired her for weeks, but he had never realized what a treasure she was, could be . . . how desirable she was . . . her exotic loveliness as fulfilling as a cup of water to a condemned man staked in a desert. Her strong, willful soul joined to his own . . . her long, lithe body molded to his hard one as if it belonged there . . . and the sensations that drove him onward were like a fire consuming him, devouring him, giving him a new sense of worth that he had never truly felt before. And she was the reason for it—her body, rocking violently against his own, consumed him with its insatiable flame.

Something beautiful and heretofore unknown was happening inside Paulina, something she did not fully understand but that she wished would never end. She was sure from the way he ground against her hips, harder and harder still, and from the beads of perspiration that dotted his brow as his cheek molded to hers, that he was feeling the same near-release deep within. Then it came, a fiery passion flooding through her . . . and simultaneously a tremor drove him against her with a violent need, before he held her close for what seemed to be an eternity . . . and she hoped would be. . . .

Though Brett felt complete and unabandoned fulfillment, he also felt something else that he hesitated to confess and that frightened him a bit. Paulina Winthrop, his wild little princess, lit a fire within him that would burn eternally. He would never be able to get enough of her, not if he lived a thousand years and she was always by his side.

But why had he thought of life when he was not meant to enjoy much more of it? His relaxed body withdrew from her and he fell to her side, taking her with him to draw her close. Paulina noticed the immediate change in his mood; her eyes lifted to study his straight profile, and her finger lifted to touch the small scar at the corner of his eye. "Was I good for you, Brett?" she asked, a little wary of the answer he might give.

His gaze met the dark green pools of her eyes, and a smile, almost sad, touched his mouth. "No . . . you are beyond good for me," he responded. "I have been granted a few precious moments with you, and I want to make you happy, as happy as a man can make a woman."

A frown touched upon her pale brow. "You speak as if some terrible foe will rip us apart. Why, Brett, why do you speak with such . . . doom?"

His gaze lifted to the darkening night, to the stars gathering overhead and gazing at them from behind the thin veil of clouds. And like a man suddenly possessed by jealousy that some form of life beside himself was enjoying the ivory beauty of Paulina's nudity, he pulled her gown over her body.

But she immediately threw it off and sat forward, dragging her hand up to untangle a lock of hair pressed against her cheek. "What is wrong, Brett?" With an angry flourish she moved back into his arms, a slim hand resting on his chest and her pert chin propped upon it. "Oh, why must you be so moody? One moment I think that you care deeply for me, and the next I feel that you are repulsed by me. You do exasperate me so!"

A grin raked his tanned features as his gaze met her

own. "I will not argue with you, princess. I want only to sleep, and to feel you resting beside me. I want only to awaken in the morning and have the softness of your hair resting across my shoulder, the sweetness of your mouth, the gentleness of your breath, against my cheek. I want only"—at this point his arm circled her shoulders and his hand cupped her breast—"to love you and make you my woman . . . again and again—"

"Like you did tonight?" A small sigh teased the hair matting his chest. "I am special to you, aren't I, Brett? I'm not just another female conquest, someone you will forget once we are parted?" She eased herself more deeply into the cradle of his arms, then touched her hand to his own, which still rested upon her breast. "I simply must be special to you. It is so important."

Brett's hand withdrew, and as she thought that he was recoiling in revulsion, his head moved to the valley between her breasts, to rest gently there. "You are not simply special to me, Paulina. I am madly, passionately in love with you. I have been since that first time I saw you on the boardwalk when you were disguised as a boy."

"And you didn't believe it for a moment," she laughed, finding a resting place for her hand against his warm cheek.

"Not for a minute," he chuckled in return. "Damn!"

Puzzlement settled upon her brow. "What is wrong?" He dropped a thick thigh across one of her slim legs. Then he took her hand and slowly lowered it, so that she would feel the hardness at his groin. "But I thought that a man could be so aroused only once in a night."

His laughter could not be contained. "Where the hell did you get an idea like that? One of those dime-store romance novels you American women read?"

She shrugged; actually, she had. But even as her laughter became a melody with his own, her legs opened to accept him, and again they sampled love's nectar . . . sweetly, completely . . . searingly.

Twelve

Paulina dreamed that night . . . of flowers in profuse bloom across a summer-warmed countryside, of her dear sister, Lillian, and of Uncle Will and Matt and Lucille. She was lost in her subconsciousness, and clinging to happy memories, her wonderful dreams, and the warm male body sleeping peacefully beside her. She couldn't imagine that life could be better, nor could she imagine being anywhere else on earth and being so happy. Here on the island, lying in Brett's arms and sharing the wonders of oneness with him, was everything she had imagined heaven to be.

She awoke from her dream early the following morning, her sleepy gaze watching her lover's profile for some sign of life. Her right hand lying gently upon his chest, she felt his heartbeat, his light breathing . . . and she was so deeply in love with this rogue that she wanted his heartbeat and his breath to be her own. Snuggling against him, she attempted to feel the rhythmic thump of his lifeline more strongly against her ear.

His eyes did not open, the pace of his breathing did not change, but suddenly, his hand was closing tenderly over her shoulder.

"Are you awake?" Paulina asked, the note of expectancy whisper-light in her voice.

"No . . . I am still asleep . . . and dreaming of a beautiful"—he paused, one eye cracking to gain partial view of her features—"dark-haired Polynesian goddess . . . half naked and running toward me on the clean white shore."

With a sharp "oof!" Paulina's slim hand slapped him full upon the chest, grinding a hoarse laugh from him. "Polynesian goddess, indeed! Your vision had best be of me, Brett McCallum! Or your next vision will be of fire and hell and the devil himself."

Rolling to his side, he drew her to him. "My fiery beauty from Turkey Gulch, Utah . . . of course, you are my goddess."

She made no move to conceal her nakedness, but again snuggled to him, her head of tawny tresses covering his torso. "Do you know what I want, Brett?"

"To make love to the best-looking man on this dog-gone island?"

"Besides that," she laughed. "I want some breakfast—eggs and ham and hot buttered biscuits, and a glass of milk so cold that tiny flakes of ice float on its surface."

"Dream on, little one," he murmured. "How about fish?"

Her crinkled nose went unnoticed by Brett, who was scanning the beach across her slim shoulder. "Fish . . . I am sick to death of fish," she pouted with becoming prettiness. "I want eggs. Do seals lay eggs?"

"Seal eggs," he mused, his eyes, touched with humor upon awakening, now narrowing worriedly. "Now, that would be one for the books." A silent wind whipped along the beach, touching them, wrapping them together, bringing with it a whiff of something that caused Brett's heart to speed its pace, to crease his brow in a severely dark frown. In a softly controlled tone he said, "Let's get dressed—"

Though he'd attempted to disguise the change in his tone, those few words frightened Paulina, so much so that her eyes lifted to scan the shadows of his face. What she saw alarmed her. "What is wrong?"

Quickly, he rose to his full height and searched the ground for his trousers. "I don't know." Pulling on the tattered garment, he tossed Paulina's equally tattered dress to her. "Hurry, Paulina . . . something doesn't feel right." Suspended on the far horizon of the sea, the pale yellow orb that was the sun seemed to dance, its delightful warmth failing to eradicate the fear and dreaded apprehension crawling through Brett's shoulders. At last pulling on his purple silk shirt missing half its left sleeve, and without looking toward Paulina's slender form, he said to her, "I want you to go to the cave . . . stay there until I come for you." Scanning the immediate area, he called to their four-legged companion, "Come here, Alujian," and to Paulina, "Take the dog with you. I will scout the island."

"You are frightening me, Brett," she said, finally arising to pull down the skirts of her dress.

"I fully intend to," came Brett's response. "Now . . . hurry. And do not leave the cave until you see me." His tone had left no room for argument, and Paulina obeyed without question.

Moving a hundred feet along the beach toward the cave, Paulina cast a quick glance over her shoulder to see Brett rapidly taking down the canvas shelters he had so carefully erected. As she rounded the closest of the smooth white boulders that would separate her from him, she saw all evidence of their existence on the island swept into the underbrush.

"I sense no danger," Paulina complained to the dog

that now began to trot beside her as she eased into a run. "I see nothing threatening. I do declare, Alujian . . . your master is so . . . so"—she fought for the right word, eventually sputtering out two choices—"unpredictable and suspicious."

Soon she entered the tunnel from the beach and the largest of the caverns where the shimmering walls mirrored the lavender aura surrounding the morning sun outside. She sat for a moment on the nearest of the boulders, attempting to catch her breath and still the rapid beating of her heart. Alujian sat several feet from her, his head cocked, his eyes watching her every movement. Then a splash of water through the inky darkness of a far tunnel beckoned him away, and she was left alone . . . to worry and to think.

As some semblance of control returned to her body, she arose and moved through the amethyst walls of the tunnel and into the quiet inner chamber where she had bathed. Water splashed against the crescent-shaped dam and the stillness of the pond was put into motion . . . waves swirling hypnotically, gently, to the outer edges and dampening the slate-black rock where she imagined she could still see the footprints she had left the day before. She approached; it was but an illusion caused by indentations pressed there centuries before, casting minute shadows toward the water's edge.

Then still another shadow, without a visible source, piqued her curiosity. She turned, fully expecting to see Brett approaching, but saw nothing human . . . or non-human. She looked about for the dog, but he had disappeared into the maze of tunnels. And she hugged herself worriedly, feeling only then the warmth of her body. Lifting a fragile hand, she was almost sure that the skin of her palm burned like the fire she was sure hung upon her temples.

Perhaps her frantic rush along the beach had heated her through; perhaps the sudden fever was a manifestation of her fear and worry. Whatever it was, she felt weak, and quickly sank to the hard rock floor beneath her.

Then the shadow again cast its image against the cavern wall and she pivoted sharply, covering the small wrench in her back with her right hand. At that same moment she caught the delicate aroma of gardenias, and a whisper through the tunnels was almost haunting . . . and yet so terribly familiar that her heart livened its pace. She heard a scratching far, far away, echoing through the silence, and knew that it was Alujian seeking nourishment. But she cared not about food, or the dog's hunt, she cared only about the source of the shadow and knew that it was not a specter created by a fevered brain.

Then she saw her, and her breath caught, strangling her as surely as if hands had wrapped themselves around her throat. There . . . dear, merciful heavens . . . there against the arch of the amethyst tunnel stood the pale form of . . . could it be . . . her lovely young sister, Lillian?

The fire consumed her within, a fragile weakness threatening her equilibrium as she attempted to rise to her feet, all the while her gaze holding the vision of her sister. Then she was on her feet, the tunnel swirling, mesmerizing and dark all around her, and yet Lillian remained in the natural light of the jeweled walls. "Lillian?" she called ever so hesitantly. "Lillian, is that you?" Filling her lungs with the aroma of gardenias, Paulina took a precarious step forward. Then she stopped to ask herself in a small voice bordering on hysteria, "But how can it be?" Then, coldly, cruelly, callously, a wind whipped through the tunnel, slapping Paulina rudely in the face. The vision of Lillian slowly faded, like a ghost suddenly made to feel unwelcome, and Paulina sank, sobbing, to the coolness of the floor. "I'm going mad," she sniffed in her first quiet moment. "Surely, I am going mad."

How is she?

Paulina looked up, surprised to see Brett, since she had not heard his approaching footsteps. "How is who?" she asked, a little confused.

"How are you?" Brett amended, sinking to one knee to take her hand. Then his fingers touched her cheek, dampened by tears. "Why were you crying?"

Paulina's hands eased across his shoulder to circle his neck. When she drew close, she responded, "I was so worried about you, and"—she hesitated to continue—"I thought I saw Lillian."

"That's impossible," he replied.

"I know. I'm so glad you're here."

"We have problems," he said without hesitation.

Drawing slightly back, Paulina asked, "What problems?"

"A royal burial party from my homeland. Someone has died. We cannot be caught here on the Island of the Royal Crypt."

Her eyes widened, her pretty features cocking slightly to the side. "But . . . they'll rescue us. We're saved."

"No—" His fingers closed firmly over her hands, holding them against his thick thighs. "We cannot make ourselves known, Paulina. To do so—"

Silence. She did not like the way his eyes lowered. "To do so will what, Brett?"

He could not lie to her. Not now, when they were together and in love and relying on each other for support and survival. The truth was the only protection he could offer right now. "To be caught on the Island of

193

the Royal Crypt is a crime punishable by death, Paulina—"
His gaze lifted, to be instantly struck by the horror on
her ashen features. "It doesn't matter how we came to
be here; it matters not that we were washed up here in
a storm. If we are caught, we will be put to the sword.
So for the next six days we must stay out of sight.
And . . . we cannot stay here. The caverns echo every
sound and they will hear us."

There was something else wrong; Paulina could see
the pain in his eyes. "And besides this ridiculous sentence of death, what else bothers you?"

"What can bother me that is worse than death?" *Not
knowing, that's what,* he mentally answered his own inquiry. He felt the sickness inside that grew from personal
loss . . . from a death in his family. If a burial party was
on the island, then he had lost a mother or a father or
a brother or one of half a dozen sisters. Until the high
priest and burial party departed, he would have to wonder if it was the kind, dear woman who was his mother,
or the staid, dignified, and yet loving man who was his
father . . . a vibrant young sister, or a self-serving, self-
centered brother who had demanded a bride from the
outside world, and who might, even now, be planning to
ascend the throne of Talantia. Until he read the name
inscribed upon the crypt, he would not know who he
had lost . . . and who to mourn.

"I asked you, Brett, what else troubles you?"

With a smile that was almost not there at all, he
squeezed Paulina's hands and responded in a husky
whisper, "Nothing . . . nothing at all. I just want us to
survive, Paulina. That is all."

"That is enough," she said. "If we do not survive, then
nothing else matters."

Lifting a strong hand, Brett was suddenly aware of her

unnatural warmth. "You're fevered," he said, his fingers easing along the fringe of her brows. "Are you ill?"

Actually, she thought she might be, but she did not want to add to his worry. "I believe I ran too quickly to reach the cave. I'll be all right."

The dog appeared, standing just outside of touching distance of Brett, as if he awaited his master's command. But Brett's only order was "Stay out of sight," and the dog ambled off, dropping to a cool, dark place against the wall as if he understood.

Paulina started to arise, but when Brett took her wrist, halting her, she explained, "You said we could not stay in the caves . . . that they would hear us."

"It'll be several hours before the entourage leaves the ship sitting out in the sea. We are safe for the time being. Besides—" Turning to retrieve a bundled canvas he had dropped upon the floor, he said, "I took the time to pick berries I found growing in the underbrush. I knew you'd be hungry."

Picking up one of the full, juicy berries, Paulina said, "Back home, berries do not ripen until mid- or late summer. How very strange." As she popped it into her mouth, she mumbled, "Wish they were in a pie."

She had the most natural ways of endearing herself to him. Wrapping his fingers around her shoulders, he drew her against him, then tasted the juice of the berry upon her mouth. "You are so sweet, Paulina."

"It is the berry," she responded.

"No . . . it is you . . . your sweet, womanly essence . . . I want you for my very own—"

"I believe"—she drew slightly back, her head cocked to the side—"that you had me for your very own last night."

"I don't mean sex," he grumbled, bearlike, "I mean

195

forever, Paulina. I can't imagine spending my lifetime without you."

Paulina drew a deep, weary sigh, her gaze easing over Brett's sharp good looks. She saw kindness—and sincerity—in the set of his jaw, a twinkle in his left eye that reminded her of the first star of night, a soft pout upon his full mouth that made her want to caress it with her own. Though he had not said it, his declaration had been as readable as one of love . . . and she knew in her heart, in her mind, in her soul, that Brett McCallum was every bit as much in love with her as she was with him. But love wasn't enough to ensure their future. That would take skill, art, and determination . . . if what he said about the consequences of being on the island was a statement of truth.

But only four years separated them from the twentieth century . . . could she believe anything as barbaric as a sentence of death being imposed simply for being cast by a freak storm upon a prohibited island?

Human sacrifices had long since been abandoned.

If only human injustice could be also.

By that evening, an exploring Brett had found a shady dell at the center of the island and a fall fed by an underground stream. There, in the confines of their makeshift quarters, he came up with a plan.

"You will what?" exclaimed Paulina, aghast.

"You heard me."

"Well, I don't think I heard you correctly."

"Then I'll repeat myself," he remarked indulgently. "We cannot build a fire to cook fish for fear of being discovered. I will swim out to the ship and stock up on supplies and bring them back."

"You'll do no such thing, Brett McCallum! Get such foolishness out of your head right now!"

He could have reminded her that he wasn't asking for her permission, but he could see that she was simply worried about him. So he said, "They'll have flour and canned milk and eggs . . . all the makings for a pie."

"And pies need ovens, too!" Softening her voice, she implored, "I don't need a pie, Brett. I just need"—leaning seductively close, her mouth grazed his cheek—"you. You are all I need, all I will ever want, all I will ever depend on."

"Without proper food you will wither and die," he reasoned just as softly, "and then it will not matter what you need or want or depend on. I'm swimming out to the ship after dark, and that's all I'll say on the subject."

"Doesn't my opinion count for anything?"

Brett's gaze connected to her own, the anger gently subdued, her mouth slightly parted, trembling, teasing, compelling him to close the distance and feel its soft moistness against his own. But he could not . . . would not . . . give her the satisfaction of thinking she had won this small battle, that she had managed to get the last word in when survival was so important to them and the food items aboard the funeral ship could ensure that survival. His hands lifted to cover her slim shoulders and his mouth pressed into a tight smile before he offered, "Your opinion counts for a lot in most instances, but not now." The smile softened. "You are speaking from the heart. I am speaking from the stomach. I'd as soon eat poisoned brambles as one more blasted fish."

There was absolutely no reasoning with him. For lack of a better response—or an instant retort—Paulina gently folded herself into Brett's embrace. He needed her stamina and her strength . . . and certainly her understanding. To deny him that would be deplorable, and

197

she cared much too deeply for him to deny him any-thing. "If your conviction is so strong, then do as you must. But Brett—" At this point her gaze lifted, though she could scarcely make out his features through the haze of tears. Thank God she had committed his image to memory. "I've always thought it silly to tell people to be careful—and it is, of course, since reasonable people would be nothing less—but Brett . . . be careful. What would I do without you?"

He smiled, that cockeyed, half-mocking, playful smile she had grown so accustomed to, and hadn't seen for a while. "I don't plan to give you the chance to find out, Miss Paulina Winthrop."

Snuggling against him, Paulina asked, "Since you in-sist on being reckless, will you do one thing for me?"

His fingers closed gently over her shoulder. "What is that?"

"Will you wait until I have fallen asleep so that I will not know that you've left?"

In the moment's silence, Brett's dark brows knitted together. When he eventually responded, "If you wish," his voice was almost reverent.

"Promise?"

Now one of those dark brows arched above a twinkling eye. "Don't think for a moment that I don't know what you're attempting to do."

"Why, whatever do you mean?"

"And don't play coy with me, Paulina Winthrop. You are attempting to extract a promise, and then you will deliberately keep yourself awake because you know I would not break a promise. Well . . . I won't fall for it."

Oh, how well he knew her! Paulina fought to keep the hint of anger from her voice as she spoke. "You're much too suspicious, Brett. If I remained awake, it would be for no other reason but that I am so hungry I could not possibly sleep. We've hardly eaten a thing all day, only a few berries."

"Enough to make half a dozen pies," he argued, looking toward the dog. "Keep watch, Alujian. Now, you"—Brett's finger touched lightly upon the tip of Paulina's pert nose—"go to sleep. I'll bring back food if it's the last thing I do."

"And it bloody well might be," she growled.

"Don't be vulgar."

In a slightly sarcastic tone she responded, "Well, hellfire and damnation, why not?" then closed her eyes against the wide expanse of his chest as if she were not even remotely annoyed with him.

The moon was round and full on the island of the midnight sun, spilling a bright light across the small lake and dappling the woodline in varying shades of gray, crimson, and gold. Brett could feel an argument building, and he knew that he should depart now. But he just couldn't be so sensible. Absently, he massaged Paulina's cool skin, then tucked his fingers beneath the scant fabric of her gown to gain more intimacy. She was everything he wanted in a woman . . . perhaps more than he could handle, he thought with a suppressed grin. She was smooth and soft and supple, she was independent and carefree, she was brave; he liked that trait in a woman. He had seen her stand up to Soapy Smith and his men that morning on the boardwalk, and he would have given his weight in gold to have heard her demand the return of her father's handgun. If he hadn't held her back, she might have gone after the man who'd gunned down Big Pat. That she had survived to the age of twenty-four was, he imagined, something of a miracle.

"What are you thinking?" asked Paulina tugging at a particularly tangled strand of her hair.

"I am thinking of you," he responded without hesitation.

"That I am something of a wasp, I'd imagine," came her softly spoken return.

His fingers closed gently over her arm. "I was thinking no such thing."

"What, then?" Her eyes lifted, but only for a moment, returning their gaze to the dance of a thousand lights across the lake. When he failed to respond, she waited to meet his gaze once again, but hesitated, though she didn't know why. In a much softer voice she asked, "Well . . . what, Brett, if it's not that I'm a wasp?"

Giving her the comfort of a small hug, he thought that he should not betray the true direction of his thoughts. Thus he responded, "I backed into a nest of wasps once. They were ugly things, reddish-brown bodies whirring threateningly through the air toward me. I got stung a half-dozen times before I jumped feet-first into a pond." Tousling her hair a little roughly, he touched his mouth in a gentle kiss to the back of her neck. "And you look nothing like one of those creatures. Hell, you've never even stung me, not once, love."

She tried not to smile, but that was a feat she could not accomplish. "How do you do it, Brett McCallum? I can be so angry with you, and you have a way about you that endears you to me even more, that chases away my anger as if it had never existed, that makes me want to turn in your arms and—" She halted abruptly, heaving a weary sigh.

"And what?" he prompted her, the sarcasm renewed in his quietly spoken words. "And kiss me, I'll bet. That's what you were going to say, wasn't it?" The fingers of his right hand eased upward, between the valley of her breasts, and came to rest against her pert chin.

200

"I could use a kiss about now . . . a kiss from the prettiest lady on this godforsaken island."

Heaving another sigh, she responded demurely, "I'm simply too tired to be kissing you, Brett McCallum. Besides"—though her face remained turned from him, she smiled, because she knew he liked her smiles—"you're a rake and a rogue, a liar and a snake."

"And those are only my good points," he chuckled, nudging his thumb against her chin. "And I am also a prince, Paulina, the prince of your dreams . . . the prince who will snatch you onto the back of his great white steed and carry you away from all danger."

"And you are the dreamer's deception, for I do not need a prince. I need a lover and a companion, just as you do. Princes need princesses, and there is not one single ounce of royal blood flowing in my veins."

"I beg to differ," he chuckled with slight sarcasm, then turned her in his arms so that she had to face him. One of his dark eyebrows arched, his gaze, darkened to the shade of the evening sky, connecting with her emerald one. Then, slowly, his left hand eased along the curves of her waist and hip, his fingers soon tucking beneath the tattered hem of her gown to ease it upward. Though her breathing all but ceased, he did not terminate the bold uncovering. "Now, what shall we do to pass the time while I am waiting to swim toward the ship?"

"I haven't any idea," she replied, her hand immediately covering and stilling his own. "But I know what we will not do!"

His mouth turned down in a comical pout. "Ah, why not?" His hand eased from beneath her own and quickly covered the flat plane of her stomach beneath her gown.

Paulina gasped. Fire lit her eyes. She wanted to draw away from him, voice her displeasure, and put enough distance between them to end his bold molestation. But her body would not move; rather, she felt the heat of passion flooding her body and working its way up the length of her spine. But when his hand moved toward the juncture of her thighs, she threw herself to her back, tearing herself away from his touch. "I said, I know what we will not do, so I suggest you listen more closely. I am still angry with you, and I think you are being foolhardy, putting yourself in unnecessary danger. Unless you have decided against swimming to the ship, then—"

Where he had been playful and teasing just moments ago—in the rich depth of his eyes—there now came a hardness. His mouth pinched into a thin line, almost as if he had pulled his lips between his teeth. He had seen this argument coming and, dammit, had not been rational enough to separate from her. Then his mouth relaxed again, his knee drew up, and his hand came to rest across it. In a childish rush of words he said, "I wasn't in a mood to make love anyway. I just thought you needed it."

Oh, now, didn't that infuriate her! "Just because all of *your* brains are six inches below your waist, doesn't mean mine are too. I made a mistake last night. I do not intend to repeat it."

All of a sudden the world ceased to exist for Brett. If a distant rumble crawled across the sky, he did not hear it. If water splashed into the lake, it did so without sound. *A mistake!* She said last night had been a mistake! "What are you saying, Paulina?" He hadn't been aware that his thoughts had formed into spoken words until her spitfire gaze turned full upon him.

"You heard me! You caught me in a vulnerable moment. I made a mistake. I never want to make love to you again!"

"I can live with that," he said. "But don't say last night

202

was a mistake. It was good for both of us, and I will believe nothing less."

"I'm sure it was good for you!" she shot back unthinkingly. "Men's loins need release. I'm glad I was there for you. But if you need release again, go elsewhere . . . go into one of your dreams and find yourself a princess."

Brett wasn't for a moment buying this uncharacteristic meanness. He came swiftly to his knees and his hands darted out, grabbing her arms and pulling her firmly to him. "I know you don't mean anything you've said. I know you care about me. I know you want to be with me, to make love to me. And I know why you're saying these things. You're worried sick about me swimming out to that ship, and you're afraid I won't return. So, my sweet little viper, spew your ugliness, your denials, and your degradations. Waste your breath, because I am not listening." Then he slung her away as if she were repulsive to him and rose to his feet. Raking his hands down the fabric covering his thighs, he continued in a hard tone. "You'll be safe here until I return. Alujian will stay with you. Do not venture away from here."

Then he turned and disappeared into the veil of darkness, disappeared before she could call him back, whisper her tearful apologies, and tell him how very right he was about her.

Thirteen

The water was cold; Brett felt that he'd been sucked into a vacuum of frigid death. His lungs burst, his nostrils flared, and a penetrating chill ate into the marrow of his bones. He could feel his body temperature plummeting, and had enough sense to realize it could be fatal.

Surely, he'd swum half a mile by now, but the outline of the boat that was his destination seemed to grow farther and farther distant the more he cut through the water. Now he wondered if he would drown, given the slim chance that he survived the cold, and Paulina would be left alone to fend for herself on the island.

Strange, the thought of her being alone sickened him more than the thought of drowning or freezing to death. And he'd seen the bloated bodies of drowned men, many times. Nothing, thus far, had been more unpleasant.

By the time he reached the hull of the ship, the moon was high overhead, though a purple haze kept its light dim. Winding his arm around the thick chain of the anchor, he attempted to still his violent trembling by drawing several long, deep breaths. Then, as sensibility returned to him, he wondered what the hell he thought he was doing.

He knew, of course, ensuring survival, and he had a second reason he had not given Paulina—his hope of finding out the identity of his deceased relation. He expected that Caspius would be aboard; for the past fifty years the old seaman had accompanied the dead of Talantia to the Island of the Royal Crypt. Brett had no reason to believe he wouldn't be aboard now. If he could find Caspius, he would be safe. Caspius would never betray that he'd been aboard, and certainly would not betray his intrusion upon the sacred island.

Soon his strength returned somewhat and the icicles began to melt in his veins. Brett began the arduous trek up the forged iron of the anchor. When, at last, his hand locked across the rail, he kept low, his eyes scanning the spotless deck. He saw no one, not even the sentry. But on second thought, what need was there for a sentry at an island inhabited only by the dead?

He thought back to the first funeral, twenty years before, when a sister had taken ill and died within three days. He'd stood upon the pier and watched this regal, ornate ship, used in the last century as a British warship, depart for the frigid sea spanning the horizon. At twelve years of age he'd been impressed by her great length of over two hundred feet, her crisp white sails, mahogany masts, and brass fittings gleaming in the morning sun. He'd watched her slowly descend into the horizon, far, far out to sea, taking from him forever the beloved toddler, Mara. Then he had turned away, tears clinging to his cheeks like vines. A reprimand from his father had awaited him: "Men do not show their emotions. You shame me, son."

An unexpected noise erupted nearby—male laughter. Male laughter? Aboard a funeral ship?

Brett sank beneath the rail, a furrow of worry upon his brow. The laughter continued, loud, raucous, guttural . . . depraved?

Aboard a funeral ship?

Something was wrong.

Just at that moment a thick, gnarled hand clamped down over his own upon the rail, pinning it in place.

Paulina huddled against the trunk of the spruce, her shiver from head to toe having nothing to do with the coolness of the night. She was almost positive that more than three hours had passed since Brett had departed, and now, against the black of night, she saw the soft golden luminescence of a campfire on the beach. Delicately interlaced with the mournful flow of the wind were scattered male voices, muted, indistinguishable, and so very puzzling, an occasional play of men's laughter.

Laughter among a funeral party? She thought not.

So, who enjoyed themselves around a campfire, if not the funeral party from the ship anchored in the sea?

The island was forbidden. Did any man dare set foot upon it, especially if discovery was imminent?

Paulina shivered from fear, apprehension, and dread . . . and the coldness of the night merely whispered over her skin, unnoticed.

A low growl erupted nearby. Alujian stood a few feet away, both front paws upon a rock, his back end in a half-crouching position, as if he considered pouncing on an unseen foe. Moonlight gleamed upon his bared canine teeth, his eyes so black they were like deep, impenetrable caverns.

Crawling across the ground, Paulina sat upon her bent legs and an arm scooted across Alujian. "What's the matter, boy? Are you worried too?'' Though the growl ceased and a wet tongue made an affectionate swipe at her cheek, she could feel the tremble in the great black body.

Then a horrid thought came to Paulina. Suppose Brett was in danger and Alujian sensed it?

But before she could allow the worry to penetrate her through, Alujian sat straight up, ceased the growl, cocked his head for a moment, and bounded across the bush that had been shielding them from the beach. As Paulina watched, horrified, Alujian pounced with all of his weight upon a large, barrel-chested man.

Dear God . . . he attacked . . . they'll kill him . . . how will I explain to Brett that the dog lost all of its senses?

Clamping her eyes tightly shut, she cupped her palms over her ears as she prayed that she wouldn't hear Alujian's death cry.

But she heard only his whine, the familiar one that indicated his contentedness, and then the men began to laugh again. Venturing a look, she saw the big man hugging the dog that was half his size.

"Alujian . . . why, you old brute!" laughed the man. "Where did you come from?"

Alujian knew the man, and the man knew Alujian. Paulina, shocked and bewildered by the jubilance of the burial party, could only look on in awe.

Ducking low, her sea-green eyes held the small group of men gathering around the dog as though nothing else existed. Hugs between them and the dog were shared all around, and as Paulina looked on, Alujian took the big man's wrist and began tugging him toward the timber-line with a low growl emitting from deep within his throat. Paulina heard it, saw the horror of the distance closing between her and the stranger, and she didn't know whether she should continue to lie low or slowly crawl backward so that she might flee toward the interior of the island. But how far would Alujian go to draw her into the circle of friends with whom he had reunited? Would he drag her out of the underbrush by the rags of her skirt and thrust her into the danger she so dreaded?

The answer was soon apparent; Alujian released the man's wrist and made long leaps across the expanse of beach and underbrush until his nose was pressed into the curve between Paulina's neck and shoulder. His tongue lapped at her cheek, then his teeth caught in the fabric of her collar and tugged. She heard the material begin to rip, and as she found the moment to thrust out her hand in an attempt to break Alujian's hold, the coolness of her palm fell immediately upon the creased leather of a man's boot. Her breathing all but ceased, and she looked warily upward.

The moonlight was blinding, forming a halo around the hatless head whose eyes gleamed like the devil's own. Then she caught her mouth in an ever so slight smile, casually withdrew her hand, and mumbled, "Nice evening, isn't it?"

No answer; her breathing once again ceased as surely as if her heart, too, had lost its rhythmic beat. Did he have a club with which he would reduce her to scarcely recognizable human flesh? Or a gun he would press to her forehead and discharge without conscience? Would a large, gnarled hand reach out to thread through her tangled hair and drag her upward? She waited, praying now, anticipating the worst and hoping that death would come quickly.

As the man crouched, and his hands dangled limply over his knees, Paulina forced her gaze to drop. Make it swift, she prayed, tensing for her execution. Don't make me suffer like this.

Then, in a voice so quiet and reverent that Paulina's head snapped up in surprise and disbelief, the big man said, "You'd be a lot more comfortable at our campfire, little lady, than sticking like glue to that ground. Here"—a hand went out toward her—"let me help you up."

When she hesitated, Alujian licked her face again, as if to assure her it would be safe to take the proffered hand. She did so, and was soon, though somewhat shakily, standing on her own two feet. Finally venturing an assessing look upon the full-bearded features, she asked the man who was much older than she'd initially thought, "Are you a pirate?"

He threw back his head and his laugh caused the mound of his belly to shake beneath his shirt. "Of a sort, I'll have to admit, lady. Indeed . . . of a sort. Now, come." He reached out his hand, making no move to touch her. "We have a grand supper of beef and roast potatoes at our fire."

"Beef?" she said in a small, strangled voice as her hand unconsciously closed over his extended wrist. "Potatoes . . . beef and potatoes? I've died and gone to heaven!" All fear abandoned her as she lifted the remains of her gown and hurried ahead of the man. "You wouldn't by any chance have an apple pie for dessert, would you?"

Chuckled the big man, "Could have the cook on board bake you up one, if you'd like."

Within a matter of moments a ravished Paulina, enjoying tender chunks of beef and steaming potatoes, listened to introductions all around. The big man was named Caspius. The others, their names immediately forgotten in her total enjoyment of her meal, were as friendly as the great black dog now sitting among them. Finally, the food consumed and the amenities ended, Paulina became the subject of their lighthearted interrogations. "Who are you?" "Where are you from?" "How did you get here?" "How long have you been here?" "Are you alone?"

And Paulina laughed. "You haven't given a single pause so that I might answer your questions."

Caspius, who seemed to be in charge, asked, "Have we asked a single question that you feel you could answer?"

Leaning back with her palms firmly upon the shore, Paulina replied, "What do you think, Mr. Caspius?" Her index finger tapped against her head. "Think nobody is home upstairs? Of course I can answer your questions." Dragging her feet beneath the hem of her dress, she continued. "My name is Paulina Winthrop. I'm from Turkey Gulch, Utah, and I was washed off the deck of a ship during a storm. I think I've been here for about two weeks—"

"Alone?"

Her brows knit in a moment of thoughtful silence. She felt the boring gazes of the men, and a hidden apprehension crawled through her. "Before I answer, may I ask you something?"

"Sure," replied Caspius, drawing up a thickly muscled leg.

"Is this a forbidden island?"

The gasps reached her ears in unison. "How the hell would you have known that?" Caspius was, obviously, surprised by her question.

"Well, is it?"

"It was, up until about five weeks ago."

"Then any man . . . or woman . . . would not be executed for being found here?"

"Not anymore."

"You wouldn't lie to me, would you?"

The hand of the man named Caspius gripped at his

chest with grand flourish. "I'd as soon rip my heart out."

"Then . . . no, I am not here alone."

"And who is with you?"

"A man who calls himself Brett McCallum—"

"Brett McCallum! Good God!" Instantly, the men began mumbling to one another, keeping their words behind hands cupped against each other's ears. Then Caspius returned his attention to Paulina. "The man you know as Brett McCallum is our prince, Kiam. When he is in your world, he is Brett McCallum. When he is in ours, he is Prince Kiam. And where is our beloved prince? It was reported to us that he had been killed."

"My world . . . your world. You speak as if you come from another planet. Tell me, what is this world of yours?"

Caspius's graveled laughter was immediately matched by the other men's. "We're not unknown specimens from a far and distant land no man will ever see, little lady. We are humans, just like you." A grin stretched from ear to ear. "But you were pulling my leg, weren't you?"

Paulina shrugged delicately. "Well, I didn't know there were princes in Alaska. It is an American territory, isn't it?"

"Seward's folly, indeed, it is. Now, are you going to tell us where our beloved prince is hiding?"

"He swam out to your boat. He wanted to find food and, I think, to find out who has died."

Wide black eyebrows joined in a deep crease atop the man's nose. "Someone has died? Who?"

"You should tell me. Aren't you navigating the funeral ship from your home port?"

Again Caspius laughed. "We are navigating a pirated

ship," he corrected her. "We, rebellious men of Talantia, have stolen her away."

Paulina absently picked at the last small morsel of beef on her plate. "Brett has told me nothing of his homeland. He has told me only of this island, and that is because he felt that he had to. Will you tell me something, so that I might know Brett a little better?"

"About our homeland?" Paulina's nod gave Caspius the encouragement to continue. "We are a small nation within the territory of Alaska, though we are not recognized as such. Many centuries ago, our people left Novgorod in Russia when it succumbed to Moscow. Since that time, Kiam's family has ruled the community. We have lived by our own laws, our own constitution, and have been undisturbed by the outside world. Kiam—our prince—is the second son of his father, and since he will not assume the crown of Talantia, then he is allowed to travel in the outside world. One of his duties is to return a woman to Talantia, to be taken in marriage by his brother, the crown prince." A sharp black eyebrow rose quizzically. "I assume that you are that woman."

So, I am wrong, thought Paulina. *That is why his name did not appear on that ridiculous document he had me sign.* Her thoughts immediately scattered; she looked up, a slight smile twisting her mouth. A painful revelation came to her—Brett did not love her; he would coldly and callously offer her as a sacrifice to his brother. Somehow, she hated the rush of tears gathering inside. She could not—would not—allow herself to be so cruelly used by the man she had thought loved her. "I assume this crown prince would not want a woman who is not a virgin."

"Prince Kiam would not *choose* a woman who was not a virgin," Caspius replied immediately. "To do so would greatly dishonor his brother. But"—he shrugged, his large, burly hands stretching out—"the matter is moot.

212

Kiam's family—his father, mother, and his sisters—have been ousted from Talantia, and his brother has established himself as dictator. That is why a few of us stole the funeral ship and took our wives and families, and our king and his family, to safety among friends near Nuklukayet."

Paulina felt that she had been caught up in a fairy tale, so unbelievable was the story being told by Caspius. "I see. And why didn't you stay with your families at Nuklukayet? Why are you here?"

Caspius dropped his eyes. "I am ashamed to say that we have come to take royal jewels from the Crypt of the Kings and Queens so that we might outfit a small army to take back our home."

"You say the island is no longer forbidden. Why?"

"Our true king lifted the prohibition. He himself gave us permission to take from his ancestors the wealth we need to organize an army. Now"—rising to his full height, Caspius slapped his thick thighs—"we must return to our ship to see that Kiam arrived there safely." Looking Paulina up and down with no intent to criticize, Caspius added, "You might wish to accompany us. There may be women's clothing in the cabin occupied by the king's family on the journey to safety."

"I was hoping you wouldn't leave me here alone," she confessed. "And I certainly have a few things I would like to say to Brett." With a short pause she added, "You don't mind if I call him Brett, do you? I do not know him by this other name."

"If he is not alive, it will not matter what you call him."

Not only was Brett alive, he was warm and dry, and his belly was full. He had not recognized the man whose

213

hand had clamped upon his own at ship's rail, but the man had recognized him. During the course of his meal, Brett had learned of his brother's insurrection and the ousting of his family. Though he was concerned, he was glad of their safety.

"I've got a woman on the island who will want some of this food," said Brett after a moment. "Could you put a longboat in the water to fetch her?"

"The other men ashore will bring her aboard," said the man who had introduced himself to Brett as Gustav.

"She has orders to hide out."

Gustav laughed heartily, though his laugh was short-lived. "Women do not obey the orders of men. I would wager she is even now among our other friends on shore."

"Is Caspius among them?"

"Caspius is our leader," proclaimed Gustav proudly. "Your father ordered that Caspius be the only man whose hands should touch the royal crypts, whose hands should pluck from them the wealth needed to take back Talantia from your brother."

"My brother is insane," mused Brett, cocking a dark eyebrow. "I do not understand how he could have accomplished the takeover."

"We will regain control. Your brother will be crushed."

Brett had been thinking a lot about this since learning of the insurrection. He himself could not return to Talantia without losing Paulina, and the small plot of land upon which Talantia stood was slowly being swallowed by the earth. Within a few years there would be nothing but a sinkhole. Talantia would exist no more. His family would be better off ending the fantasy life of royal dynasties; it was certainly what Brett had wanted all his life. And he would be free to take Paulina as his wife. If the sovereignty of Talantia were restored, he would not have that option.

"Let him have the doomed Talantia," said Brett after a considerable pause. "We can make a new life for ourselves at Nuklukayet. Alaska is growing by leaps and bounds. Yes . . . give my brother Talantia. The people who have remained will wise up and move out, and he will be alone."

"But—" Gustav could hardly find his voice. "Do you mean this, my prince? Your father . . . he is the one who thought you would want to return to Talantia. You have always been so loyal, even in the face of your brother's extreme hatred for you."

"I thought you told me your father was killed by a grizzly on Denali?"

Brett turned sharply in his chair, more than a little surprised to see his ragamuffin Paulina standing there. He hadn't realized how thin she had grown, eating fish and berries these past few days, and she was gaunt and pale. Guilt flooded him; he should have taken better care of her. "I—I—" Now he was the one who could not find the means to speak.

"Well?" Despite her fragility, Paulina's voice was firm and strong. "What are you doing, Brett McCallum, or is it Prince Kiam? Trying to come up with still another lie? Perhaps you have two fathers? One who was killed by a grizzly, and one who has established himself as a king? It's possible, I suppose."

Caspius slipped into the large dining cabin and skirted the long table toward Brett. "I'm glad to see that you're alive. Your father never gave up hope."

Without taking his eyes from the now-silent Paulina, Brett responded, "I see you've found my companion—"

Leaning close, Caspius whispered huskily, "I've a feeling you've made her more than your companion . . . my prince."

Paulina did not hear the words spoken by Caspius. All she knew was that she had met a man named Brett McCallum in Skagway, a man who had professed to be a guide and who was going to take her to find Millburn Hanks. But since leaving the wild port city, she had learned that he was anything but a guide. He was a sneak, and a liar . . . and a—a—oh, who knew what the hell he was! So in a scarcely contained voice, she asked him, "Did you ever intend to help me find Millburn Hanks, or was that just a scheme to get me away from Skagway? To get me married to a brother who must be a monster?" Though she tried hard to keep her emotions in check, tears flooded her eyes. "I thought you cared for me, Brett. But everything you have said, everything you have done, has been a lie." Lifting her eyes to Caspius, who stood silently at Brett's side, she asked, "Will you let me off at first port? I want to be as far away from your bastard prince as I can get."

With that, she fled onto the deck, sobbing bitterly, and a stunned Brett found the will to jump to his feet. Instantly, the hand of the hulking Caspius landed upon his shoulder. "Let your woman cry. Give her time to think. She will realize the error of her ways."

"But—" A lump as large as Denali rose to Brett's throat. "I love her, Caspius."

"I know."

Paulina wasn't sure why she was crying. It had been many days since she'd first discovered that Brett was not what he would have had her believe. Perhaps it was the relief of being rescued, of being fed decently for the first time in two weeks. Perhaps she was just now reacting to the fact that she had not saved herself for marriage. And perhaps she was merely lonely for Lillian, Uncle Will, and Matt. Perhaps she just needed Lucille's plump shoulder to cry upon.

Caspius approached and stood silently by for a moment. Only when her tear-sheened eyes lifted to his own did he say, "I'll show you to a cabin where you can rest and be alone, where you can find a fresh change of clothing. Perhaps you'll feel better."

In a small, strangled voice, she replied, "Thank you," and followed him the length of the great ship until a cabin stood open to her. Though small, it was elaborately furnished, with a bed, an armoire, a chest, all bolted firmly to the planked floor. Her feet soon stood upon a thick white rug and she remained motionless, listening as the door closed behind her.

Throwing herself upon the plush feather mattress, she relished its comfort so that for a moment the flow of tears stopped. But physical comfort was not a total salve, and the tears came again, fresh and warm upon her cheeks, tickling along the curve of her mouth and finally dropping onto the white linen bedcover. She wished she were back in Turkey Gulch, standing up against the Bartletts as she and her kin had always done, refusing to be intimidated and driven out, refusing to give up what was rightfully theirs. She wished she were right now enjoying one of Lillian's soft, sisterly hugs, wished she were fussing at Uncle Will for drinking too much whiskey, wished she were chastising Matt for the small mischiefs he got into with unsurprising frequency. She wished she could feel the planked boardwalk of her hometown beneath her feet, wished she could crinkle her nose in distaste in the face of Mr. Tillford's ever-present cigar. Oh, dear Lord, she wished she were reading a telegram from her mother and looking forward to her first visit in seven years. She wished for anything, anything familiar, anything that would help her forget that Brett McCallum was a liar and a rogue and a deceiver . . . and the man she loved with all her heart and soul.

Yes, that last declaration . . . that is what she wished most to forget.

Because he was part of her now, just as surely as was her life force, just as surely as was the breath she breathed and the steps she took, and the pain that filled her so fully that she thought she would explode into a million tiny fragments.

She had never felt such grief.

She had never felt such loneliness.

And she had never thought she could love so deeply and fully as she loved Brett McCallum.

And hated him just as much.

Caspius, knowing full well what was on Brett's mind as he moved toward the door, issued still a second warning. "I said you should leave the lady to her solitude. You've hurt her and lied to her and deceived her. She needs time to think and sort things out."

"But she must understand how much I love her," came Brett's agonized response. "I would give anything for her . . . I would give my life for her if it came to that." In a moment of rage Brett pounded his fists upon the table. "But she knew on the island that I was not a guide. She overheard a conversation I had with Captain Pericles aboard ship. Why, then, is she so angry. Why, then, does she want to be rid of me?"

"She knows now that you were taking her to our homeland to be your brother's wife."

Brett looked up quickly, his eyes dark and angry. "How could she know that?"

218

"Because I told her," Caspius calmly told him.

"Why, dammit? Why did you tell her?"

"Because she would have found out eventually."

"Not from me, she wouldn't have. I had already decided not to return to Talantia, but to become part of her world, to make her my woman and my wife. There was no need for her to know that I was taking her to Talantia to become my brother's wife." Rising to his full height, Brett again moved toward the door. "I must go to her."

"Don't," Caspius warned again. "Give her time."

Brett, of course, knew that Caspius was right. But he abhorred these moments apart from her, these minutes that would become hours that might possibly become days, and he could not bear the thought of the horrors that would manifest within her. If she would listen to him, understand the predicament he had faced when he'd realized how much he loved her . . . if she could understand that he wanted to make her his woman; if she would have him, then, perhaps, she would not hate him so.

Damn! Damn! That was what ate him up inside, the fact that she might hate him.

He couldn't bear it.

She was all he had ever wanted in a woman.

She had to believe that he loved her.

"I am going to her," he said with a note of finality, and certainly one that left no room for argument. "If you try to stop me, Caspius, I'll—" He left the threat hanging. Meeting the pale, warm brown eyes of the man he had known all his life, he knew that Caspius would not interfere.

If anything, he was loyal.

* * *

By the time Brett stood outside Paulina's cabin, his convictions had all but vanished. Pressing his elbow to the doorjamb, his knuckles raked his teeth, back and forth, back and forth, his dark eyes narrowed, yet free of anger. The short distance separating him from her was like a thousand miles; he could almost have reached out his hand to touch her, and yet the softness of her skin would not have been his reward . . . only ugly, lethal emptiness. She might as well have been back in Utah.

He wanted to go into the cabin, to hold her, to soothe her and whisper words of love and adoration against her hairline, but he was afraid of being rejected by her. She was the most important person in his life, and without her, he felt empty, powerless, like half a man. What would he say to her? Forgive me? I am but a man; with faults and vices, and bad habits. Forgive me, because I am an inconsiderate bastard who has no right to expect anything from you, especially your love and your understanding?

No . . . no . . . she would not want to hear it. Balling his fist so tightly that his fingernails cut into his palms, he turned away, retraced his steps, and stood at ship's rail. Perhaps Caspius was right; she needed time alone.

But in the meantime, his own personal agony would rip him apart inside.

Paulina had felt the presence on the other side of the door and had suspected it was Brett. Part of her wanted to see him, to throw herself into his arms and profess her love, but the more rational part of her wanted to hate him, to hurl insults and abuses and never, never trust him again.

Then he had moved away, and whatever she might have done was lost to the silence and solitude of her cabin. So she returned to her prone position upon the bed and rested her cheek against the warmth of her palm. She could feel her heart beating . . . th-thump, th-thump, th-thump . . . would it cease, and would she be aware of it, knowing that she was dead and amends could not then be made? Had Brett really done anything so hideous that she should put him out of her life for-ever?

Close your eyes, Paulina. The order echoed through her brain as she forced herself to obey. *Think rationally. Don't be so judgmental. You have made mistakes in the past too, and always you were forgiven.*

Before she quite realized it was so close upon her, sleep came, deep, warm, peaceful sleep, and all sounds of the night, all worries in her mind, and that rhythmic, irritating thump that was her heart became part of an-other world, a world she had visited often, a world where anything could happen . . . and possibly would.

The world of dreams.

Part Three

Is it but a dream, or is it reality?
If I knew for certain, would I be free?

Fourteen

"Wake up, sleepyhead. We're entering Dutch Harbor."

Paulina lurched from her sleep so quickly that a sharp pain shot through her temples. There stood Brett McCallum, pulling on a tan jacket and quickly combing back his dark hair. She looked at him as if he had lost all his senses. "You get out of here, Brett McCallum. I don't ever want to see you again."

He turned, a surprised grin beginning to form on his mouth. "What's gotten into you? You asked me to wake you in time for supper."

"I did no such thing. I told Caspius I wanted to be let off at the next port. You were right there . . . you heard me. Now, get out!"

"Who the hell is Caspius?"

How dare he play dumb with her! Did he think she was so distraught that he could convince her the last two weeks had never happened? Well, he had better think otherwise! Her father didn't raise any fools! "Don't be ridiculous. He rescued us from the Island of the Royal Crypt."

"Island of the Royal Crypt?" His pleasant, rolling chuckle drew her attention right away. "Good Lord, woman, do you have some ridiculous book beneath your pillow that you've been reading? Now, come on. Supper is served only until seven."

As her eyes cleared, a very startled Paulina looked around. Rather than the small, elaborately furnished cabin aboard the funeral ship, she saw stark gray walls and a few ordinary furnishings. Beyond the walls, she heard the loud, guttural churning of steam engines, and the voices of people . . . children among them. What was happening to her? Had she gone stark raving mad?

As he continued to groom himself, Brett McCallum mumbled, "That must have been some dream you had. No wonder you tossed and turned all afternoon." He had spoken coolly, but now, reflected in the mirror across his shoulder, were the tearful eyes of Paulina, as she slowly lowered herself to the bedcovers. He turned, quickly covered the distance separating them, and sat on the bed beside her. "Hey, you really are upset. Why don't you tell me about this dream you had?"

"It wasn't a dream. You're attempting to pull off some elaborate hoax!" Then she looked up, asking almost timidly, "You are, aren't you?"

"Suppose I am. Why don't you indulge me and tell me about your dr—I mean, your adventure. Tell me just as if I were a curious bystander."

"You're teasing me."

"No I'm not. Just tell me." When she hesitated, he added, "Please?" in a childlike voice.

"You don't want to hear it." Catching her trembling lip between her teeth for a moment, she quietly added, "You'll just laugh at me."

"No, I won't, Paulina."

She looked up, a little surprised by the sincerity and the concern in his eyes. "I dreamed we were on a ship called *Crown Prince of Talantia*, and that your name was really Prince Kiam. I dreamed we were tossed into the sea during a terrible storm and we ended up on an island where your royal dead were buried. There—" For a moment she studied his eyes, trying to detect laughter in them, but seeing only a quiet concern that gave her the incentive to continue. "There was a great black dog named Alujian with us, and we were all having to live on fish and berries. Then there was an insurrection in your country and your father the king sent two of his most faithful men, Caspius and Gustav, to the Island of the Royal Crypt to take the jewels to finance an army and retake Talantia from your evil brother. You were taking me to Talantia to be his queen, but then we—" With a small gasp she caught her words, just as she was about to relate the most vivid part of her dream. Oh, dear, didn't it happen . . . that sweet, wondrous, erotic night on the beach when they had made love?

"Then we what?" he prompted her, the concern still in his voice.

Lowering her eyes, she responded, "Then we fell in love." Venturing a small, shamed look into his vivid, unsmiling blue eyes, she said, "It's silly, isn't it?"

He wasn't sure whether she meant the dream or the fact that in her dream they fell in love. He chose not to embarrass her further by questioning her meaning. "No, it isn't silly," he said, his hands gently massaging her arms through the fabric of her blouse. "Sometimes dreams seem so real that it's hard to believe they're not. But I promise—" At this point, he smiled. "I am not a prince. There is no great black dog. We've met no one named Caspius or Gustav, and my father—as I told you— was killed by a bear on Denali. We are on a stinking steamer coming into Dutch Harbor for a two-day layover in Unalaska, and I, Brett McCallum, a commoner, rake, snake, and poor excuse for a guide, am taking you to

227

Nuklukayet, and then northward on the Yukon until we find your Mr. Millburn Hanks. Now"—he rose to his feet, ending politely—"I would like to escort the prettiest lady aboard into the dining room of this awful tub. Unless you've made another date?"

Rising, and sweeping back her thick, tangled hair, Paulina thought for a moment, then said reminiscently, "You know . . . I miss that dog."

And Brett, laughing, gave her a hug.

Several times during the course of the meal, Brett caught Paulina daydreaming. He thought how pretty she looked, her thoughts so far away, her eyes like emeralds, her full, puckered mouth parting almost absently to accept modest bites of her meal.

"You're still thinking about your dream, aren't you?" asked Brett, spreading butter on half a biscuit.

Silence. Her eyes lifted to his own, then her brows slightly arched. "Sorry, did you say something?"

"Are you still back on that island?"

"It was just so . . . so real, Brett. I mean, you should have seen the caves. I went swimming in a pool that was as warm as water heated on a stove. I found beautiful treasures and brought them up, and you wouldn't let me keep them. We were there for two weeks, from the moment we were washed overboard until Caspius took me out to the ship. And the strangest part of all, I knew your thoughts just as if they were my own. I knew what you were doing even when we were apart."

Only one part of her narration really caught his attention. "Oh? I got left behind on the island?"

"No, of course not. You had swum out earlier to find food."

Pushing aside his plate, Brett took her hand across the

table. "Do you know what would have happened if we'd been in these freezing waters for more than a few minutes? We would have perished. Our body temperatures would have plummeted so low that we could not have lived." When embarrassment, because she, an educated woman, hadn't thought of that, touched her cheeks, Brett smiled warmly. "And I think it is charming that you have such a vivid imagination, Paulina. It is charming, indeed." Leaning close, he added, "Are you sure we didn't engage in any hanky-panky on that island of yours?"

Quickly, she withdrew her hand from the cover of his own. "Why, Brett McCallum, is *that* the only thing on your mind? I do declare—" Stabbing at the peas on her plate, she impaled several, then scraped them unceremoniously off on the edge of the plate and waved the fork at Brett. "I just don't know why I put up with you."

Dimples cut into Brett's cheeks as he smiled. "There, that's the Paulina I remember. Sharp-tongued and nasty-tempered. Welcome back from that blasted island, little lady."

Unalaska Island in the Aleutians was probably still as lonely and desolate as when the Russians had first sighted it in the early eighteenth century. As the steamer *Iron Ice* pulled into the Dutch Harbor port, Brett saw very few ships taking shelter at the isolated pier. Since its fur-sealing days had ended, Unalaska served little purpose except as a refueling stop.

What there was of the village was laid out in a sharp military fashion, the clean white buildings symmetrical and complimentary to the snow-capped mountains beyond. The villagers, mostly of Lapp and Russian descent, were friendly and accommodating, and the layover passengers from the *Iron Ice* were made welcome at a small shelter run by an Eskimo woman who never smiled and bobbed her head in response to all attempts at conversation. Befriended by an anthropologist named McQuesten, Paulina and Brett settled in to a partitioned lodge to pass the next two days. Paulina settled in with other women, and Brett with the men.

Paulina did not like the wind-scourged island of Unalaska. It was impossible to stay warm, even in the spring of the year, and the fire in the grate was frequently killed by the wind. Finally, several of the women pooled their strength together and stacked tables against the paneless windows. So much for second-class accommodations, Paulina thought. Next time I'll find a rich guide, someone with enough money in his pocket to put us up at a boardinghouse not being run by the financial skin of its teeth.

That evening, called to a meal in the main room of the lodge, Paulina joined Brett and the thin little man, McQuesten, at a table off in a corner. McQuesten jumped up quickly and pulled out a chair for Paulina. Casting a narrow glance toward the still-seated Brett, Paulina said, "Thank you, Mr. McQuesten. It is always such a delight to meet a chivalrous gentleman. You *must* be from the mainland."

"Minnesota, to be exact," responded McQuesten, returning to his chair. "But I've been traipsing all over the world for so many years that I've near forgotten what she looks like."

"Oh?" Only now did Paulina's gaze cut from Brett's. "You're an anthropologist, aren't you? What has brought you to Alaska?"

"I'm charting the colonies of the Inuits, those who have mated with Russians and Laplanders. I'm being financed by the University of Massachusetts."

"I see."

Brett interjected. "But you don't want to talk about mating, do you, Miss Winthrop?"

Paulina cast a warning look in his direction. "Indeed. I'd much rather discuss the extinction of a certain breed of two-legged snake."

Brett smiled, drawing his hand up to cover his chin. "Any snake I know?"

McQuesten, who had failed to recognize the insult, asked rather enthusiastically, "Has a new breed of reptile been discovered this far north? I would be most interested, as a professional man, you know."

Brett laughed. "I think the snake she's referring to is me. Miss Winthrop and I have not seen eye to eye on certain matters."

"Of course not," Paulina continued the bantering. "I never could get my eyes that low to the ground." At that moment a grim-faced Eskimo woman set a plate of food in front of Paulina. Looking at the plates of the two men, she said, "You both look hungry. Let's eat, shall we?"

Later that evening the three of them walked out of doors, seeing the sights of Unalaska, until the winds, howling down from the north, forced them indoors once again. McQuesten seemed to enjoy the constant bantering of insults between Paulina and Brett, and managed to throw in a couple of his own, always in Paulina's defense, which surprised Brett since he and McQuesten had become fast friends.

It was certainly a night for surprises. Scarcely had McQuesten left them alone in a private parlor of the lodging house before Paulina moved into Brett's embrace as casually as if they were lovers. When their gazes met, she managed a small smile as she said, "You do know that I enjoy teasing you, Brett McCallum. Half of what I say I certainly do not mean."

"And the other half?"

Her fingers moved over his thick muscles, until they were stopped by the bend of his arm. There they rested, all the while her gaze strangely, admiringly, continuing to hold his own. "Well, I'm sure there was a certain amount of truth in what I said to you."

"Perhaps," he conceded, surprised—and delighted—by her moment of amiability. "And what has brought on this good mood?"

"Being with you," she responded, and was immediately besieged by renewed surprise. "I mean it, Brett. When I overlook your faults, you're really not so bad. And . . ." She shrugged slightly, her eyes dropping to a button on his shirt held there by what appeared to be a single thread. "You do need taking care of," she continued, plucking the button from the fabric. "See? You'd have lost this had I not noticed. I'll fetch my sewing kit from my canvas bag."

Brett would not allow her to pull away from him. Taking her wrist, his fingers massaged the soft skin above her palm. "Don't go." With gentle coaxing he soon got her to sit beside him on a large divan. "I thought we could just sit here and talk for a while, like two civil people."

Settling back, Paulina laughed softly. "And what would two people, who have been anything but civil to each other, have to talk about?"

"Oh—" Linking his fingers behind his head, Brett grinned. "You might tell me the real reason you want to find Millburn Hanks. You haven't said so, but I don't think he's your father . . . not really."

"What makes you think so?" Although she tried to maintain firmness in her voice, she felt her eyes lowering in shame nonetheless. He was much too astute, or had she simply failed to be careful in keeping her lies sorted out?

"Because most of the time you call him Millburn, and if you were his daughter, you would always have referred to him as Father, or, out of respect, as Mr. Hanks. But it was Millburn."

"You're right, of course. He isn't my father."

"Will you tell me why you want to find him?"

"Does it really matter?"

"Since I'm not being paid, I think it does."

Paulina chose not to remind him of the marriage contract. He still thought she was unaware of the true identity of the intended groom.

Stretching back his arms, then slapping his hands to his thighs, Brett dropped back into the comfort of the divan. "I'd hate to think I was taking you to a man you wanted to kill. You were god-awful determined to get back that gun Soapy took from you. And you did say it was your father's. Ol' Millburn wouldn't be doing whatever he's doing along the Yukon without a weapon. So why don't you tell me why you are so desperate to reach this Millburn Hanks."

She really had not been entirely truthful with him. But she had a reason—she could not bear the thought of him laughing at her, ridiculing her, and making her feel like the total fool. She imagined that he might enjoy that. He had certainly taken every opportunity to embarrass her since their first meeting, and what reason did she have to believe he would not do so now?

Her eyes lifted; their gazes locked. She did not see the familiar gleam of ridicule, did not see that outrageous smirk playing upon his mouth. But just in case it happened, she looked around to make sure there was not a witness lurking about. She could hear no sounds from beyond the single door, only the call of a wolf far off in the mountainous region of Unalaska Island.

It really wouldn't do any harm to tell him the truth about her mission. But was she willing to lay all her cards on the table? And if he knew the goal she was expecting to accomplish back in Turkey Gulch, would he end up on the floor, laughing so hard that he wouldn't be able to catch his breath?

Then again, how would she know how he would react if she did not get it over with? Perhaps he would surprise her. Perhaps there would be no ridicule at all, and no breathless laughter as he rolled on the floor, unable to control himself.

But who was she kidding?

He was like every other man. He didn't think a woman could accomplish anything without the support of a man.

"What are you thinking?"

She caught her breath, so surprised was she by his softly spoken words. "Oh, I—well, I was wondering if you really, ummm, what is the word I want?"

"Something as simple as *care*?"

"Yes, that's it. I wonder if you really cared why I need to find Millburn."

"Of course I care," he said, a little hurt by her doubt. "I care because I do not know if this Millburn Hanks is a dangerous man, and if you will be threatened by him. I don't want to endanger your life, Paulina, and if I thought I was, I would take you no farther—"

"But Millburn is an old pussycat!" she declared a little more hotly than she'd intended. "He wouldn't harm a soul . . . no, not Millburn. He was my father's closest friend, and—"

When she hesitated, lowering her eyes, his fingers

234

eased beneath her chin to again lift her face. "And what?"

"He was the only witness to my father's murder. If I can return Millburn to Turkey Gulch to testify in court against the killers, they will go to the gallows, and Turkey Gulch will be free of its greatest menace. Don't you see, I must bring him back! Not only for my father, but for my town. They are depending on me and I simply cannot let them down."

"But why you, Paulina? By your own admission you were schooled to be a teacher. I've seen nothing less than the behavior of a lady in everything you do. I can't believe that someone more qualified couldn't have taken this journey."

"But I must do it! It's a matter of honor. And it's a matter of—" Was this the moment, the moment to confess her other motive? The one that might send him into hysterical laughter upon the floor? Well, the subject had been brought up, why not get it over with? "If I bring Millburn back to Turkey Gulch, the city council will appoint me to complete my father's term. Right now one of his murderers is holding down the job, and I want it. I want it so badly I can taste it!"

"And what is this job?"

"City marshal." All right. Go ahead and laugh, Brett McCallum. Get it over with so that we can go on with what has to be done.

But he didn't laugh. Rather, he took her hands and enveloped them warmly between his own. "You know, I saw a strong, determined lady back there in Skagway, the way you stood up to Soapy Smith. I think you would do a fine job as city marshal."

She looked up quickly, trying to see humor that might indicate he was making fun of her. But she saw only sincerity, and even a touch of admiration. It made her smile. "Do you really think so?"

"I wouldn't have said it if I didn't. But—" She should have known there would be a catch. A certain hardness came to her eyes as they continued to connect to his own. "Don't forget that you've vowed to marry."

Her lips pressed impudently together. "So I did." But she had no intention of keeping such a promise. She had given it only so that Brett would take her to the Yukon. Paulina tried to bite her tongue, to keep from quipping something she might later—or even immediately—regret, but it was much too painful. So with carefully chosen words, she continued. "I fully intend to keep my promise, Brett McCallum, but I never promised to *stay* married . . . now, did I?"

"It won't be necessary to make such a promise. The marriage will be extremely short-lived."

"What?" She sat forward, so surprised was she by his almost nonchalant declaration. Although she remembered her conversation with Big Pat, and knew the marriage was not to Brett but another man, she felt a strange, unexplainable need to continue playing the game. "Then why do you want a wife, Brett? If you merely wanted . . . that . . . for a few months, you could get it from any woman. Why do you want marriage, and why to me?"

He was certainly wrong in thinking that they were being honest with each other. Could he now be honest and not expect to feel the slap of her hand against his face? Shrugging, he continued in the same matter-of-fact tone. "Did I tell you about my friend Gruff? I've known him for about seven years, and during those seven years he's saved my life countless times. Before the past winter he'd never asked me for anything in return, and now my friend is dying and there is only one thing he asked of me." Silence. Brett drew forward, dropped his elbows onto his parted knees, and lightly linked his fingers. Paulina said nothing, but he could feel the almost intimidating gaze of emerald eyes upon his profile. "Gruff has less than a year to live, Paulina. He asked me to bring him a wife from Skagway—"

Paulina shot to her feet. Turning away, she drew her hands against her waistline, then balled them into fists. This was too, too familiar, and again she remembered her dream in all its vivid details. An arranged marriage . . . The dream must have arisen from her learning of a sick man's need to take a wife and make his last months unforgettable. So why did she feel such shock now to hear Brett confessing his plans. The marriage really didn't matter, since she did not intend to go through with it. But now the cold, callous manner in which Brett told her of his plans made her blood run both hot and cold at the same moment.

How should she handle it? With shock, disgust, or with indifference? She turned to face him, seeing him instantly brace, as he had once before when he'd expected her to slap him. But she had no intention of resorting to brutality. Rather, she quietly returned to the divan beside him, a small, knowing smile playing upon her mouth. "I won't tell you how I knew, Brett, but I am quite aware of your plans to marry me to your terminally ill friend."

"There is no need to betray a confidence. The only other person who knew was Big Pat." He attempted to take her hand, but she would not allow it. "And are you sorry you signed the consent to marry? And are you disappointed that it isn't me you are marrying?"

She felt a need to inflict pain, and that was confusing to her, because she also felt a sudden warmth rush through her, taking away the coldness that his confession had caused. She wanted to be in his arms, holding him, having him hold her, feeling the fiery roughness of his mouth against her own. But she was confused by her feelings because logic dictated that she should hate him, that she should be running as far away from him as she could possibly get. Mentally chastising herself for the rebellious emotions welling within her, she calmly said, "No, indeed, I am not disappointed. To be truthful, I am relieved. The thought of being married to a man like you makes me cold inside."

Brett wasn't sure what he had expected her to say, but this certainly wasn't it. In a moment during which the heated swell of anger filled him, he was on his feet, dragging her up to press against him. The coolness of her eyes annoyed him, though he knew not why. Everything he had said should logically have produced this look of undeniable loathing. "You know damn well that you want to be with me, Paulina. You know it! Why do you deny it?"

Paulina felt a certain victory. She had angered him; she liked having this control. His eyes were now a dark royal blue, his mouth pressed into a thin line, the tick at the corner of his eye uncontrolled. In a quiet moment in which she enjoyed her victory, her hand rose to his neck, where she could almost feel the tiny hairs bristling. His muscles beneath her hands, which were now moving boldly over him, were so taut, she was sure they would tear open from the strain. Puckering her mouth, she took a moment to drop the button into the pocket of his shirt.

Then she smiled, and the dark fury flooding his features was her reward a thousand times over. Drawing her index finger to his tightly pressed mouth, she said, "Oh, is poor little Brett McCallum angry? That mean old

Paulina! She treats you so badly! How shall we punish her, hmmm?"

The door creaked, but Brett's broad shoulders blocked her view. She strained to see, but he would not permit it. Without turning, he warned, "This room is occupied. Please give us some privacy," and in response the door gently closed.

"That was very rude," quipped Paulina, extracting herself from his embrace. But when he snatched her wrist and kept her from putting distance between them, she again pressed herself to him, snapping, "Let me go, Brett McCallum. If you don't, I'll scream."

"Go right ahead. But there is one thing I forgot to tell you."

"Oh? And what is that?"

"I spread the word around that you are an obstinate wife who refuses to do her duties to her husband." He hadn't, of course, but it sounded fairly convincing. "Everyone feels sorry for me and wonders why I put up with a—" He took delight in saying, "Cold wife."

Don't let him know he's prickling you, warned her little voice inside. *He'll feel a tremendous satisfaction.* "Well now, isn't that funny, Brett. I told everyone that you were a wife-beating husband, and several of the men told me that all I had to do was scream, and we'd need a shovel to scrape you off the floor."

How it happened, neither would ever know, but their cruel banterings, lies, and insults had suddenly metamorphosed into an arousing sexual game. She pressed against him, and his hands moved swiftly to her back to pin her in place. He was breathing so heavily that Paulina could almost see the expelled breaths, but it only magnified the heated river suddenly moving within her. Her mouth close enough to his own to taste the sweetness of a kiss, Paulina whispered, "I'll make a deal

239

with you, Brett McCallum. If we can reach Nuklukayet without—"

When she hesitated, an intrigued Brett asked, "Without what?"

She smiled coyly, sensually, seductively, her fingers easing across his shoulders and closing over his taut muscles. "Without making love, then I will marry your friend Gruff and I will stay with him until he is gone from this earth. I will be a wife to him in every way. This I swear to you . . . if we—you and I—do not make love before then."

He did not widen the distance as he asked, "And what makes you think that isn't the easiest deal I've ever made?"

"Because you want me, Brett. I see it in your eyes, I feel it in the hardness of your body, and"—her smile, though malicious, was so charming that Brett pulled her even closer—"here, Brett," she continued, her groin pressing softly against his hard one. "And there will be no rules. No rules at all, Brett McCallum."

"Am I to assume that you will try your mightiest to seduce me?"

With a small, cynical laugh, she replied, "Seduce you, Brett McCallum? There will be no need. You want me; I know it."

Blast it! He wanted her even when she was slinging her insults and degradations. He had wanted her from the first time he'd seen her, wearing men's baggy clothing. He wanted her so badly that he had dreamed about her night after night after night, and had imagined as many times again what she looked like beneath that tight-fitting frock she wore. The more she had reviled him, the more he had wanted her.

And now would he be able to deny himself the pleasure of a seductive siren?

He thought not.

Now would be the best time to refuse to accept her challenge.

"All right, you've got a deal."

Fifteen

Paulina was so proud of herself. She couldn't have solved the problem of Brett McCallum and his puffed-up ego better if she'd spent a year working on it. Of course, she had no intention of allowing him to make love to her—nor would she want him to—and now she wouldn't have to worry about him even trying to get her alone. He would certainly avoid her like the plague, because he wanted her to marry his dying friend.

Which, of course, she had no intention of doing either. She felt sorry for the critically ill man, but not enough to be his wife. Perhaps by this time he'd found a pleasant, round-faced, willing woman to satisfy his needs. Paulina surely hoped so.

Now all that needed to be accomplished was the trip to find Millburn Hanks. She had no more problems facing her, and Brett had other things to concentrate on. Perhaps he, too, had found a woman to satisfy his male needs tonight.

Paulina grimaced, unsure why the picture forming in her mind displeased her so. She didn't want him for herself—she really didn't!—but she didn't like thinking that he might be lying in the arms of another woman just then. She remembered how she'd felt when he'd so willingly accepted the whore back in Skagway that had cost her the last two dollars to her name.

But who was she trying to kid? She'd thought about nothing else but Brett McCallum since the first day she'd seen him in Big Pat's Saloon, and she had dreamed an entire adventure about him, an adventure in which they had made sweet, wonderful love, and it still seemed so real to her. She could taste the sweetness of his kisses, feel the full strength of him filling her. The memory of his breath upon her cheek was as real as if he were there with her, that very minute, and they were pressed together, man and woman, about to be together again.

Her senses reeled, reminding her that she stood in the common parlor like some kind of daydreaming dolt. She was glad of the lack of audience, because she wasn't really sure how she would have explained herself. So, pulling a weary sigh deep into her lungs, her feet began to move again.

As Paulina crept into the women's sleeping quarters, she felt a little disheartened. She had wanted Brett McCallum to assume that she would rather die than make love to him; she had heard something recently about using reverse reasoning—and yet the very idea that he wouldn't so much as look at her *that way* made her miss the playful bantering already. Well, she'd just have to see what tomorrow brought.

Looking around the semidarkened chamber, she saw that women were sleeping peacefully—one even snored loudly enough to wake the dead. If at all possible, she would soon join them in slumber. Then she thought again about how her father's snoring, drifting toward her in those long-past years even through three walls, had kept her awake well into the predawn hours.

There were too many things conspiring to keep her

awake that night. Parted from her by a community room, Brett McCallum might also lie awake, staring at the ceiling, and trying like hell to figure out how Paulina Winthrop had gotten the best of him that night.

Slipping under the covers of the cot, she whispered, "Good night, Brett. Happy dreams."

But Brett was wide awake. Rather than retiring for the night as any reasonable traveler would, he had accompanied Walter McQuesten to the only tavern in Unalaska. There the two men sat, hunkered over two glasses and a whiskey bottle at a small corner table, talking about things that would only interest men.

Women . . .

"You say she's like no woman you've met before, McCallum? How is that?"

"Blast, Walt. You don't mind if I call you that, old man? Hell, the woman's just plain mean. And manipulative. Do you know how unattractive that is in a woman?"

"You like her very much, don't you?"

Brett looked up, a grin spreading his mouth. "I like everything about her. You know, I'm thirty-five years old and I always thought I'd die alone and unloved. A bachelor, I thought! But Paulina makes me doubt that I will. She has her own goals for her life, but I sure wish I were one of them. I'd leave Alaska—again—if I thought she wanted me. I wouldn't mind my woman being the marshal of a place called Turkey Gulch, Utah, even if I was wearing an apron behind a counter in the local drugstore."

McQuesten laughed. "You've got it bad, young fellow. And you don't appear the type who'd readily be admitting all this if you didn't have one too many under your belt."

Brett looked up, arching a dark eyebrow. "Think not, eh? Well—" Bringing up his glass he swallowed its contents in one gulp. "Let's see how much looser my tongue can get."

McQuesten was extremely thin, his lips much too large for his face. When he opened his mouth to accept a swallow of his drink, it appeared that the glass itself was being consumed. And every time he tipped back his head, his spectacles shifted toward his forehead.

Brett had been watching intently, and was a little surprised when McQuesten suddenly exclaimed, "Ahhh . . . I'm ready for another bottle. How about you, McCallum?"

"Did I tell you about my friend Gruff?"

McQuesten snapped his fingers, calling to the bartender, "Another bottle over here." Then to Brett he replied, "I don't believe you did. If it's a long story, we have all night."

"He's dying."

"I'm sorry." The bartender set down the fresh bottle, quickly departing. "Anything a good doctor could do for him?"

"Nah." Brett took the bottle and poured whiskey into both their glasses. "He's got something growing inside his head. Gruff refuses to leave Nuklukayet, and the only doctor there can't do anything but feed him enough opium to dull the pain. Still, ol' Gruff has his good days. And when he has those good days, he wants a woman."

"Any women in Nuklukayet?"

"Not any that ol' Gruff would take a second look at. I promised him I'd bring him one from Skagway."

"I haven't seen you with any woman but Miss Winthrop." A small light went on inside the anthropologist's head. "Oh, I see . . . you're taking Miss Winthrop to him. You're taking a woman to him that you want for yourself." When Brett's mouth pressed firmly, and no answer seemed forthcoming, McQuesten continued quietly. "And that's why you're here, drowning your sorrows in the bottle."

"I just don't know what to do, McQuesten," said Brett, his voice uncharacteristically melancholy. "I promised Gruff, but I don't want him to have Paulina. Hell! Tell me I'm a selfish bastard."

"No, you're just an unfortunate bastard in love."

"But the woman's impossible. Hell, I told you she was mean as the dickens. But it's my fault. I've lied to her and deceived her."

"I'd be willing to bet she's seen through you, McCallum. Deceiving a woman is like trying to sneak sunrise past a rooster."

The high-pitched voice of a small, jittery man suddenly drew their attention. He entered, slapped a few coins on the bar, and ordered a drink in a tone that contained more pomposity than a much larger man could have backed up. Then the man turned toward the other patrons in the bar and exclaimed, "I have a woman outside needing a man! Anyone here interested?"

A big, burly man laughed. "For the night, or do you mean forever?"

"Forever," said the squeaky-voiced man. "She came here to get married, but the man took one look at her and fell over dead."

The men in the bar mumbled among themselves, quietly echoing, "Not me . . . hell, no . . . get lost, buster. She must be one ugly fleabag."

Brett's curiosity got the best of him. He asked, "What interest do you have in the woman?"

The man picked up the drink he'd paid for and sauntered toward Brett. "My business is bringing women to Alaska for men who ain't got any. You interested?"

McQuesten interjected, "The woman must be god-awful ugly to keel a man over dead."

The female-broker, as he proudly called himself, replied, "Jes' the opposite. The woman's a real looker, an' the prospective husband had a bad heart. Got so excited thinkin' about the weddin' night that he dropped dead at the altar." Looking to McQuesten, he asked, "You interested?"

"Not me," he laughed, cutting his gaze to Brett. "How about you?"

"I got more woman than I can handle now," Brett said, shrugging. "But if I were interested, how much do you want for her?"

"Nothing. The fee was paid by the now-deceased Mr. Penny. I just didn't want to abandon the woman here. She ain't got no money."

McQuesten recognized the look in Brett's eyes. He'd seen that same look in the eyes of children running home with an abandoned puppy or kitten to plead for its reprieve. Leaning over the table, he said, "Now, McCallum, seems to me you've got enough trouble on your hands."

"Where is the woman?" asked Brett.

"On the boardwalk just outside."

"Could I talk to her?"

"Sure."

Brett stood, ignoring both a warning glance from McQuesten and a glum shaking of his head. Exiting the saloon, he found a petite, dark-clothed woman sitting on a whiskey keg, clutching a tattered canvas bag to her lap. He approached. "I understand you've got some problems." Pretty, wide brown eyes lifted to his own. "Could I talk to you for a minute?"

She nodded her head, and Brett, pulling up a stool, sat in front of her. He made no move to touch her, and let out a deep sigh as he prepared to speak.

Paulina finally sat up. She'd been trying for the past hour and a half to go to sleep, but the snoring of the heavyset lady beneath a quilt made that impossible. Slipping her feet into the coolness of her shoes, she took the blanket off her cot and moved from the room.

So sleepy was she that she didn't immediately see the man sitting beside a lamplit table reading a book. Nearly bumping into him, she drew slightly back, saying apologetically, "I'm terribly clumsy," and with a smile, "Do pardon me, sir."

The man might have been forty, though it was hard to tell. A gray-peppered goatee and mustache hinted at maturity, and yet there was not a single telltale line in a face strangely pale, as the face of the grim reaper might be if painted on a canvas. He smiled in return. "Couldn't sleep, could you? Not surprising. I can hear the lady's snoring all the way in here."

"I was looking for another place to sleep," she said, dragging the blanket close and hugging it to her. "Is there another room here where women sleep?"

"There is a small room over there," he responded, pointing. "I understand from the matron here that it is usually the maid's room, but she's away visiting a sick brother."

"Do you think she would mind?"

The man smiled. "I wouldn't think so."

As the man's smile lingered, Paulina was suddenly eager to be away from him. With a softly spoken "Thank you," she backed away, then turned and entered the small, darkened room. Very little moonlight permeated

248

the chamber, though she could see the dark outline of a small bed and a chest beneath the single window. The whole room smelled musky, but she thought that perhaps the snoring would be easier to live with here. Then, as quickly as she wondered whether she should leave, the odor subsided, and she was left with the need to sleep peacefully. So she approached the bed, drew back the covers, and sat down, quickly casting off her shoes and slipping into the bed. Dragging the quilt she'd brought with her over her slender frame, she snuggled down to begin her search for sleep.

A sound echoed nearby . . . a book closing, a lamp being snuffed by a quickly blown breath, booted footsteps upon the planked floor. Her eyes wide and cautious, she thought they approached the door of the room where she rested. But then they retreated and she breathed a sigh of relief. Though the man had seemed pleasant enough, he'd made her skin crawl and she hadn't liked the way a grin had played insidiously upon his mouth.

Now she regretted her impulse to find a quiet place to sleep. At least the presence of the other women provided some sense of security. She could have brought her canvas bag with her, and the gun that had been her father's. She felt vulnerable, stupid, idiotic.

Paulina lay awake for quite a few minutes, listening for the return of the footsteps. But as time passed, she began to relax, and the day's activities soon played upon her eyelids, forcing them down. She breathed lightly, trying to open her eyes now and then, but it was virtually impossible. Quite before she realized it, sleep was upon her.

Instantly, she returned to the Island of the Royal Crypt, to the cool, sandy beach, the deep, dark caverns and the amethyst walls glistening with beauty. She could hear the dog's playful barking as he splashed in the shallow currents of a pond. She could feel the warmth of the sun upon her features, and the breeze wafting coolly over her shoulders. Then his hands were there, easing up her arms to cover her shoulders, and his softly expelled breath tickled against her hairline.

He was the Brett she wanted, the tender, sensitive, loving one. Not that lustful brute taking her to Nuklukayet. She wanted the Brett who was a prince, not the one who was an insensitive ass. She wanted the Brett who whispered endearments against her ear, whose hands awakened her passions and whose body molded so perfectly to her own.

But conflicting emotions tugged within her. On the one hand, she felt the swell of happiness at being with whichever Brett happened to be around. But on the other hand, she felt that she was smothering, and that he was the one smothering her. She tried to come out of her dream, because she knew that she would die if she didn't. She could not breathe, and she could feel her heart beating more rapidly.

Paulina lurched from her sleep. The smothering had not been in her dream. Perched above her was the dark outline of a man's body, and across her mouth his hand pressed hard enough to cut her lips against her teeth. She tried to scream, but could manage nothing more than a soft whimpering sound. She would have struck him, but in her sleep he had pinned her wrists together and now used one of his strong hands to pin them at her side.

"Don't scream!" he warned between tightly clenched teeth. "I won't hurt you!" When she managed a tiny, trembling nod, the hand across her mouth loosened somewhat. But she dared not scream. "You tell McCallum that Gafferty is watching him. Do you understand me?" When she nodded once again, he pulled his hand away from her mouth an inch or so and ordered, "Who will you tell him is watching?"

In a strangled voice, she whispered, "Gafferty."

The hand covered her mouth again. "Now I'm going to slip out of here, and if you scream—" Rather than complete the threat, the sharp tip of a knife settled against the tiny pulse at the side of her neck. "Understand, lady?" Again she nodded, and as quickly as he'd been upon her, he disappeared into the outer room.

As Paulina drew in a long, trembling breath, she heard the echo of the assailant's boots leaving the house. When she was sure the unknown menace was well away, she flung herself from the bed and was quickly back in the room with the other women. There she dropped to her knees beside the empty cot and attempted to still her violent trembling.

"Dear Lord," she mumbled as warm tears rushed down her cheeks.

Brett entered the lodging house with McQuesten just after midnight. He felt light-headed from the whiskey he had consumed, and just irritable enough to have been rotten company for anyone other than the tolerant McQuesten. He was about to enter the gentlemen's quarters and seek a good night's sleep, when Paulina rushed from the ladies' area and into his arms quite before he could brace himself for the attack. He might have fallen had a wall not been conveniently at his back.

"What the hell—" His hands rose to roughly grip her arms, though he did not attempt to put her away from him. "I thought you were angry with me." Then he noticed the tears, felt the quaking of her body against his own, and his voice softened. "What's wrong,

Paulina?" When she failed to respond, he shook her, irritated by his own lack of self-control. "I asked you what the matter was!"

"A man—" was all she could manage to utter, and when he ripped her body from his own, so that their gazes might meet, she explained further. "I was sleeping over there because the snoring was keeping me awake." Her eyes motioned to the small servant's room. "A man came to me—"

Brett's eyes were suddenly as black as fury. "Did he hurt you? This man . . . who was he?"

"N-no, I am unhurt. He wanted me to give you a message."

"What message?"

Paulina drew in a deep, steadying breath and whispered, "He said to tell you that Gafferty is watching you."

Brett paled so visibly that McQuesten, eavesdropping from the doorway to the gentlemen's quarters, quickly approached. "Are you all right, McCallum?"

Brett could not move; his hands, firmly gripping Paulina's arms, were frozen in place. Even when she attempted to pry them loose, he could do nothing more than stare at her with ashen horror. Then she complained, "You're hurting me, Brett," and his fingers jerked open.

"You must be mistaken," he muttered, the horror deepening. "You must have gotten the name wrong."

"Gafferty," she sniffed, a little annoyed that he'd believe she could make such a mistake. "It's not a common name like Smith or Jones, but I did get it right."

"You can't have," he argued, his voice firmer now. When McQuesten would have dropped his hand to his forearm, Brett moved away from both of them. "It's impossible. It can't have been Gafferty." But even as the

252

words of argument spilled forth, Brett felt his past coming back to haunt him. He wasn't sure how it could be, but here was the horror being spoken as casually as an order at a restaurant. "Gafferty is watching you."

Paulina was now a little worried; she'd never seen his features so drained of color. She put her hand out, and when her fingers touched his arm, she felt him jerk away as if she'd startled him. Then she said, "Brett, you're frightening me . . . even more than he did," and his eyes moistened as they turned to face her. Only then did she see the agony etching his features. Only then did her heart go out to him so completely that she forgot the fright the man Gafferty had given her.

"Brett, who is this man? Why does the mention of his name have you so spooked?"

Brett turned his gaze to McQuesten and quietly said, "If anything happens to me, will you see Paulina—Miss Winthrop—to safety?"

"Of course," said a glum McQuesten.

Again Paulina rushed into his arms. "You're frightening me, Brett. Oh, why . . . why are you doing this?"

"Because—" His fingers pressed over her shoulders and drew her slightly away, betraying again the agony in his eyes. "You claim you were approached by a man named Gafferty and—" He hesitated, a tremble that he considered anything but manly settling in his voice. Drawing a deep breath, he continued. "This man is dead, Paulina. I know . . . I buried him myself eleven years ago."

"But perhaps he wasn't dead."

"He was!" Brett shook her, though his roughness instantly became a gentle caress.

"How can you be sure?" interjected McQuesten. "Perhaps the man wasn't dead."

"Because he laid in the July sun for three days before

253

I buried him. And you can imagine the condition he was in by that time."

Paulina shuddered, so revulsed was she by the picture forming in her mind. "Well, there has to be some explanation."

And McQuesten offered, "Yes, McCallum, there has to be."

But Brett wasn't so sure.

Three days later

In just a few hours the steamer *Iron Ice* would come into view of the Pribilof Islands. It would pick up passengers at St. George, then St. Paul, and would begin the last trek of the journey across the Bering Sea and dock, finally, at St. Michael.

Paulina was lonely. Except for McQuesten's occasional company, or a brief chat with another passenger, she'd seen very little of other people, especially Brett. He kept to himself, and often she found him standing at the ship's railing, staring out to sea. He had taken a separate cabin on this leg of the voyage—and she wasn't sure whether it was because of the challenge she had made or because he was worried about the man Gafferty, who had not been seen since that night. Paulina had decided that if this menace found a way to contact her again, she would not relay the message to Brett. She had missed him too much, especially at night. Before reaching Unalaska, she had lain in her cot and listened to him sleeping across the room from her. Yes, that is what she had missed most.

But her dreams were very much alive. Always, their adventures ended in lovemaking, and she had finally come to realize that there was nothing she wanted more than to be in Brett's arms, loving and being loved by him. Now the chance of this was dim. If it wasn't Gafferty sending him into his solitude, then it was her cruel challenge . . . and she wished to the almighty that she had never made it. She hadn't been worried about Brett's trying to make love to her; she had worried that he wouldn't.

She had been making casual conversation with the young mother of three children when she saw Brett enter his cabin a dozen yards down the deck. He had not seemed to see her; in fact, he'd seen very little of anything these past few days. Giving her polite excuses to the passenger, Paulina moved down the deck. Standing at the door to Brett's cabin, she knocked and immediately heard, "Come in."

He seemed surprised to see her. She stood in the doorway until he raised his hand, giving his permission for her to enter. "We'll soon be docking at St. George," she said, informing him of something he already knew. She wasn't quite sure what to say to him. "Do you know how long we'll be there?"

"Not long enough to disembark," he said a little stiffly. "Why? Did you need something?"

"No, Brett." Closing the door, she leaned gently against it. "I only need you to tell me what is wrong. I can't stand it when you don't talk to me. I would rather we were fighting than for you to be so silent."

"I'm sorry," he said, still aloof. "I don't mean to trouble you."

Silence. Paulina immediately thought how handsome he was. His hair was freshly washed, his shirt startlingly white against the deep blue of his trousers. He'd polished his boots recently, and the gleam of their toes matched the gleam of his eyes. Were it not for the angry press of his mouth, he would have stood a most appealing figure before her. But he seemed hard and cold, and she couldn't stand it.

"Would you rather I found another guide?" she asked, breaking the moment of silence.

To which he responded, "Why, for God's sake, would I want you to do that?"

Shrugging, she replied, "I just thought maybe you would."

With slow, deliberate steps, he closed the distance between them. When his hands rose to cover her shoulders, their caress was gentle, his forehead lowering to her own. He said nothing for a moment, but seemed content merely to hold her. Then he said, "Forgive me, Paulina. I don't mean to neglect you, and I certainly don't want you to think I would be willing to turn you over to another man. If you think for a moment I no longer want you—" His words faltered; his body stiffened and he drew away, almost as if he regretted his moment of weakness. "I told you I would see you all the way to the Yukon, and I will do just that. I might be many things—" He turned to face her now, a rather melancholy smile touching his mouth, "I might be everything you initially thought I was, but . . . I keep my word."

Giving him no warning, Paulina was in his arms, her head pressed against the wide expanse of his chest. "We have several hours before we reach St. George." Softly, seductively, she looked up. "Plenty of time, Brett, to"— again, she hesitated, but not even long enough to take a breath—"make love."

"So that you will not have to marry my friend Gruff?"

Dropping her head against his chest again, she hugged him tightly. "I will even do that, Brett. If you want me to marry Gruff, I will do it."

"I have your word?"

"My word," she murmured. "If I break it, may the breath leave my body and my heart cease to beat."

The silence suddenly roared like thunder. Paulina could hear the rhythmic thump, th-thump of Brett's heartbeat against her ear. Even as she closed her eyes, relishing the gentle nearness of him, she expected him to rip the door open and sling her out on deck. She mentally braced herself against just such a response, but as the moments slowly passed, she felt that so had the moment in which he might have done just that.

Then gently, slowly, fluidly, he swept her into his arms and held her, his eyes narrow yet soft, his mouth full and unsmiling, the taut muscles of his arms cradling her slender form.

And he turned toward the small, narrow cot.

Sixteen

Brett's knee touched the bed. Motionless, he held Paulina for moments that seemed like hours, the only movement the darting of his eyes as they swept back and forth over her features. Then another movement, one totally inappropriate: a smile turned up the corners of his full mouth.

"Thought I would fall for it, did you?" he asked in an even, husky whisper. "Thought I had let my brains drop below the beltline?"

She was at first too stunned to react. Then, as his words fully soaked in, she struggled from his arms, her buttocks first hitting the bed, then her feet the floor. She wanted to scold him, to sling insults and, of course, denials, but her brains were, thank heaven, hanging in there between her ears. A smirk caught upon her mouth and, righting herself, she drew her hands to her hips. She would not—could not—admit that she'd never been more sincere in all her life. She truly wanted to be with him, and if it had been his wish afterward, she would still have married his dying friend.

But at the moment she could not think of anything clever enough to save face, so she pivoted smartly, drawing up her skirts as she did so, and began a retreat from his smiling countenance. Only when her fingers circled the doorknob did he suddenly loom behind her, his hand covering her own. "I am right, aren't I?" His words were softer now, free of the sarcasm. "You were trying to win your wager?"

Even as she wanted to laugh, to sling a very humiliating "Yes, of course!" at him, neither the emotion nor the words would come. She stood there, feeling very much the idiot, and quietly said, "What does it matter? You've made it very clear that you don't want me. I can accept that."

With a firm hand he forced her to face him, his fingers easing beneath her chin to coax her gaze to his own. But although her face lifted, her eyes remained downcast. "You know that I have been worried sick these past few days—and you know why. But Paulina, when I held you in my arms just moments ago, you were the only thing on my mind." Still, her eyes did not rise, and now her mouth slightly trembled. "Blast it, woman, I'm sick and tired of always having to fight with you. Every time we're together, it seems to be a challenge of wills, a challenge to see who can best who. If I thought we could be together, love each other, and it could be for no other reason but mutual pleasure, I'd have you on that bed so fast, you wouldn't be able to catch a breath."

Finally, she was able to respond. "Just like any other woman, Brett?"

Irritation gathering inside forced him to shake her gently. "No, not just like any other woman! I would already have had any other woman! You are different. Paulina—" Instantly, his words softened, and he pulled her to him. "Blast it, I've taken care of the problem of Gruff. I met a woman our last night in Unalaska and she's aboard this vessel this very minute, going to Nuk-

259

lukayet to marry Gruff. I saw you talking to her yesterday in the dining salon."

Paulina looked up, disbelief marking her features. "You mean Miss Perkins?"

"Yes, Miss Perkins. She came north to marry, and the man she would have married died. She was stranded, so I paid her passage to St. Michael, and she will travel with us to Nuklukayet—"

"I don't believe you."

Putting her slightly away from him, he stretched out his hand. "Then go ask her. She's in Cabin Twelve."

"But you don't have any money."

Instantly his hand came up from his pocket with a gold money clip holding what appeared to be several hundred dollars together. "Just don't ask how. I have my ways."

"I'd imagine gambling booty," she said. "Isn't that how men like you usually get money?"

He shrugged, turning away from her to tuck the money back into his pocket. "Since I'm a liar, cheat, and gambler, why don't you go find other company? I'll get some sleep before we come into port."

This sudden mood of indifference didn't sit well with her. She quickly covered the short expanse of floor and stood between him and the bed. "I just happen to get along quite well with liars, cheats, and gamblers, Brett McCallum. And in case you've forgotten, I get along quite well with princes too."

This last statement evoked a smile from him. He took her arms and pulled her to him. Strangely, she did not attempt to separate from him. "You never did tell me if we made love in that dream of yours." When her mouth pressed into a defiant line, he shook his head knowingly. "I thought so." Then, "Did I seem to enjoy myself?"

She wouldn't give him the satisfaction of an answer.

Rather, she turned, sauntering toward the door as though he hadn't spoken at all. When she did eventually speak, she might have been remarking about the weather, so casual was her tone. "Do you think that when we reach St. George I might be able to purchase a few toiletries, soap, and a new toothbrush . . . perhaps a bottle of cologne? I promise to send the necessary money back to you when I return to Turkey Gulch."

"I believe I said we won't be able to disembark. But if there's a trading post, I could ask the captain to pick up a few things. I heard him remark that he has to meet a company officer for a few minutes."

She turned, tucked her hands into the small of her back, and leaned gently against the door. "That would be nice. Thank you. I'll go to my cabin right away and make a short list." Then, with tears beginning to form on her lower eyelids, she quickly opened the door and fled from him.

Too quickly, in fact, for Brett to call her back. He had seen her eyes glistening like sun-touched emeralds, her mouth trembling ever so slightly, the way her slender form had tensed as she'd pulled the door open. Placing a damp palm to his forehead, he ground it back and forth several times, then turned to the small cot. *Blast it, Paulina! What am I to make of you?*

He pondered it for a moment, then sat on the bed, slapping his palms to his knees as he continued to think. Why weren't there any answers? Why was she so cold and cryptic one moment and so warm and tender the next? She made him dizzy wondering from one moment to the next what to expect from her.

And all the while his body reacted physically—and painfully—to the sensual nearness he had shared with her just moments before, a nearness that could have been blessedly fulfilling if only he had allowed it, if only he had broken down his defenses and allowed her to get the better of him.

Well, one thing was for certain, he knew, rising sharply to his feet. He owed her an apology, and by George, before another two minutes passed, he was at least going to give her that.

When he exited onto the deck, he saw many passengers hanging over the rail, watching a great herd of humpback whales move gracefully through the sea. There, half a dozen people down the deck, stood Paulina, and when her gaze turned suddenly to his, she turned and quickly entered her cabin, shutting the door behind her. Scarcely had ten seconds passed before Brett was knocking on the door.

"Go away," she said from the interior. "We have nothing to say."

"Can we talk?" he asked softly, a little embarrassed that someone might overhear. When a gentleman turned to stare at him, he turned his back and scowled, "Let me in, blast it, or I'll tear the door down."

Silence. He heard shuffling from within and then the door opened. As he entered, she turned her back to him and marched toward the cot, dropping to it with a very impolite, "Harumph!" Then, "What do you want, Brett McCallum?"

His glare was almost contemptuous. Drawing a breath surely meant to return a small degree of self-control, he replied, "You're the most exasperating woman I've ever known."

Paulina fell back, supporting herself on her elbows. Her feet kicked out in an almost childlike way. "My goodness, did you come down here just to tell me that?"

Instantly, the groaning of the steam engines, the laughter of children out on deck, the incessant rumble of human voices, seemed to cease to exist. Brett could hear nothing but her sarcasm, see nothing but the smirk upon her mouth, and feel nothing but a boiling of fury from deep within. If she had meant to rile him, she had done just that, because his self-control went the way of a brutal wind, and he was immediately before her, dragging her up from her cot. "I came to tell you that I was sorry for the way I treated you, but you know what, *Miss* Winthrop. I think I'd rather die first."

"Be my guest!" she snarled. "But do it somewhere else! I don't want your decomposing corpse stinking up my cabin!"

"I don't plan to decompose!" he shot back with equal ferocity. "I plan to become a zombie—a walking dead man—and every time you turn around for the rest of your life, I'll be there!"

Puzzled shock registered, but only for a moment. "I've never heard of any such abomination!" When she attempted to break his hold, his grip tightened. "If you don't let me go, a certain part of your anatomy will feel anything but pleasure!"

"Is that right?" With an ugly smirk he threw her backward to the cot, immediately falling atop her. "Go ahead, draw that knee up now! If you can!"

His fury was as dark as night, and somehow it took away the insults and the sarcasm. Her lips parted, but she could not reply. The very nearness of him was doing something to her—even his heated words affected her in a way that she could not explain. Where she should have felt cold and repulsed inside, she felt a river heating and a wrenching in her heart that was almost painful, but wonderfully so.

She saw, too, the immediate change in his mood. His gaze had not wavered from her own, but it had softened, then hardened, then softened again as though he were fighting demons inside. She knew he did not do it deliberately, but the assailing pressure of his body against her own had slackened, though it was still imprisoning, and his hands, just moments before roughly pinioning her wrists, had begun, instead, to caress them.

Paulina watched, bewildered by her own emotions, as a glaze she could not recognize captured his eyes. If she'd been required to speak just then to save her life, she would not have been able to accomplish it. She was so lost in the raw masculinity of him that all their bitterly bantered insults couldn't have been less important.

Brett knew only that he felt a warmth ignoring the threads of their clothing and intoxicating him all the way through. He could feel the softness of her breasts burning into him like fire. He expected that at any moment their clothing would ignite and burn away, leaving their bodies pressed together without rude barriers.

Paulina felt her breath coming in small gasps. When her mouth rose, so that she might feel the softness of his own, she knew she was trembling violently, but she could not control it any more than she could push him away. Then her knee rose, her thigh pressed to his hard, muscular one, and she found her now-freed hands wantonly traveling to his back, dragging up his shirt and exploring the moisture-sheened muscles.

Their kisses were shared with fierce craving, again and again, bruisingly, caressingly, taking away their breath in one fluid sweep. A storm swept them together, and when a groan erupted deep within Brett's throat, she felt the simultaneous seeking of his hands beneath the hems of her skirts. As her hips rose against him, as his rough fingers dipped into the honeyed warmth of her, she washed into the sea of passion, all emotions gone except the one that compelled—demanded—that her body be sated completely, uninhibitedly, mesmerizingly sated.

Taking the front of her gown in his gentle hands, Brett eased the stays apart, immediately drawing a sweet, tender breast into his mouth to taste it, to savor its softness . . . from one to the other with lusty intensity, and the pain consumed him, body and soul, as her rapidly drawn breaths and erotic thrusts of her body against him made the hasty removal of his trousers an inconvenience that again ripped a growl from him.

When the maleness of him was no longer restricted by the threads of his trousers, he positioned himself against her . . . there . . . taking a moment to rip down the offending barriers of her underthings to cast them aside like rubbish. A single stay held her gown together at her waist, and he used his teeth to unfasten it. Then he again pinned her wrists above her shoulders and fiercely, brutally, roughly claimed another kiss. "Tell me—" he murmured. "Do you want me, Paulina?" But even before she could possibly have answered, partial penetration was accomplished, and her momentary gasp of shock and horror and dread-filled anticipation invaded his mouth as he took from her the sweetest of kisses.

Paulina was so enflamed by what was happening to her that she could not have slung him off even if she had wanted to. She cared only that his eyes were soft and lustrous, his mouth possessively claimed her own, and that his hands had now eased beneath her back to bring her passion-sensitized breasts against the hardness of him.

She knew this man, knew his movements, his techniques in the art of lovemaking because she had been with him before, on the Island of the Royal Crypt, and because of the erotic reality of her dream, she was not afraid as the fullness of him eased deeper and deeper into her. She welcomed him, closing her eyes so that his kisses could trail over her eyelids, the fiery warmth of her cheeks, returning to capture her mouth in small, teasing kisses. All the while she waited for the pain, so that it could be over and she would be free to enjoy this tantalizing naughtiness with him.

Then, just as she wondered if it would ever happen, he drove into her with brutal force and she was seized by a wave of tremors. But the pain lasted no longer than the blink of an eye, not even long enough to shed a single tear, and she arched her hips to accept him fully, to enjoy the male stroking of him within her.

As he gyrated against the delicate spread of her hips, Brett's fingers tunneled through Paulina's thick wheat-colored hair, drawing it to his mouth to feel its softness. Gathering its masses to her shoulders, he patiently settled them there, like brilliant bursts of sun penetrating the clouds. The muscles of his body jerked, and his hips thrust deeper and deeper still, so that as he felt the explosive culmination collecting within him—and within her own hips that easily matched his racing rhythm and pace—his hands circled her thighs, to press them hard against him.

Then, even as they both wished the lovemaking would go on forever, never ending, Paulina was quickly filled with the joy of him. With a tiny moan she accepted his gentle kiss, and as his palms rose to cradle her head, his cheek rested lightly against her own. The erotic pulsating of his seed as it filled her seemed to go on without end, even when they lay clinging together, unable to withdraw from each other's arms, even as Brett's sharp masculine features seemed suddenly to be chiseled in stone against her smooth, damp ones.

His rapid breathing slowed; Paulina, too, tried to recapture her lost ability to breathe. She could imagine nothing more wonderful than Brett easing upward on the cot, then gathering her to him so that they might lie together in the aftermath of their love, and she waited for him to make the move.

But it did not happen. Just as quickly as the passion had come upon them, culminating in their lovemaking, he was now withdrawing from her. Shocked, her feelings a little hurt by what appeared to be his indifference, she saw nothing at first but his hard, dark features, and his eyes that were deliberately turned away from her.

Then her gaze lowered and a gasp ripped from her throat. She had never imagined a man's maleness to be so large, especially after it had been sated, and she quickly clamped her eyes shut. When she ventured to open them again, he had pulled up his trousers and was now refastening his belt.

A strangeness glazed his eyes; a mixture of regret, intense pain, and an emotion she could not read, but that embarrassed her. Instinctively, Paulina's hands moved to gather to her the bodice of her gown, and then to sweep her skirts down over her nakedness. Tears collected in her eyes as she sat forward, only now realizing what had happened. She had made love to this wild, reckless Alaskan rogue standing before her, straightening his appearance with outrageous apathy.

When she buried her face in her hands, he turned sharply to her, growling, "What the hell is wrong with you?" And when she began to weep, he was immediately on one knee before her, attempting to pry her hands away. "Don't you think if I could recapture these past moments that I wouldn't have let this happen?"

She sniffed back her tears. "But why?" she asked with childlike innocence. "I wanted to make love to you, Brett. I truly did. And—"

When she hesitated, he asked in a softer tone, "And what?"

267

"I don't understand how you could withdraw from me as you might withdraw from a whore you had paid. I thought we would lie together, holding each other, enjoying a few moments and—" Shrugging gently, her eyes closed. "Savoring the warmth and comfort of each other."

"Romantic notions!" he growled, immediately regretting the outburst. To make up for it, his fingers gently entwined among her own and he drew them against his mouth, kissing each at the place where a ring might have been worn. "I failed you," he offered after a moment. "All I cared about was satisfying myself. I didn't think that—" Guiltily, he looked up, catching the puzzled gleam of her emerald eyes. "I should have taken it slower, since it was your first time."

She wondered how he knew, what telltale signs she or her body had given him. Had it been the momentary pain that had fragmented upon her features? Or had it been her ineptness and inexperience? To think that it was the latter embarrassed her deeply. "I'm sorry—it is my fault. You'd think that at my age I would know how to please a man."

He chuckled as his arms circled her, his cheek resting in the warmth between her breasts. "Blast it, woman. Don't make me humble myself. Don't make me admit that you are the best thing that has ever happened to me." Then in a softly masculine tone he added, "I promise, Paulina, the next time it will be better. The next time I will pleasure you as you have never been pleasured. The next time I will have you soaring among the clouds, and wondering if you will ever again return to earth."

Her hand falling gently to his thick, dark hair, Paulina touched a kiss to his forehead. "All these promises, Brett McCallum, my rogue and my guide. Aren't you afraid you might break them? Suppose I am a cold, heartless woman who cannot truly enjoy a man's love.''

He looked up quickly, his face frozen between bewilderment and a slight smile. ''There is nothing cold about you, Paulina,'' he was finally able to say. ''Take me into your lair anytime, and I will be your willing slave.''

''You know, Brett McCallum, that I don't like you one bit.''

''Yes, you do,'' he argued with deep feeling, his cheek pressing lightly to her tawny head. Then he drew back, so that their gazes might meet.

His smile was warm and friendly; and Paulina saw something gathering in the rich depths of his eyes.

She knew in her heart what she hoped it might be. . . . Love.

Gafferty stood in the recess of the dining salon, watching the door that had swallowed Brett McCallum whole. He imagined that in the time that had elapsed he could have fornicated with the woman half a dozen times. She was a pretty thing, he had to admit, but Gafferty wanted Brett to suffer pain, not enjoy the pleasures of the flesh.

Gafferty had been careful to avoid being seen, either by the woman or the man who was his blackest foe. He would stalk him like the panther stalking the hare, and at the end of the hunt Brett McCallum would be the one lying dead. He, too, would feel the scorching warmth of the sun for three days before his putrid flesh was thrown into a hole. Gafferty had waited eleven years to wreak his vengeance, and he would do it with slow, methodical calculation.

Seeing Brett McCallum exit into the evening light, Gafferty drew back into the recess, pulling up the collar of his leather coat. He hated the man, hated the fact that the past eleven years had treated him kindly, hated that McCallum had enjoyed his life when he himself had not. He'd change all that, even if it killed him—again.

Watching Brett move in the opposite direction and soon disappear from sight, Gafferty eased from his hiding place. In a matter of moments he stood outside the door, hiding the woman from him, then raised his knuckles and gently knocked. From the inside the woman's voice called, "Come in, Brett."

Gafferty wasted no time in entering, closing the door behind him. The woman—he knew by eavesdropping here and there that her name was Paulina—stood with her back to him, her hands busy before her straightening her possessions in a narrow sea chest. Patiently, he waited there, and when she finally turned, he grinned with macabre intimidation, the knife he had held to her throat just days ago now plucking at the dirt beneath his fingernails. In the moment that shock registered and as she might be preparing to scream, he warned, "I could open a vein, Miss Paulina, before a single sound escaped your lips."

Paulina, indeed horrified, backed toward the chest, eventually landing with full force upon it. "Wh-what do you want . . . Gafferty."

"You gave McCallum my message?" he inquired, the pale drone of his voice scarcely requiring an answer. The only one she could offer was a slight nod, and he continued in his same tone. "Good. And I suppose he told you that I am dead?"

"He told me that he buried you, but of course, that cannot be possible. Can it?"

"I don't look dead, do I?"

Actually, he was an extremely sallow man except for the tips of his ears, and the tender skin of his mouth, which had a bluish tint. He appeared frail, but Paulina instantly remembered how strong he had seemed holding her down upon the bed just a few nights ago. Gripping the edges of the sea chest between fingers almost as white as his own, Paulina managed to say, "Whatever is between you and Brett McCallum is none of my business. I would thank you to leave my cabin posthaste, and not to bother me again."

Gafferty chuckled, approached, and settled onto the edge of the cot, just a foot or so from where Paulina sat. Instantly, she came to her feet, but his hand dashed out, capturing her wrist. "Mighty brave, eh, little lady? How'd you get tied up with a man like McCallum?"

"He's taking me to"—her words instantly faltered; dare she betray to this antagonist her—their—destination?—"to find a man who was a friend of my father's." Her heart raced frantically, like the fragile wings of a hummingbird escaping the prowls of a cat.

When he felt the tremble vibrating through her soft skin, Gafferty observed, "Good, you're afraid of me, little lady," then released her wrist. "As well you should be." He came to his feet, resuming the task of picking at his nails with the knife. "I would suggest that if you don't want to see McCallum die, that you part company real quick-like."

Lifting a defiant chin, Paulina said, "Why are you telling me this? You know I will tell him that you're aboard this ship. You know that I will warn him of your malice and your threat. So if you truly mean him harm, why don't you wish to strike without warning rather than giving him notice through your intimidations of me?"

"Because I want him to be real scared. I want him to know I'm watching and waiting for my chance. That's why."

Paulina knew not from where the courage came. "I

don't believe you're this man Gafferty. I believe you've heard something about Brett's past and that you're using it to get to him. Perhaps you have a vendetta against him, but you're not Gafferty!"

In one surprisingly swift move the man's hand went into and out of his jacket. When he grabbed Paulina's wrist again, she dared not move, because the full length of the razor-sharp knife now rested against the tender flesh of her arm. Squeezing her wrist to force her hand open, he dropped a gold medallion and chain onto her palm. "You give this to McCallum, little lady, and you ask him where he last saw it."

She flung it back. "Give it to him yourself!" Tipping his hat in a short, sarcastic manner, he turned, tucked the knife into a sheath at his belt, the medallion into his pocket, and exited the cabin.

Paulina heard him begin to whistle. Frozen in place, she listened as the sound disappeared into the distance.

Was he, indeed, using her to get to Brett?

Or was she the true victim of this sick, demented man?

Seventeen

Paulina was surprised by her own calm as she sought out Brett in the dining salon. When she called him aside, he seemed a little annoyed at having to leave the company of the men to whom he was talking. Still, he smiled pleasantly when they were alone at another table. "I thought you were going to take a nap before we docked, Paulina?" Then, before she could respond, "Are you hungry?"

"No," came her immediate answer. "Brett—" She hesitated, looking into his eyes for a moment, then down for a much longer length of time. Twisting a handkerchief against the folds of her gown, she informed him, "Gafferty sought me out in my cabin just moments after you left."

A most intimidating span of silence followed. Brett's only visible response was the stilling of his chest as he seemed to hold his breath. When he did not otherwise respond, Paulina looked up. Only then did he heatedly ask, "What game are you playing, Paulina? I don't believe you've ever seen Gafferty. Did Obadiah tell you about him in Skagway? He's the only one who knew about Gafferty . . . and Obadiah knows as well as I do that he's dead. He helped me bury him that day."

Shock registered as fully as if she'd suddenly been slapped. Her body drew taut and she bristled back at him, "What do you mean? What could I possibly have to gain, Brett McCallum, from making up this . . . this antagonist?" She wished she'd kept Gafferty's medallion now.

"I have no bloody idea." Darkness hung upon his brow like a storm brewing, threatening to release its fury on a peaceful world. "The next time you mention Gafferty to me, you're on your own."

With that final word—and a stupefied Paulina looking on—he shot to his feet and joined the men, his mouth easing into a tentative smile just as if nothing had happened.

As she arose and left the dining salon; tears clinging to her lower eyelids, Brett McCallum did not so much as cast a look in her direction.

Three hours later Paulina watched Brett move along the gangplank with the captain. She knew they'd be in port at St. George for only an hour, and from what she could see of the settlement, which served mostly fur traders, all that was there could be viewed in half that time. There was, though, a small trading post, but she couldn't imagine that Brett would pick up the items she'd asked for now that he was so angry with her. Perhaps he was seeking a change of pace from the boat, a luxury the other passengers were not being afforded.

But he surprised her. Not only did he bring her the soap and other items she'd asked for, but he came early to her cabin the following morning, when they were well under way to St. Michael, and invited her to take breakfast with him. Though he was cordial, there was a tension between them thick enough to fog spectacles, if either were wearing any. She had very little appetite for what might otherwise have been a satisfying breakfast of ham, eggs, biscuits, and cold milk. Her attempts to converse with Brett were met by short, cryptic replies or vague silences, so she gave up, leaving the table without touching her plate. As she exited the dining room, she saw him jabbing at her uneaten portions with his fork.

She'd had just about enough of his unwarranted accusations. So she sought out the captain, a round man with ruddy, smiling features, who was more than willing to put aside his present duties to answer her inquiries.

"A Mr. Gafferty? Miss Winthrop, I don't remember such a name on the passenger manifest. Tell me, what did he look like? Perhaps he is known by another name?"

"A thin, sallow man, about forty or forty-five. His hair was light brown, not very thick, but long—to his shoulders. And he has a silly little goatee."

Captain Johns pressed his brows into a thoughtful frown. "I just don't recall such a man, Miss Winthrop." Then, patting her wrist comfortingly, he added, "But I'll keep an eye out for this phantom passenger."

She knew then, from his referral to Gafferty as a "phantom" and by his paternal, condescending smile that Brett had already filled him in. Perhaps he had asked the captain about him and, receiving the same reply, had told him of Paulina's claiming to have seen such a man. A little embarrassed by her own suppositions, Paulina excused herself and returned to her cabin.

But she sat there for only a moment before realizing that she wanted to be anything but alone. So she again left the cabin, and soon knocked on the one occupied by the young lady known to her only as Miss Perkins. She suddenly felt an overwhelming guilt that she'd never cared enough to ask her first name.

She heard an emotional "Do come in" from the interior, and entered the cabin. Miss Perkins, sitting on the bed, suddenly straightened, and her fingers, pressing upon a single sheet of paper, eased beneath the ruffles of her skirt.

Paulina saw that she had been crying. Quietly, she approached, then sat upon the cot beside her, gently taking her hand. "Would you like to talk?"

Rather than respond, Miss Perkins asked, "How old do you think I am?"

With a smile Paulina replied, "I would say thirty, perhaps thirty-two—"

"I'm forty-five," came the petite lady's response. "And it's not *miss*. I suppose by law I'm a Mrs., although my husband and I have been divorced for many years."

"What is your first name?"

"Ruth."

"Well, Ruth, if you want a husband, I see nothing to cry about. Brett mentioned to me that his friend Gruff is fairly close to fifty, and"—Paulina closed her fingers over Ruth's slim hand—"you are a woman who, I believe, will greatly please one of these rough Alaskan males. But I suspect you are running away from something. Won't you tell me what it is?"

Without hesitation, Ruth replied, "My daughter."

"Oh?" Then, "Don't you love her?"

Withdrawing her hand, Ruth moved to her feet, losing the sheet of paper she'd been hiding against her gown. Bending to pick it up, she held it almost lovingly to her breast. "She is the dearest thing to my heart. I would have given my life for her. I still would. But—" Shrugging, she continued, the tears gathering once again in her brown eyes. "She doesn't love me. Since her marriage she has wanted nothing to do with me. She feels that once a woman marries, she has no need of her

276

former family. I've tried to adjust to her indifference and her lack of care for me, or for any member of our family. But—" Ruth's hand eased out, and she held it there until Paulina took the sheet of paper. When Paulina hesitated to read it, Ruth prompted her. "Go ahead. Read it. Then you will understand why I can no longer go through this with my daughter. It is best to break all ties. It is best that she and I never see each other again."

Paulina felt that she was imposing, but at Ruth's insistence, she read the letter supposedly written by her daughter. It was, indeed, a hateful letter, accusing the mother of spreading lies through the family and saying that her two-year-old daughter—Ruth's granddaughter—was horrible and destructive. She had accused the mother of being on the warpath, of "spreading boundaries," whatever that meant, and then, cruelly, coldly, and callously telling her that "it's best that we keep our distance." Finally, the daughter informed the mother—and Paulina could almost hear the vicious sarcasm in the words—that a second grandchild would be born in the spring. With tears gathering in her own eyes, Paulina handed the letter back to Ruth. Shuddering, she replied, "If this is what a mother can expect of her grown children, I don't think I'll ever have any. Ruth, I am so sorry."

Quietly, Ruth returned to the cot, then gathered Paulina's hands between her own. "Please, don't let my sadness upset you. I should never have imposed my troubles on you. I just want to be as far away from Minnesota as I can get."

Instantly, Paulina thought of Walter McQuesten, since he, too, was from Minnesota. "Don't you think things might get better with your daughter, Ruth?"

With a regretful smile Ruth replied, "Perhaps, one day, but . . . it's too late. I no longer trust her. I cannot take her viciousness any longer. I have to think about myself now." Immediately, Ruth's tone brightened. "So, do you think Gruff will still want me when he finds out that I'm a middle-aged woman who can't even maintain a relationship with her grown daughter?"

Paulina laughed. "I do believe he will. A good man looks into the heart. He does not look at age or at background. You have a good heart, Ruth, and Gruff is a good man."

"Oh? You've met him?"

"No, but—" Paulina looked deeply into Ruth's eyes, trying to see the passage of time that would hint at forty-five years. There were no telltale lines, no dark circles, only a tiny little line between her eyebrows that might have taken root through sadness. Paulina knew then that Ruth would be a very good friend, and she had someone to confide in when Brett proved to be too much to handle. So, withdrawing her hand, then patting Ruth's, she continued quietly. "If he's a friend of Brett's, he's got to be a good man."

"And with him I will make a new life for myself, and I'll be the best possible wife. If we are married for half a century, he will never regret that he married me."

A puzzled frown etched into Paulina's pale brow. She looked into Ruth's sad but expectant eyes, wondering if she'd heard her correctly. Surely Brett had— Oh, but of course he had. He must have! For a moment she cut her eyes downward, fearing that Brett had not told Ruth what she had every right to know. With that firm conviction deeply imbedded within her, she looked up again. "Ruth, Brett did tell you that Gruff is dying, didn't he? That he has less than a year to live?"

She did not hesitate to respond. "Yes, he told me."

"But you just said—"

"I know what I said, Paulina. A woman can hope, can't she?"

Paulina had never seen so much strength in so fragile a woman. An eternity of admiration gathered inside her for this determined, indomitable woman. With renewed gaiety she replied, "Certainly, she can."

"And Mr. McCallum? Do you love him as I suspect that you do?"

Lowering her eyes, Paulina easily responded, "Yes, with all my heart."

Brett McCallum felt like the dog biting the hand that fed it. He loved Paulina—that was a revelation he had just forced himself to admit—and he knew that she cared for him, perhaps even loved him in return. He had absolutely no doubt that she had indeed been visited twice by a man who had described himself as Gafferty, but he had a reason for the false accusation he had made against her. If this "phantom" was attempting to make himself known through Paulina, perhaps he would stop if, the next time, she admitted to him that Brett had accused her of lying. His only way to protect Paulina was to hurt her, and by hurting her he hurt himself even more deeply.

But he had to maintain the façade of ire if he was to protect her from this menace unseen by everyone except her.

Brett had seen her leave the dining salon, and even across the dim space he had noticed the gleam of tears in her eyes. After she'd exited he'd sought out a waiter and had asked him to box the breakfast she had not eaten.

Now he moved along the deck with the paper-lined box held carefully in his hands. When he stood outside her cabin door, he knocked, but she did not respond. So he moved toward the rail and watched the tossing sea along with other passengers. Time passed, a few seconds, or a few minutes, perhaps even an hour, he wasn't sure, and he did not turn when he saw her exit Ruth Perkins's cabin and quickly enter her own without ever having seen him standing there. He gave her a moment, then knocked and was surprised when she immediately jerked the door open. He managed to look a little guilty when she sniffed back tears.

Holding out the box, he said, "I had a waiter salvage your breakfast. I want you to eat it."

She pivoted smartly, soon settling onto the cot with her back to him. "I am not hungry."

"I insist that you eat it."

"You are not my father."

The door closed. His booted feet began to move, halting beside her. The box was gently placed upon her lap. "Eat it."

"And what will you do if I don't?" Still, Paulina did not look up. "Beat me?"

His shrug went undetected by her. "Now, that would be a new experience for me."

Giving him no time to brace himself, Paulina threw the box aside, shot up and was immediately in his arms. "Why are you such a brute, Brett McCallum? One minute I think you truly care for me, and the next you are calling me a liar and treating me just like"—she fought for the words—"like an irritating little sister. Don't you care for me, Brett? Oh, don't you?" Emotion had eased into her softly spoken entreaties, and Brett was quite at a loss for words. "I just don't know why I should care though," she continued after a moment. "When you've taken me to Millburn, I probably won't ever see you again. You'll probably delight in putting as much distance between us as possible."

Suddenly, the one porthole blazed with morning light as the ship turned into the sun, and Paulina's features were illuminated. She closed her eyes, and a tear broke from her lower lid to begin its gentle travels along the smooth contour of her cheek. Instinctively, Brett's finger moved to catch it, and she turned her face from his touch.

"Don't do this, Paulina." He had the gall to sound pained . . . and innocent of all wrongdoing.

She would not allow him to turn the tables and make her the villain—or villainess. "Do what?" she finally answered, disguising her grief in the high pitch of her voice.

Brett McCallum released a harsh groan. "Don't shut me out."

She spun back, surprised. "Shut you out? You've got to be out of your small, ignorant mind, Brett McCallum. If anything, I've tried to include you in everything. I have kept no secrets from you. And what have I gotten for my honesty and forthrightness? Accusations, unfounded accusations!"

A frown abruptly claimed his features; guiltily, he looked away from her. "I'm sorry."

He could easily have said *Drop dead,* so indifferent was his tone. Before she could catch herself, her palms landed upon his shoulders, pushing him back. "Get out, Brett. Just get out of my sight! You and I have nothing to say to each other."

And so the last word was left at that. For the following two days, until they reached St. Paul Island, Paulina avoided all Brett's attempts to be civil, or to make amends. Her scathing looks had followed him like Captain Ahab on the trail of Moby Dick. If he didn't love her, he wouldn't care how she treated him.

But—and he silently groaned as he admitted it—he had missed her, in more ways than one.

Brett slept through the docking at St. Paul, where they picked up a handful of passengers bound for St. Michael. When the steamer was again under way, he gave the *Iron Ice* an hour to ply her way into the open sea before venturing out on deck. He had skipped breakfast and now his stomach was snarling its protests at being denied food. He entered the dining salon, took a plate, and went through the buffet, taking portions of the most appetizing offerings, then moved through the tables toward the captain's table. "Mind if I join you?"

Captain Johns jovially replied, "Have a seat, Mr. McCallum. I just sat down myself. The cook outdid himself this morning."

Brett scrutinized the captain's plate. If he'd just sat down, he was a speedy eater, because his food was half eaten. Placing his knife and fork at his right side, Brett began salting and peppering his food. "How long until St. Michael?" he asked.

"With no mishap, a week. We should be in sight of the mainland within three days."

"Good. I'll be glad to get back home to Nuklukayet. And I'm sure Miss Winthrop is getting tired of the ship—"

"Miss Winthrop! What do you mean?"

"She's been short-tempered. I believe she needs to get her land legs back."

"I believe Miss Winthrop has gotten a jump on you there, Mr. McCallum. She left ship at last docking."

Brett, who had just taken his first bite of food, now choked on it. Balling his fist, he hit himself in mid-

282

chest. "What do you mean? Surely it wasn't Miss Winthrop. There were no plans to leave ship at St. Paul."

"She left, sir."

Brett bit his tongue to still the annoyance he felt at the captain's indifferent tone. "Did she leave alone?"

"Another woman was with her."

Coming to his feet, he knocked his chair over, though a swiftly moving hand caught it before the floor did. Other passengers, looking on, were ignored. His booted feet quickly traversed the planked floor, and within moments he was knocking at Ruth Perkins's door. Surprised to hear her say "Come in," he pulled the door open.

"I was told you'd departed ship at St. Paul with Miss Winthrop."

"Not me," Ruth answered, swinging her feet to the floor. "She has left? She said nothing."

"Damn!" Brett's hand swept to his forehead, then remained there as he tried to think and to rationalize her actions. Why the hell had she left ship, and who was the woman she had left with? Though his thinking was muddled, one thing was for sure: Paulina was in danger. As he left Ruth's cabin, he mumbled, "I'll have to get the captain to turn back."

But Captain Johns staunchly refused. As far as he knew, the woman had left of her own accord. "She appeared in no distress when she left the ship," he remarked to Brett. "She was smiling, and, it seemed to me, in quite a good mood."

"How far are we from St. Paul?"

"Too far for you to swim," came the captain's response. "But if we meet a southbound ship in the next day or two, you might hitch a ride." Captain Johns, with Brett stomping angrily at his side, entered the wheel house. There, a helmsman politely nodded, then gave

283

the controls over to the captain. At this point Johns said, "If you'd like, I'll have one of the roustabouts begin a search of the ship for her. Then, if you don't find her, I'd suggest you go on about your business, Mr. McCallum. The little lady apparently wished to part from your company."

Just at that moment an explosion rocked the steamer, sending both men staggering into the boiler-iron wall of the pilot house. Righting himself, then yelling above the screams of panic from the outside, Brett said impatiently, "If it's not an incident that'll sink us, I pray to God you'll have to turn back to St. Paul, Captain Johns."

As if in answer to his prayer, a steamboat mate rushed into the pilot house, his face soot-covered. "An engine blew, Captain. Mr. Moore says she'll not sink, but we'll have to turn back to St. Paul."

"Thank God," mumbled Brett.

And Captain Johns remarked casually, "It looks like lady luck is on your side today, Mr. McCallum."

In the ensuing confusion following the explosion, Brett learned that two people had been thrown overboard. When the identity of one, a roustabout, was made known, Brett overheard another roustabout explain, "No matter . . . he was just an Irishman!" And the second, a female passenger, was plucked from the icy waters and immediately revived by the only medical man—a veterinary specializing in injuries and diseases of horses—who happened to be aboard. The "luck of the Irish" did not hold up to scrutiny that day, because the roustabout was not found, and by nightfall he had been presumed drowned. The search ended and the crippled *Iron Ice* turned its fore to the south.

Since seven men had been burned or otherwise disabled by the exploding boiler, Brett did what he could to keep the remaining engines going. By the time the crippled steamer entered the shallow waters of St. Paul's northern side, he was almost too exhausted to breathe. But from somewhere deep within he summoned enough strength, soon finding the captain looking over the damage that was done.

"How long before she's seaworthy?" came Brett's question.

"I would say we're stuck here for a couple of days," responded Captain Johns, his voice crisp with annoyance. "We have all the necessary parts to put her back in service. Time is what we need now. Just time." Somehow, he managed a smile. "You'll be wanting to find the young lady. I'll have one of the men take you ashore. I would suggest that you avoid the seal harems. They'll be protecting their young this time of year."

Brett chose not to remind the captain that he'd lived in Alaska most of his life and was very familiar with the ways of the indigenous wildlife. He nodded politely, saying, "I'll wait on deck until your man lowers a boat."

Once he stood on the iron deck, he leaned against the rail and only half heard the groans and complaints of other passengers. He was sick with worry for Paulina. What on earth could have motivated her to leave the ship at such a desolate place as St. Paul Island in the Pribolofs? Except for a few natives and the pods of seals and other wildlife, the islands were virtually uninhabited. And who was this mysterious woman who had disembarked with Paulina? He had not noticed her making friends with other passengers, except for Ruth Perkins, and he couldn't imagine that she would leave the ship with just anyone. Was she so angry with him that she would jeopardize her safety simply to put distance between them? And had she abandoned her hopes of finding Millburn Hanks and taking him back to Utah with her? Brett didn't think so. She'd come too far to give up.

Was it that blasted marriage contract he'd had her sign? Was that why she was fleeing from him? Or was it because they had made love, and he had not lain with her in its aftermath as she had wanted? Blast! Didn't she know that he felt like a rat—no, worse than a rat—because of that?

He really wasn't sure why he had wanted to part from her so quickly that day. She was everything he had wanted, and from that moment on he could not imagine ever sharing the experience of lovemaking with any other woman. If he had his way about it, she would never return to Turkey Gulch, Utah, to take the job of town marshal and strap a pistol to her hip. He wanted her to stay in Alaska with him, to experience life and togetherness and the love that would accompany their every waking dawn. He imagined that given time, she would grow to love Alaska as much as he did.

Still, if she simply *had* to return to Utah—

He had left Alaska once before, to join the army.

Would it really be so difficult to do so again?

His friend Gruff was his last emotional tie to Alaska, except for his love of the land and the people. But Gruff was dying.

Damn! He didn't want to have to think about that.

A hand landed upon his shoulder. He shot up, so startled that an arrow of pain lanced through the entire length of his frame. "Sorry, gov'ner," said a ship's mate in a strong cockney accent. "I spoke ye'r name, but yah dain't hear."

"Sorry." He gave the man an apologetic smile, brief but sincere. "Are we ready to shove off for the island?"

"If yah be ready, gov'ner."

"Give me a moment." At that point Brett moved toward the cabin occupied by Ruth Perkins. Knocking, he instantly heard her voice, and entered. "I'm going over to the island to look for Paulina. I just wanted you to know I'd be gone for a while."

"I'll pray for you," said Ruth.

And Brett, smiling, unsure really how to respond to that, nodded as he slowly pulled the door to.

Within a half hour the beach of St. Paul was only a few pulls of the oars away. He could feel the salt air of the bounding waves spraying upon his face; his nostrils filled with the smell of a thousand seals; and his heart pounded with fear that he would not find Paulina.

In the span of the few hours since the *Iron Ice* had sailed from her southern border, could she have caught another ship?

Was it possible that he might never see her again?

No . . . no! He refused to believe that.

She was in his blood now.

And he *would* find her!

Eighteen

Gafferty had immediately taken Paulina to the grass and adobe hut of an Irish hermit named O'Caine, who claimed a preference for the solitude of St. Paul over anywhere else on earth. Now, as a very frightened Paulina watched, Gafferty climbed out of his female attire and began washing the flesh-colored paste from his features that had given him the deceptively soft look of the woman he had professed to be aboard ship. That was the reason the captain had not noticed a man fitting Gafferty's description. For the most part, he had paraded among the crew and passengers as a woman and had not donned the false goatee, except to accost Paulina. Now he was trying to wipe away all evidence of his female identity. Paulina thought the lipstick smeared on the towel looked horribly like blood.

Which is what now trickled down her left side beneath the fabric of her dress. Gafferty had discreetly pressed a knife into her to force her off the ship, and the tip of it had pierced her just below the armpit. But the tingle of pain caused by the small wound was not the reason for the tears gathering on her lower lids. She was so frightened of this macabre little man, she was almost sure she would faint.

Though Gafferty—a master of disguises—was deeply engrossed in changing his gender from female to male once again, he did notice Paulina gently sway. Cutting her a sharp look, he accused her, "You're trying to make me feel bad about taking you, eh? You swoon and I'll just let you knock yourself out on the floor and lay there. An', well, when my friend O'Caine gets back from the well, he just might take advantage of a lady what's taken leave of her senses. You know what I mean, eh?"

His cruelly spoken words gave her a moment of strength. She straightened, only the light-headedness affecting her now, though she managed to keep it under control. "I'm not going to faint. I just felt a little dizzy, that's all." Not only did his cruelty give her physical strength, she felt a strong rebellion now flooding her within. Lifting her chin, she said, "I don't know why you have taken me when it is Brett McCallum you want. If you think for a minute he will come back for me, you are mistaken. He loathes me."

The dress and bonnet deposited on the floor, along with a long, pale brown wig, Gafferty now began buttoning his shirt and rolling down the legs of his trousers. "He won't have any choice but to return. I sabotaged the engines of the *Iron Ice*. She'll be back, and so will McCallum. And then you know what I'm going to do?"

Paulina shrugged, as if it didn't matter one way or the other. "Kill him, I suppose."

But when the maniacally grinning Gafferty responded, "And not real quick-like either," Paulina felt shock replace any other emotion that might have otherwise settled upon her features. Gafferty noticed, of course, and as he used the tip of his knife as a comb, dragging it back and forth through his hair, he continued in his taunting tone. "I'll put a bullet in his thigh right about here"—a bony finger jabbed into his upper

leg—"an' then about an hour later, I'll put one here."
Now the finger jabbed into his left shoulder. "And then,
next mornin' bright an early, when he's been jerkin' an'
moanin', I'll put a bullet square between his eyes, just
the way he did my"—the amendment skittered from his
mouth—"just the way he did me."

If he thought she hadn't noticed, he was sadly mistaken. Her chin lifted, though not consciously, to a
haughty angle, and the left corner of her mouth turned
up slightly. She was still fearful, but now she thought
she understood better. This man was not *the* Gafferty
who had supposedly survived an attempt to kill him, but
perhaps a cousin or a brother or, depending on *the* Gafferty's age, a father or a son. But why have her believe
he was a man Brett had known beyond a shadow of a
doubt was dead, unless it was for the purpose of having
him doubt his sanity. Yes, that must be it. He wanted
Brett to worry and to fret, and even to wonder if Gafferty
had, indeed, been dead that morning when he'd buried
him. But Paulina didn't believe for a moment that Brett
would be so careless as to bury a man who was still
alive . . . and he had assured her, without actually having to give grueling details, that he had every reason to
believe he'd been dead when he'd shoveled dirt over
him.

"What are you thinking, little lady?" Gafferty's eyes
narrowed treacherously, demanding the attention of
Paulina's soft green ones.

"I was thinking that you've gone to an awful lot of
trouble to make things bad for Brett . . . and the ship-
ping company who owns the *Iron Ice*. Do you have a
vendetta against them too?" When he curled his hand
as if he wanted to hit her, she continued hastily. "But,
of course, that's preposterous, isn't it? It's Brett you
want . . . only Brett."

290

Gafferty grinned then. He really wasn't an ugly man, but the way his mouth turned up made him unattractive. When he sauntered toward her, she tensed, then immediately hoped that her posture had not been visible. She did not want him to know how afraid she was, because it might give him more leverage. His hand went out, then gently traveled along the fringe of lace at the bodice of her gown. "This is a very pretty dress. The color is becoming—"

"Oh? Do you want to wear it? I'll gladly trade."

Where the grin had been remained only a vicious sneer. "Think you're amusing, do you? Well, see if this amuses you—" Before she could stop him, his hand shot beneath the bodice of her gown and roughly sought her breast. Just at that moment—thank God, Paulina thought—the man O'Caine returned, and Gafferty jerked his hand away. From the side of his now-twisted mouth he said, "Don't think this is over, Miss Winthrop."

It'll be over when Brett comes after you! she thought ruefully, wondering if it would, indeed, happen. He was probably twenty miles out to sea at that moment, and possibly not even aware that she was gone. Gafferty had said he'd sabotaged the engines aboard the *Iron Ice*, but he appeared much too frail to have accomplished that. Then again, she remembered the way he had held her down that first night he'd made himself known, and the brutal strength he'd employed to drag her across this cold, isolated island. Looks were deceiving; Gafferty was the perfect example of that. He might have been able to accomplish the sabotage after all.

But would the crew have allowed him anywhere near the engines, especially dressed in women's clothing? Or in that disguise, had he managed to seduce one of the crew? Now, that would be one for the books, wouldn't it? He was a desperate man. Paulina felt that he could accomplish anything if he put his mind to it.

He had certainly accomplished taking her as his prisoner. She was at his mercy and—

"Are you all right, Miss?"

She looked up, her thoughts scattering to the wind. The man O'Caine swiped a knitted cap from his head—to be polite, she supposed—and smiled comfortingly. "I really don't know," she responded after a moment.

"You don't worry about a thing, Miss. Won't let no harm come to ye while ye'r in my house. Would ye like a cup o' tea?"

"Real tea?" she asked, smiling back, and hoping he was sincere in his promise to keep her safe.

"Real tea, straight from the China boat," he replied.

"Don't you be mollycoddlin' that woman," warned Gafferty, settling into a straight-back chair.

O'Caine, a large, lumbersome man who walked with a slight stoop, failed to respond, but Paulina could see that he was not afraid of Gafferty. He shrugged off his warning as if he'd known him long enough to have reason not to fear him, and that gave Paulina a certain degree of comfort in itself. While O'Caine set a pot in a brick grate, Paulina began to watch the howling wind outside the single window and through the wide slats of the door. The terrain of the island was rough, and the lone tree that she could see grew at a peculiar angle, along the ground almost as if the howling wind had dared it to touch the sky. She could see the southern beach from there, and the large, bobbing bodies of a seal harem and its young—slick brown bodies that also scarred the shallow waters for a good hundred yards out from its breeding ground. A large basket just outside the weathered slats of the door was filled with freshly dug clams, and she wondered if that would be supper.

She knew the islands were in a natural storm track of the North Pacific, though she didn't know the frequency of those storms. She had heard that they could be fierce, and she didn't relish the idea of being caught in one. Then she looked toward the man who appeared to be a gentle giant.

"O'Caine?"

He did not look up from the water that was now coming to a boil. "What, Miss?"

"How long have you lived here?"

"Nigh onto ten years now. Since I left"—the sentence ended abruptly, and he quietly repeated—"nigh onto ten years."

"Are we due for a storm?"

He was now pouring the water into two cups, and Paulina wondered which of the men would not get one. "Storm, Miss? Not anytime in the next couple of days, I'd say." Lifting the egg-shaped sieve from one cup, he dropped it into the other. "Sugar, Miss?"

"A teaspoon," she replied.

"You two sure are bein' chatty," said Gafferty, reaching down for a whiskey bottle, then popping the cork and lifting it to his mouth. "Goin' to serve crumpets with that tea, O'Caine? With lacy little lap cloths an' pinky fingers flickin' at the air while ya sip?"

Silence. O'Caine stirred the contents of the cup, then brought it over to Paulina. "Careful, Miss," he cautioned. "Cup's real hot."

The wind blew hard, rattling the shaky timbers of the cabin and, she thought, attempting to lift the sod and straw roof. The cup was, indeed, hot, and Paulina used the folds of her gown to protect her hands from its heat so that she could grasp the handle. When she ducked as if trying to evade the howling wind, Gafferty released an idiotic laugh. "Real skittery, ain't you, little lady?

293

What's the matter? You think the wind's goin' to carry you away?" Then in a malicious tone he added, "You ain't that lucky. You'll be stayin' right here . . . with me an' O'Caine. An' he won't be able to protect you if I decide to hurt you. You better believe that, little lady."

Instinctively, her eyes cut to the quiet man. An almost imperceptible shake of his head reaffirmed his promise of protection, and she lowered her gaze. Steam rose hypnotically from the cup of tea which she now brought to her lips. But it was still much too hot, and she began to blow small breaths upon the pale brown liquid.

As Gafferty dragged his feet up to a small stool and rested his head back, Paulina began to feel more at ease. She knew that Brett would find a way to help her. She had to believe that he cared enough. It was important to her, for without Brett she felt that she had nothing. Her family was many miles to the south, and except for Brett she was alone here. *Oh, please . . . please, Brett, help me. Come back for me. Find a way.*

Male voices snapped her from her moment of thought. O'Caine stood at the door, preparing to exit, and she only then realized that Gafferty had demanded to know where he was going. Giving Paulina an apologetic look, he said, "A man has private business to attend to every now and then, and after that I'm going to check on my goats." He cut his eyes away before he could see her gentle pleading that she not be left alone with Gafferty. He knew what the man was like. Surely, he wouldn't leave her in danger. When O'Caine spoke again, Paulina looked warily up. "Come to the door, lady. I'll show you where the outhouse is, should you need it."

When she stood, gingerly setting her cup on a small table, Gafferty warned, "Don't be gettin' no wild ideas about runnin' away."

"It's too damned cold!" retorted Paulina in a momentary need to project defiance.

On the small covered porch O'Caine made a pretense of pointing to a small building a dozen yards away. But, so that only she could hear, he said, "Don't you worry none about Gafferty. He's all huff an' he's—I don't know the word for it, if there is one, but he can't be with a lady, if you know what I mean."

She cast a quick glance at the still-reclining Gafferty. "You mean—"

"Be with a lady . . . like that."

A pale hue rushed upon her cheeks. "Oh, I see."

Departing, flicking a thick wrist, O'Caine said, "Now, you go on and drink your tea. It'll warm your blood."

Paulina reentered the breezy cabin, then took up the cup of tea. She considered flinging it in Gafferty's face, burning and shocking him enough so that she could make a getaway. But her feeling that O'Caine was going to help her was strong enough that she chose not to resort to such tactics. She didn't know where the feeling came from, but O'Caine didn't appear to be the kind of friend a man like Gafferty would have. He seemed as uneasy around Gafferty as did Paulina herself.

Perhaps he would try to get a message to Brett. Somehow—

"What are you thinkin', little lady?"

Paulina started, her eyes instantly connecting to those of Gafferty, peering narrowly at her from beneath the rim of the hat he had now placed on his head. "Nothing, I was just wishing my tea would cool a bit so that I could drink it."

"Sure," he laughed. "Sure . . . an' thinkin' about throwin' it in my face, ain't you?"

Now her wind-colored cheeks darkened to the color of ripe apples. She quickly turned her gaze to the landscape visible through the slats, only then noticing the specks that were white anemones and red rhododendron scattered across the lowlands. "I'd never do such a wicked thing . . . even to a man like you."

Gafferty's eyes narrowed even more, and the cynical smile crawled across his face again.

But she didn't notice. She was much too busy sipping her tea . . . and stilling the mad racing of her heart.

Brett was only dimly aware of the stinging wind. He moved over the rocks, toward the interior of the island, and as he reached an isolated hut, he approached, made inquiries of the natives, all of whom had been friendly to this point, then moved on. Paulina had to be somewhere on the island, and he knew he would find her. It was only a matter of time.

An Eskimo had told him at the last hut that no ship had departed from the island in the interim since the *Iron Ice* had embarked. Brett felt confident in the fact that Paulina *had* to be somewhere nearby. The island was small; a man could walk across it in a very short while.

He knew he had only two days to find her. His last word with Captain Johns had been to elicit a promise not to leave without them, but all Johns had promised was the time it would take to repair the engine. Then the *Iron Ice* would sail, with or without Brett McCallum and Paulina Winthrop.

And that didn't sit well with Brett.

He knew that Paulina was eager to reunite with Millburn Hanks, and he was eager to see Gruff again and assure himself that he was still alive. He had promised Gruff a wife—a role Ruth Perkins would fill—and he couldn't bear the thought that Gruff might die while he was away. He hated unfulfilled promises, and he hated it when his friends died.

But Paulina was his main concern right now. She was somewhere on the island with a strange woman, and though he had no reason to believe she hadn't left ship of her own accord, he still had a deep feeling that she was in danger. He felt it in his heart and crawling through his shoulders, like heat and ice, all at the same time. He needed to see her, to hear her explanations and to convince her to return to the *Iron Ice* with him.

Then again, he wouldn't have to coax her if he confessed his true feelings for her. If he could resist the urge to say *Be sensible and return with me*, and simply say, *Return with me Paulina, because I love you*, he felt she would be more prone to listen.

A man approached. Brett stopped short, his thoughts scattering to the brisk north wind. Squatting, Brett pretended to be brushing something from his boot, but his other hand moved discreetly toward the pistol at his waist. From beneath the brim of his hat he watched the man's approach. Brett's eyes were narrow and suspicious, and his fingers opened and closed an inch or so from his weapon.

O'Caine paused a half-dozen feet away from the stranger. Settling his hand just above his own pistol, beneath the thick fabric of his jacket, he looked first to Brett, and then to the north and south of him. Then he said, "Need some help there, stranger?"

Though the voice was polite and free of malice, Brett was taking no chances. As he rose, he kept his hand on his weapon. "I'm looking for someone," said Brett, leaving the statement without details for the time being.

The two men seemed to square off against each other, narrowed eyes meeting narrowed eyes, both of their gun hands, obviously, settled cautiously upon weapons. "You wouldn't by any chance be looking for a lady by the name of Winthrop, would you?"

Just the mention of her name caused Brett's heart to skip a beat. He wasn't sure if it was relief or dread that had caused the pain to grab him within. Now he replied, "That's who I'm looking for." He might have been speaking of the weather, and immediately chastised himself for the lack of concern the man might think he recognized. Still, he didn't want to give this man leverage if he were thinking about using Paulina as a bargaining chip.

"Then you'd better come and get her," said the Irishman, his hand only now dropping from his weapon.

Brett's, too, left the cool hardness of his weapon, though the caution remained with him. He approached and stood several feet from the man. "You've got her?"

O'Caine grinned. "Got her and don't want her. I don't like people. Name's O'Caine." A large, calloused hand was extended, and when Brett took it, he continued. "You're probably wondering what I'm doing here on the island. Well, I'm not real sociable . . . been here for ten years or so, trying to protect the seals from the murderous humans clubbing them toward extinction." Dragging his hand back, he turned to the south. "Come along with me if you want the lady back."

But as O'Caine started to move, Brett's hand darted out, catching him upon the arm. "Why do you care about Miss Winthrop? What's in it for you?"

O'Caine gave him a strange look. It might have been officious, even rude. "What's in it for me, young man, is getting back to my solitude. I told you, I don't like people . . . not men, and not women. If you come and take her off my hands, I'll be alone, the way I like it. Now"—the grin crept back to the craggy, middle-aged face—"you going to make me happy, or you going to stand there like a dag-nabbed, bumbling fool?"

"Well—" Scorching blue eyes were softened by the mid-afternoon sun. Brett, too, grinned. "I reckon I'll make you happy and take the dag-nabbed female off your hands. In fact, I'll take the other off your hands if she's in trouble too."

"What other?" asked O'Caine, a little annoyed at the thought of still another female interrupting his peaceful lifestyle.

"The one who left ship with Miss Winthrop."

O'Caine threw his head back and laughed heartily. "Don't know about another lady." The wind grabbed at his cap, but a hand rose to hold it down. "What'd you say your name was?"

"Didn't—McCallum."

"Like I said, don't know about another lady. But if you want the one I got, then come with me."

"Then she is alone?"

"Didn't say so, did I?"

Brett was becoming a little annoyed. "And you didn't say she wasn't either."

"So I didn't."

Brett wanted to ask if she'd been with a man named Gafferty, but if she had been, this man would have said so.

Then . . . maybe not.

Though Brett moved at a steady pace beside the shorter, stouter man, he maintained an edge of caution, his gaze constantly watching to the left and right and his hand once again settling on his weapon. When O'Caine made an idle remark about whether he would be shot in the back if he moved ahead between two large boulders, Brett responded, "Not unless there's somebody behind us ready to shoot us both."

"Well, I didn't see nobody else, so I'll rest easy that I'll be alive at the end of the day."

"Tell me—" Brett moved cautiously over the rocks, slipping once on a patch of ice that had not yet thawed. "Did Miss Winthrop mention a man named Gafferty to you?"

Brett thought that O'Caine's pause was terribly suspicious. "Miss Winthrop didn't mention nobody's name," he said after a moment. "She just come around and I fixed her a cup of tea. Then I decided that I'd better see if somebody was looking for her."

Now Brett was more confused than ever. If Paulina hadn't left ship with another woman, and the person who'd identified himself to her as Gafferty hadn't been responsible, then what the hell was she doing on the island when she should have been aboard ship?

Blast, the woman was beginning to pose a problem. He wanted to kick himself in the britches for falling in love with her.

Paulina lurched from her sleep. Gaining her bearings, and quickly remembering where she was, she couldn't believe that she had been so careless as to fall asleep in Gafferty's presence. Now, as she looked around, she saw that she was alone and would be able to concentrate on other things besides the fear she'd felt for the insipid little man. Far, far across the island she could hear the occasional bark of a seal, the wind howling so fiercely, it was like a breathless whistle and, a little closer, vague human voices. Male, she thought. The voices came nearer, but fearing that Gafferty was close by, she did not attempt to rise, to watch the approach of the men whose dark outlines she could not see against the blinding light of the afternoon sky beyond.

300

She was stiff and sore from sleeping in the uncomfortable chair and wished she were brave enough to rise and arch her back. But her gaze continued to dart here and there, waiting for Gafferty to make his reappearance and threaten her with the very sharp knife that had cut her side. No, she wasn't that brave. So she sat there and suffered, though she did shift on her buttocks and feel the tension slowly subside.

Then she saw the two men part company, one, who she was almost sure was O'Caine, moved off to the right and soon disappeared from her view, and the other moved toward her. Was it Gafferty? She didn't think so, because he was a much larger man. Then the wind whipped his hat from his head, though his hand was quick enough to retrieve it, and the sun shone upon his sable-colored hair. With a short, almost painful gasp she shot from her chair, her trembling fingers rising to cover her mouth.

"Brett?" But could it be? Had Gafferty been telling her the truth when he'd claimed to have sabotaged the engines aboard the *Iron Ice*? Had she been put in this isolated cabin as bait by Gafferty, who had been only too sure that Brett would come back for her?

Fear surged through her, darkened her eyes, made her dizzy with dread, and when Gafferty did not make a reappearance, her feet began to move, slowly at first, then picking up speed so that within seconds she had flung open the door and leapt toward Brett, calling his name over and over.

Immediately she was in his arms, being held against the iron hardness of his chest. "What the hell are you doing here, Paulina?" he choked out, his mouth gently trailing kisses over her forehead even as his words were harsh.

"Gafferty . . . Gafferty brought me here."

The gentle caresses immediately ceased and his hands, tenderly holding her to him, now braced, hard and unyielding, against her back. "What do you mean?"

"He forced me off the ship and said he wanted you."

A shudder crawled through Brett McCallum's tall frame. Slowly, he gripped Paulina's upper arms and forced space between them. His eyes became as dark as the midnight sky, and his mouth pressed into a thin line. "You're a damned liar. And I demand to know what game you're playing!"

Her mouth fell open in shock and her eyes, bright with love and relief just moments earlier, now filled with tears that immediately caressed her cheeks in their downward flow. "Why would you say these things. Surely, O'Caine told you—"

"O'Caine said nothing!" He flung her back through the doorway, refusing to catch her when her heel caught at the threshold and she half fell. But he wanted to . . . God, he wanted to, and his muscles jerked instinctively in his need to protect her. "He said he wanted to get you out of his hair. He said nothing about Gafferty! I mentioned the name to him . . . and he said nothing! Nothing, do you understand?" His rough desire to put distance between them had sent her into the house, where she now sat in the nearest chair. She was too stunned to answer, too hurt to rise. When he moved away from the door, then barked, "You'd better get your butt in gear, woman! We're returning to the ship!" he'd put a hundred yards between them before she was finally able to move.

But his long strides quickly put more distance between them, and she did not even attempt to catch up to him.

Right then, she hated him more than she'd ever hated anyone—even the Bartletts.

Why had O'Caine left out the most important details

of her captivity? Why hadn't he admitted that Gafferty had brought her there against her will?

She looked around, wishing she could see him so that she could demand an explanation. Then she called, "O'Caine, where are you?" and prayed that he would answer. But he did not . . . and her heart sank.

She saw no one . . . not O'Caine . . . not Gafferty . . . only the tall, brooding, and very angry Brett McCallum moving like an enraged stallion over the ground a hundred yards ahead of her.

So she dropped her tearful eyes and hugged herself to ward off the viciously stinging wind. She did not attempt to disengage the disheveled strands of hair from her face that made it almost impossible to see.

She swore right then that for the rest of the time she and Brett were together, he would not again hear the sound of her voice.

She hated him.

Hated him!

Nineteen

The promised silence that would have robbed him of the sound of her voice lasted all of fifteen minutes. He had reached the rocky seashore, then dropped to a crouched position, cursing beneath his breath because the *Iron Ice* sat five hundred yards out into the bay and no one had bothered to come for them. For almost two hours he watched for a longboat to head for shore, but none did. He saw movement on the deck of the boat with its engines silenced, but he and Paulina were as far from the thoughts of the crew and passengers as salted snails.

And even worse than being ignored was Paulina, pacing back and forth on the rocks behind him, giving him a good piece of her mind and thinking it important to remind him every few minutes that he was as worthless as pyrite. He wished he were a violent man; he would have throttled the she-devil and put himself out of his misery!

"Well! Don't just stand there, Brett McCallum! Do something! Wave your arms and get their attention." After a pause she grumbled in a louder voice, "Well, aren't you going to do something?"

From the corner of his eye he could see her skirts, the

way her hands fell arrogantly to her slim hips, the way her emerald eyes danced like jewels tumbling down a precipice. When her foot began to tap upon a smooth bit of rock, he growled, "Do shut up, Paulina Winthrop. You're becoming something of a bore!"

"A bore am I?" A toe jabbed into his right hip. When he did not react, the foot went out to repeat the action, but immediately found itself snared by one quick-moving hand. Before she could maneuver away from the culprit, she found rocks beneath her bottom. She was too angry to feel the pain, and a slim ivory hand went out to viciously pinch his arm through the fabric of his shirt.

"Dammit, woman!" He shot to his feet, rubbing the stinging flesh. "That hurt like hell."

She made no move to arise, but bent to gather the folds of her gown between her parted legs. "I fully intended for it to hurt, Brett McCallum. Why do you think I did it?"

He grumbled, "I thought you were never going to talk to me again. And I was so looking forward to it."

"I knew that!" she snipped. "If my voice grates on your nerves, then I shall recite the Gettysburg Address. Fourscore and seven years ago, our fathers brought forth—"

The recitation suddenly ceased, made impossible by the flesh of his palm rudely clamped across her mouth.

Her eyes were livid, their expression all the reward Brett needed for the small act of brutality. He had clamped his palm down hard enough that her teeth would not be able to find a place to cut into his flesh if she should suddenly feel the need to retaliate.

But she did not try to bite him. She used a much more effective weapon to bring him down, the one thing in the world he could not stand up against without having

305

his heart pierced. Turning quickly, he moved a few feet away from her and tucked his hands into his pockets.

Paulina wasn't sure where her tears had come from. She usually held her own very well when bantering insults with Brett McCallum. Now she sat upon the rocks, crinkling the folds of her gown between her fingers, wishing she could pinch herself and awaken from her terrible nightmare. She had been forced off the *Iron Ice* at knifepoint by a man who might or might not be sane, and had been forced to endure hours of fear and hunger, none of which Brett McCallum believed had even happened. Yes, that is what had caused her tears—fear and hunger; she couldn't remember the last time she'd had something to eat.

She couldn't look weak in front of him, and have him thinking her a whimpering child. So she announced haughtily, "I'm starving. I'd like a big slice of apple pie, Brett McCallum, and a tall glass of ice cold milk."

He looked out toward the ship, a smile etching onto his features. In a low, polite voice, he replied, "And I wish I could give it to you, Paulina. There might be something to eat back in O'Caine's cabin." He listened to the delicate sounds of her arising, the crinkling of skirts, the smacking of a small palm upon the rock as it found a steady perch, her foot slipping into a crack and quickly extracting itself. In his same bland tone he asked, "Shall we go back and see what he has in his food cupboards?"

"It seems rather rude to rummage through a man's house, doesn't it?"

He listened intently as she sniffed back the last of her tears. "He said he'd be gone for a few days hunting and to treat the place like home." He took a step in the direction of the cabin, then paused. "Are you coming?"

Paulina moved to his side. "Of course." Then, "If

there's a fresh apple pie in the cupboard, I wouldn't want you to eat it all before I could get a bite."

He laughed, something he didn't think he would ever do again. Instinctively, he dropped a long, muscled arm across her shoulder, then withdrew it. As the distance closed to the small cabin, they engaged in polite talk, about mundane things that neither was really interested in. He enjoyed Paulina's small, childlike laughs, as rare in these past weeks of traveling as fine porcelain. For the moment, his anger with her was forgotten.

They soon found canned goods and a piece of meat that could not be identified. It smelled fresh, though, so they put it in a skillet with a little dried onion and pepper and within half an hour they were sharing a meal.

With her stomach full, Paulina soon settled against a small, comfortable settee covered in bear hides. "They won't leave us behind, will they, Brett?"

Her inquiry, after so many minutes of silence, caused him to stir in the chair he occupied. "They know we're here, and it'll be a couple of days before the engine is repaired. No, they won't leave us behind."

She started to tell him that Gafferty had sabotaged the engines, but Brett would not want to hear it. Since she'd uttered a small sound, and Brett expected her to say something, she mumbled, "I'm as full as a tick on a spotted hound, Brett McCallum. I don't know what that was we cooked, but it was good!"

"Might have been a spotted hound," he remarked casually, a cockeyed grin easing onto his mouth.

She watched him from beneath the fringes of long, pale lashes. How quickly his moods changed; for that matter, how quickly her own changed as well. One moment he was furious with her, and the next, they were like best friends sharing a casual moment. Becoming aware of his steady gaze, Paulina dropped her own, color

307

suffusing her cheeks like a bright dawn. Closing her eyes, she remembered her adventure-filled dream and the excitement she and Brett had enjoyed on the Island of the Royal Crypt. There were many times when she couldn't believe she had dreamed the most wonderful moments of her existence, and she liked to think that Brett had pulled off an elaborate hoax, that his royal ship, the *Crown Prince of Talantia*, plied the waters of the North Pacific just out of sight of the lumberous *Iron Ice*, waiting to take her back on board. She still missed the dog; he couldn't have been her imagination. She could still smell the musky odor of his fur when she'd buried her face against him. She could remember the look of perplexity in his chocolate-brown eyes when the crab had pinched his nose.

"What are you thinking?"

"I miss Alujian—"

"Who?"

"The dog. You remember, the dog on the island. I wonder, Brett." Sea-green eyes turned in his direction. "Do you think that such an island might really exist? That there might be a mystical land far to the north?"

He chuckled. "Of course, Paulina, in your wildest dreams."

She looked toward the slats of the ceiling, and the sky beyond the wide cracks. Sighing wistfully, she closed her eyes and remembered every vivid detail of her dream. Then a familiar aroma drifted toward her, followed immediately by a familiar voice.

Paulina dear, dear sister. Reach out for me. I know if you really try, you can reach out and grasp my hand. Oh, Paulina . . . please, please try.

Paulina sat upright, her fingers closing so tightly over the arm of the settee that her knuckles bared white. "Did you hear that, Brett?" He grumbled, making no further response, and she knew he was trying to catch some sleep. "Brett, I heard my sister's voice. Didn't you hear it?" Instantly, she felt a pressure upon her arm, then a vicious pain shooting into her shoulder, and she tried to wrench it away, to withdraw it from the brutal, invisible fingers hurting her. But her hand would not move, and she felt the pressure of someone holding it, massaging a path along her arm. Tears popped into her eyes; she wanted to scream for Brett to help her, but she felt terribly foolish. Nothing held her hand, or touched her arm, and she closed her eyes, thinking that if she willed it, this unseen intruder would go away. She swayed against the heady aroma of gardenia, her sister's fragrance, hating it, seeing it as an enemy.

Then, without any warning, the frightening sensation ended. Fearing that it would return, she shot up from the settee, flew across the room and settled onto Brett's lap before he could possibly have made a defensive move. "What is this for?" he asked, his hands claiming her small waist. "You'd think you liked me a little."

"A little," she echoed, resting her head against his shoulder. "I just want to be with you."

"You're trembling."

"No, I'm not." His nose nestled into the soft skin at her hairline; his delicate breaths tickled her and she shrugged her shoulder against him. "Do stop it, Brett McCallum," she fussed without feeling. "I'll have none of your intimacy."

"Won't you?" he murmured, a small kiss touching her cheek, then traveling a path to her pert nose in its approach to her puckered mouth. She instantly drew her lips between her teeth, leaving a straight line. When he did the same, then touched the thin line of his mouth against her own, her instant laugh released her soft lips to his caress. "Now, isn't that better? We're not like two toothless old folks trying to steal a kiss? Hmmm?"

Pressing her cheek to his own cool bronze one, she whispered, "I feel like I'm in a dream, Brett, that none of this is real. Not the sea, the islands, the *Iron Ice* . . . not you . . . not me. It is as though time has flown away, leaving a safe, comfortable void for us, and we cannot possibly be touched by the real world. Even our perils"— her voice softened as she remembered his prior anger, an anger which prevented her from elaborating—"even they are not real," she continued, snuggling against him, locking her fingers over her wrist at the back of his neck. "I believe that from this moment on, if anything treacherous happens, we should simply close our eyes and think happy thoughts. What do you think?"

How is our Paulie this morning?

Paulina's head snapped up again. "Did you hear that, Brett? It was Big Pat's voice. He's the only one who called me Paulie."

Brett's hand went up, roughly drawing her head back against him. "Big Pat is dead, Paulina. You couldn't have heard his voice." She was trembling again; the kiss he stole at that moment was his attempt to still it. But she drew back, fire emitting from her emerald eyes so viciously that he felt the painful heat.

"Don't take advantage of me, Brett McCallum, just because I'm hearing voices. I'm not daft!"

"No," he agreed. "You're lonely. Which is why you're hearing the voices of people you love—your sister, Big Pat." He drew a sigh. "But why delve into dreams for comfort, Paulina, when I am here with you?" When he attempted to take another kiss, she slipped from his lap and turned away from him. He sat forward, his fingers linking together over the space between his parted knees. He watched her move nervously about the small

310

ramshackle cabin, flicking her fingers over items strangely free of dust, looking into cupboards she had not looked into before, and kicking out at a rotting bit of rug upon the floor.

But it was only when she drew a long, wistful sigh that she heard Brett move, then approach and enclose her within the circle of his arms. "Stop pacing about, Paulina. You're as nervous as a treed coon."

She accepted the intimacy, her hands moving to the small of his back. As her head gently fell to the broad expanse of his chest, she murmured, "I should be tired, but I'm not. I should want only to tuck myself into a comfortable bed, but"—lifting her eyes to his bold bronze ones, she smiled seductively—"I want only to lie in your arms and be loved by you. I want only to feel your body against my own and to know that you care about me, Brett." Drawing a sweet sigh, she added, "I just want you to hold me."

He grinned, pulling her roughly to him. "Blast," he whispered huskily, "and I thought you wanted to make love."

Lifting her smiling features, she said, "Well, we didn't find a pie in O'Caine's food cupboards, and if you want dessert, I think you might find me as pleasing to the palate as sweetened apples and pastry."

He drew back a little with feigned shock, even as his fingers lifted to tunnel through the rich masses of her hair. "We cannot be so engaged, my lovely," he groaned. "Someone might come from the ship, and you would never live down the embarrassment—"

"Oh? What embarrassment is that?"

"An unmarried lady in her altogethers being caught beneath a male rogue in a compromising position? What embarrassment is that, indeed!"

"I wouldn't be embarrassed." She shrugged as she responded, her smiling lips puckering playfully. "Would you be?"

Before he could be aware of her movement, her fingers had tucked into the waist of his trousers. "You're getting a tad thin, Brett McCallum." Gently, she tugged on the coarse fabric. "Your trousers are getting loose."

The door burst open, nearly knocking it from its rusty hinges. Paulina drew back with such a start that she thought she would faint. As Brett pivoted sharply, his hand moving instinctively toward his sidearm, Paulina felt herself falling to the hide-covered settee. There in the doorway stood three of the crew from the *Iron Ice*, the sky beyond like a blinding light magnifying the sizes of their dark silhouettes.

"Mr. McCallum, sorry it took so long to come for you. I see you found the young lady."

Brett righted his attire, then dragged his holster toward his right buttock, out of the way of his hand. When his gaze cut to Paulina, she arose, soon moving to his side. "The engine is repaired?" he queried of the larger man, the one now moving toward him and eyeing the small cabin as he did so.

"Nay, take a couple of days. I thought you'd be more comfortable aboard ship. Miss Perkins has inquired about the young lady."

"But the young lady and I were just going to"—instantly, a horrified Paulina dug her elbow into Brett's ribs, causing him to gasp out the completion of his declaration—"take a little nap."

Lifting her skirt as well as her pert nose, Paulina moved past the men and into the coolness of the day, appalled that Brett would even consider telling strange men about their plans for intimacy. It never occurred to her that he had been teasing, and that he would never have been so ungentlemanly. "And we can nap quite well aboard the *Iron Ice,* in our separate cabins."

"But we could share a cabin again," a smiling Brett McCallum reminded her even as he continued to rub the assaulted rib.

"You'll have to, Miss Winthrop," announced one of the crew. "We've taken on a new passenger who needs your cabin."

She turned now, her eyes like green ice as they held Brett's mute gaze. "Excuse me, Mr. McCallum, but I believe I will share lodgings with Miss Perkins, and you can have your cabin to yourself."

"But—" He started to issue the protest, then thought it would please her too much. He couldn't have that! "And I think that will suit me fine, *Miss* Winthrop. I find your company terribly boring." One of the crew laughed, but Paulina's scathing look instantly suppressed it. "And furthermore, I'm tired of all your primping."

The insult went right past her head, her concentration on the ground just outside the door. Then she bent, picked up a small object, and brought it up very close to her eyes. "Well, look at this. If it is genuine, I've found quite a valuable treasure."

Seeing a flash of green, Brett looked immediately at his right hand. Then he approached, snatched the large square-cut emerald from between her fingers, and dropped it into his pocket, along with the ring he had removed. "It's mine." When her gaze lifted with noticeable argument, he dragged the ring from his pocket and showed her the empty setting. "See . . . it *is* mine! Do you think I'd take something away from you that was rightfully yours?"

"I've never seen this ring," she responded, attempting to take it from him. "Where did you get it?" Then, smiling maliciously, she continued. "From one of the interred corpses on the Island of the Royal Crypt?"

"My emerald is real," he sneered, passing her in the doorway close enough that his torso grazed her softness. "Your dreams are just that—dreams!" As he marched across the smooth rocks toward the longboat swaying in the sea, he tried to reason out his thoughts. He wasn't sure why he always fought with Paulina. She was the most desirable woman he had ever met, and he could envision her as his wife and the mother of his children. He wanted her to be part of his life because, dammit, he knew he loved her. But he couldn't seem to let go of his independence, and admit to himself, finally, that a beautiful, sensual woman was worming her way into his heart. He needed the moments of tense anger between them, because without it, he would be putty in her hands. He didn't like to admit that though, and he would rather die than have her aware of his deep feelings for her.

She was a puzzle to him. How could she be the most sensible woman he'd ever encountered one moment, and a scatterbrain the next, catching the aroma of her sister's gardenia fragrance and hearing her voice as clearly as one might hear a piercing wind? He wanted to take her by the shoulders and shake the dickens out of her, but he wanted to hold her close, feel the rapturous heat of her body against his own, and taste the sweetness of her full, moist mouth. He wanted to be as far away from her as the moon, but he also wanted her always to be near enough to fill his vision when the need so struck him.

Blast it! Blast it, what was wrong with him? Was he going as daft as she apparently was?

He feared that he was.

* * *

Paulina made the threatened move to the small cabin inhabited by Ruth Perkins. While the two women became fast friends, Brett McCallum wallowed in his solitude, hating it. He had made himself a part of the crew in its efforts to repair the engines, simply so that he would not have to think about Paulina, and the fact that the words she had spoken to him in the doorway of O'Caine's cabin—*From one of the interred corpses on the Island of the Royal Crypt*—were the last words she had spoken to him.

In his leisure moments he attempted to sit near enough to the two chatting women to hear the sound of Paulina's voice, even when she spoke with vicious sarcasm because she knew he was eavesdropping.

Thus he was surprised when the second night in the bay, when he finally collapsed onto his cot for a few hours sleep, that the alluring beauty crept into the cabin and quietly approached him. He watched her from beneath the fringes of his sable-colored lashes as she stood in silhouette above him, then silently took a step back to close the door. There was only the dim light of the late evening reflecting through the porthole to betray to him the sensual allure of her standing there, contemplating something that he could only guess at. He wondered if she'd tucked a knife into the back of her skirt, for there her hand now went. Her features were lit with a pale glow, her skin as iridescent as dawn over Denali, and he watched in fascination as she quietly, wondrously, allowed her gown to fall to the floor, betraying her radiant nudity.

Brett's breathing suddenly ceased. He wanted to pinch himself to make sure he was not dreaming, but when she climbed onto the cot and cuddled against his side, he caught the whiff of freshly washed hair and her natural essence with the power to intoxicate him.

Her breasts burned hotly against him; it was almost impossible to ignore her, as he was trying so hard to do. When her fingers lifted, then wrapped through the short, thick strands of his hair, easing toward his temple, he closed his eyes, hoping that the dream would never end. She had not spoken a word; her actions said everything he wanted to hear.

If she was trying to get a reaction from him, she had only to move one of those seductive hands down the length of his body. He felt that he would explode with want of her, but stubbornness was as alive inside him as his desire was, for the moment, exercising some degree of control. He wanted only to rip off his clothing and turn her beneath him; he wanted only to fill her with his aching maleness and punish her for tormenting him so wickedly.

But it would hardly be punishment! She was the one doing the seducing. She was the one whose bold little hands explored beneath the threads of his clothing, now popping the buttons of his shirt and easing beneath the waist of his trousers. She was the one arousing him to heights he didn't even know existed.

And he was enjoying every delicious moment of it!

His body burned with aching. He took a long, deep breath, praying that she wouldn't disappear like a spectral mist that had simply come upon him by chance. When she offered her mouth to him, he tasted wine-sweetened kisses, caressing him wildly, lingering passionately, teasing, playful, enchanting him as he desired to be enchanted. This seductive siren was everything he needed in the deep darkness of his cabin, and beyond the porthole he was scarcely aware of the light of the midnight sun.

When one of his hands moved to claim her, to feel the heat of her body, one of her hands covered it, halting

316

its bold movements. She shook her head slowly as if to say, *This is my adventure, my pleasure . . . and whatever happens is my choice.* So he simply lay there, her willing victim, and his body, racked by lust and desire, was her playground to do with as she pleased.

A low, steady knock at the door jarred him. Snapping his eyes open, he suddenly realized that he was alone.

Blast! Blast! This couldn't have been a dream! Blast! And he was having a good time.

Foolishly, he looked to the side of the cot, thinking that his sudden movement had knocked her to the floor. But he was alone in the small cabin, and the persistent rap at the door continued, causing him to come to his feet, traverse the short distance, and jerk the door open.

There stood Paulina Winthrop . . . fully clothed!

Blast!

His gaze narrowed; he wanted to lift his fingers and claw away the crimson suffusing his cheeks. God! He couldn't bear the thought that she might know he'd been dreaming about her.

"Mark my word, Brett McCallum," she instantly launched her attack. "I will not speak to you again after this night, not even if you threaten to draw and quarter me! I hired you to take me into the interior to find Millburn, and I'll not have any more of your sassy, arrogant, patronizing, sarcastic tongue! Do you hear me?" When he hesitated, humor lighting up his masculine good looks, she snipped, "Well, do you?"

Want to make love, Paulina? "Yes, I understand. Now"—he took a step back, his hand moving up on the door to push it to—"get off my back, will you?"

Her foot was immediately in the door. "If I am ever on your back, Brett McCallum, you will be only too aware of it!"

317

Come in . . . strip off your clothing. "Get your foot out of the door or you'll lose a few toes."

"Don't threaten me, McCallum!"

Fall back to the cot . . . we'll begin where we left off. He faced her now, his eyes like onyx. "What the hell is this, Paulina? Was your only purpose in disturbing my sleep to sling a little more of your viciousness? Frankly, I'm sick of it! Either come in and disrobe, or get your damned foot out of the door."

The foot snapped beneath the hem of her dress. "I'd as soon disrobe for a snake!"

"I slither well," he said with a small laugh. "Or don't you remember?"

With a shove a lumberjack might have been able to accomplish, Paulina was inside the cabin, looking into the face of a very surprised Brett McCallum. "I'm game! Remind me how well you slither."

He grinned wickedly. What the hell was she up to? Was she trying to trick him, or was she just a merciless little witch teasing him with her allure, her charm, and her threats? "Very well," he took the bait. "Get out of your dress."

She lifted finely arched eyebrows the color of sand. "Oh? You can only slither when the woman is naked?"

Perplexion settled onto his swarthy features. "Of course. What did you think I meant?" He thought her a bold little thing, standing there with a foot tapping beneath the hem of her skirts, her hands drawn arrogantly to her slender hips.

"I thought you would drop to your belly and slither, Brett McCallum. Why do you think I came in here? Surely, you didn't think—" Her gaze cut toward the messy cot where he'd apparently been napping. Then she looked up into his features, seeing the color instantly suffuse them. "Oh, so you did think we'd make love!"

Turning toward the door, she added, "Sorry to disappoint you."

He moved swiftly to block her exit, his hand going up to the door. "I won't be disappointed, Paulina. Because you will not leave here until I get what I want!"

"Sorry!" she spat out at him. "I will not make love to you! And that is final!"

He drew back, feigning surprise, attempting like hell to salvage what was left of his dignity. "Love?" he finally uttered. "Hell, I thought you had a sandwich in your pocket."

He made her smile with genuine humor even as she instantly suppressed it. "Listen to me, Brett McCallum, because I will not repeat myself. I will not make love, I don't have a sandwich in my pocket, and I want you to stop teasing me! Also, I—"

Before she could utter another sound, he drew her into his arms and kissed her deeply. It mattered not that she fought him, that he could feel her teeth attempting to bite his tender flesh, that he had to lock down the leg she would raise in attack against him, that her fists now pummeled against him in an unsuccessful attempt to stop his assault.

"If you do this . . . Brett McCallum . . . I shall never speak to you again!"

"I can live with that!" he growled against her hairline, immediately relaxing his hold. "But, blast it, Paulina, if you don't want to be with me, then flee now, while you have the chance." She stood in the circle of his arms, her gaze picking over his dark, clean-shaven features. When she made no move to part from him, he murmured, "So be it," then stole another sweet, delicious, tormenting kiss.

Twenty

Paulina stirred to delicate wakefulness, her arms stretching into the air and her back simultaneously arching. Was it already a new day, a cool northern morning gently infiltrating the room where she lay? Her eyes crept open, seeing at once the blur that was a window and heavy muslin curtains hanging in rags on either side of it. But beyond, against the fringes of the wild Alaskan wilderness, clusters of buttercups and moss campion hugged the ground in profuse bloom, taking away the wildness of the land and reminding her of home.

Home . . . Had it been so long ago . . . so many, many miles behind her that she had looked into the ruddy features of Uncle Will and assured him she would be all right? Had it been so long ago that Lillian had hugged her and pleaded with her not to go? Had that day truly existed when a youthful Matt had begged to go along and keep her safe?

Sitting forward, Paulina hugged the coolness across her shoulders, then her eyes scanned the room for a moment. She could hardly believe that three weeks had passed since she'd attended the early morning wedding of Ruth Perkins and Gruff, whose formal name she had learned soon after arrival was Calvin Bosworth.

Had it really been three weeks since she'd last seen Gafferty, or even felt his presence?

Three weeks since she'd last spoken to Brett McCallum?

And that had been the hardest part.

Propping herself on the pillow as she contemplated arising and facing the day, Paulina thought back to the trip aboard the *Iron Ice,* sleeping one cabin away from Brett, the silent meals spent together, with Ruth chattering away and attempting to break the tension, her refusal to make direct eye contact even as Brett had glared at her. And now they were at the cabin where Gruff and his new bride seemed as happy as mating magpies, and Paulina wasn't sure how to get across to Brett that she was eager to begin the search for Millburn without actually having to speak to the rogue.

She knew he was deliberately making it hard, if not impossible, for her to accomplish that end, and she imagined that it was his way of forcing her to talk to him. Certainly, he wasn't going to volunteer to resume the journey to the Yukon River and Millburn's location until she actually asked him to.

She refused . . . simply, outrageously, flat-out refused! He owed her an apology . . . and by doggie, she would get it!

The door opened. With Brett standing there, glaring down at her, she drew the covers over her bodice. She said nothing, of course, as he silently approached and threw a newspaper atop her drawn-up legs. "Thought you'd be interested in this . . . news from the States." When she continued to make eye contact, her hand moving to retrieve the paper, he said, "Gruff and Ruth have gone over to Pokie's cabin. They'll be there for the day, visiting." Still, she did not reply, though her mouth did part when an ugly smirk turned up a corner of his mouth. "And I've got the whole blasted day to make you talk to me . . . and believe me, pet, I have ways." Instinctively, defiantly, her nose lifted into the air. Taking up the newspaper, she quickly scanned the first page. When it seemed that she would lay it aside, Brett said, "Page three . . . bottom right corner." Turning the page, her gaze moved over the headlines, then settled on one: MURDER IN TURKEY GULCH, UTAH. Her heart caught between beats as she quickly read:

Last month gunfire erupted in an alley of this once-thriving town and moments later the bodies of the Bartlett brothers were found facedown in the dirt. The elder, Lester, who had just been appointed marshal, had been shot seven times. Earl Bartlett received five shots. There are no suspects in the slayings. A special session of the town council the following morning resulted in the appointment of Miss Lillian Winthrop as town marshal, a position promised to her absent sister, who had wished to complete her father's term. The late Marshal Sabin Winthrop was gunned down in 1895, and it was suspected that the Bartletts were responsible. In other news from Turkey Gulch, businesses are being rebuilt following the fire that swept through the town several weeks ago. It was suspected that the fire began in the Winthrop mercantile and quickly caught the vacant buildings. Plans to build expensive town houses in Turkey Gulch were suspended by eastern investors following the death of the Bartletts and all properties have been reclaimed by town residents. This newspaper has been asked to appeal to Miss Paulina Winthrop to return home to Turkey Gulch.

"So, do you want to go home?"
Paulina did not look up from the paper but read it once again. She was angry with Brett, too angry, in fact,

to answer him, and yet she wanted to. Even more urgent was the instinct to throw herself into his arms and enjoy his embrace, but she could never give him *that* satisfaction. He was a snake and a charmer, and she wouldn't be his victim.

She cast the newspaper aside as if she were totally indifferent to the news she had just read. She wouldn't let Brett McCallum think that he had done anything to please her. After all, the newspaper article had informed her that the mercantile had been destroyed by fire. She could only hope that no one had been injured, though she reasoned that the article would have said so.

When Brett saw that she was not going to answer him, he turned. "Sorry your throat hasn't recovered sufficiently for you to talk. One of our neighbors came by this morning and I purchased two dozen eggs and a side of pork. I'm preparing breakfast—eggs, ham. Ruth made a pan of biscuits before they left. There's also cold milk, but you can't have any unless you place an order." Turning, he grinned across the space separating them. "And the order can't be written. Nor can you point. It'll be necessary for you to use that prattling female tongue."

She opened her mouth to protest the insult, but immediately halted any flow of words. He was trying to bait her, of that she was sure. Thus, she crossed her arms, then cut her eyes from the doorway where he stood.

When he left—and she really wasn't so sure that she'd wanted him to—she began to think about these new developments. If Lester and Earl were dead, then there was no reason to bring Millburn back to Turkey Gulch to testify against them. Still, it would clear the record if he could relate how the Bartletts had gunned down their father in the dead of night. Paulina hoped that the brothers rotted in hell; they deserved it even more than Brett McCallum did.

Oh, Brett . . . Brett, why can't you try harder to make me speak to you? Can't you see that I'm terribly hard-headed, but I've missed you terribly, and that I love you and want to be with you and hear your whispered endearments against my ear? You falsely accused me of creating Gafferty in order to torment you, and yet you have never given me a reason why I would do such a despicable thing. You have been so cruel to me these past few weeks. You must know how I care for you. You must feel the love I have for you. And yet you continue to treat me like an irritating little sister, even after we made sweet, tormenting, delicious love.

"Want that breakfast?"

Paulina jerked from her daydream, so sure he had read her thoughts that a telltale crimson rushed into her cheeks. Her palms went immediately up to cool them. *Paulina . . . Paulina, it is your imagination. He heard—felt—nothing!* But when her gaze lifted and his boyish grin was her reward, she wondered if, indeed, he had known her thoughts as surely as if they'd been his own. *Don't be stubborn, Paulina,* her little voice said to her. *Answer him, or you'll go hungry.* But she simply couldn't do it and with a hastily raised wrist flicked a hand at him in dismissal. With a hearty laugh he retreated, pulling the door to as he did so.

"I hate you, Brett McCallum . . . I truly hate you."

The door jerked open; a smiling masculine face peered into the room. "I heard that . . . you talked to me. You said"—at this point, his hand went over his heart for playful, sarcastic emphasis—" 'I love you, Brett McCallum . . . I truly love you.' "

"I said I hated you!" With a small gasp, Paulina's fingers covered her lips. *Blast . . . blast!* she thought, employing his favorite expletive. *He forced me to talk to him.* "Well, since the era of silence is ended, I *will* have some of that breakfast you're cooking."

Brett bowed with grand flourish. "Aye, my lady, your wish is my command."

"I hate you," she huffed again.

"Yes, I know," he laughed, retreating once again. "I can tell."

Paulina drew in a deep breath and held it until she was sure her face had turned beet-red. She had said that Brett McCallum would not hear the sound of her voice again, and now she had broken that promise. She was angry enough with herself to eat oatmeal as just punishment. Then she got the whiff of strong coffee, and the pleasing aroma of it brought her up from the comfortable bed. In the following moments she bathed her skin from a ewer of clean water, brushed and plaited her waist-length hair, and drew on a comfortable dress Brett had picked up in St. Michael three weeks back. Then she turned, nearly stumbling over the wood case containing the last of the seven bottles of whiskey Brett had brought from St. Michael for Gruff. She recalled Brett's fondly spoken order: "Drink it straight only when you're in pain," and she could see by the five empty bottles placed back in the case that Gruff had been in a great deal of pain. He was not otherwise a drinking man.

As Paulina turned to the door, following the aroma of the coffee, Gruff's pet caribou cow poked her head in the paneless window. "Go on, Penelope," said Paulina, flicking a slim hand at the friendly creature. "I'm sure Gruff left you plenty of hay."

Penelope did not withdraw until Paulina had given her a familiar pat below her antlers. As Penelope's trotting hooves withdrew from the cabin, Paulina left the bedroom and entered a small, overly warm kitchen, where Brett McCallum turned eggs with a spatula. "How do you like your eggs?" he asked.

"Cooked," came her reply, and when he looked narrowly toward her, she sniffed, "And don't you give me that smug look, Brett McCallum!"

"Smug? Me?" came his laughing reply. "I don't know what you're talking about. I'm just cooking eggs." Brett was so glad to have her talking to him once again that he didn't mind her own smugness. Although her little escapade at O'Caine's cabin in the Pribilofs had outraged him, as had her explanation for it, he had not enjoyed the moments of silence that had followed. All his efforts to converse with her had been met with blank stares and rebellious looks—until that morning. He wondered what other pleasures she might have in store for him that day.

As if she had read his mind, she warned, "And don't you dare try to be friendly with me—and you know what I mean—Brett McCallum. I'll have none of it."

Rather than respond, he pointed out, "Since you really have no reason to find Millburn now, I imagine you'll be wanting to go home?"

"Oh . . . I still want to find Millburn. He might like to know he can come home to Turkey Gulch, and no one is going to hurt him." Just at that moment Paulina got a strong whiff of gardenias, reminding her of Lillian. "Do you smell that?"

He did not look up from the chore of spooning the scrambled eggs in equal proportions onto the two plates. "Gardenia . . . yes, and—don't tell me—just like your sister wears. Well, love, she isn't here, just like she's never been here before when you thought she was close by."

Silence. Paulina did not appreciate the mocking tone with which he had spoken to her. He was feeling his oats, simply because she had broken the barriers of silence and was once again conversing with him. Well, she could still be quite sparse with conversation, as he would soon find out.

Momentarily, the plate was put on the table before her. With a curt "Thank you" she took a biscuit from the basket on the table and began to spread freshly churned caribou butter upon it. Brett joined her at the table, and in the intimidating span of quarter of an hour they breakfasted together without saying a word. She did not look into Brett's eyes, but she knew they were glaring at her from beneath the dark, hooded brows. When, at last, her plate was empty and her stomach full, she stood from the table, announcing, "I'm going for a walk."

"What about the dishes?"

"What about them?" she asked, moving toward the door. "They'll be here when I return." Then she exited into the clear, crisp morning, determined to put enough distance between her and Brett McCallum that he wouldn't even have the chance to muddy her thoughts.

Penelope joined her as she moved onto a foot trail through the forest of white spruce. All around her the wind blew, and across the timberline she could see a rain squall advancing, though it still seemed a long way off.

Soon she cut off the trail and through the meadow toward the base of a nearby mountain. There she found a smooth white boulder and sat, Penelope wandering off to nibble at a patch of campion moss. From where she had perched, Paulina could see the valley before her, the widely spaced spruces separating her from Gruff's cabin on the Yukon, flowering shrubs, and a single eagle circling in the sky. All around her lay the silence, the utter stillness of the region, a silence that swept along with the vibrant green of spring and scattered with the wind.

Now that she was alone—save the foraging caribou cow—she really didn't think much. Brett was in her mind and, strangely, she gave very little thought to home and family. Had time and distance hardened her? She hoped not. Nothing was as precious to her as Lillian and Matt, Uncle Will and her very dear friend, Lucille McWhirter.

For the first time in many weeks she felt that they were safe. The Bartletts were dead, the investors had withdrawn, and Turkey Gulch would thrive the way it had before the Bartletts had tried to buy them out. One last loose end to be tied together was reuniting with their mother and learning why she had left them and Father. Then her life would be whole again.

But for the time being Paulina knew what troubled her—Brett McCallum. Though she had been very angry with him these past three weeks because he had not believed her, she still had wanted to be with him. That infuriated her because she felt that her body was her worst enemy. She had lain in the cabin aboard the *Iron Ice*, in the hotel room in St. Michael, and slept beneath the stars while they had traveled inland, and all the while she had wanted to be in Brett's arms. If it hadn't been for the presence of Ruth Perkins, she would probably have given in a long time ago. She remembered the times that Ruth had wandered away from camp, claiming a need for solitude, and Paulina had known that she'd wanted to give her and Brett time to heal their old wounds and misunderstandings.

Paulina enjoyed the mountain, the clean air, the call of the wildlife, the birds flying overhead. She leaned back, closed her eyes, and before she knew it was drifting in and out of sleep. When some close presence finally forced her to full alertness, the sunshine had slid from her features, and the storm hovered immediately overhead. Three hours of the morning were suddenly behind her.

Without warning the tiny hairs on the back of Paulina's

neck prickled up. It had nothing to do with the wind; rather, it was an odd, depressing, frightening feeling, and her eyes scanned the woodland and the mountain behind her. That was when she saw him, sitting on a boulder twenty-five yards or so up the mountain, surrounded by moss-and-lichen-covered ground in a grove of white spruce.

Her heart beating frantically, she fought the urge to scoot up from the boulder and break into a run. He would immediately overpower her, though, and he might hurt her for running from him. Though he had been a terrible menace since the first night she had laid eyes upon him, so far he had not really hurt her. She didn't imagine that was his intention anyway.

Gafferty plucked the dirt from beneath his fingernails with the ever-present knife. "How you been doin', Miss Winthrop?" he drawled. "Missed me?"

"Does one miss a swarm of mosquitoes?" she asked in a soft, even tone, then answered her own question, "I wouldn't imagine." She lifted her eyes to the man, who was diminished by the size of two massive boulders rearing up on either side of him. The glassy light of the sky behind him made everything stand out, and with the rain squall washing in, the cloud patterns changed the lights and colors of the horizon. But Paulina couldn't concentrate on the beauty of the country; her eyes were on the petty, intimidating Gafferty who had been dogging her for the last thousand miles.

Suddenly—and she wasn't sure what brought it on—she wasn't afraid anymore. He might have, indeed, been a swarm of mosquitoes, something that would prickle and annoy but certainly would not frighten its victim. Paulina didn't even fear turning away from Gafferty now, knowing that he was at her back and that he held in his right hand a weapon that could easily pluck the life from her. It was rather a strange feeling, knowing he was there and not being afraid of him, and she felt that she had control of her life.

She could hear his bootsteps approaching, slowly, methodically, trying to frighten but failing miserably. She was beginning to believe he didn't really exist; after all, she was the only person who had seen him. Yes, that must be it, he was an apparition born of her imagination. She needed only close her eyes and wish him away . . . and he would vanish.

Paulina closed her eyes tightly, and through her mind softly flowed the order *Go away, Gafferty. Go away, Gafferty.*

"Paulina?" So startled was she by the familiar voice that she nearly toppled from the boulder on which she was sitting. Her eyes flew open, and instantly her gaze connected with the softly controlled and narrowed one of Brett McCallum. Quickly, she looked to the left and right, then across her shoulder, but except for Brett, no one else was about. *Dear Lord, it worked. I wished him away and he vanished, just like that!* "What on earth are you doing out here? Daydreaming?"

Her timid smile was followed closely by a familiar blush rising in her cheeks. "I guess I was," she said, her tone strangely soft. "But what else is there to do?" Just at that moment a playful breeze wafted up the mountainside, carrying on it the strong fragrance of gardenias, Lillian's aura, and Paulina suddenly felt just as playful as that precocious breeze. Thoughts of her dear sister did not fill her with loneliness; rather, she felt happy and free, and ever mindful of the dark, brooding monolith of a man who hovered over her, the familiar look in his eyes making her want to be pressed to him without the rude barriers of clothing. Tucking herself into his arms, she cooed, "Hold me, Brett. Tell me that you care about me . . . tell me that we will be together forever."

Though his body tensed, the hand that had risen to her shoulder continued its soft caress. "Forever, Paulina? I thought that would be the last thing you wanted from me."

"Why would you think that? Don't we enjoy being together? Haven't we made beautiful, passionate love? Haven't we proven how much we care for each other? Oh, haven't we?"

Brett looked up the face of the mountain. Something strange and eerie hung upon it, like gossamer ghosts. The approaching storm had moved slowly, but now it began to tumble upon itself, black and gray mounds of threat covering the sky to the north and immediately overhead. Putting Paulina slightly away from him, Brett said, "Come, we need to get back to the cabin. This is going to be an angry storm."

As Paulina allowed him to take her hand and coax her into a brisk walk, she looked back over her shoulder. Nowhere did she see Gafferty. Nowhere did she see any evidence that he had been on the mountain. Could her imagination have run so rampant? Actually, she prayed that's all it was.

Brett's booted feet were now easing into a run. Holding fast to his hand, Paulina matched his pace. Just as they exited the stand of slender spruce and entered the clearing where the cabin stood, the first great droplets of water splashed hard against her skin. As the cabin swallowed them whole, the sky opened up and the wind and rain slashed against the now-shuttered windows. Hurriedly they rushed to and fro, double-checking the shutters, putting down pans where drips could be expected, and running into each other at every turn.

Finally, a laughing Paulina dropped onto a hide-cov-

331

ered divan and outstretched her arms, too exhausted to think about anything.

Soon Brett eased into a sitting position beside her. His fingers rose to the gentle pulse at her temple. "You are flushed," he remarked. "I made you run too fast."

"It's good for me. Keeps my bones limber." Turning her eyes to him, she smiled gently. "And you, Brett McCallum? Is that a bit of color I see in your features, also? I do believe you're getting too old to cut the mustard."

With a growling laugh Brett roughly pulled her into his arms. "Mustard, blast! I'm not too old to please the woman I adore!"

Paulina peeled herself from his arms, then found her footing in one swift move. "Oh, if only that woman were here, you could prove your bold assessment." Suddenly a face appeared in the window at the far wall, a macabre, grinning face that had been dogging her trail for weeks. Pointing a finger, a now-wide-eyed Paulina stuttered out: "A man . . . a man is prowling outside . . . I saw his face at the window."

Without a moment's hesitation Brett was pulling the door open. Paulina did not move so much as a muscle when she heard his hard bootsteps treading over the ground outside, then circling the cabin. Presently, he returned, his hand raised to his sable-colored hair. "He must move fast, then. I saw no one." Narrowing his eyes, he accused her, "Or could it be that you're playing your little games again?"

The accusation smarted, of course, though she tried her best not to let it show in the narrowing of her own eyes as they held his intense gaze. Was he attempting to bait her into an argument . . . and even more important, was it her fault that Gafferty moved too quickly to be caught by his prey? She could allow this moment of tension to metamorphose into a full-blown argument if she chose. But—she smiled—she wasn't in the mood for a good argument, even with the one man who most stirred her to that unattractive occurrence.

"Actually, Brett McCallum—" Sarcasm settled into her quiet voice even as she felt the tremble of fear beginning to flood her entire frame. Gafferty managed to do that to her. "I was trying to get rid of you just long enough to decide what to prepare for our lunch. The side dishes of course. You did stir up a rabbit, didn't you?"

Pinching his full, attractive mouth into a thin line, he responded, "Didn't feel like hunting today. Gruff left a slab of bacon in the smokehouse."

"Then, will you fetch it? I'll cook it up and throw some sliced potatoes into the grease."

Brett noticed the sarcasm slightly ebbing, the fear inching into her voice. It took him slightly off guard, and he wasn't sure what tone of voice to use himself. He approached, his hands soon settling on her upper arms. Only then did he notice the tremble racking her body. "What is wrong, Paulina? You are trembling."

"I am not," she smarted, instantly turning to face him. "I just felt a little chill across my shoulders, that's all."

His look narrowed; doubt settled upon his dark brow. Crossing his arms, his feet apart in a careless stance, he continued to look at her, his gaze combing her pale, lovely features, the thick, windswept masses of her hair, then inching downward over her slender frame. God only knew what force drove him then, for suddenly his right hand eased out and captured her left one, and with all the sincerity of a dedicated preacher at a baptism, he murmured, "Marry me, Paulina. Marry me tonight."

He had expected some response, of course, but he had not expected her to flee in tears. Almost before he realized she had moved, her skirts were swishing through the exit door and her gentle sobs racked the rain-swollen morning. Recovering his senses, he turned to go after her, and when he, too, exited into the vicious course of the storm, she was disappearing into the stand of spruce toward the mountain where he had just moments ago found her sitting.

He called, "Paulina . . . Paulina—" and the gentle sound of her name was lost in the heavy Alaskan storm. "Paulina—" he called again and again, his booted feet edging into a full run toward the sanctuary she had sought several times in the three weeks they had been at Gruff's cabin on the Yukon.

As he rushed to the mountain, the rain subsided into a heavy mist. When he did not find her, he sat upon the boulder, sure that he could feel the warmth she had left there earlier, and tried to think. His thoughts were scattered though, and he could not get a feel of her presence at the base of the mountain. His eyes swept the meadow where rhododendrons grew, scanned the sterile spaces among the modest army of young spruce and toward the river where the current broke and thrashed with torment and wandering. He saw her nowhere, and it frightened him.

Where would she have gone?

A frantic need to see her, to know that she was safe, filled him inside. He stood for a moment, his feet apart, his eyes closed, and his hands clenched into fists, trying to imagine where she might have gone. *Where are you, Paulina? For God's sake, where are you?*

Then it hit him—the small cabin the Sullivans had built a quarter mile through the woods. He and Paulina had walked there the week before, and she had been intrigued by the simple, carefully laid out plans of the cabin built of split young spruce trees. She had wandered inside, touching walls sanded to the texture of fine linen, touching furniture with such smooth lines she could hardly believe it had all been hand made. She had loved the cabin. She said that it would be a wonderful place to live if one had a notion of remaining in Alaska. She said she felt safe there. She said—

Taking a deep breath, Brett turned to the south woods. Yes, he would find her there, her fingers easing over the smooth walls and intricate patterns of the furniture . . . her eyes glazed with tears . . . the tremble of emotion settling into her throat.

Yes . . . yes, he had to believe it. She was there and she was safe.

In the next few moments Brett broke into a run, as panicked and yet deliberate as a fleeing buck. Nothing could have stopped him then in his quest, not quake or storm or man.

He wanted to be with Paulina.

He felt that his life depended on it.

Certainly . . . his heart did.

Twenty-one

Paulina liked the large, roomy cabin. Brett had told
her about the Sullivans, a man and his wife, who had
built the two-story structure just three years before. The
balustrade of the stairs had been brought overland to
add a civilized garnish to the otherwise rustic structure,
and the rooms had been laid out much in the fashion
of the Victorian homes she had seen in New England.
The Sullivans had been young and determined to make
a home in the Alaskan wilderness, but the stillbirth of
their first child had sent the disillusioned and grief-
stricken couple retreating in defeat. Brett had told her
that the last word he'd had from them was that they had
settled down in Mississippi and founded a new-order
church.

Now she sat upon a plush though dusty divan,
dropped her head back, and closed her eyes. She could
almost hear the laughter of Pearl Sullivan, wood being
chopped on a block by her husband, Tad, and if she
really concentrated, the soft whimper of the child they
might have cherished filled the dusky air of the spacious
parlor. A lady's delicate fragrance whisked by her . . . a
ghost from the past . . . and far beyond the timberline,
the storm was gently hushing.

Sniffing, she was able to staunch a fresh flow of tears. Tears! What was it she was crying about? Oh, yes, Brett McCallum, always the lovable rogue who had stolen her heart. How casually he had asked her to marry him . . . perhaps it was that casualness that had sent her fleeing in tears and shock. *Marry me, Paulina,* the rogue had said. He might easily have said *It's raining outside.*

Marry him . . . Mrs. Brett McCallum . . . Paulina McCallum. It sounded nice. But living twenty-four hours a day with him, bearing his children, feeling the chill of an Alaskan winter barrel into her flesh and fill her bones—was she up to it? Indeed, did she love him that much?

The answer to that one came easily. She loved him with all her heart and all her soul, and she could imagine no more wonderful future than being his wife and having him as her husband. He kept her constantly on her toes wondering what he would do next. He made her feel warm and comfortable and secure. He loved her the way she had always imagined a man could love a woman. Only one man existed who could tame her wild, adventurous heart, and that man was Brett McCallum.

But was she ready to be gentled, to be domesticated . . . to be a wife? What had happened to her ambition to be the marshal of Turkey Gulch, Utah? Was it no longer important to her? Could she live in his beloved Alaska and never again think of home and Lillian and Lucille, Matt and Uncle Will and those grumpy old men of the town council? Was she willing to give up the life she'd had before, the life that had been her father's and her father's father's and before that a half dozen times as far back in her history as had been recorded in their family Bible?

And what of Brett McCallum? He'd had and lost one wife. He'd been a wanderer, an adventurer, he'd once been a cavalry officer. What other revelations would there be? Would there be any that might manage to drive a wedge between them and cool the love they had for each other? But did she really care what was hidden in his past?

There was, of course, the question of Gafferty. Brett had been so vehement that he'd died, that he'd buried him with his own hands. But the man dogging her trail was as much flesh and blood as she was. He was no vision created by an overactive mind. He was a renegade antagonist who seemed to be able to appear and disappear at will. He could make his presence known to her without effort, and hide it just as easily when Brett—or anyone else—happened upon the scene. Though she knew that Gafferty was just as much a threat as he had been weeks earlier, she'd learned not to broach the subject of him to Brett. Though he'd given her every reason to keep the secret of Gafferty's reappearance in her life, she felt guilty that it was necessary.

Why couldn't Brett put his faith in her, believe her, and help her overcome the problem of Gafferty? He had accused her of lying and inventing this nemesis simply to prickle and annoy him. And, along this same vein, could she marry a man who did not trust her and believe in her? She thought not.

A hand landed upon her shoulder. With a small cry she was on her feet, reeling from the dizziness the sudden move had caused. As she attempted to focus, she saw a familiar stance, dark hair, and, focusing more, narrowed black eyes that seemed strangely blank and without feeling.

Brett McCallum had forced calm upon himself when he'd seen her through the cabin window. Now he stood separated from her by the large divan, his eyes glaring at her as if she'd done something wrong. But he was simply attempting to chase away the annoyance he felt within, an annoyance that had settled in when the panic had fled. "I was worried about you, Paulina. Why did you run away from me?"

"Because you're a rogue and a rat, and because I hate you more than oatmeal!"

Dark eyebrows raised quizzically. "Hell, all I did was ask you to marry me. And for that I am a rogue and a rat deserving of your hatred?" Forcing a moment of humor, he added, "And hating me more than oatmeal at that! Imagine how my ego feels right about now?"

She truly wanted to be angry with him, but almost instinctively a smile turned up the corners of her mouth. Quickly, she suppressed it, but the frown she attempted to drag onto her face had no legs on which to stand. "I do hate you," she said, but now her words were insincere. Again she tossed herself upon the divan and immediately he bent to touch his cheek to her own. She enjoyed the coolness of it, warming ever so gently against her flushed one. But even as she wanted more from him, she whispered, "Don't touch me, Brett . . . please, don't—" Her actions did not match her words; closer she pressed her cheek, then she sought the hot caress of his kiss.

Wrapping his fingers through her thick, damp hair, Brett slid over the divan, then drew her to him. Though she again said "Don't—" her lips opened to accept the teasing caress of his tongue against her own. His breath was warm, rushed, and yet gentle upon her cheek, and when his right hand slid roughly beneath the bodice of her gown to cup her breast, her body instinctively arched against his touch. His mouth imprisoned her own, capturing, lingering, teasing her softness with lusty nips. Then, with her breath coming in small gasps, his mouth moved over her chin and the slim column of her neck, locking to her passion-peaked breast now freed from her bodice.

Immediately she felt the swell of him hard against her thigh and, in one quick move she was on her feet, dazed and disoriented by the passion she wanted from him and yet loathed at the same moment. "I told you to stop!" she snapped at him, catching the arm of the divan to steady herself. She only halfheartedly attempted to cover her exposed breast, and when she looked at him, fire emitted from a frosty gaze. "Do you think that every time we are together I want to do—" With revulsion she spat out, "That!"

For a moment Brett could not come to his feet. A brutal ache in his groin prevented him from moving at the moment, and all he could accomplish with any flair at all was a lethal look. Even words were lost, because he feared if he tried to speak, nothing would come forth but an angry groan—or, worse, a silly squeak.

Paulina seemed to sense what had happened to him. In a teasing, sarcastic tone, she said, "What's wrong, Brett McCallum? Big old bad wolf grab you in the loins?" Then, wanting only to prickle him further, her hands rose and gently cupped the sides of her breasts. "I've got something you want, don't I, Brett? Don't you find me desirable? My goodness, that old wolf did render you helpless."

Giving her no moment for planned evasion, Brett was on his feet, his hands grabbing her wrists as she was forced backward. Only when her back was firmly against the wall, and her mouth pressed rebelliously, did he say, "Helpless, am I? We'll just see, my pet!"

Without prelude, without the moments of teasing caresses and warm awakenings, Brett caught both her wrists above her head, then freed himself from his trousers. Roughly dragging her skirts up and her underthings down, the hardness of him was positioned against the warmth of her thighs. With a small groan Paulina clamped her legs together. "This is rape!" she spat at him. "Get your filthy bands off me! Now! Do you hear me? Now! Now!"

His movements stilled instantly, his hand withdrew from the warmth of her thighs, and he dragged his body away from her. His eyes like lethal weapons, he quickly drew up his trousers and fastened them. "You're right . . . we wouldn't want to break any laws, would we?"

Paulina was mortified. She had expected to fight off a man determined to have his way with her. The very fact that he would withdraw so easily, leaving her as unfulfilled as he himself must surely be, was so horrifying that she felt a panic quicken inside her. As he turned away and beat a hasty retreat toward the door, she was at his back, pounding him so viciously that he half fell to the floor. In his efforts to fend off the attack, his arm gave way from beneath him, landing him full upon his side. Managing to turn to his back, he grabbed for her flailing fists but did not catch them until they had dealt several blows to his face.

"Dammit, woman!" He felt the warmth of blood at the corner of his mouth. Paulina was like a she-cat thrashing through underbrush, so wild and entrapped that all reasoning was lost. He could not see her face through the thick, tangled masses of her hair, nor the mouth that spewed groans and expletives in small, catching breaths. But now that he had her hands, he felt her strength gently waning. When, at last, she collapsed into an exhausted heap atop him, he was sure that an hour had passed.

It hadn't, of course. Her little fit had lasted no more than a minute or so. Now that she was quiet, her breaths no more than soft moans, his hands moved in a caress across her shoulders. He made no move to separate from her, but allowed her anger to subside slowly. When she lifted her head, then dragged the strands of hair back from her face, he calmly met her tearful gaze.

Paulina saw at once the blood trickling along Brett's jawline. With a carefully placed finger she touched the warmth of it. "Did—did I do this to you?"

A cocked smile, without malice. "Accidentally bit my lip. I do that sometimes."

Instantly, Paulina's mouth touched his own, even as the fingers of her right hand drew up a bit of her skirt to wipe the blood. "I'm sorry," she murmured. "Truly, I'm sorry. I didn't mean to hurt you. Did I hurt you anywhere else?" Slowly, a slim finger lifted to an eye, now beginning to redden. There, she kissed him gently. "Anywhere else?" The finger slid to his right cheek and the area was kissed. "Anywhere else?" And now, hesitating only slightly, the finger returned to his now-parted mouth. When she had again kissed him there, she said, "Have I ever told you what a big baby you are?"

"Lots of times," he responded, drawing her ever closer. "Are you still angry with me?"

Quick kisses trailed over his warm cheek. "Furious," she replied, gathering her legs together and falling to the side of him. The floor was hard, but it didn't matter. Silence compelled her to lift her gaze to his firm profile. His dark brows were pinched together, as were his lips. When her hand dropped to his chest, she could not feel the rhythmic rise and fall of his breath, as if he had deliberately held it. "What's wrong?"

Again silence. His mouth pinched tighter, his brows furrowed more deeply. After a moment he replied, "You are right, you know. I almost did rape you. I've—" Regret caused his speech to halt, just for a moment, before he resumed. "I've never done anything like that, and certainly not to someone I love. I apologize."

"You goose—" she chuckled, a slim index finger caressing the soft skin of his upper lip. "Perhaps you were being terribly rough, but I did—do—want you. And I believe you know it. It's a shame"—gently, she shrugged against him—"a shame my hateful attack has quelled your desire for me."

Slowly, mechanically, his head turned, and when his gaze connected to her own, he murmured, "What makes you think my desire is quelled? I want to make love to you, but I don't want you to beat me in the face again. Blast . . ." Now a grin raked across his good looks. "Can't have this handsome puss messed up by a she-cat!"

Instinctively, her fingers went to the scar at his temple that a grizzly had left there years before. "I'm sure that I wouldn't—couldn't—hurt you this much. Why"—a smile turned up her lips—"my fingernails are an awful disgrace." Flanging her fingers, she showed him her nails, two broken off and the others needing to be filed smooth. "See what the wilderness has done to me?"

Brett laughed. "What would a marshal need with fingernails anyway?" Then he pulled her across his body and held her warmly against him. His fingers eased into the tangled strands of her hair and made a halfhearted attempt to comb it. The heat of her womanly curves penetrated the fabric of their clothing and caused a chill to crawl along his skin. Raising a thigh against her slender hip, he continued to massage her scalp and comb the tangled strands.

"Why did you ask me to marry you, Brett?"

The question, after the moment of silence, caused him to jerk. "Call me a madman if you will." His attempt at humor was unsuccessful. He immediately sighed deeply, then continued. "Because I cannot imagine life without

343

you, Paulina. I don't want you to go back to Turkey Gulch. I want you to stay with me."

"But my family is there. You have none here. And . . . Gruff will not be here long, you know." Drawing a shallow breath, she said, "Do you put much stock in 'Whither thou goest I will go?' and is Alaska so important to you that you would not consider moving farther south . . . perhaps to Utah?"

"I love Alaska. I have always planned to die here."

"Where you die is your business, Brett McCallum. I am asking about life, where you will live it . . . and with whom you will enjoy it."

He was immediately struck by her logic. True, he had never thought about Alaska in such a loyal sense beyond its being his burial ground. His shallow breathing slightly increased, and dropping his palm to her slim shoulder, he responded, "Utah . . . Alaska . . . hell, I'd live anywhere on earth with you, Paulina. Anywhere, even a cave, even your"—now he chuckled good-naturedly—"even your blasted Island of the Royal Crypt. I liked that place. Didn't you?"

She had told him so much about the island of her dream that she was sure he knew it as well as she did. Softly, she said, "I especially liked the warm pond beyond the amethyst walls. And Alujian liked it too."

"Oh, yes, that crazy dog you befriended. Wonder what ever became of him?"

"He's all right, safely tucked away in my dreams and my memories."

"I would like to be there too. Promise you will give me a special place—in your heart."

Without making her intentions known, Paulina drew up, dropped her hands onto her thighs for a moment, then, smiling, began removing her simple gown. As Brett watched the magnificent unveiling of her, she removed her shoes, chemise, and the pantaloons he had rudely violated just moments before, and soon stood naked before him. He had never seen such beauty—the tiny waist, small, firm breasts, lovely, round hips all held together by flesh that was as flawless as smooth porcelain. Her hair was wild and pale, forming a halo around her oval features, wide, passion-filled emerald eyes and full, sensually parted mouth. Then, as he watched in awe and wonder, she dropped to her knees once again and began pulling the ties from the front of his shirt.

"What are you doing, Paulina?"

"Seducing you," she responded, her mouth trembling so slightly. "Don't you want me to?" When she saw the tightly controlled pleasure lighting his azure eyes, she smiled her own pleasure.

He said nothing for a moment, then seemed to enjoy saying to her, "I believe the roles have reversed, my pet. You are raping me, are you not?"

"Rape . . . rape . . . rape! What an ugly word! We are making"—at this point, her voice seductively softened— "sweet, passionate, tormenting, wild, and wicked love. Doesn't that sound like"—a soft, sensual series of kisses teased his mouth—"pure, unadulterated adulation?"

"Pure, heck, what?" Brett growled a laugh, his hands moving up so that she could easily remove his shirt. "Sounds more like fun to me."

Brashly, breathlessly, she offered, "Want me to help you out of those trousers?"

Within moments, he, too, was free of his clothing. As he turned roughly over, dragging her with him, the howling wind outside the cabin sent a splatter of rain that had settled onto the sill across their heated, entwined bodies. Both, simultaneously, drew in a quick, surprised breath, then broke into laughter together.

Brett wanted her so badly that he thought his body

would explode. Roughly positioning himself between her thighs, his hands almost impatiently caressed her soft, round breasts, arousing them quickly to firm peaks. He groaned with pleasure, his back arching as her fingers teasingly journeyed along his spine. She seemed as impatient as he, for now her thighs rose and hugged his slender hips.

Then his body drew up; he was kneeling between her legs and lifting her hips. His eyes raked her slowly, methodically, as if he were visually exploring every erotic inch of her slender frame and wondering if he did, indeed, want her. When her eyes narrowed quizzically, he seemed to sense what she was thinking, for now he said, "Yes, I want you, Paulina . . . but I want to see the treasure that you are, and the treasure that we shall be together."

A coy smile; Paulina's gaze held his own for a moment, then moved fluidly over the wide expanse of his chest, the inward curling of the hard muscles lowering toward his stomach, and there . . . to his commanding manhood so close to entering her that she ached with want of him.

"Now—" she whispered seductively, siren-like, "you torture me, Brett."

His gaze was passion-filled, his flesh darkening to the color of bronze as he lowered his torso to cover her own. Positioning himself, he eased into the warmth of her— there—and withdrew only a little when a short gasp reached his ear. "Did I hurt you?"

"You've never hurt me," came her reply. "We belong together, you and I. I love reacquainting myself with the rhythm and pace of your loving ways, Brett McCallum."

His hands cupped her warm, flushed cheeks, his mouth touching first one translucent violet eyelid, and then the other. For the moment he stilled his masculine

346

movements within her, and she enjoyed the attention his caresses gave to her features . . . the trail of teasing kisses . . . the way his fingers eased into her hair like combs, the playful growl as he captured one of her earlobes and gently kneaded it between his teeth, and then gave the same attention to the other. Then his kisses were moving along the slender column of her throat, his tongue drawing a circle around each of her passion-peaked breasts.

"You are so beautiful," he murmured. "Every man's dream."

"I don't want to be every man's dream . . . only yours."

"And so you are," he chuckled softly, the brilliant sparkling of his eyes as their gazes met fusing straight through to the core of her heart. "And when you think you will burst for want of me, then, only then, Paulina Winthrop, will I ask again for your hand in marriage."

Her body tensed; ceased to move. Arching both of her fine eyebrows, she gave him one of those familiar looks of feigned annoyance. "Oh?" Instinctively, her hips arched, and he began to move within her again, slowly, tormentingly, all the while holding her gemlike gaze. "And you think you are man enough to have me begging for your masculine attentions?"

"Aren't I?"

Rather than respond, she deliberately matched his rhythm and pace, thrusting . . . thrusting quicker . . . quicker . . . and she called his name, "Brett . . . Brett—" in a breathless rush that matched the intensity of his rhythm. Her eyes closed, then fluttered open, scanning his dark, handsome face as he seemed to grow still and rigid and, quite before she knew it was near that point, he was filling her with his seed. Then, as before when they had made love, her own desire rocked her body in deliciously tormenting spasms as she arched to accept him fully.

If the wind howled beyond the window, neither heard it. For them, there were no sounds outside the laboriously shared breathing just now beginning to slow to a gentle pace, and the creaking of the planks beneath the dusty rug upon which they lay. Then, as their senses reeled back from somewhere far past time and reality as they knew it, the sounds of the wilderness sifted back to them, to remind them that they were not the only two people left on earth . . . though their love seemed to create that perfect union and block out rational thoughts of others like them . . . past the fringes of the Alaskan countryside, where they shared the ultimate joy of man and woman.

Only then was Paulina able to sift back through her thoughts and remember what he had asked her. Quietly, pressing herself to him, she said, "Yes . . . yes, I will marry you." And when his head snapped up, and his eyes narrowed as though he were not sure that he had heard her correctly, she added, "And whither though goest, I will go. For it matters not where we chance to reside, as long as we can always be together . . . whether it is in your world, or my world . . . or at the ends of the earth, it matters not. Yes, as long as we are together."

He grinned his pleasure as he sat forward to take her in his arms and feel the soft, willing, naked warmth of her against his torso. "I am not the richest man on earth, but I love you enough to promise that I will make you the happiest woman on earth, Paulina Winthrop. You will want for nothing that is in my power to give you. And I will never be far away. Whenever you call my name, I will be here. This I promise."

"There will be times," she whispered against his dark

hairline, "when we will be apart. But they will be of short span."

He drew back only enough to see all of her face, to press the vision of it into his mind. "You do love me?"

"Not only do I love you, Brett McCallum, but I like you too. My father said that like is as important in a relationship as love, and he said that should I find the right man, to make sure that he—"

Instantly, Brett's finger pressed to her lips to silence her words. Then his lips replaced the pressure of the finger and he stole the sweetest of kisses, though it was offered so readily, it could not be considered stolen. But he liked to think of it so, just as she had stolen his heart.

When at last a breath of space separated them, Brett tousled her shaggy mane of trailing hair. "I think we could both use a comb," he laughed, sweeping back his own sable-colored hair. "And"—he looked down, at both of their nakedness—"we had better put some clothes on before someone happens by. I wouldn't mind so much, but my modest little Paulina . . . she would faint from shame."

"You're probably right about that." Paulina offered her own gentle laughter. Sweeping herself gracefully to her knees, she retrieved her gown from the heap of their clothes. When she began to pull it over her head, Brett tucked his head into the bodice she'd pulled over her own, halting her efforts. Grinning at him within the shadows of her dress, she said, "We'd look pretty silly to that interloper, wouldn't we, Brett McCallum?"

"Have I ever shown you the way Eskimos kiss?" At that point his nose moved softly back and forth against her own. "Do anything for you?" he asked, a grin turning up his mouth.

"Not as much as this," she responded, her mouth

seeking, finding, and pleasuring his own with teasing caresses. "And this—"

Her hand boldly moving along his muscled thigh and touching his again-aroused manhood brought forth a groan, and he pulled her roughly to him. "What are you trying to do, Paulina?" Then a teasing smile lit his eyes. "Unless . . . well, I'm willing if you are."

With feigned shock and a clicking of her tongue, Paulina pulled her dress between their bodies. "I do declare, Brett McCallum. You're an animal . . . you feel the instinctive need to mate, and nothing else matters to you at the moment."

Dragging the gown from between them and tossing it across his shoulder, he grinned again. "I think you're the one who initiated this bout of foreplay, but if it comes to a vote as to whether we do or not, then I'll certainly second it."

Playfully, Paulina's arms scooted around his neck and her body molded gently to his own. "Suppose someone should find us here. An Eskimo, perhaps—"

"No Eskimos." His nose gently nuzzled her own.

"A hunter?"

"No hunters."

"How do you know?"

"No gunshots."

"Gruff and Ruth?"

"Visiting. Besides . . . he's never been here—"

"A wolf, then?"

"Couldn't open the door—"

"Pooh!" Her body pressed closer, her mouth touching, caressing, drawing ever so slightly back from his own. "You have an answer for everything. Why is that?"

"Because . . ." His hand moved along her womanly curves, over one of her buttocks, then circled, lightly touching her . . . there. Then he eased her to her back

350

and covered her body with his own. Instantly, and she welcomed him eagerly, he was within her once again. "Loving you is worth all the risks," he murmured against her pale hairline.

And the renewed session of loving, gentle at first, slow and methodical, quickly moved toward rough, exhilarating wonder, and Brett found himself outpaced by her eagerness for their coupling.

Suddenly, the room was awash in shadows, cool ones . . . hot ones . . . and the rain began again, though gentle now . . . for all the intensity of love's storm was within the abandoned cabin.

Not outside it.

Twenty-two

The following morning, when Ruth and Gruff returned to the cabin, Gruff went straight to bed, feeling "under the weather," he said. His skin was unusually pale, which made his bulbous nose seem even larger and darker, and even his thick, prematurely white hair seemed to have thinned in the day and a half since they'd been gone. For two days Gruff stirred in and out of sleep, restless and agitated one minute, sedate and peaceful the next. Since their marriage just two weeks before, Ruth had grown especially fond of the lovable, oversize Alaskan who preferred to be called Gruff, rather than his given name of Calvin. She sat at his bedside constantly, leaving for no more than a minute or two at a time, and Paulina brought her meals to her at Gruff's bedside.

They were all sure that Gruff would be gone within hours, which was the reason that visitor after visitor from the neighboring homesteads and settlements trekked in and out of the cabin. But by the afternoon of the second day, he began to stir and became lucid for the first time since he and Ruth had returned from their neighborly excursion.

Still too weak to stand, he sat in a comfortable rocker

and allowed Ruth to feed him his first meal in those two days. "How'd I get so lucky?" asked Gruff, the twinkle in his eyes matching the smile upon his mouth as he gazed at his lovely mate. "You came here and you agreed to be a dying man's wife, and what will you get out of it, Ruthie? Widowhood, and loneliness. I didn't have no right making you marry me."

"You didn't *make* me marry you," said Ruth, smiling, even as tears rested, unshed, behind her eyes. "In case you didn't know, we are all dying, just some of us sooner than others. In these two weeks, husband, you have given me more joy than I've known in a lifetime. Now, hush and eat your stew."

At that point Paulina stuck her head in. "How about a visitor?" she asked, moving across the floor when Gruff raised his hand to motion her in. "How are you feeling today?"

With a loving look to Ruth, he responded, "Much better. I have a good nurse." Then, with a smile, "What are you and Brett up to?"

"I'm going to insist that he take me upriver to find Millburn."

"Ah, you don't need to be doing that."

That remark surprised Paulina, because Gruff knew how important it was to her to find Millburn and take him back to Turkey Gulch. "Well, of course I do," she said a little roughly, immediately softening her voice. "That's the initial reason I came to Alaska . . . to find Millburn."

It was supposed to have been a surprise. Now he had no choice but to tell her. "You don't need to find him."

A puzzled look met his gaze. "What do you mean?"

"Ruth and I saw Millburn Hanks last evening. I told him you were 'in town' and he said he'd be here on Saturday."

"You saw Millburn?" she asked incredulously. "But I didn't know you knew him. You said nothing—"

Ruth interjected, "He didn't know him, Paulina. He came up and introduced himself. It was as if he were compelled to do so by a force none of us could explain. Almost as if he knew—"

Paulina was elated. She clapped her hands together once, and then linked her fingers. "How is he? How did he look?" An innocent, childlike excitement added a pleasing lilt to her voice.

"Like a man named Millburn." Gruff laughed weakly. "He seemed a fairly spry fellow to me."

When Brett entered the room, wiping sweat from his brow, the result of half an hour at the woodpile, Paulina leapt at him, her arms circling his neck. "Did you hear that?"

"Hear what?" he asked, drawing her against him without inhibition. "Did I miss some excitement?"

"Millburn will be here on Saturday."

"Oh, that. Yes, I know."

She drew away, a little miffed that he possessed this knowledge, whereas she had not until five minutes before. "What do you mean? You knew—"

Looking toward Gruff, he said, "I thought it was supposed to be a surprise."

A shrug lifted Gruff's broad shoulders, the look on his face saying *you know how women are,* without his having to speak the words. "Didn't have much choice. She said she was going to insist that you take her northeast on the Yukon to his camp."

"Insist, was she?" Brett laughed, drawing Paulina back into his arms so that a kiss could touch her forehead. "What is it about women that no matter how pleasant a surprise is going to be for them, they just can't stand it

354

unless they know everything the men in their lives know."

"Oh, hush—" Paulina twirled from his embrace, then smiled for both men before fixing her gaze upon Ruth. "And you conspired with these brutes," she said. "How could you, Ruth? I thought you were *my* friend."

"I am," responded Ruth. "That's why I kept mum."

When her gaze again lifted to Brett's, Paulina saw the true depths of his love for her, like a clean, blemish-free surface of crystal over his azure gaze. Quietly, she tucked herself into his arms, caring not that he was sweaty, and then whispered, "How empty was my life before I met you, Brett McCallum."

"I don't know . . . how empty was it?" With teasing affection he asked, "Now, what has brought about this revelation?"

To which she responded, "Just long past due, I think, Prince Kiam."

"What?" His look hinted that he might possibly think she'd lost her senses, but immediately, his mind snatched at a past conversation they'd enjoyed. "Oh, that's right . . . the island in your dream. At least you made me a prince rather than the villain."

"You could be that too, at times," she chuckled, turning in his arms and dragging his hands to her waistline. "If you two are all right, I'm going to make this devil of a man take me to that cave at the base of the mountain he's been telling me about."

"Go along, youngsters," Gruff said.

"Youngsters! I never thought I'd be hearing that at my age—"

"I wish I was thirty-five again," said Gruff.

"Why?" The single word was uttered by Ruth.

His eyes narrowing with loving pride, he looked into

Ruth's eyes and said, "Because then I'd have another fourteen wonderful years with you, wife."

Quietly, sadly, Brett and Paulina, linked together in an embrace, left the small bedroom where the newlyweds held hands and gazed at each other with the kind of love that under normal circumstances would have taken years to nurture to perfection.

Paulina wasn't especially fond of the mountain where Brett took her. It was where she had seen Gafferty, an encounter she still had not told Brett about. But she didn't want to think of that, because it made her angry with the man she loved for not believing her. Since she hadn't seen Gafferty in a few days, she was hoping that his image against the mountain had been nothing more than a mirage.

Or was he simply lying in wait, like a wolf watching a rabbit from the shadows of a timberline? A shudder crept along her spine. When Brett made a comment, she said simply, "Someone must have stepped on my grave."

To which he replied, "Nonsense."

Now they stood at the wide entrance of a cave, she looking in and Brett standing with his back to it as if he had suddenly detected an unwelcome presence. "What are we looking for in here?" asked Paulina.

"We're not looking for anything," he said, turning back. "There is something about a thousand yards into the cave that I want you to see."

Her curiosity was certainly piqued. "Will I like it?"

"You will love it."

Gathering her against him, he moved into the cave, smiling as she clumsily attempted to match his longer strides. He slowed down and coaxed her into the dizzying darkness.

Paulina was a little surprised; the cave reminded her a lot of the one she'd discovered on the Island of the Royal Crypt. The wide, expansive walls appeared a dark purple, darker even than the amethyst ones of her dream cave, and water trickled down, making her remember her dream in vivid detail. But unlike the cave of her dream, this one was cold and damp and dank, and she couldn't wait until she had seen what Brett wanted her to see so she could get back out into the cool sunshine. She imagined that a bear as big as a house would charge out of the shadows and reduce her to stew-size chunks.

"What are you thinking?" asked a solemn Brett, maneuvering her now into a tighter darkness of the cave.

"About stew."

"Hungry?"

"No." Just at that moment the narrow tunnel opened into a large cavern lit by sunlight. After several precarious minutes in the darkness, Paulina had to lift her hand to block out the painful brilliance. "Are we outside once again, Brett?"

"No . . . we are deeper into the cave."

"But how—"

"Look up—"

She followed the direction of his raised arm and immediately saw short, wide breaks in the ceiling to the right of the great cavern. Now she was more curious, because she felt the heat of a summer day chase away the cold she had felt. Then she saw it . . . the most magnificent structure she could have imagined. For there, spanning the rocky floor of the cavern for thirty feet in every direction was a miniature castle, complete with towers, gardens, and moats and tiny armor-clad knights on splendidly bedecked horses, damsels hanging from open windows, kings and queens . . . green trees, cobbled roadways, shops and markets and water wells scattered here and there.

"How absolutely marvelous," she whispered. "Did you build it?"

"Gruff built it, carved the stones for the castle and the city . . . the figures are all of white oak . . . but I believe one of our female neighbors, probably Mrs. Larkin, made the clothing for the wooden dolls." Carefully, Brett stepped over the low, long wall keeping the city together. Bending, he picked up one of the dusty horses with its regal black knight and handed it to her. "The detail is magnificent," he continued. "The armor is sheet metal. Gruff made that too. But this"—Brett returned the horse and stood to approach a tower of the castle—"this is what I wanted you to see."

"As if this isn't enough," said Paulina, still so deeply in awe she could scarcely drag her voice above a whisper. She watched as Brett removed something from the tower, then turned toward her. Standing before her, grinning, he handed her a doll that was scarcely seven inches high. Paulina's eyes widened with equal wonder as she gazed down upon the exquisitely carved features.

"Yes . . . she looks just like you, Paulina."

"It's amazing. It could be me! But how—" Looking up, she said, "You didn't say anything when we first met."

"You will notice the lack of dust on this one. Gruff carved and painted her just a week before we arrived. He told me about it only after he had seen you for the first time."

"So that is why he was so speechless when first we met. And I thought it was because he thought a woman had finally snared you." Moving gingerly through the castle grounds, Paulina returned the miniature figure. "This is your castle," she said to the figure, turning into Brett's arms. "And you are my castle."

"I thought I was your prince,"

"That too . . . Prince Kiam. You know—" Resting her chin against his hard chest, her hands circled to his back. Mischievous green eyes lifted to his darkly hooded ones. "I was really angry with you back then, when you would have sacrificed me in marriage to your tyrannical brother."

Brett swooped her into his arms, then moved outside the perimeters of Gruff's miniature castle. Soon he dropped her onto the smooth surface of a boulder and eased beside her. "It is strange how dreams work, isn't it?" he said after a moment. "You learned that I wanted you to marry Gruff, and in your dream you made Gruff a mad brother. And me . . . I should be flattered that I was your prince."

"You would have liked Caspius. Why, when I thought he was going to cut me in two with his sword, he merely offered me a delicious meal of meat and potatoes . . . after you had fed me nothing but fish and berries for nearly two weeks!"

With a hefty growl Brett swept her into his arms and held her close. "Dreams . . . dreams . . . Miss Paulina Winthrop. I am happy to share them with you!"

Something had been bothering Paulina of late, something ugly and black and which she really didn't want to bring up. But she simply had to know. It had been many weeks since she'd gotten only half the story from Brett, and now she felt that she would burst in her need to know everything. Was it the time to bring it up? Or would it darken his mood when it was especially good? He had been happy enough to bring her to a place that meant a lot to him because his friend Gruff had built it. She looked deeply into his loving gaze. She knew in her heart that he wouldn't mind sharing that painful part of his life with her. "Brett?"

"Ummm?" His cheek rested warmly, gently, against her own.

"Will you tell me what happened that day when Gafferty was killed?"

He drew back a little, surprised by the course their conversation had taken. "Why? What made you think of it?" When she hesitated, he asked, "Have you seen him again?"

She wanted to tell him the truth—that she had, indeed—but she remembered the past moments when it had angered him so. Therefore, she fibbed. "No, I am just curious. We spoke of it only once in the Pribilofs, and I have been curious. If I were to know what happened that day, perhaps I could forget about it and not dwell so deeply on it at times."

Trouble sat upon Brett's dark brow. The only reason that Paulina would dwell upon it was that she had seen Gafferty again. If she had, then why was she not telling him the truth? Then he stopped to think: He had not given her reason to trust him. He had accused her of lying so many times that she was now afraid he would do so again. Quietly he asked, "Tell me the truth, Paulina. Have you seen this man who identified himself to you as Gafferty?"

He was looking for a reason to be angry with her. They'd had such a lovely day, he'd brought her to see Gruff's castle, and there was so much left to enjoy before the brief interlude of night. She simply couldn't spoil his mood. "No, I promise you—" She'd discreetly crossed her fingers within the folds of her gown. "I just want to know. Curiosity, you know?"

"All right, I will tell you, and then we will never speak of it again. It is a part of my life that makes me hurt inside."

"Because your father was killed?"

"And . . . because I killed a man that day." A short pause brought silence to the vast cave. Far away, the distant rumbling of thunder could be heard. "That day—"

Paulina heard the words he spoke, the melancholy, the anger, and the regret. The regret, how darkly it echoed his words. She said nothing during the ten or fifteen minutes it took him to relate the painful story of his youth, and when he had finished, she looked tearfully up and said, "I'm sorry I brought it up. Can we forget it now and go on with our day?"

He did not have to force his smile. Her plaintive request captured his heart. "Miss Paulina Winthrop, our day is just beginning." And with renewed happiness he jumped up from the boulder, took her hand, and pulled her along as he eased into a half-run.

Moments later, a laughing, exhausted Paulina crumpled to a heap on the grass outside the cave, hugging the painful wrench in her chest. "Brett McCallum, you're trying to kill me!" she accused him, then pulled him down to the grass beside her. "I knew you didn't like me!"

"I'd like you even if you were wearing blue shoes!"

Surprise instantly touched Paulina's features. "Now, what on earth made you say that?"

"When I was a little boy"—Brett claimed her hand and held it fondly—"we lived in San Francisco for a year. That's where my mother's family lived."

"And your mother now runs a boardinghouse there."

"Yes, anyway, there was one little girl at the school I attended who always wore the same pair of blue shoes. I can't tell you how many times the toe of those blasted shoes bruised my shins! The little imp disliked me . . . and I was a runt back then. She easily outweighed me two to one." He grinned boyishly. "So now you'll know that if we have a daughter, we can't ever buy her a pair of blue shoes."

"Oh?" Paulina scooted to her knees and took Brett's other hand. "I could tell you a little verse my mother told me when I was a girl that will make you change your mind, that will wipe that ugly memory from your mind."

"I'll bet you can't."

"Take you on for a dollar."

"Deal."

Quietly, Paulina recited the poem from her childhood:

> Little blue shoes mustn't go,
> Very far alone, you know.
> Else she'll fall down or lose her way,
> Fancy what would mother say?
> Better put her little hand,
> Under mother's wise command.
> When she's a little older grown,
> Blue shoes may go quite alone.

"And what other charming verses did your mother tell you?"

"How about this one:

> "The wind, the wind, the naughty wind,
> That blows the skirts on high.
> But God was just and blew the dust,
> Right in the bad man's eye."

Brett laughed, "Now, that's my kind of verse. Just call me the wind!"

"I love you, Brett McCallum."

"Of course you do," he teased, pulling her roughly against him. "I'm the handiest thing to fulfill your woman's sentiments!"

"No, I truly love you, Brett."

How beautiful were the words falling from her lips. He held her close, caressing her tender flesh beneath his palm, feeling the wind rush through her hair and touch the coolness of his features. "And I love you, Paulina, with all my heart and all my soul. I don't want to live another day without you in my arms. As God is my witness, I will never hurt you and I will always protect you. I will even"—laughter slid into his tender words— "let you pass your childhood poems on to our sons and daughters."

"We'll have many," she responded.

"Half a dozen or more! I was an only child, a dull, boring existence! No brothers to wrestle with, no sisters to protect from older bullies. I don't want that in our family!"

Turning, Paulina fell against him, drawing her feet beneath her skirts. "Tell me about your mother. Why does she live in San Francisco rather than here with you? Have you seen her lately?"

"She's very fragile, couldn't take the bitter cold. Father understood though, and let her go. I haven't seen her since my army days, and then only briefly."

"Wouldn't you like to see her again?"

"Of course. She's a warm, gentle woman, and I love her very much. Besides"—Brett's embrace strengthened—"I want her to meet the woman I will marry."

It was still an alien feeling, knowing that she would become a bride, when she had always thought herself too headstrong for such sentiments. She had asked for the job of city marshal in Turkey Gulch. Now that didn't matter, and Brett did. When his embrace became even firmer, an attempt, she thought, to coax a response from her, she said, "I think I will like your mother."

"And your mother? You've really never said too much about her."

"My mother—" Though Paulina didn't feel the same degree of bitterness that Lillian did, it was there nonetheless. "She left us about seven years ago . . . the summer that I was leaving to attend school in New England. That is where her parents live. All I remember is she and Father talking late into the night . . . and Mother crying. The following morning she was gone, and Father would never explain. Lillian and I hear from Mother quite often, but she doesn't visit. Always she said she would, but she'd change her mind. I have a feeling that something happened between Mother and Earl Bartlett, something ugly and immoral."

"What makes you think that?"

"Something Earl said after Father's death. I didn't like his tone, and I certainly didn't like what he was implying. I am hoping that Millburn might know something, since he had been the closest friend my parents had. I fully intend to ask him."

"Do you realize how much we have in common parentwise?" said a thoughtful Brett. "Both of our fathers are dead, mine killed by the grizzly, yours murdered. Both of our mothers left for their own reasons and we hardly see them."

"And we are both willful and stubborn and determined to have our own way," laughed Paulina in an attempt to lighten the moment. "Oh, Brett, Brett, I do so enjoy being with you."

"You'd better, since you're going to be my wife!"

She turned against him, her mouth seeking the warm gentleness of his own. "I will be the best wife you've ever imagined, Brett. I will."

"And I will be an adoring husband. Promise me that if I ever do anything to annoy you, you will tell me and not brood silently over it. I hate getting the cold shoulder and not knowing what for."

"You should know by now that I usually speak my mind."

"And do you!" Rising, offering his hand, Brett felt the warmth of her fingers slip onto his palm. Thunder grumbled across the skies, and clouds tossed over themselves in their northerly travels. "We're in for a summer storm. Want to stick it out here, or run for cover?" But the rain began to splatter in large droplets, robbing them both of the decision. Firmly grasping her hand, Brett dragged her back into the darkness of the cave.

There they waited, chatting about pleasantries of their separate pasts, sharing a special hope for their future together, huddled together upon the cool, dry floor, watching the storm pound the earth outside. So driving was the rain that Paulina thought the base of the mountain would float away, leaving the rest to crush in on them.

But it didn't matter what course the mountain took. She was in Brett's arms, and that was all that mattered.

Gafferty waited out the storm in his own sanctuary, the abandoned cavern very near the top of the mountain, where an old prospector had once lived. In the several weeks that he had been in the region, he had stocked the shelves there with whiskey, canned goods, and smoked meats he'd purchased at the nearest trading post four miles away.

He had been patiently waiting, but now he was tired of the chase. It was time to put his plan into action. He had kept track of the four people living at Gruff's cabin, and by eavesdropping, snooping, and joining into casual conversation among folks here and abouts, he had learned their every move.

He needed only wait until the man named Gruff died; folks had hinted that it would be soon now. The woman Ruth was part of his plan, and even he had a conscience. He would not disrupt her life as long as she was unselfishly taking care of a dying man. With him out of the way, he had only the two women to deal with, and the man he would kill, Brett McCallum.

He was angry with Paulina Winthrop. Since she and Brett McCallum had been getting along fairly well, he suspected that she hadn't told him of his recent visit to the mountain. He had counted on her telling McCallum everything, and the fact that she possibly hadn't made him want to punish her.

He would have to deal with that later.

For now he had a dying to wait out.

After that the women would fall easily into his plan.

Then the greatest reward of all.

Brett McCallum . . . dead.

Twenty-three

Paulina sat at the edge of the stream, absently tossing stones into the shallow water. A dozen yards or so to the right, a waterfall splashed down steps of stone, and there a long tress of algae clung to a rock, waving hypnotically back and forth in the falling water.

The cabin was a dismal place to be. Gruff had taken another bad turn, had been in and out of delirium, and Paulina had been forced to separate herself from Ruth's grief for an hour or two. Though she'd spent these last ten hours constantly at Ruth's side, giving what comfort she could, she still felt guilty for the moments of solitude she enjoyed . . . or really didn't enjoy in view of the circumstances.

The shade of a cottonwood pressed coolly upon her skin. She began to rub her arms briskly in an attempt to bring a little warmth to them. All around her the forest wore its frock of rich summer green; an alder clung to the crumbling edge of a hill, its exposed roots dangling in no form or fashion. She imagined that they were the tentacles of a beast all mortal beings would be forced to face one day, Gruff sooner than others.

The beast was death, and it frightened her more than anything she had ever imagined.

"Paulina Winthrop! I've looked everywhere for you!"

She pivoted on her buttocks to face Brett as he advanced on her. "Well, you knew I wouldn't be far." And in a quieter voice, "Am I needed?"

Now beside her, he stooped, his hands draped across his knees. "No. In fact, Gruff's a little better. He's sitting on the porch now, and Ruth is trying to get him to eat."

Paulina dropped her cheek against his thigh, then her hand circled his knee and rested there. "It's sad when someone dies, Brett," she half whispered. "I was thinking about my father. You would have liked him."

"You speak so fondly of him that I'm sure I would have."

"There is no other way to speak of him." Paulina could tell that Brett had something on his mind even without seeing his eyes, which were the mirrors of everything he was. Looking up, she asked, "You have something to tell me?"

"Just that there's a visitor at the cabin to see you."

Her slender form snapped up, her features so touched by warm emotion that it made Brett smile. "Millburn? Is Millburn here? But he wasn't expected until Saturday."

" 'Tis here and now, Paulina girl! Not Saturday!"

Paulina turned so quickly that a wrench caught in her chest. Hugging it, her gaze cutting across the stream to the trail on the other side, she saw the tall, lumbering figure of her father's closest friend emerge from the shadows. So tightly did she grasp Brett's knee as she shot up that he said "Ouch," and she didn't even notice.

With a happy cry she dragged up her skirts and bounded across the shallow stream, throwing herself against Millburn with so much enthusiasm as she sought a hug that she nearly knocked him off balance. In his usual manner he acted a little annoyed at her show of emotion, and Paulina immediately drew back, though her moment of embarrassment did not reflect in her voice.

"Millburn . . . old Millburn Hanks! You don't know how far I've traveled to find you!"

"Yes, I do, Paulina girl. Yes, I do."

Brett watched in silence . . . the reunion between old friends making him happy inside. He came to his feet only when Paulina pulled Millburn toward him. "You've met my friend, Brett." She did not notice the hurt darken his eyes, because if she had, she would have immediately amended her description of their relationship. "Brett, this is Millburn. Millburn . . . Brett McCallum."

"I know." Brett took the man's hand. "We met in passing at the cabin."

"How'd you know who I was?" asked a curious Millburn.

"Before I got out of hearing range, I heard Ruth speak your name." When Millburn gave him a narrow look, a sheepish Brett added, "I don't eavesdrop. Sorry, I guess I forgot to stick my fingers in my ears."

"You'd of looked a little peculiar, young man," said Millburn without cracking a smile.

Though his eyes shone like glass, Millburn's features were, characteristically, as expressionless as stone. Paulina remembered him sitting at the table with her parents, discussing the passing of friends and acquaintances and showing not the least bit of remorse or grief. Questioning her father, she had been told, "He grieves in silence. No one sees his tears, but he sheds them. On the other hand, he'll be overjoyed to see you after a time, but he'll scarcely show it, if at all." She could see no emotion in the firm set of his features as his gaze eventually returned to her, but Paulina had no doubt whatsoever that he was overjoyed to see her. She felt it in her heart. It was important, because she had traveled so far. To think, for even a minute, that he was annoyed that she'd bothered was absolutely unacceptable.

"So, Paulina girl, why have you come all this way?"

The three of them moved casually toward a long, thick log that had fallen during the winter. Paulina took a seat first, taking Brett's hand to coax him to the rough timber beside her. Millburn sat on the other side of her, his eyes squinting against the morning sun.

"At first it was to implore you to come back to Turkey Gulch," she responded to Millburn's inquiry, "and testify against Earl and Lester."

"What makes you think I had anything to testify to?"

"Because I know you witnessed Earl gunning down my father that night."

"You know no such thing." He'd spoken roughly, though without feeling. "If I had, indeed, you and Lillian were in the East when he was killed and could not possibly have known what I did or did not see."

"I did some investigating after Father's funeral. You left Turkey Gulch the morning after he was killed. Any person in his—or her—right mind would have assumed that you knew something about it."

Millburn had been living with the guilt for the past two years. Yes, he had seen the Bartletts that night, tracking his good friend along a dark street. He had seen Lester stand silently by while Earl shot him in the back . . . and, damn, Earl knew he'd witnessed it. Had Millburn not fled Turkey Gulch, he'd have been the next victim.

In a quiet, hoarse voice Millburn responded, "And suppose I did see something, and suppose I did leave because of it. You said it was the initial reason you came after me. Ain't it the reason now?"

"Earl and Lester were ambushed and killed. There's

no need to testify against them now, except that your testimony will put the suppositions as to my father's killers to rest . . . finally. When I learned of their death, I wanted to let you know so that you could come back to Turkey Gulch—if you want to, of course."

Brett moved so suddenly that it startled Paulina. Her look was soft, and yet still demanded an explanation. "I feel like I'm eavesdropping on two old friends reuniting," he said after a moment, his gaze sliding between the two people. "I'll go on back to the cabin and see if I can do anything to help Ruth."

He'd sounded almost rueful, and Paulina took the moment to think back over what had been said in the few minutes since Millburn had arrived. Then she realized she'd referred to Brett as "friend," and certainly, that description needed to be clarified. He was much, much more than a friend, and he should know that better than anyone. Thus, taking his hand and holding it fondly, she said, "If you must go, my love, I'll be along shortly." Then she looked to her left and said to Millburn, "I believe I neglected to tell you that Brett and I will be married. We share everything." And lifting her adoring eyes to Brett, she softly added, "Even our pasts."

Millburn said, "Well, you are a lucky man, McCallum."

To which Brett teasingly replied, "No, she's a lucky lady." Squeezing her hand, he separated from her, then turned, took a few steps, and waved back at them.

When he was out of sight, Millburn said, "Where'd you meet the young man?"

Paulina had been watching the forest, her gaze narrowing to catch the last sight of Brett as he merged into the shadows. She wished that he'd stayed. "In Skagway," she responded, looking back to Millburn.

"Skagway? Did you ever meet Soapy Smith?"

With a humorless laugh Paulina commenced to tell Millburn of her experiences with Soapy. She told him everything, including how Brett had been shot in the leg and Soapy had let her believe she'd done it when, in fact, one of his men had fired the gun. Then she looked to Millburn and asked, "Why did you mention Soapy?' "

"Rascal got himself killed. Read about it in a paper coming out of St. Michael."

"Soapy's dead? How?" Paulina had thought the scalawag was invincible. Surely a mistake had been made. It had to be someone else. "Are you sure it was Soapy?"

Paulina was not sure what compelled her to leave the cabin in the early morning darkness that would last no more than three hours. A soft mist rose about her ankles as she moved slowly, quietly making her way across the clearing and into the woods. Reaching the stream, she lifted her skirts and traversed it. Scarcely fifteen minutes later she was entering the Sullivans' cabin.

She wasn't sure whether it was the darkness that made the cabin seem different, but now the boards seemed old, the hinges rusty, and a nail protruding from one caught on her dress as she closed the door.

The darkness created noises that had not existed before, and Paulina suddenly regretted her decision to leave the cabin. Though Gruff was a little better—she'd heard him and Brett mulling over the chess set as she'd slipped out—she felt a terrible need to escape and seek solitude. Millburn had not yet returned from Nuklukayet, and she was sure—if her memory served her correctly—that he would seek the nourishment of the saloons before returning to the cabin.

A creak outside.

Paulina, who'd been about to drop to the wide, dusty

divan, reeled about, facing the door separating her from the outside darkness. Could it be Gafferty? Oh, what a fool she was to have left the cabin!

In a moment of bravado she approached and jerked the door open, stepping out to the porch and attempting to see through the veil of shadows that was the forest. Though she saw nothing, she wanted to assure herself that she was, indeed, alone, and moved across the clearing, a painful tension easing into her shoulders as she skirted the timberline. The twigs of an alder whipped gently across her neck as she made her way around the darkness.

In a calm, low voice, she called, "Come out, come out, wherever you are." Expecting no response—truly, she didn't—she was startled when the weeds suddenly parted and a small gray rabbit scurried out of her way. As it was enveloped in the rising mist, she drew her hand to her throat and patted it roughly, fussing at herself, "Paulina, it's your fault your heart is beating at a frantic pace. You were foolish to come out here alone!"

Now finding the silence unnerving, Paulina hurried back to the Sullivans' cabin, traversed the steps, and closed herself within the security of the walls. Aware of the musty smell, which seemed to close in and nauseate her, she covered her nose and mouth with a warm palm, then fluttered her hand in the tight air. "Why, in heaven's name, did I come here?" she continued to fuss.

She had seen matches a few days earlier, the same day, in fact, that she and Brett had spent wonderful moments together, and now searched for them on the mantel. Ah, there they are! Old newspapers, though almost black with the passage of time, soon sprang to life as she tossed one of the matches upon the logs that probably had been there since the Sullivans' departing.

With the shadows skittering along the walls, brought

from hiding by the gentle flames licking at the hearth, Paulina became aware of the dust covering everything, settling, even, upon her skin as she moved about.

She had thought the cabin warm and sad, and yet comforting; now it emitted a mysterious, cold aura that she could not dispel, and certainly could not explain. Though the logs had quickly caught, and the warmth was replacing the cold within the room, she shuddered. "Someone walked on my grave again," she muttered, settling onto the divan and trying not to hear the haunting sounds of the night without.

The shiver remained in her shoulders, yet over the span of an hour or two . . . or three . . . she really wasn't counting, not so much as the whisper of another human being invaded the tranquility of the room. Outside, an occasional stir hinted at the presence of a nocturnal creature, and the wind whipped through the trees with a greedy need to keep things stirred up. But Paulina felt only comfort in the wind and the creatures of the night, and in her solitude. Soon she stirred herself, left the cabin as dawn's light began to filter through the ragged gossamer at the windows, and now made her way back to the cabin she shared with Brett, Gruff, and Ruth. She entered through the kitchen, causing both male heads to snap around in surprise.

Brett said, "I thought you were sound asleep."

To which she replied, "I just took a little walk." She favored both men with a pleasant smile. "Would you two chess-playing champions like breakfast?"

"Shall I assist?"

Ruth emerged through the curtains separating kitchen and living room, still rubbing her sleep-filled eyes. She bent across Gruff's shoulder and gave him a peck on the cheek. "How are you this morning, husband?"

"Blasted rotten," came Gruff's response, though an undertone of affection touched his words. "This young whippersnapper has beaten me seven times in a row. You'd think he'd have more respect for a dyin' man." And grinning to Brett, "An' let me win at least once!"

Brett laughed. "I don't give away victories, you old rascal. If you want it, earn it . . . if you can." Then, taking a moment to feel a little neglected, he said to Paulina, "Why is it that Gruff deserves a morning kiss from his woman and I don't?"

Pauline arched both her eyebrows, her look almost sarcastic. "Oh, well, did you ask Ruth for a morning kiss?" Then they all laughed, and in the flurry of morning laughter Paulina bent, eased her arms around Brett's shoulder, and kissed him warmly. "There, is that better?"

"Yes"—he pouted boyishly—"but it won't take the place of breakfast." Drawing back, Paulina clicked her tongue. "Well, it won't!" he continued. "I'm famished. How about you, Gruff?"

"Maybe a cup of coffee and a flapjack. I ain't really that hungry."

Making a social event of breakfast seemed to have become a way of life at the cabin. When Millburn came in halfway through Gruff's meal of seven flapjacks, the occupants of the cabin burst into laughter. "What's so funny?" asked a serious-faced Millburn.

"We were just wondering," Brett said, "how long it would be before you broke up this event."

The reference was to the noonday meal yesterday. In the middle of conversation Millburn had extracted from his pocket the most offensive item any one of them could imagine—one of his hand-rolled cigars, made of tobacco grown directly in horse manure. They were all sure the tobacco leaves had absorbed the full brunt of the fertilizer's odor.

"Ah—" A rare note of laughter echoed in Millburn's deep voice. "I'll try to keep the blasted things in my pocket."

And they laughed again, dispersing only when, by habit or instinct, Millburn lit up half an hour later.

As Brett chopped more firewood for the cabin, Paulina walked with her old friend in the forest that morning. Together they sat on the boulder against the mountain where she had last seen Gafferty, and now Paulina brought up the subject that had been bothering her for seven years—her mother.

"Why did she leave, Millburn?"

"Who is that, Paulina girl?"

"You know who . . . my mother."

"Oh!" Silence. Millburn raked his hat from his scant head of graying hair, then cupped it across his drawn-up knee. A world of thought flooded his mind as he remembered the years before the very beautiful Laura Roxbury Winthrop had left Turkey Gulch. Had it already been seven years?

"Did Father still love her?"

In his moment of thought, Paulina's inquiry startled him. "Love her? Paulina girl, your father adored her."

"Then why, Millburn. Please—I'm twenty-four years old, no longer a girl. I need to know so that I can understand."

He did not hesitate to respond. "Very well." He did hesitate a moment after those two words. "Your mother was a victim of the most heinous crime, Paulina, rape."

"Rape!" Paulina shot from the boulder so quickly she felt faint. She turned shocked and bewildered eyes to Millburn. "My dear, beautiful mother? By whom!" She spoke the question as though she would immediately take up a gun and kill the offender. When Millburn hesitated, she repeated, "By whom?"

Millburn lowered his gaze, his knuckles bending upon the boulder as he quietly shook his head. "By Earl Bartlett."

"A Bartlett! I should have known!" Paulina was furious; she wished the Bartletts weren't already dead so that she could rush home and put a bullet in Earl herself. But, gaining a moment of calm, she asked, "But surely Papa understood. He did not send her away because of that!"

"He didn't send her away, Paulina. It was only after she"—he hesitated, a whisper easing into his usually gruff words—"after she discovered that she was carrying a child . . . and that it was Earl's."

"A child. Dear Lord—" Paulina turned away, attempting to shield her tear-moistened eyes from her old friend. "Papa sent her away because of a child?"

"He didn't send her away. It was her choice to leave, and there was nothing he could say or do to make her stay. She didn't want Earl to know about the child, but he found out, and that is why she had to remain in hiding in the East. To this day only her parents—your grandparents—know where she is."

Paulina swung back, a world of pain in her eyes. "My word, Millburn. I have a half—"

"—Brother," Millburn finished the statement. "His name is Garrett, and with your father's permission, he is registered as a Winthrop. With the Bartletts dead, no one ever need know that he is anything other than a Winthrop, including the boy himself."

Tears now flowed freely down Paulina's cheeks. "How do you know all this, Millburn?"

"Because I visited her after your father's death. And we have kept in touch ever since." At that point he extracted a wad of letters, held together by a paper band, and handed them to Paulina. "Here, I want you to read them, and then you will understand everything. And I know you haven't felt as strongly as your sister. Perhaps you will harbor no bitterness at all toward your mother. She loves you dearly. You and Lillian—and her son, Garrett—are more precious to her than anything. And you will understand that she has missed you terribly. Had it not been for the Bartletts, she would have come home years ago." When Paulina began to cry gently, her shoulders rocking with emotion, the usually staid Millburn drew her into an embrace. His bony hand gently massaged her back, then patted it paternally. "You cry if you want to, Paulina girl, but you remember, you have a mother who loves you, and a little brother you need to get to know. You and Lillian, I know the two of you have a world of love within you, and that little boy, though deeply loved by his mother and his grandparents, needs the two of you."

Just at that moment Brett emerged from the forest and quickly approached. "Come back to the cabin, Paulina. Gruff"—his words were rough with emotion—"Gruff's on his way out."

"What? But he just—" Paulina felt the grief filling and quaking within her. "He just consumed eight flapjacks. He was fine."

"He's going," Brett reiterated, taking her hand. "You too, Millburn. He wants to see you too."

Hardly had ten minutes passed before they were around Gruff's bedside. Ruth, her fingers tightly linked as she fought back tears, sat in the chair beside him. Brett stood back, the emotion dark upon his features. Millburn, felt sad but out of place, as if he hadn't known Gruff long enough to be part of his dying. And Paulina, stood behind Ruth with her hand resting on her shoulder for comfort.

"This is it," mumbled Gruff. "I know it this time." Raising a weak hand, he summoned Brett to him. "Over there—the board in front of that old chest, look under it, old friend." Quietly, Brett moved toward the chest, stooped, and pried up the loose board. There, resting side by side, were two small wooden chests with brass trim. "Take them out," ordered Gruff, and when they rested on the edge of the bed, he said to Ruth, "The gold in these boxes is worth about twenty thousand dollars. I want you to have it." Looking to Brett, he said with a small grin, "I know you don't need it. You have all the treasure you need in that sweet little lady right there." Fondness lit his eyes as he looked to Paulina. Then he turned his gaze to Millburn. "You ain't got a woman here in Alaska, Hanks, an' I'm here to tell ya, my Ruthie is one fine lady. I'd be obliged if you watched out for her and made sure she'll be all right. I wouldn't even mind if—" He left that thought unspoken, but the four people surrounding him knew what it would have been.

"Can I get anything for you, husband?"

"Naw," growled Gruff, though affectionately. "But ya might shoo these folks out so's you an' me can be alone for a while."

Approaching, taking Paulina's hand, Brett coaxed her into the kitchen. When Millburn had joined them, he and Paulina sat at the table while Brett poured the three of them cups of coffee.

The minutes passed; they were only vaguely aware of the quiet mutterings of the two people beyond the curtain, and once, giving them hope, a male laugh reached into the kitchen. Could he come out of it again, as he had several times these past weeks?

Yes, yes, perhaps . . . but would it only prolong his agony?

Then the muttering became silent, the three people in the kitchen looked from one to the other, and Ruth's sobs, muffled by the blankets resting over Gruff, told them that it was over.

Tears filled Brett's eyes. He drew up from the table and walked out to the porch. Paulina, weeping herself, gave him time alone, and her hand scooted across the table to find comfort in Millburn's.

She looked up when Ruth emerged from the darkness beyond the curtains and leaned against the door facing with her hands tucked into the small of her back. "He's gone," she said, emotion fragile upon her voice. "Where is Brett?"

"He's on the porch," responded Paulina, rising to give Ruth a hug. "I'm so sorry."

"I know," said Ruth, drawing back, taking Paulina's hand to hold it warmly for a moment. Then she moved toward the exterior of the cabin to talk to Brett and tell him where Gruff wanted to be buried.

Brett turned when Ruth approached and her hand touched his forearm. Gently, he held her, saying, "We all loved him, Ruth. Thank you for making him so happy."

"I'm afraid he wasn't very lucid," said Ruth, stifling her tears. "He said he wanted to be interred in the room with the castle."

Brett smiled sadly. "He was very lucid. There is a castle, Ruth, and if that's where Gruff wants to be, then that's where he'll be."

The following morning, four very somber people, joined by mourners from throughout the region, gave

Gruff the kind of funeral he deserved. Then, with two sticks of dynamite at the entrance of the cave, the walls were brought in, dropping a hundred tons of rock onto the cave's front entrance. Wrapping his arm across Paulina's trembling shoulders, a quiet Brett said, "No one will ever disturb Gruff's peace. Not as long as this mountain stands against the sky."

As the dust and debris settled, they turned toward the cabin that had been Gruff's home, sat at the table, and spoke fondly of Brett's old friend.

And occasionally, a breeze would stir within the cabin where no window stood open . . . and they knew that Gruff was still there.

It was where he had been happy. And it was where he would remain.

Twenty-four

Two weeks after Gruff's funeral, life began to return to normal at the little cabin facing the Yukon River. Ruth had decided to stay rather than return to her former life with a daughter who considered her a hindrance . . . or so she explained. Both Brett and Paulina suspected the real reason was that Millburn had asked her to stay. Ruth had learned to love Gruff in the few short weeks they'd spent together, but she was especially fond of Millburn. Dear Ruth deserved a second chance, and Paulina hoped that it might be with a good man like Millburn. Ruth managed, in those long, lonely days following Gruff's burial, to display the lovely depths of her character.

"What?" Brett stared at the small trunk of gold Ruth held out to him. "I'm not taking that. It's yours, Gruff wanted you to have it."

"You were his best friend, Brett. Please, Gruff would have wanted it."

Brett remained adamant. "No, that was not his wish."

"We were all with him in his last hour. You saw how much pain he was in. You know that he wasn't thinking clearly."

At that point Paulina approached, tucked her arms

into Brett's, and smiled sadly when her gaze met Ruth's. "You heard Brett. You were Gruff's wife, and you gave him much happiness in his final weeks. The gold is yours, Ruth."

Brett dropped his hand onto Paulina's. "You have heard my little woman," he said fondly. "And I believe the matter is closed."

The box, growing heavy in Ruth's arms, found a resting place on a small table. "Well, I still have a while to try to convince you," she said, "because there is too much gold for one person here, and Gruff would have wanted it this way. Besides—" Clicking her tongue in gentle admonishment, she added, "What on earth am I to do with it?"

Smiling, Brett lifted his nose into the air. "I'm getting a strong whiff of that bacon Millburn's cooking. How about if I escort two fine-looking ladies in for an Alaskan breakfast?"

Paulina laughed, "Bacon and eggs and biscuits, sounds like a Utah breakfast to me."

And Ruth chimed in, "Sounds like a Mississippi breakfast to me."

When they joined Millburn in the small kitchen, he said, "I have to agree with Paulina. This *is* a Utah breakfast."

Over the span of half an hour, the four of them made a social event of breakfast, chatting, laughing, reminiscing and remembering Gruff, with Brett relating to them some of the pranks his good friend had pulled over the years. The mundane morning event, made into the highlight of their day, might never have ended had Millburn not extracted from the pocket of his shirt one of the odorous cigars that could drive people out faster than a single, sick old polecat.

As polite amenities saw Brett, Ruth, and Paulina move

into another room, Millburn asked, "Hey, where you goin'? We were just gettin' started on this conversation."

Paulina said, "I have to mend a torn dress."

Ruth added, "And I have to help her."

At which time Brett chimed in, "Me too."

And they all laughed—Millburn too, because this happened every time he lit up. As he sat alone at the table, staring at the swirling smoke of his cigar, he mumbled, "Hell, I oughta give up these things. Ain't real good fer my social image."

As the morning moved toward noon, Millburn and Ruth prepared to leave the cabin to journey to the site of Millburn's camp farther east on the Yukon. He had wanted to show her the large cabin he had built, and the "magic" spot in the Yukon shallows that had yielded a goodly amount of gold.

"Gold! Gold! Gold!" fussed Ruth. "Men are so preoccupied with gold!"

Shrugging, an indulgent Millburn said to Brett and Paulina, "We'll be gone until tomorrow evenin'." Millburn winked. "So you two can have some privacy."

A crimson-cheeked Paulina had said, "Now, what would we need privacy for?"

And Brett said simply, "Thanks, old man. We'll find something to do, I'm sure."

Millburn teased, "My chess set's under the kitchen table."

Ruth reminded him, "But there are two pawns missing."

"I hate chess anyway," said Brett, waving farewell to his departing friends, his other hand hugging Paulina's shoulder. When they were at last alone, he said, "How about if I cook you the best lunch you've ever had."

Paulina chuckled. "Isn't cooking *woman's* work?"

"My experience with women," Brett laughed in re-

turn, "is that *their* work is anything they want to do."
Then he pulled her to him, embraced her as would a
lover, and whispered, "And I know you can do anything
you set your heart to do, Miss Paulina Winthrop. You
are the strongest, bravest, sweetest, most sensual woman
I have ever known in my life."

She enjoyed the musky, manly scent of him for a moment, until he, laughing, pulled her out into the day of
endless sunlight, temporarily forgetting the lunch he
had promised her. Still, though summer was upon them,
the cold kept its grip on the Yukon, and the wind bit at
Paulina's tender flesh. But she scarcely felt it, for she
was enveloped by the warm glow of Brett McCallum and
nothing could penetrate the aura they created together.

Thereafter, they set about doing the little things they
had told Ruth they would do. But when Brett dug the
hole to plant the stripling spruce Gruff and Ruth had
brought home that same week he'd died, he found the
earth frozen solid a foot into the ground. Taking up a
pickax, he was able to dig the hole out another six
inches, enough to support the young spruce as it took
root. Gruff's pet caribou assisted in the chores until
Paulina, exasperated by her mischief, shooed her away
from the garden they were planting for Ruth. But
Penelope immediately returned, and Brett set about
building a fence around the garden and reinforcing it
with the chicken wire from the uninhabited coops. Not
a single chicken Gruff had brought from St. Michael last
summer had survived after the wolves had gotten a whiff
of them. Gruff had given up; wolves *didn't* like turnips
and cabbages nearly as much.

Brett was startled from a thoughtful mood when
Paulina quietly approached him from behind and her
arms circled his waist. The hoe he'd been leaning upon
fell to the ground. "What were you thinking about?"

asked Paulina, her cheek caressing his back through the thick fabric of his shirt.

"Gruff and chickens and wolves," said Brett, turning to take her in his arms. For a moment he studied her features, her cheeks glowing against the cool wind, her thick, loose hair waving gently beneath his hands. Right now her eyes were as green as the grass laid flat by the breeze rolling along the ground, and adoring . . . and expectant. "And what are you thinking about, my pretty lady?" he asked in a husky tone.

"About you and me and an empty cabin, a warm bed and a willing woman. What else do you think I might add to my list of thoughts?"

"A willing man?" A dark eyebrow arched; a devilish smile curled his mouth. "But one who might need a bath if he becomes a viable choice on your list."

Paulina tucked herself against him. "You smell like a man. But"—she eased back, a smile playing upon her full, sensual mouth—"that is quite a tub in there. Big enough, I'd wager, for two."

When, indoors, Brett again insisted on a bath, Paulina checked to see if there was any hot water left in the kitchen. For the next few minutes Brett hauled in cold water and Paulina stirred the coals in the stove. Several times he paused to hold her close, to kiss a warm cheek or nuzzle against her hairline. "We'd better hurry with that bath. The big bad wolf is getting impatient."

Paulina promised him, "A bath—especially one that is prepared for two people of opposing genders—can be quite a pleasurable experience. Just be patient, Brett McCallum." When he shuddered, Paulina raised a quizzical brow, the smile she might have favored upon him deliberately suppressed. "Has the very idea caused a shiver to crawl over your flesh, McCallum?"

"No—" he said, grinning, pulling her close and

squeezing. "Makes me shake all over just thinking about it. Is that hot water ready yet?"

Paulina saw then that Brett had built a new fire to warm the cabin. Its glow permeated the kitchen as she turned in his arms and said, "The water is hot. If you will add it to the bath, I shall climb out of these dusty clothes." When she started to draw away, his hand scooted to her back and again she was against him, feeling the warmth, the raging heat of his prowess. "Let me go, Brett McCallum," she said, feigning indignation, "or I shall faint right here and you'll never—"

"I'll never what?" A grin raked his masculine good looks. "See you without these rags again? I think not!"

Her cheek brushed his as she pivoted away from him. "Get on with that water, Brett, and don't burn yourself. I promise you'll have better things to concentrate on than pain!"

Then she half ran into the rustic parlor where the large tub waited patiently in a corner, and she began removing her dress.

Using a folded towel to take up the black iron pot, Brett was soon adding the hot water to the tub. All the while he watched Paulina disrobing . . . first the dress . . . then her shoes and stockings and now . . . she sat on a small stool and began untying the laces of her chemise. Looking up, she asked with a smile, "Are you spying on me, sir?"

And he replied, "But not without your blessing—"

"I beg to differ—" The teasing tone remained in her voice. When she started to pull off the chemise, Brett approached, taking both her hands to hold them in his own.

"Let me do that." His hands eased beneath the thin fabric and rested on her slim shoulders. With one fluid move the smooth white flesh was exposed and he deliberately paused over the soft curves of her breasts. His gaze held her own boldly, lovingly, with promises reflecting in its depths. How lovely were her features framed by the mass of pale tresses, like golden clouds. Bringing them up in the palms of his hands, he buried his face in their rich softness.

He wanted only to explore her supple curves and smooth flesh. "Now, what were we going to do?" he asked, lifting his head, his voice low and lusty.

"Take a bath," came her soft response. "At least . . . I think we were."

He grinned almost malevolently as he swooped her into his arms for a moment, then turned with her. "A bath," he mused. "A nice hot, milky bath. I suppose you added some of that oil to the water?"

"I did," she replied, her voice blank of emotion, but a merry twinkle shone in her emerald eyes as their gazes met. "Do you mind?" Oh, what was this about baths and oils and whether they were going to take one or not? Paulina knew only that her flesh was both hot and cold at the same moment, and a fierce longing deep within reminded her how very aroused she could be by the nearness of this man. The manly aroma of him was like a drug . . . fogging her mind and yet clearing it at the same moment . . . fogging . . . clearing . . . and she wanted only to be held close by him.

But then the unthinkable happened. With a husky laugh Brett McCallum dropped her into the bathtub and the oily, sudsy water splashed hither and yon. As a very surprised Paulina gripped the sides of the tub, unable to see through the limp strands of hair now covering her features, Brett's hand covered the crown of her head and she was immediately pushed beneath the water. But just as suddenly, as she prepared to berate him—perhaps, even, to call him an impolite name—his clothed body was covering hers and his mouth was seeking the roughest of kisses.

"Oh! I hate you, Brett McCallum. Why do I put up with you?"

"No, you don't hate me—" Straightening himself, he pulled off his shirt, then threw it to the planked floor, where it landed with a dull, wet thud. And when his hands moved to pull her soaked chemise from her, she slapped his hand away. "What? You've changed your mind? Well, heckfire, little lady, what did I do?"

His silly, forced western drawl elicited the smallest of smiles. Again she slapped him, this time upon the broad, naked expanse of his chest. "You know what you did! You dropped me into the tub and now look. We have a mess to clean up!"

"It'll soak through to the ground," he laughed, his effort to remove her chemise, this time, meeting with success. When Paulina made a feeble attempt to cover herself, he took her arms and pulled them onto his shoulders. "Don't be shy, little lady."

She could not maintain her façade of being indignant no matter how she tried. Her smiling mouth touched his own, then softened to accept the teasing hunger of his caress. Between his playful nips, she murmured, "How is it . . . that some horrid thing you do . . . like dropping me in the tub . . . only . . . makes me . . . want you more?"

"Because I know you, Paulina Winthrop." His hands slipped into the waist of her pantaloons and eased them down. As her legs came together and upward between his own, the pantaloons became airborne, landing atop his discarded shirt.

"Your only asset, Brett McCallum," she laughed, tucking herself against him once again, "is still in the barn."

"Why, you little hussy!" he laughed. "And you told me you were a lady."

"I am a lady. Really, I am."

"Real ladies don't talk like that!"

"What did I say?" She would have smiled, but her heart was pounding fiercely. Lifting her fingers to trace a path along the fringe of his damp hair, she coaxed his mouth to her own and kissed it gently. "I said I wanted *all* of you lying against me, Brett McCallum."

"But you didn't use those exact words," he continued in his teasing tone.

At that point her hands dropped to his shoulders, traced a line over the taut muscles of his arms, then pulled together to circle each of his dark nipples. As he watched, smiling, his flesh tantalized by her sensual touch, her fingers soon eased beneath the waist of his trousers and a button popped, then two . . . then three.

"All right," he groaned, rolling his eyes as though he found her actions intolerable. "I'll take them off. Why didn't you just say so?"

The bottoms of her feet touched his belly, and she used the leverage to push herself away, giving him more room. When he hesitated, that boyish grin again turning up the corners of his mouth, she insisted, "Well . . . go ahead. I'm not in the way, am I?"

Soon, laughing at his own clumsiness as he found the tub a tad small for maneuvering, Brett slung off the heavy denim trousers. Now his toe traveled along Paulina's inner thigh, and when it suddenly emerged from the suds, she grabbed and held on fast. "Oww!" He made a feeble attempt to withdraw the captured toe, and when that failed, reached over and pulled her against him. "Capture my heart, woman. Leave my toes alone!"

"Oh? Sacred ground?"

"No, tender ground. I stubbed one of them getting out of bed this morning. Don't you remember?"

"I was sound asleep," she continued the playful bantering. "Do you want Paulina to kiss it for you?"

"No." He grinned boyishly, his finger tucking into the corner of his mouth. "But I'll take that kiss right here. I'll even pucker up if you'd like."

His playful pucker ended when her mouth touched his gently, caressing, tasting, demanding. Her fingers lifted to his thick sable-colored hair and then traced a path along his jawline. With a small, sensual smile, she said, "I really should insist that you shave this sandpaper face before—"

"Before what? he prompted her when she fell silent. "Before you allow me to kiss you?" Just at that moment his hand moved over the side of the tub, returning with a straight razor and the bar of soap. Handing her the razor, he sudsed the soap between his hands, then slapped it to his face. Sitting, grinning out at her from the cloud of soft white covering the bottom half of his face, he said, "You will now see how much I trust you. I'm going to let you shave this handsome mug."

Paulina looked first at the razor, then deeply into his eyes, before easing to her knees between his thighs. "Shall I start at your throat? Or—" Without warning, she pinched his nose between her thumb and forefinger, lifting it up. When he grumbled, she quipped with teasing affection, "Don't be such a baby."

Brett had never thought being shaved could be so sensual. But Paulina had a way of doing it that made his body ache for want of her, the way her fingers grazed his jawline, making a path for the razor, the gentleness with which she turned his face, first to the left and then to the right, the careful method she employed to make sure the hair was left even at his ears, and the way she grinned when his throat was all that was left to be shaved.

"Don't look at me like that, pretty lady," Brett warned, suppressing a grin in an effort to appear threatening.

"I'm just wondering . . . are you *sure* you trust me?"

"I do," came his short, firm response.

When she continued, Brett had that I-can't-believe-I'm-doing-this look, and yet, a few seconds later, the razor put aside, he realized that not once had she nicked him, something he himself had never accomplished. Now it was time to take her in his arms and hold her and love her and tell her how precious she was to him.

Resting her cheek against Brett's, Paulina murmured, "That's better. You won't scrape all the flesh off my face now."

"And other delicious body parts," he murmured.

The tub became a playground . . . masterful strokes and caresses . . . female responses . . . hot, sensual kisses . . . and when, long before the water began to grow cold, Brett drew up, stepped from the tub, and picked up Paulina as if she were weightless, they were both ready for the wonderful continuation of their love. Within moments he eased her to the bed, covering her wet body with his own, then again found her mouth in a deep, commanding, roughly erotic kiss.

She purred with pleasant pain as his mouth sought and found her passion-sensitive breasts, to caress circles around them, the hardness of him resting against her and, unconsciously, her thighs eased apart to allow for him. Fire consumed her; almost greedily her fingers massaged the hot expanse of his chest, then circled to draw him closer. How persuasive was the passion of this man—this rough-and-ready Alaskan—and she wanted only to join to him, like liquid fire.

"Are you ready for me?" asked a husky-voiced Brett McCallum.

"I was ready for you in the tub," she murmured, her pretty mouth easing into a most coy smile. "Am I a hussy or not?"

He had aroused a fury within her, and when at last the full, commanding maleness of him slipped inside her, she felt wild, unabandoned rapture seize her body from head to toe. This was what she wanted for the rest of her life, to be Brett's woman, and to know that he was the man who would forever please her.

He began to move within her, his slim hips grinding against her own, the ease with which she matched his rhythm and pace coursing them toward a vastness of no return. Her erotic caresses traveled the length of him, and it pleased her that she could bring that special look—that dark, fiery passion—to his face.

Melting together in arousing splendor, they lifted to ethereal planes and reeled together in splendid ecstasy. Blinded by their mutual passions, they spiraled together toward the riveting storm their own bodies created, and now, with her heart pounding as fiercely as his own, she felt the seed of his passion fill her . . . and again—because they were made for each other—her own tremor joined his until they lay in exhausted splendor.

With their breathing slowing in gentle harmony, Paulina eased her fingers into his dark, damp hair. His body remained joined to her own, and might have remained like that if a sound had not erupted from the clearing outside.

Just before he hastily withdrew from her, his fingers painfully gripped her shoulders. Now she watched him at the window, the nakedness of him silhouetted against the light he had dragged into the room by parting the black curtains.

"Dear God—" he mumbled.

And a worried Paulina, hopping from the bed with a blanket clutched modestly to her, asked, "What is wrong?" When her gaze followed the direction of his own, she said, "It's just a silly old bear. He'll go away when he finds nothing to eat. Come—" When the huge beast ambled into the woods, her fingers circled her lover's wrist, "Let's go back to bed."

But with a mighty groan he freed himself from her touch, then roughly drew his fingers through his hair. "No . . . I've got to go after him."

"Why? For heaven's sake." She didn't like the way his eyes had narrowed, his mouth pinched, and an almost lethal darkness eased into his features. Placing her hand gently upon his arm, she asked, "What is wrong, Brett?"

"It's him!" he barked, turning, retrieving a pair of dry trousers from a rack and pulling them on. "He's the one—the six-toed bear—that killed my father. I have to kill him." Lifting his gaze to her ashen one, he rudely reiterated, "I have to, dammit! I don't expect you to understand!"

"But how can you know it is him?"

"Because—" His teeth gritted. "He has a bare, burned patch on his rump. He's the one." Then, following a pause, "He's definitely the one!"

That seemed to be the last word. He was not even interested in her redressing, an event he had always liked to watch before. Now it was as if she were the least important aspect of his life, and that frightened her. She had never seen him so possessed.

Brett settled at the table to load the rifle. Paulina, standing in the doorway, did not have to force the tears into her eyes. She could not help them. All she could think about was Brett going after a murderous bear that had killed his father, and being killed himself. Why, dear Lord, why had the beast returned after all these years? Was she destined to find the love of her life, and to him lose him to an obsession that had clung to him for all these years? Did he care so little about her that he would risk his life? His father was dead; surely, the grizzly's life span would end soon. It wasn't immortal, for mercy's sake! Why couldn't Brett let nature take its course?

Brett felt the intimidating silence, but his mind was on the mountain where the bear would be. Paulina would have to understand how much this meant to him. He had sworn to bring down the grizzly that had killed his father, and all of his hunts for the past ten years had not yielded so much as a clue as to either its whereabouts or its fate. Now he had seen the beast, seen its six toes standing rigid against the wind, seen the place where a campfire had burned off the fur, and he would bring it down just the way it had brought down his father.

"Don't go, Brett. Please—"

He looked up, his eyes narrowing, his mouth pressing into a thin line of disapproval. "I have been easy to live with, haven't I, Paulina? Whatever you have wanted I have given you. Whatever you've asked me to do, I have considered it, and I have done it if it seemed right to me. But the grizzly and I have had a long understanding. We have both known that it would come to this."

"For Pete's sake, Brett! It's an animal! It has no power of reasoning beyond instinct." In a softer voice she continued. "It simply came back to a place where it had known excitement . . . perhaps to the place where it wishes to die."

Putting aside the loaded weapon, his eyes narrowed

even more. "I guess you consider killing my father excitement. Perhaps it was for that beast. Now it is time that I enjoy that same excitement of the kill."

Unable to restrain her fear—and her sorrow at the very thought of losing the man she loved—Paulina rushed into his embrace, knocking his rifle away from its prop against the table. "Please, Brett, will you make me beg? Is that what you want? To make me humble myself and beg you to stay here, where it is safe? To stay in my arms? Do you want me to drop to my knees?" When she made the move to do so, he gripped both her wrists and dragged her against him.

"You could beg . . . you could drop to your knees . . . you could cry . . . you could even swear to leave me . . . but—" Instinctively his mouth found her own, though she pressed her lips and refused to yield to his caress. "You must understand, Paulina . . . this is something I *must* do! It has nothing to do with the way I feel about you."

She pulled away, turning childishly, her mouth pressing into a much more impudent line. "Then go! Don't worry about me, and please, don't let me stop you!" But when she heard his pause, the rifle being picked up, and his small sigh as he turned toward the door, she pivoted quickly back and rushed into his arms. He did not lay aside the rifle, but drew it snug against him. "If you must go, my darling, promise you will come safely back to me!"

Now his tone matched the soft caress of his fingers against her back. "I believe that is a promise I can make and keep, Paulina. After all, haven't I promised you a husband? And"—he grinned, hoping he might lighten the moment—"aren't I the one with the rifle?"

"And your father had a rifle when the grizzly killed him, didn't he?"

There was no denying that, and no putting her mind at ease. He stood slightly back from her, then drew her close once again to caress her mouth in a soft, sensual kiss. When he broke physical contact moments later, he left the cabin without looking back.

Paulina did not go after him; she remembered her father saying once that you should never watch a friend— or loved one—depart. To see them disappear from sight was unlucky. So she turned, picked up a dustcloth, and began flicking at the sparse furnishings of the cabin with an emotion closely resembling anger.

Ruth would be back tomorrow. She'd had so much sorrow in her life in these few short weeks that Paulina did not want her to see tears.

And trying to hold them back was even harder than not rushing after Brett with one last plea that he not pursue the murderous grizzly. Giving herself the afternoon to grieve, she lay gently upon the mattress she had shared with Brett and wept until exhaustion made it impossible.

Millburn and Ruth had been forced to turn back to the cabin at just past seven that evening after finding the nearest crossing over Cale's Ravine destroyed by a mysterious fire. He could see the burned remains of the bridge a thousand feet down the steep ravine. Something was going on, something that he did not want Ruth to see was worrying him greatly. So when Crocker Atterby happened by soon after the discovery was made, Millburn sent Ruth back with him. He stayed at the ravine to explore, and to travel to the next crossing four miles down to see if the same damage had been done there.

Toward midnight, with the sun still high in the sky, Crocker politely saw Ruth to the door of her cabin. Saying good night, he removed his hat and waited for her to enter before beginning his journey to his own cabin half a mile through the woods.

The darkness itself was almost blinding inside the cabin. Ruth saw that Paulina had drawn the black curtains, something done only when sleep was being sought. Though she had planned to relax with her needlework for an hour or so until she was tired enough to sleep, she chose not to disturb the tranquility of the cabin. Brett and Paulina must be asleep.

She used what little light permeated the room at the edges of the black curtains to tidy a few things in the kitchen. Though Paulina had washed the supper dishes, she had neglected to put away the array of spices and had not returned the milk to the cold cupboard.

Then a door opened. Surprised by the movement— since she thought that Brett and Paulina were asleep— Ruth turned sharply. The slim figure of a man stood in outline against the cabin door. Raising her hand to eyes already adjusted to the dark interior of the cabin, she attempted to filter out the blindness of the light beyond him. "Who are you?" she asked. "Mr. Atterby, is that you?"

"Just a man who needs assistance," hissed a low male voice. "Will you be so kind as to point out the way to Cale's Ravine?"

"Of course," responded Ruth. Though a little wary of a man who would enter another's dwelling without first knocking, Ruth eased past him and onto the planked porch. And then, only then, did she recognize the features so vividly detailed to her by Paulina. She started to scream, but instantly Gafferty's hand was across her mouth, smothering her.

"You don't scream now, little lady," warned Gafferty, "and I'll remove my hand." She nodded, her terrified gaze lifted to his pale, milky features. When her mouth was uncovered, Gafferty ordered, "Call out to Paulina."

"No!" she bit back, and immediately his knuckles were digging into the small of her back. Timorously, she called out, "Paulina," and when the knuckles pressed harder, she called her name in a firmer voice. With tears flooding her lower lids, Ruth warned, "If you hurt her, I'll kill you."

Gafferty laughed. "You'll have to stand in line, little lady."

A sleepy Paulina emerged from the bedroom, rubbing her eyes. "Ruth? Are you back already?" Then she saw them at the cabin entrance and she froze, becoming instantly alert. She knew the man; she'd seen him on the mountain that day, with the sun shining behind him the same way it did now. "Gafferty! Let her go this instant!"

"Certainly." As he released Ruth, she moved across the room and was immediately drawn close by Paulina. Gafferty said, "It's you I want anyway. Come with me, Miss Winthrop." The beady eyes narrowed.

She had no choice; the rifle was lethally aimed. "Where are we going?" Firmness settled into her voice.

"Up the mountain."

"Why?"

"None of your business." Gafferty's rifle made a wave, and he stepped back from the doorway.

"Now, you two come outdoors with me."

Paulina felt the violent tremble rocking Ruth's body. She held her close, coaxing her toward the door. "Don't worry," she soothed. "We'll be all right."

When they stood in the clearing, facing Gafferty, the man ordered of Ruth, "Now, you go on . . . scat. I have no need of you."

"You must be the one who burned the crossing at Cale's Ravine." When he did not answer, Ruth looked

399

to Paulina for reassurance. "Will you be safe? Oh, how can you be?" she softly spoke the questions.

"I'll be all right," said Paulina, tears misting her eyes in spite of her resolution to be strong. "Please, go to safety."

Hesitatingly, Ruth parted from her after one last embrace, then turned alone toward the trail cutting through the forest. Paulina watched her go, fearful for her own safety and for Ruth's, because she didn't like the way Gafferty seemed to be readying his weapon. Then the realization struck her. Just as Ruth reached the woodline that would have enveloped her in its safe darkness, Gafferty raised the rifle. A single shot was fired before Paulina could clear the distance to hit the rifle from its deadly aim. Instantly, Ruth screamed, then fell, clutching her shoulder.

With a horrified scream Paulina started across the clearing toward her, but Gafferty's slim, strong hand snatched her wrist, halting her progress. Sobbing, dropping to her knees, Paulina watched as a frightened Ruth dragged herself into the darkness of the woods and disappeared.

Twenty-five

Paulina wasn't sure which of them was in more danger: Brett, who was in pursuit of the murderous bear, or she, with Gafferty's rifle pressed painfully at her back. She stumbled along the trail, occasionally catching her balance by grabbing for one of the prickly limbs jutting from the mountainside. Gafferty said nothing, but occasionally the rifle would press into her back to rudely coax her along. Far down the face of the mountain she could see the gentle swirl of smoke from the cabin where she and Brett had lain in gentle splendor just that afternoon.

Tears popped into Paulina's eyes as she remembered her last sight of Ruth, dragging herself through the woods with a bullet in her shoulder. Damn, Gafferty, damn him to hell if dear, sweet Ruth should not make it to safety.

"Why are you doing this?" she asked, the question instinctively falling from her tongue, so deep was her need to know. "You cannot be *the* Gafferty that Brett buried eleven years ago. So who are you? Why are you doing this? For God's sake, I have a right to know."

Before he came to an instant halt on the trail, Gafferty grabbed Paulina's shoulder, throwing her off her balance. She stumbled, then fell against a sharp edge in a boulder, tearing her skirt. Gathering the jagged tear in her right hand, she dropped tearfully onto the only smooth section of the rock.

"You want to know, do you, little lady?" said Gafferty, the butt of the rifle snugly tucked into his armpit. Drawing his foot up to a fallen limb, he grinned across the short expanse of space separating him from Paulina. "*The* Gafferty, as you put it, was my only brother. Him and me, we grew together in our mother's womb, an' when we was growin' up not too far from here, we was never more'n a few feet apart. When he was sick, I was sick. When he was happy, I was happy. An', blast it to hell, the only time we was apart for more'n a day, he run into McCallum. By the time I learned what happened to my brother, he'd been in the ground for a month, an' what was left of him weren't fit to be moved to the cabin where we grew up together, an' where our mother grieved herself to death over him. So I've had a lot of years of hate brewin', an' I'll see McCallum dead, or I ain't fit to draw breath."

"But he told me that it was your brother who tried to kill him. Brett was already grievously injured by the bear, and your brother was—"

Gafferty straightened so quickly that Paulina's words instantly halted. Murder reflected in his small hazel eyes; she knew it would be wise to hush while the opportunity was there. Now the rifle made a sweep toward her. "Get up. We've got a long way to go up this mountain."

Drawing in a heavy sigh, Paulina pushed herself up, looking first to Gafferty, then toward the rocky escarpment that formed the side of the mountain half a mile up. How far would this beast of a man take her, and what was his intention when he reached his destination? She was fearful for her life, and for Brett's as well.

She moved mechanically, only half aware of the cold wind threatening to unfoot her. She hugged the side of the mountain and stepped precariously over the rocky trail. But the menace of the mountain was small compared to the intensity of the embittered, maniacal man treading behind her.

Murderous thoughts began to penetrate Paulina's brain. Suppose she should pretend to fall and swipe out at Gafferty with her foot, sending him over the side of the mountain. Would she be able to live with the fact that she had taken a human life?

But was Gafferty human? If anyone deserved to die—

"What you thinkin', little lady? Thinkin' about how you can kill me?"

A chill crept through Paulina's shoulders. She remembered the day at the remote cabin in the Pribilofs. He had known then that she wanted to throw the cup of hot tea in his face. Now he could read her thoughts just as surely as if they were his own. Perhaps she should try to clear her mind—because this insane little man could step into her head and know everything that she was thinking. And she didn't like that idea one bit.

She continued to move, and now her thoughts were of her beloved Brett. Ruth would reach one of the settlements—the dear woman had to!—and word would be taken to Brett that Paulina was in danger. He would come for her.

Just at that moment a movement ahead on the trail startled her and she stumbled, falling, and scraping the palms of her hands. A mountain goat had suddenly gotten the strong whiff of approaching humans and was beating a hasty retreat up the mountain. While Paulina picked small pebbles from the wounds on her hands, the goat disappeared over a knife-edged ridge.

Brett, I'm so afraid. The declaration ricocheted through her brain several times, though she stood, smoothed her crumpled skirts, and began to move with the strength and dignity of rebellious pride, paying no heed to the rifle now pressing into her back once again.

Brett bent low in the underbrush; a hundred yards across a wide, rocky clearing, the grizzly lumbered toward a small stream. He knew this great, slothful creature was hungry, being too slow to be an effective predator for caribou, moose, and Dall sheep, so it would either seek out ground squirrels in the burrows, or turn on man, its preferred nourishment. Instinctively, Brett touched the scar at his temple and traced the raised ridge of it into his hairline. He would gladly have taken a thousand such scars if this murderous beast had not taken the life of his father.

Brett held his rifle at the ready. He was too far away to kill the bear with one shot. So he arose, shook one knee, and then the other, to relieve the stiffness, and began skirting the clearing. He kept the wind at his back, so that the astute nose of the bear would not pick up his scent.

The bear began to grunt; Brett ducked low again. It was rooting in a squirrel burrow, but as Brett watched, the small, quick animal darted out another entrance and stood up, boldly watching the weak-eyed grizzly who could not see its small prey across the short expanse of ground.

Then, giving no warning, the bear's great head lifted. It grunted at the air and took off in a clumsy run toward the far side of the clearing. As a startled Brett gathered his wits about him, the bear disappeared into the under-brush.

But as he started in pursuit, his foot caught in still another squirrel hole and he fell to one knee, wrenching his ankle. He stifled his cry of pain but sat upon the ground, rubbing his hand inside his boot to survey the damage. He didn't think it was broken, but he had been injured enough times to know that the ankle would swell. In preparation, he took his knife from the sheath at his waist and cut the leather of his boot at the outside of the ankle. Then he sat for a moment more, attempting to gain his bearings.

A thrashing in the underbrush behind him caused him to turn on his knees. A man he knew only as Wooly exited into the clearing where he sat. He left his rifle on the ground, feeling no threat from the man.

"McCallum—"

Brett forced himself to his feet. "Yeah."

The man dragged at scruffy facial hair, the characteristic that had given him his nickname. "Gruff's new wife come to our cabin. She got shot by a fella at her place."

"Hell," mumbled Brett. "Is she all right?"

"Just a flesh wound. My woman's takin' care of her. But she tells me this man who shot her took your woman and headed up the mountain."

So still was Brett's heartbeat that the life might have been instantly snuffed from his body. "He took Miss Winthrop?"

"That's what she says." When Brett dropped to one knee, Wooly asked, "You all right?"

"Sure," said Brett without looking up. "Did Ruth say who the man was?"

"Said your woman called him Gafferty."

Good God! The color drained from Brett's features. His

405

thoughts scattered through his head as he remembered all the times she'd told him Gafferty had come to her and he had called her a liar. He had believed her sometimes, though she hadn't been aware of that. If only he had trusted her. If only he had believed her. If only—

He shot up from his knee, his brow pinching as the pain of the ankle jerked through his leg. "Thanks for bringing me word," he said to the silently waiting messenger. "If you'll keep Ruth at your place, I'll—"

"Want me to get some of the men together to help you, Mr. McCallum?"

"No." Brett gritted his teeth; his knuckles wrapped around the cold steel of his rifle were bone-white. "This is something I have to do myself. Just take care of Ruth, will you? And tell her I've gone after Paulina. She'll be worried."

"Sure, Mister. But I think you're bein' a mite foolish."

Turning toward the mountain—and the direction in which the grizzly had gone—Brett issued one last order, "Don't send anybody up after me. I'll be down with Miss Winthrop, by damn."

As he disappeared into the timberline across the clearing, Wooly mumbled, "Or you'll probably both be dead, Mr. McCallum."

Gafferty mumbled at Paulina's back, "You're slowin' down, little lady. I'd pep up my step if I was you."

"Well, you're not me!" she smarted. "And I'm tired! I want to rest."

When it appeared that she might move off the trail, Gafferty's rifle hit against her left hip. "You just keep walkin'."

Only now, with the distance closed between them, did Paulina get a strong, heady whiff of liquor on Gafferty's breath. Boldly, she asked, "Did you drink your whiskey, or did you douse yourself in it? You stink to high heaven."

Gafferty laughed maniacally, retrieving a silver flask from the inside pocket of his jacket to offer her. "If you wanted some, little lady, why didn't you just say so? I'd be glad to share."

"I'd as soon drink from a flask made of possum entrails!" she huffed. And when he again shoved the flask at her, she slapped his hand away. Instantly, that same hand drew back to hit her, though the man wielding the power immediately had second thoughts. His beef really wasn't with the woman. She was merely the bait to get him his true prize, the bastard who had killed his twin brother.

"Just keep goin' an' keep to the trail."

"Where are we going?" Paulina asked, feeling a moment of bravado. "We are either traveling blindly, or you know where you're going. I have a right to know also."

"You have no rights, little lady," Gafferty replied, taking a swig of whiskey from the silver flask. "Your personal bill of rights has been terminated, an' the constitution ain't been written that gives you any rights at all. Just keep movin'."

"And if I don't?"

"Then I'll leave a real fancy female carcass for the bears and the foxes to nibble on. By the time McCallum finds you, there'll be pieces of you scattered through the woods."

Lifting her chin, Paulina sniffed, "If you're trying to scare me, you've done a good job." There were times, she surmised, when there was more advantage in telling the truth. If Gafferty knew she was frightened, he might slacken his guard, and perhaps she would have an opportunity to escape. Yes, yes, it sounded like a viable plan. She would appear to be frightened; if she tried hard enough, she was sure she would be able to shed tears.

She forced herself to shiver—the cold made the chore easy—and occasionally she would think of her father's death, and tears would pop into her eyes. When Gafferty spoke, she listened and responded appropriately, and once—she was very proud of herself for that bit of dramatic acting—she dropped to the trail and sobbed against her arm. Gafferty backed off then, mumbling something about "giving her time to compose herself." And Paulina, so terribly weary from traveling up the face of the mountain without adequate moments to catch her breath, took advantage of that lull in the journey to rest.

Only too soon, though, they were on the move again. The hours passed . . . two . . . three . . . four . . . the afternoon sun disappeared to the west side of the mountain, and the shadows were frosty and uncomfortable against her exposed skin. In the more southerly parts of the world, night would be falling. As she continued to move just inches ahead of Gafferty's rifle, she feared that dear, gentle-hearted Ruth had not made it to another settlement. She tried to shut from her mind the horrible vision of Ruth bleeding to death in the forest somewhere. She had placed all her hope in Ruth, and for that she felt terribly selfish. If Ruth did not reach help, then Brett could not possibly know she was in danger. She began to accept the imminence of doom rather than the rescue she had been so sure would happen. She was equally sure now that she would die at Gafferty's murderous hands.

Soon they reached a small cabin built into a rocky precipice of the mountain. Only when she had entered did she realize the small façade of timbers built in the shape of a cabin was merely an entrance to a large cave.

Bits and pieces of broken furniture were strewn about and a large, lopsided shelf bore canned food and a few kitchen implements. A grill placed over a mound of rocks seemed to have been used for cooking, and when she watched Gafferty move toward it, she saw that the center was hollow and that a few embers of wood and charcoal still burned. So this was where Gafferty had lain in wait, and prayed for the opportunity to begin his revenge against Brett.

When Gafferty did not stop her movement, she dropped onto a mound of straw covered by a torn and faded quilt. Stretching to her full length, her hands pressed to the soft straw, she watched Gafferty move about, managing to perform a few mundane chores around the cave without putting the rifle down. The only light flooding the chamber came from the single window of the cabin façade, but that was quickly fading as dark clouds blocked out the sunlight.

Though Gafferty was the greatest danger she had ever faced—and certainly she wanted to remain alert—Paulina felt her eyes closing. She wanted only to sleep, to escape the fear that had kept her moving ever ahead. They must have traveled five miles up the precarious face of the mountain that day, and every muscle in her body ached as if it had been torn from its roots. Her hair was a tangled mass, and her swipes at her cheeks throughout the day had left them feeling gritty and tender to the touch. Her palms burned, so abraded were they from her fall that day, and her dress was scarcely more than a series of rags hanging from her slim form.

She willed away the remainder of her strength and tried to relax, her eyes constantly watching Gafferty. Only once did she close them tightly, when he approached a far wall of the cave and unfastened his trousers to relieve himself, and that might have been the only moment that day when she'd truly felt safe. Now he was washing his hands in a tin bowl, and when he had dried them on the tail of his shirt, she saw him approach the makeshift stove where a fresh fire burned. Presently, he approached and carefully set down a bowl. Rising on an elbow, she saw a crooked spoon sinking into a pile of steaming beans.

She was hungry enough to eat frogs. Nonetheless, when she sat up to eat, she found herself strangely controlled, a decent length of time taken between each spoonful of beans she put in her mouth and washed down with the water Gafferty brought to her.

When she had eaten the last of the beans, Gafferty approached to take the bowl from her. "Want more?"

"No," came her short reply. "Is it all right if I rest here?"

Gafferty flicked his wrist at her. "You go on to sleep. I ain't goin' to hurt you. It's McCallum I want."

Paulina drained the last of the water, then handed the glass to Gafferty. "How long will you keep me here?"

"Until I have McCallum." Gafferty grinned widely, maniacally. "I reckon by the morning he'll be mine."

"Don't count on it," said Paulina, settling onto the quilt. "He's not going to stand still and let you shoot him."

Gafferty rose from his knees and began to put distance between them. "We'll just see about that, little lady. Yep, we'll just see."

Brett was weary, hungry, and fearful. He moved up the face of the mountain, following not only the scent of a human monster who had taken Paulina away from the security of their cabin, but also the grizzly whose large pawprints steadily creased the soft, rain-swollen

410

earth. The indentation of six toes on the front paws made his skin shudder as he recalled their brutal strength slashing out at him so many years ago when he had tried to save his father. But even as the six-toed grizzly had laid him flat, with wounds that would have been fatal had he not been found by the man Gafferty, his father lay dead just a half-dozen feet away from him.

That day would be forever embedded in his memory. He wasn't sure what had snapped in Gafferty's mind, but immediately after dressing his wounds, the man had fallen to his knees, clutching his head and screaming as if the devil himself had impaled him in the fires of hell. He had gone on a rampage, slashing out at Brett with a thirteen-inch blade, and Brett, rifle lying against his right leg, had begun firing. First he had hit him in the leg, and when the man had continued to advance on him, he shot him in the shoulder. Finally, with the knife slashing close enough to leave the impression of wind against his chest, Brett fired one last shot. The man dropped dead across his knees and, after Brett pushed him off, the two of them lay there for three days, Brett drifting in and out of consciousness, and Gafferty decomposing beneath the hot sun flooding the side of the mountain.

The memory of it was gruesome; to this day he did not know what had made the man go berserk and attack him. He knew only that he'd had no choice but to kill him.

Now, who the hell was this bastard calling himself Gafferty, who had taken his beloved Paulina onto the same mountain? Could it be a father or a brother, or a friend who had waited in the silence of eleven years to wreak vengeance? And why now, after all this time? It was a question he would ask himself throughout the night as he traveled on and on up the mountain in search of the woman who was his love and his life.

And a question, too, that Paulina woke from a light sleep to ask the man.

He pondered her question for a moment, then dropped down along the rock wall and drew his knees up. His palms drifted along the smooth bore of his rife. "Why'd I wait eleven years?" he echoed Paulina's words. "Well, didn't have much choice." The silver flask made a reappearance from his pocket. But when he went to take a swig, he found that it was empty. "Ever hear of a penal colony?" He'd asked the question just as if an answer was neither required nor wanted.

"Of course. It's a prison, usually a working one at a remote place such as an island."

"Ah, yes, an island, a low, palm-covered island, fifteen square miles of living hell. Unfortunately, I killed a French citizen and was tried by French justice. I spent ten years at this tropical paradise in the Atlantic ocean."

Paulina knew her history. Quietly, she said, "Devil's Island?"

"Well, it certainly wasn't Angel's Island!" A hard bitterness rose in Gafferty's throat. "Shall I show you the whip wounds, the scars of the irons that surrounded my ankles and wrists? Would you like to hear how I survived by eating roaches during a two-year stint in solitude?"

Paulina shuddered. "No, I don't think I would."

"Well, now you know why I waited so long to come after McCallum."

"But when . . . how did you find him?"

"Saw him in Skagway one afternoon, but he didn't see me. When he booked passage for you and him, I booked passage. Didn't seem like much fun killin' him outright. Thought I'd have a little fun with him first."

"But how did you find out he had killed your brother?"

"That weren't hard. Read the records at the constable's office when he reported the death. Justifiable homicide some bastard had written in a small block labeled Disposition of Case. If McCallum were justified in killin' my brother, then I'll be justified in killin' him."

"But your brother went berserk. Brett told me about that day, and I heard the regret—the horror of it—as he told me the story. He never wanted to kill your brother. But one moment your brother was helping him, dressing his wounds and giving him water to drink, and the next moment he was turning on him with a knife. Surely, you must have some idea as to what made him turn like that? You were raised with him, for heaven's sake! Surely you had witnessed similar behavior!"

Reverie overcame Gafferty. Slowly, the light of the single lantern faded and his mind wandered back in time, through the years and the seasons, beyond the accursed Devil's Island where he had died a thousand deaths, back to the days when he had been a youngster, growing up with a brother who looked and acted as he himself did save one characteristic that his identical twin had not exhibited. His brother had suffered from "spells," their mother had called them. He would be rational and friendly one moment, and the next he would be clawing at invisible demons in the air, digging at his face with stiffened fingers, and attacking any living thing that came into contact with him. At those times their mother had told him to "run away until your brother comes to his senses," and he always had.

Neither he nor his mother had known what had brought on the "spells," but they had always had the good sense to distance themselves from them. His brother had suffered one of his spells that day, unfortunately, when a grievously injured young man had rested next to a rifle. Perhaps if he hadn't been injured he would have been able to handle the flailing madness of the man who had initially helped him, without having to put three bullets in him and ending his life.

No, dammit, no, he could not make excuses for Brett McCallum. Regardless of the circumstances, he'd had no right to kill his brother. He had to die. It was imperative. He would not be able to sleep peacefully at night until his brother's killer had been brought to justice. If the law would not bring him down, then he would. He owed it to his brother.

And it would be done if it was the last thing he accomplished on this earth.

Gafferty thrust away his memories, turned his small, watery eyes to Paulina, and took a moment to remember the question she had asked. Then he responded, "No, little lady, weren't no more gentle man in the world than my brother. That's why I know McCallum killed him in cold blood, and that's why McCallum has to die. An' you mark my word, what the law didn't accomplish, I will. Nobody kills somebody of my flesh an' gets away with it. 'An eye for an eye, a tooth for a tooth.' So it says in the Bible itself."

"The Bible also teaches forgiveness," said Paulina, resting her head on her hand. "Or doesn't that matter?"

"Don't matter a bit." Stretching into a prone position, Gafferty coldly ordered, "Go to sleep, an' quit preachin' at me. Tomorrow I got a killin' to do."

414

Twenty-six

Paulina awoke to a blinding light against the single window of the cave's man-made façade. Covering her eyes as they focused on this rude intrusion, she pushed herself into the circle of light flooding the straw and quilt where she'd slept that night. Was the world bursting into flame? If it was, strangely, she was not afraid.

"Come to the window," came an eerie, familiar voice. "You might want to witness one of our visual spectacles."

Slowly, curiously, Paulina rose, smoothed down her crumpled skirts, and eased toward the window where Gafferty stood. The awe of the magnificent lights momentarily took away her fear of the man's ever-present rifle.

Standing at the window, she looked out to the northern sky of early morning. An abyss of heavenly fire lit the horizon. The heavens spewed forth nervous flames of light, so very high that she was sure they must be scorching the stars themselves. Quietly, she asked, "Is a distant city burning?"

Gafferty laughed. "Nothing quite so man-made. What you are witnessing is the aurora borealis, one of the great natural mysteries of this world, little lady. Enjoy it now, before you begin to grieve for the loss of your love and will be unable to concentrate on this beauty.''

She did not hear his words; the magnificent curtain of light had blocked out the mundane threats of the nervous little man. She stood for the longest time, watching the shimmering luminescence, the reds and blues and violets, the greens and various pinks pulsating against the dawn light, and she thought that heaven and earth had combined to create a wondrous glow.

Brett McCallum had been shamelessly dreaming of Paulina, languid and erotic, her full sensual mouth slightly pouting, her eyes wide and hypnotic, the sheen of dew-kissed emeralds beckoning him into their mysterious depths. In his dream he had seen her free of clothing, tall, slim, blemish-free, curvaceous hips and small waist, firm, uplifted breasts, slender arms welcoming him into their fiery embrace.

He didn't want to awaken from the dream, not ever, not if it meant that she would disappear into the dark, misty shroud slowly beginning to envelop all that was in his mind. The silence giving him the moment to stare lustfully upon her was beginning to stir, and while he fought it with all his mental might, the world rudely returned to him—and in his thoughts, he cursed it.

The great beams of light comprising reality seemed to pass directly over Brett's head as he detected a distinct guttural sound. With the lights shimmering against the morning, the huge grizzly he'd been stalking—and that had been stalking him in return—now stood over him, its massive forepaws stretched out menacingly. Brett felt his breathing suddenly cease, and the bear, whose height seemed to touch the northern lights, lumbered forward, in a murderous frenzy.

Just as the huge paws pounded upon the earth, Brett was out from under him, using the toes of his boots to move on all fours into a stand of timber. The bear snarled and growled, his large body moving from side to side like a giant, odorous pendulum. Saliva slung off its bared teeth as he thrashed into the underbrush after Brett. Shocked by the attack that had snatched him from his sleep—and the beautiful dream—snatched him so quickly, in fact, that his rifle had been left behind, Brett watched the long claws of the beast's front feet stab into the ground, closer and closer, driving him toward a precipice of the mountain. Death seemed imminent; he wondered if a prayer might help.

But just as suddenly as the attack had begun, the bear now backed off, a move that resulted in its back foot treading upon, and snapping into, the rifle that was Brett's only protection. Though it aborted its pursuit of Brett for the moment, it continued to roam through the clearing, and soon dropped to its huge, scarred buttocks, seemingly intent on staying for a while. Muttering an expletive, Brett settled against the trunk of a massive spruce, to think about his next move.

He knew, of course, that a man would be foolish to continue his pursuit of the bear without a weapon. He knew, too, that bringing down this massive killer was tantamount to touching the northern lights with an extended finger. He had planned to terminate the hunt until he had rescued his beloved Paulina, but the bear hovering so near at hand seemed to have other plans. Hell! What was he to do now?

He sat very still, continuing to think, and not altogether rationally. The bear was a dozen feet away, parted from him by the thickness of brambles, and Paulina was somewhere on the face of the mountain with a man just as dangerous as the six-toed grizzly. He needed his rifle to hunt down both predators, but again he looked at the rifle that had been snapped like a brittle twig. The bear had taken care of that.

Blast! Blast! He should have taken the fellow up on that rescue party. But he'd been too damned proud. He'd wanted to accomplish both ends without the assistance of another man, and now not only was Paulina in danger, but he was in danger of losing his life to the grizzly. That made him worth far less than a damn to Paulina, and he knew—blast it, that's what bothered him the most—that she was depending on him to rescue her. Even now, in her captivity, she was watching for him with expectant eyes. He knew it in his heart.

Though Paulina knew that Gafferty was a danger to her—and to Brett—she had foolishly begun to view most of his threats the same way she viewed a hissing house-cat—too small really to do damage beyond a few ugly scratches and menacing growls. The man was like a cha-meleon, able to change its spots to suit its needs—she couldn't help but remember the female garb he had donned in order to maintain virtual obscurity aboard the *Iron Ice*. She wondered why he hadn't come right out then and killed Brett—if that was, indeed, what he in-tended to do—but he had remarked that he liked cat-and-mouse play. He had waited a long time—eleven years—and the hunt was almost at its end.

"How'd you like the northern lights?"

Paulina looked up, though she continued to blow on the surface of the hot tea Gafferty had given her. "They're beautiful. How long will they last?"

"Days . . . weeks . . . nobody knows, but from one day to the next they'll completely change. No one knows why, but I have a theory about it."

418

For lack of an alternate interest at the moment—and the subject might keep his mind off Brett McCallum—she asked, "What is your theory?"

"My guess is that they're the result of charged particles steaming from the sun, particles caught by the earth's magnetic field and funneled toward the north and the south poles. They collide there and scatter gas into the upper atmosphere, and that is what produces the distinct lights and colors."

Paulina thought she'd been thoroughly schooled in virtually every subject available, but she'd heard nothing about charged particles, magnetic fields, and gases in the upper atmosphere. Gafferty hardly seemed the sort to be spewing scientific jargon. For lack of an argument, she replied, "Well, I certainly can't come up with a better explanation."

"Women ain't supposed to be smart," jeered Gafferty, taking a long drag from a bottle of whiskey. "Supposed to cook and please their men and birth young'uns and maybe now and then socialize with others of their kind so they can gossip about the neighbors."

Paulina sipped the tea, her gaze cutting across the rim of the cup to touch upon Gafferty's pale features. "Well, I would suppose that some women don't fit the social standards you have mentioned. It would be a rather boring world if they did."

"That's the trouble with some women, 'specially women like you. Think they can go traipsin' all over the world an' doin' the things that men's supposed to be doin'. But you'll get your reward, little lady. Reckon you'll die a dried-up old spinster wonderin' where your youth went."

"My, aren't we in a lovely mood this morning?" said Paulina in an instant of bravado. Just at that moment the handle on the mug she'd been holding broke clean, as if the heat had suddenly loosened the glue, and the tea spilled onto her skirts, immediately soaking through to her bare skin. She jumped up, a pained scream breaking from her mouth.

As the female cry echoed across the mountain, the grizzly ceased to be Brett's main point of attention. He scooted to his knees, his ear alerted to the direction of the only sound in the dreadful silence of the mountain. It was Paulina; he knew beyond a shadow of a doubt, and his heart wrenched painfully as he wondered what could have made her scream like that.

The grizzly, too, paused in its taunting hunt of the ground squirrel and lifted its brownish-black nose to sniff the air. It paid little attention to Brett; rather, it got a strong whiff of vulnerable human fear, and the lumbering beast began to move.

Brett watched as it exited the clearing on the north side. When he was sure it was well on its way up the mountain, he scooted from his hiding place and was soon beside the rifle, surveying the damage. It was broken clean in two, completely useless, and with a low, frustrated groan, he threw the pieces as far as his strength allowed.

Then he stood to his full height, the rage so great inside him that he was sure he could tear the murderous grizzly in two as easily as it had ripped apart his rifle. But he couldn't worry about that predator now; his beloved Paulina was somewhere up the mountain, and she needed him.

He began to move, oblivious of the treacherous north wind that whipped all around him. He found the trail and began his ascent of the mountain. He would not stop until Paulina was safe and in his arms once again.

Paulina stood at the window, dabbing at the scalded skin of her thighs with the salve Gafferty had thrown to her. She was more annoyed than anything, though the burns were bad enough that they would surely blister. Engaged in treating the wounds, she tried to ignore Gafferty at the far side of the cave, cleaning and reloading his rifle.

Actually, Paulina was surprised that he would allow her so near the exit. But when she ventured a look toward the door, she saw that it was bolted and secured by still a second lock that would need a key. There was the window, but it was so small that by the time she broke out the glass, she would probably shred herself to pieces trying to squeeze through. She was, effectively, still Gafferty's prisoner, and if she did manage to escape, she wouldn't know which way to run to get away from him. When she saw a rickety chair sitting beside the window, she turned and asked Gafferty, "Do you mind if I stay here and watch the lights?"

Rather than respond, he flipped his wrist at her and continued cleaning the rifle. She sat and watched the lights, now resembling the rays of a powerful searchlight. It moved steadily, no evidence of flickering or rapid movement. For what seemed the span of half an hour she watched the beam slowly change, one side fading out, at times perfectly transparent and at others very bright. Then she began to study the door again, cutting her gaze every now and then toward Gafferty to make sure he was not watching her. The latch through which the key lock rested seemed loose on the side board. Would she be able to rip open the bolt, snatch the key lock from the half-rotted board, and escape before Gafferty got to her? She studied the window; could she break it out and make her getaway before he was able to grab one of her ankles? She thought not.

Still, she could not sit there and simply do nothing. The pain of the burn was beginning to subside, and her skirts were drying. Now the lights were the least of her concerns. For in the shadows of the timberline an eighth of a mile down the trail, she saw a human form emerging.

Her heart quickened its beat, her knuckles now turning white as her fingers gripped the arms of the chair so firmly that she felt pain. Through the dirty window-pane she watched him, waited for him to get closer, prayed that it was Brett, and hoped that Gafferty would not approach her. A nervous gaze cut momentarily to him. He did not look up, but was studying the bore of his ever-present rifle. She watched the man move on the trail, the nervous lights of the aurora borealis seeming to change the shape of him and the color of the clothing he wore.

He must have seen the cabin entrance in the side of the mountain at about the same moment she recognized that it was Brett. She saw that he had no weapon—unless he had tucked a pistol into the back of his trousers—and that alarmed her. Would she be able to sit quietly by the window and not react should Gafferty cease his activities and move toward her? Again she thought not.

Then, as she watched in horror, the giant grizzly exited the woodline several hundred feet behind Brett. And when he turned, freezing in place as the menace made itself known with a loud, long bellow, Paulina was pounding against the windowpane and screaming with all her might. "Brett! Dear God . . . Brett! Brett—"

She had not realized she'd vocalized her fear until Gafferty's hand was upon her shoulder, wrenching her away. Now the vicious devil of a man stared out the window, releasing his own maniacal growl as he feared the bear would rob him of his vengeance.

His pale, strong fingers wrapping around Paulina's wrist, he was jerking open the bolt and tearing the key lock from its hinge. Within moments she felt the cold air ripping against her tender flesh as Gafferty dragged her onto the trail and farther up the mountain.

In a moment of boldness she screamed out, "Brett . . . Brett—" hoping more to sway the bear's intention than to make him aware of her presence. She looked back just as the timberline swallowed her whole. The great furry menace, its nose lifted high in the air, dropped to all fours and came in pursuit. She breathed a sigh of relief; Brett was safe for the time being.

Gafferty pulled her along, caring not a whit that brambles and twigs tore at her tender flesh, snatched at her skirts, and ripped them asunder. He pulled her ever higher . . . until, at last, they stood on a rocky precipice with the trail and the timberline on one side, and nothing, save the frigid mountain air on the other. He stood there, his chest distending and collapsing, over and over, and his nostrils flaring over the extended rifle. He waited, and Paulina knew for whom he waited. It was simply a matter of time.

The grizzly was first to make an appearance. As its huge frame emerged from the forest line across the trail, it rose on its hind legs, sniffing at the air, saliva dripping from its bared teeth. When it began to move toward them, Gafferty slowly lowered his rifle, fired, and put a bullet in the screaming creature's left shoulder.

Then Brett emerged from the shadows and stood on the trail, surveying the scene and trying to decide what to do.

Gafferty's forearm was now so snug against her neck that Paulina was sure she would choke to death. Steadily, he eased toward the precipice, dragging her protesting weight with him. "Don't do this," begged a breathless Paulina. "Let me go, for God's sake, there is no way out for either of us . . . except death, if you do not cease this insanity—" She had lost one of her shoes; now, her bare heel scraped along the rock and she could feel the flesh being slowly skinned off.

Brett's power of speech went the way of the wind. The man standing at the edge of the precipice could have been the Gafferty he had killed eleven years ago. But that man was dead . . . his flesh had been putrid when he'd finally had the strength to drag him into the grave. So this man had to be an identical twin. Either that, or he was going mad.

Slowly, Brett skirted the rocky precipice, until he could see Gafferty and Paulina standing precariously at the edge. The grizzly, too, moved, so that it was again between Brett and Gafferty. Supporting itself on its back legs, its massive height blocked Brett's view of his beloved Paulina. The bear was furious; its head bobbed back and forth as it seemed to contemplate its next move. The wound Gafferty had inflicted was bleeding profusely. When the murderous beast turned toward the man and his prisoner, a quick-thinking Brett picked up a rock and threw it, hitting the six-toed bear just above the stub of its tail. It did not turn; rather, it continued on a slow, lumbering, and lethal course toward the people standing on the edge of death.

Gafferty screamed in mortal fear, and as he attempted to turn the rifle to shoot the beast once again, the weapon discharged, hitting Paulina in her upper arm. Too stunned to cry out, or even to feel the pain, she continued in her attempt to pry Gafferty's arm loose from her neck. She felt darkness surrounding her; she never even saw the grizzly approach.

As Brett watched in horror, the grizzly pounced upon Gafferty, and all three went quickly over the ledge. Brett heard the male cry droning to silence as it fell, and before he could pull his senses together to move toward the precipice, a pair of dull thuds were heard far down the mountain. Trembling so violently he could hardly move one foot ahead of the other, he slowly approached the precipice.

Just at that moment a slim, pale hand attempted to gain a hold on the sharp edge and Brett made a grab for it. As he eased toward the precipice, he saw the bloody, mangled bodies of man and beast on a flat surface of rock half a mile down the mountain. Cutting his fear-darkened gaze, he saw the lovely oval features of Paulina, and her tear-sheened eyes transfixed to his.

His hand surrounded her own, crushing her fingers; she could feel it, strong and damp, clinging to her slim one with all its might. That hand . . . Brett's hand . . . holding her own as if nothing in the world mattered at that moment.

"Hold on, Paulina, hold on." Though desperate, his voice was soothing, and Paulina, feeling the cold wind dragging at her skirts, attempted to gain a foothold on the icy face of the mountain. But nothing was there, only the sharp ledge cutting into her shoulder and across her left breast.

"Ruth—" she mumbled. "Ruth is hurt."

"No," he said soothingly. "She reached help, and now she is being taken care of by friends."

Paulina closed her eyes, relieved to hear the news. Then she opened them, met Brett's strangely dark gaze—was it fear?—and said, "I am lost, Brett." How gentle was her voice; she might just as easily have been waking from a long, peaceful sleep to greet a new day. "But I am not afraid."

Her tone, almost one of acceptance, frightened Brett more deeply than the menace of either Gafferty or the bear who now lay dead on the mountain. "No, you aren't lost. Remember, my love, if you fall, there will be nothing to catch you . . . only eternity, but if you hold my hand . . . hold it with all your might and strength . . . then you will know only my love and my adoration. Fall, and we will not see each other again. Hold on, and I will pull you into my arms . . . forever."

So softly spoken were his words—and his promises—that the acceptance that had filled Paulina's heart slowly dissipated. She began to struggle now, struggle with all her might for survival, her eyes lifting, adoringly, to share the strength reflecting in Brett's darkening eyes. Yes . . . yes, she held the hand of love . . . below her was eternity and darkness and a netherworld without him.

But no, no, it could not be! She ceased her struggles immediately. There . . . there against the impending darkness of the night a city appeared, a city surrounded by silence, houses and well-defined streets, and trees. Against the sky there rose tall spires over huge buildings that appeared to be ancient cathedrals. She could hardly believe it, because it had not been there before . . . and could not be there now.

"Come, Paulina, give me your other hand."

"There is a city"—her eyes cut to the brilliance of the silent, miraculous civilization—"we could go there for help."

"There is nothing there." But, dear God, dare he believe the mirage that stood before him as his gaze followed the direction of her own? There was, indeed, a city where none existed, and the silence surrounding it was almost deafening. Gritting his teeth, shaking his head in an effort to free his mind of the mirage, he again begged of Paulina, "Give me your hand."

She looked again to the silent city of Alaska, then into Brett's eyes, and again at the wondrous sight shimmering against the horizon. What did she want? The miracle of an apparition . . . for surely that was what it was . . . or did she want a lifetime of loving in Brett's arms?

And was the choice really so hard to make?

Closing her eyes, she willed away the pain in her shoulder; though her arm felt limp and lifeless, she attempted to lift it. So surprised was she to feel it moving, her eyes came open, her gaze connected to Brett's, and slowly the arm floated upward. Though it seemed that an eternity had passed, she knew it was only a matter of seconds before Brett's other hand firmly grasped her own. The pain was excruciating; she bit her tongue to keep from crying out.

Like an eagle taking to wing from the highest cliff, she felt her body lifting, embracing the azure sky and touching the love that was the essence of Brett McCallum.

Part Four

Awaken, sleeper, from your dream of dreams
This world awaits you,
with its lulls and its extremes

Twenty-seven

The aroma of gardenias, the stifling embrace of an overly warm room, a heaviness in her chest that made it almost impossible to breathe—these were the things Paulina now felt. A thousand tons of rock had settled onto her eyelids, and try as she might, they would not open. At the moment, only one thing in her life was certain—the hands gently holding her own were Brett's. She'd felt their loving touch too often to be wrong about that.

Slowly, the world began to awaken all about her . . . a soft mattress beneath her back was comfortable . . . a deep, throaty masculine voice muffled by the thickness of walls was vaguely familiar . . . glasses clinked, the way she remembered in Big Pat's Saloon . . . a gunshot far away caused her muscles to jerk.

And the hands continued to envelop her own, hands that gently massaged, hands that moved occasionally to touch her forehead, hands that eased along her cheek and touched her mouth with familiar loving.

Oh, yes, yes, my beloved Brett, you have drawn me from the jaws of death. Your love has saved me. Why can't I remember the moment I felt again the earth beneath my feet, recall the instant security of your arms holding me, the lull in time when your words of love and adoration whispered with husky emotion against my hairline. Why can't I remember these things . . . oh, my beloved Brett.

"Dear Lord, she's coming to." A familiar voice . . . female, refined, softly sad, carried like dusky lavender with each spoken word. Am I dreaming, my dear, precious Lillian?

But of course she was dreaming. Lillian was half a world away from the treacherous mountain ledge that had almost taken her life. She was alone with Brett; even the mattress beneath her back was imagination. It was his arms in which she rested, and when her eyes opened, she would surely see the shimmering lights of the aurora borealis dancing beyond the fringes of darkness. She needed only lift her lids to witness the wonder, the awe, the fascination. And to see the sad, expectant features of Brett McCallum hovering worriedly over her.

She inhaled a deep breath, feeling warm again. But that, too, was her imagination, for it was surely the crisp air of the mountain she had drawn into her lungs. Then, savoring the precious enjoyment of her reawakening, her eyes slowly opened. His look, filled with surprise and mystery and disbelief, greeted her awakening, though she could scarcely see it through the impenetrable blur she immediately tried to shake away.

"Brett," she whispered, surprised at the hoarseness of her voice . . . or was it her voice? She really wasn't sure. The weakness clung to her, making it impossible to move even a finger of the hand lying, covered by his own, upon her waistline. "Brett—" she whispered again.

Moisture fell from his eyes, then, as the realization sank in, a smile widened his mouth, causing the dimples to deepen in his cheeks. "You're awake . . . thank God . . . thank God."

Only his features were visible to her; all else beyond his shoulders was a dark blur, and though she felt dazed and disoriented, she knew that she must have passed out, for darkness had fallen and taken away the curtain of nervous lights that was the aurora borealis.

"Paulina, can you hear me?"

She looked quickly about, if, in her weakened condition, that was even remotely possible. Not only was the magnificence of the northern lights gone, but she could not see the silent city that had beckoned to her from beyond the edge of the cliff. Her gaze narrowing worriedly, she said, "I must have had a terrible fright on the ledge. I can scarcely speak."

He said nothing at first, but his brows furrowed into a frown and his eyes cut to the right. "Paulina, do you know where you are?"

"In your arms," came her laborious response. "Where I should be. I looked down and I saw the silent city . . . and eternity, Brett, and then I looked up into your face, and I saw love . . . and I knew I had to live."

At that interlude someone approached. "What is she talking about?" asked this strange, detached, and yet familiar voice.

"She must have been dreaming," responded Brett. "She must have somehow heard us talking about the mirage seen by the Duke of Abruzzi on Mount St. Elias. Remember, it was reported in the paper earlier this week."

"I believe she simply had a very good dream," chuckled the male voice behind him. "And you were there, McCallum, sharing it with her."

Paulina heard the voices, but she couldn't sort them out. What were they talking about? Why would the man beyond the fringes of darkness think she had been dreaming? And why was she aware of the delicate scent of gardenias once again? Perhaps she was now lapsing into sleep, and was beginning to dream.

Lillian could bear it no longer. She stepped forward, her powder-pale features bending over those of her sister's. "Paulina? Can you hear me? Can you see me? It is your sister, Lillian."

Her face devoid of emotion, Paulina responded, "Lillian . . . dear, dear Lillian . . . you are in my dream."

Then a familiar, exasperating click of the tongue. "No . . . I am here. Paulina, you have been in a—"

Suddenly, Brett's fingers closed over Lillian's arm, and when their gazes met, he shook his head. She seemed a little miffed at having been so suddenly quieted. This was her sister, after all.

Paulina felt sluggish; again her eyes gently closed and she sought sleep. She wanted to be with Brett, to feel his arms about her, and to know that he loved her. She'd been on a long journey and had shared with him the adventures of a lifetime. Now it was time to return some degree of normalcy to her life, and to forever be the kind of wife she had sworn to be to him, just as he had sworn to be an adoring husband to her. She had just stood on the edge of death, and it had drained her strength completely. Though she didn't want to sleep— and thus to dream—she knew that sleep was exactly what she needed then.

"I'm sorry, Brett—" Her words were soft and slurred, and when he shook her she was a little surprised. Though her arms felt as heavy as lead, she was able to lift them and surround his shoulders. Pulling herself weakly into his arms, she promised, "I will sleep for only a little while. Then we will return to the settlement."

Brett was almost frantic. She was talking out of her head, and all he could think about was losing her again to the coma that had claimed her for the last nine weeks, since Soapy Smith's henchman had shot her. He turned an agonized look to Lillian. "She's slipping away again," he said.

Just then, Dr. Gafferty rushed into the room and forced Brett away from her. He was a pale, thin, nervous little man whose eyes looked as large as saucers through the thick lenses of his spectacles. Bending over, he forced open each of Paulina's eyelids in turn, then drew his fingers to his chin as if deeply concentrating on his prognosis. Then, with a smile, he calmly announced, "She's out of the coma. I suspect she'll fully recover."

Lillian drew her linked fingers against her mouth and muttered, "Thank Providence—"

And from the doorway, an emotionally torn Big Pat echoed, "Yes . . . thank Providence," then returned to the patrons in his saloon to announce the good news. Presently, a loud round of raucous cheering echoed through the walls.

Brett was still a little skeptical. "Are you sure, Dr. Gafferty? She's awfully still."

Dr. Gafferty assured him, "Despite what you might think to the contrary, a comatose state is very draining on the patient. She may sleep for most of the next two or three days. It's to be expected. But"—Gafferty's fingers clamped roughly over Brett's shoulder—"I wouldn't worry if I were you, young fella."

Skagway's only physician excused himself, picking up his black bag as he left. At that time Lillian asked, "Might I speak to you alone, Mr. McCallum?" Politely offering his arm, Brett followed her into another room. When they were alone, Lillian said, "I want to thank you for sending for me, Mr. McCallum, when my sister was injured. I know I have been here only two weeks and that you have been with her for the nine weeks since her injury and have taken care of her—"

"With Big Pat's help," said Brett, interrupting. After these two weeks Brett was still not sure whether he liked Lillian. She was smug, critical, a little too nervous for his taste, and her condescending tone, as though she considered him little more than an uneducated backwoods hillbilly, thoroughly ruffled his feathers. "I think I know what you're getting around to," he continued after a moment, "and I admit that you can take care of your sister by yourself, as you have reminded me on a daily basis for the past two weeks. But I'll be perfectly honest—"

"I don't think you have it in you!" Lillian quipped rudely.

Brett, inhaling deeply, chose to ignore the insult. "I don't know how it has happened, but I have learned to care deeply for Paulina. I won't leave her now." He hesitated to continue. "I may never be willing to leave her."

Lillian drew in a short, startled breath. "What are you saying, Mr. McCallum? Surely, you are not suggesting that you are in love with my sister?"

"I am saying that it is very possible, Miss Winthrop."

"That's preposterous! Before her injury you'd known her for only a couple of weeks—"

"I told you I could not explain it . . . but she and I are kindred spirits. I believe we belong together."

"Men! I do declare!" scolded Lillian. "Well, I'll just have none of this silliness. When Paulina is well enough to travel, she is returning to Utah with me. And I dare you to try to stop me from taking her home!"

"I won't try to stop you," promised Brett without malice. "But I will ask her to stay." After Paulina had been shot, Brett had wasted no time in sending a message to her sister in Utah, and in these two weeks since she'd arrived, she'd been almost hostile toward him. He had not understood the reason for it, but had chalked it up

436

to a clash of personalities. He had been too worried about Paulina to let it worry him, and thus he had not questioned her in an effort to learn the source of her hostilities. Now, with Paulina's recovery imminent, he did not feel that barrier standing between them. Crossing his arms, he leaned against the closed door. "What have I done to make you dislike me so?"

"You've done nothing," came her instant reply. "I just don't think it is good for you to get so attached—"

"Or is it not good for *you* if I get attached?" While she contemplated an answer, Brett studied the woman who was several years younger than Paulina. She was pale, her waistline slightly thick, and her hair coarse and swept sternly up, though he could see that in a few years she might give her much more beautiful sister some competition. He imagined that she'd be a hellion of a wife.

Lillian's look of indignation only slightly changed the direction of Brett's thoughts. Though they looked as different as night and day, he saw similarities between the two sisters. He could almost see the glowering of Paulina's eyes in the way Lillian looked at him.

"I just don't know why you can't go about your business, Mr. McCallum. Paulina is my sister, and I will see that she is taken care of. You needn't concern yourself further. Paulina no longer needs you."

With a small groan, Brett pushed himself up. "I will let her tell me that herself. In the meanwhile—" Turning to leave, he flipped his hat onto his head. "I'm going out to round up a bit of broth. Paulina will be hungry soon. If she awakens, please tell her I'll be back shortly." As a matter of courtesy, he asked, "Could I bring you anything?"

When she curtly answered no, he left the room, looking in on Paulina once more before leaving the building.

* * *

Through the blur of her tears Paulina was unable to identify the lady who entered the room. When Lillian sat down and attempted to make physical contact, Paulina tucked her hand into the covers of the bed. "Who are you?" she asked. "Why are you here?"

"Paulina—" A moment of annoyance eased into Lillian's voice, but she instantly suppressed it. "It is Lillian, your sister."

"But it cannot be." In a quiet moment Paulina recalled all the times she had felt Lillian's presence . . . on the Island of the Royal Crypt in the most realistic dream she'd ever had . . . aboard the vessel *Iron Ice* . . . and many times during the trek across the Bering Sea and the mainland of Alaska. But how could she be here now? Paulina looked around, but she could not see the room through the haze of her tears. Was she in Gruff's cabin or was it the abandoned cabin the Sullivan couple had occupied? She couldn't remember.

Oh, why couldn't she remember? Where were the magnificent lights, and the silent city?

Feeling terribly confused, Paulina allowed Lillian to take her hand and hold it fondly between her own. "Paulina, don't you remember anything? Don't you remember being shot?"

"Well, of course I do. It was only this morning. Gafferty . . . Gafferty fired the shot just as he slipped from the ledge. He took me over with him and I almost died too. Brett saved me."

"For heaven's sake, Gafferty is the physician who has been treating you for the past nine weeks. And that scalawag McCallum! Must he always be your redeemer?" Instantly, Lillian, regretting her outburst, softened her voice. "I don't know what you're talking about, Paulina.

It's been just over two months since you were shot by a man named Buckeye Puckett right here in Skagway."

This was all too much for Paulina to handle. She didn't know why Lillian was lying to her, and certainly, she couldn't understand how she had gotten to the interior of Alaska, but suddenly, she felt anything but comfort in her sister's nearness. "Where is Brett?" she asked, closing her eyes. "I need to see Brett."

"That rascal has gone to—"

"I'm right here. Broth had already been brought to the saloon." Brett cut Lillian a scathing look before saying to her, "Could Paulina and I have a moment in private?"

"But—"

Again the glaring look, cutting Lillian's protest short. Lifting a haughty chin, she stood, preparing to stomp from the room like a scolded child when Paulina took her hand and coaxed her back down.

"Lillian, as soon as I can confirm something with Millburn, I believe I'll be able to tell you some things about Mother and why she left Turkey Gulch. Then perhaps you will understand and you won't always be so angry with her."

"What could Millburn possibly know about Mother?"

Paulina reminded her, "He was Father's and Mother's closest friend. I believe that if any confidence would have been made, it would have been to Millburn. Please—" Gently, Paulina patted her sister's hand. "Just let me find out for sure—"

"Another of your silly dreams!" quipped Lillian.

"Perhaps," said her sister indulgently, unable to stop tears from moistening her eyes. "Just be a good girl, and let Brett and me talk for a while."

With still another scathing look in Brett's direction, Lillian withdrew from the room. Taking the chair beside

Paulina, he set down the bowl covered with a linen cloth. Then he took her hand and held it warmly. "Now, what are these tears about?" A gentle finger wiped them from her cheeks. "If it's because you're hungry, I brought some broth."

"I'm sorry about Gruff, Brett."

His surprise was instant. "What? How did you know?" Then, "Lillian told you?"

"What do you mean, how did I know? We were with him when he died."

"No, Paulina—" Emotion choked in Brett's throat. "You were here—we both were—and Gruff died at his cabin. It's been only a few days since I got the news. You—somehow you must have heard us discussing it when you were in your coma."

"No—" Her voice was firmer now. "No, we were with him. Your friend, Gruff . . . just before he died he pointed to the place in the floorboard where he had hidden more than twenty thousand dollars in gold."

"You had to have overheard me discussing that with Big Pat."

"No . . . no." Why was he speaking of Big Pat when they had both seen him die? The tears renewed, her eyes now like dew-covered emeralds against unblushed porcelain. "You are trying to tell me that I was in a coma, and I don't know what game you are playing, but—but, Brett, you and I spent three wonderful months together. We were with Gruff . . . we were!" His perplexed look caused her to sharply echo her own words. "We were!"

Brett's azure eyes narrowed. She was so convinced that they'd been together. How could he prove it was but a dream? "All right, Paulina. Then tell me, what does Gruff look like?"

Not one single moment of hesitation passed before she started to speak. "Tall, rather odd-looking . . . his nose is very large and bulbous, and he has a ragged scar beginning right here"—a slim finger lifted to a point at mid-forehead—"and it cuts through here and ends here at his jawline." With that exertion her hand weakly fell into the folds of the blanket covering her. "And though he is—was—only in his mid-forties, his hair was snow-white. Thank God he had Ruth to love him in his final days."

Brett was at a loss for words; she had, indeed, described Gruff, even knowing the name of the woman he had married three weeks before his death. He tried to think back, to remember if he and Big Pat had discussed Gruff to that extent, but he didn't think so. When his surprise receded, he asked, "What else do you, ummm, remember?"

"Shall I tell you about Gafferty? Will that convince you?"

"But Gafferty is your attending physician—"

"No, no, he is a ruthless predator. He—he shot me . . . he was going to kill you . . . and when the bear attacked, both of them fell off the mountain and died. Don't you remember how you buried his brother eleven years ago after he had tried to kill you? Three days after the bear killed your father? Oh, don't you remember?"

Never in his life had Brett felt that he'd faint, but now he thought he might. He was sure his heart had slowed to a fatal pace. "Paulina, that did happen, but the man's name was Forrester. You must have heard me and Big Pat talking about it and you associated Dr. Gafferty's name with the incident." He managed a smile, solely for her comfort. "Everything can be explained, I promise you." When she looked as if she might cry, he said, "Why don't you tell me the story of this For—ummm, Gafferty, who was up on the mountain with us?"

441

Her eyes narrowed; slowly, her head fell back to the pillow. "Why?"

"Because you need to talk, and I am willing to listen." Slowly, she began. "Eleven years ago Gafferty came upon you when you'd been grievously injured and your father had been killed by the grizzly. Then you and Gafferty—"

Though she continued to speak, his mind wandered back to that time when he'd had to kill Forrester or be killed himself, reliving each vivid detail as she related it to him. He heard her, yet he did not hear her. In the eleven years since the grizzly attack, he had spoken of Forrester's death only once, and that had been to Big Pat more than three weeks before. Though Paulina had been in a deep coma, somehow she had managed to hear the story and had remolded the details to fit her dream. There was no murderous, revengeful brother. Forrester had come from England, where he'd grown up in an orphanage and there had been no relatives. He had simply had too much to drink and had gone into a fit of rage.

But suppose she had not heard his discussion with Big Pat? Was it possible that she had taken a spiritual trip during the nine weeks she had lain comatose upon the bed in the back of Big Pat's Saloon? Had she somehow climbed into his mind and shared his thoughts with him? He shuddered as he silently explored the possibility . . . and the impossibility. . . .

"Brett?"

His thoughts snapped back. "Yes?"

"Did you hear me?"

"Every word," he said truthfully. "And I'll be dad-burned if I can explain it, other than your hearing me and Big Pat talking about it." Taking Paulina's slim, pale hand, he remarked, "No one, not even a physician, knows what goes on in the mind of a person who is lost to sleep. You had a dream, Paulina . . . only a dream. And"—he grinned now—"thank you for letting me share the experience with you." Shrugging, he assumed a façade of indifference, but it was just that. "One day I will tell you about Forrester, and you will understand why I had to kill him."

"I already understand, Brett. You were defending your own life."

"Yes but we'll still talk about it. I want you to know everything there is to know about me. Though that might be impossible."

"Nothing is impossible, Brett."

The sudden change in her tone took him aback. "What do you mean?"

"I am saying, Brett, that I spent three months with you. I know everything about you . . . everything."

"Nobody can know everything." But she knew the story of Forrester, though she'd attached a different name to him. "I do hope we got along during this time we spent together . . . out yonder."

"Oh, we fought. But"—a smile caught upon her mouth—"we also loved . . . and loved completely."

A little embarrassed, he grinned. "Did I enjoy myself?"

"You asked me that before, you know, when I told you about the Island of the Royal Crypt. I didn't answer you then, and I shan't answer you now."

"Island of the Royal Crypt . . . now, that sounds intriguing."

Big Pat's appearance could not have been more inopportune. Brett was sure he'd have gotten better details of their time together. The bear-sized bartender stood in the doorway, grinning down at Paulina. "How about a visit from an old friend?" he asked.

She narrowed her eyes, attempting to focus. That

voice . . . the outline of the large man whose features she could not distinguish. No, no, it could not be. Hesitantly, she asked, "Big Pat?"

And he was across the room, kneeling beside the bed to take her hand. "It's me, to be sure," he continued with his toothy grin. "I sure was worried about you."

Paulina looked as if she'd seen a ghost. Though pale already, she paled even more, prompting a worried Brett to ask, "Are you all right?"

But if she heard him she gave no indication of it. Slowly, again hesitating, her hand moved out to touch the smooth, round cheek below Big Pat's twinkling right eye. "You're not dead? But I saw you . . . we saw you . . . when we were leaving Skagway that morning—"

Still grinning, an emotional Big Pat answered, "I've heard about that dream of yours, little lady." A big, burly hand lifted to cover her own, a kiss landing upon her palm. "I'm just as alive as you are."

"I—I really believe I might have died, and *this* is all a dream, Big Pat. If this is heaven—"

Big Pat laughed, but deep emotion echoed within it. "This ol' saloon's been called a lot of things, Paulie, but never heaven."

Standing, he gave her hand a paternal pat and laid it gently against her waistline. "Maybe this black-hearted rogue"—he'd spoken the slur affectionately as he'd looked to Brett—"can convince you this ain't heaven."

Immediately, a frown pressed upon her brow. As Big Pat retreated, she looked deeply into Brett's eyes. "If I dreamed, then—"

"Then what?"

"Then Soapy Smith is still alive."

"Unfortunately."

"What day is this?"

"June twenty-sixth—"

With a small shrug Paulina said, "Well, he won't be in a few weeks. He's going to shoot it out on July eighth with a man named Frank Reid. Soapy will be killed outright, and Mr. Reid will die twelve days later."

"And how can you possibly know this, Miss Paulina Winthrop?" Brett deliberately suppressed his humor.

"Millburn told us a few days ago. Remember those newspapers wrapped around the seven bottles of whiskey you purchased for Gruff in St. Michael? Millburn found the story there and told us about Soapy being killed."

"That was some dream you had, Paulina."

Again she shrugged, and this time a slight smile accompanied her effort. "Yes, I know . . . but I can keep dreaming, can't I?"

"Indeed, you can. Maybe—"

When Brett hesitated, Paulina prompted him. "Maybe what, Brett?"

"Maybe you'll be around in July to see if ol' Soapy really bites the bullet?"

"Are you asking me to stay?"

Just at that moment Lillian entered. She'd been waiting silently in the hall, preparing to interrupt just such a course of conversation. "You'll be going home with me when you're strong enough," she told Paulina. "I spoke to Dr. Gafferty a while ago"—Brett knew that was not true—"and he says you'll be ready to travel in about three weeks."

"Why must I go home? The council has appointed you to complete Father's term as marshal—"

Lillian's mouth gaped. She shot daggers at Brett as she accused him, "You told her? I had asked you not to! It was my news to tell!"

"I told her nothing," came Brett's soft reply. "How did you know, Paulina?"

445

"I don't know." She looked genuinely askance. "I know that Lester and Earl are dead too."

"You told her that? Mr. McCallum, how could you!" Lillian stomped her foot in quite a childish fashion, and at that moment Brett found it hard to see any semblance of a marshal in Paulina's younger sister. Paulina, yes, Lillian, no.

"Brett has told me nothing of the goings-on in Turkey Gulch," Paulina said. "I don't know how I knew. I must have heard somehow when I was asleep." Looking again to Brett, she asked, "Are you asking me to stay?"

He paused, his mouth twisting as if he were deep in thought. Then he linked his fingers and brought them below his clean-shaven chin. "Alaska's a big place . . . beautiful in the summertime . . . I would like to show it to you, Paulina."

Smiling her pleasure, she responded, "I feel that I've already seen it, but . . ." The smile broadened. "I would like to see it again. Yes, I'll stay for a while."

Lillian huffed. "Paulina, you can't! What about Uncle Will, what about Matt and Lucille?" She paused, asking more dramatically, "What about me?"

"Hush, Lillian." Her gaze transfixed to Brett's amused one, she eased her hand atop his. "You've got everything under control back in Turkey Gulch. You're rebuilding the mercantile—"

"You told her about the fire too?" Lillian lashed at Brett.

But Paulina gave Brett no time for fresh denials. "You're the marshal, and Uncle Will can teach you how to use a gun. Millburn knows he can return to Turkey Gulch without Lester or Earl shooting him down and"— her other hand eased beneath Brett's, so that it was enveloped between them—"I'm a big girl. Brett will take

446

care of me." Then she eased into his arms and whispered against his hairline, "Won't you?"

"You bet, pretty thing," he murmured in return. "But first—" Lowering his voice so that the impudent, foot-stamping Lillian would not overhear, he whispered, "But we'll stick around here for the next couple of weeks . . . to attend ol' Soapy's funeral."

When Lillian charged from the room like an enraged bull, Paulina said, "She's not usually like that, Brett. She's really very sweet."

"It's all right," he laughed. "She reminds me of another lady I met just a few short months ago."

Despite her weakness, Paulina felt the crimson creeping into her cheeks. "Was I so childish?"

Just at that moment a great black dog bounded into the room, his front paws literally attacking the side of Paulina's bed and forcing Brett to let her go. Surprised at first, a now-beaming Paulina hugged the dog. "Oh, Alujian, Alujian, it's so good to see you again."

A startled Brett had never seen his dog—who had up to this point disliked all humans except him—take to anyone. "His name is Prince. I guess you two have met before."

"Well, that explains part of my dream," remarked a quiet Paulina.

"What part?" inquired Brett.

"The part in which you were a royal prince."

"Oh . . ." He grinned boyishly. "Being a prince sounds rather dull. I'll save the title for the dog."

"Yes . . . we are old friends," said Paulina, caressing Prince's ears and the rough fur between them. "Aren't we, Prince?"

Then the dog quietly moved away, his tail still wagging as he dropped into a corner.

"Now, where were we?" asked Brett.

447

"I think I asked you if I was really so childish."

"Oh, yes, more so," he responded. Then, taking her again in his arms, he said, "I could hold you like this forever, Miss Paulina Winthrop."

"I think I could give you that, Brett, if you wanted it."

He knew it was exactly what he wanted. Closing his eyes, he could almost feel, see, touch, hear . . . remember the long adventure he had shared with Paulina in her dream. He could feel the coolness of the sand beneath his feet as he had walked, hand in hand, with her along an isolated beach . . . taste the fiery sweetness of her mouth upon his own as they had made love . . . he could feel the frigid air of the Bering Strait whipping back his hair and tantalizing her own so that his hands were drawn into its rich depths . . . everything was as clear to him as if he had truly been there with her.

Perhaps he had.

Perhaps the dream continued . . . and he could, indeed, look forward to forever with Paulina.

"Forever—" he murmured after his long, thoughtful pause. "Yes, forever . . . and this time it will be for real."

You know, Brett, that I am a virgin.

Forever will last . . . which is more than I can say for other things.

"Did you hear that, Brett?"

"I heard nothing," he chuckled, holding her close. "I heard nothing but the echo of promises, Paulina. The echoes of forever—"